# FADE TO BLACK

Right on cue the dogs started howling even more, if that was possible.

"This is ridiculous," said Bradley. "I can't work with this."

"It's worse than usual, even for her."

"Don't you think you ought to go check on it? Maybe she's been murdered in her bed."

"My recollection, she could take care of herself in bed."

"Suit yourself, but this is not working for me."

So I agreed to take a look. I wasn't surprised nobody answered the door. Nobody'd answered the phone. I climbed over the short front fence. Right away challenged by six or eight snarling, hysterical dogs. With crazy eyes and bad vibes.

I inched my way around the side of the house, then climbed to the pathway that led around back. The dogs alternated running at me and away, definitely spooked.

And right on the money, no big surprise, floating in the heart-shaped pool, the no longer any-shaped Teri.

Hate when that happens.

# ROUGH CUT

## Stan Cutler

A SIGNET BOOK

SIGNET
Published by the Penguin Group
Penguin Books USA Inc., 375 Hudson Street,
New York, New York 10014, U.S.A.
Penguin Books Ltd, 27 Wrights Lane,
London W8 5TZ, England
Penguin Books Australia Ltd, Ringwood,
Victoria, Australia
Penguin Books Canada Ltd, 10 Alcorn Avenue,
Toronto, Ontario, Canada M4V 3B2
Penguin Books (N.Z.) Ltd, 182–190 Wairau Road,
Auckland 10, New Zealand

Penguin Books Ltd, Registered Offices:
Harmondsworth, Middlesex, England

First published by Signet,
an imprint of Dutton Signet,
a division of Penguin Books USA Inc.

First Printing, November, 1994
10  9  8  7  6  5  4  3  2  1

 REGISTERED TRADEMARK—MARCA REGISTRADA

Printed in the United States of America

PUBLISHER'S NOTE
This is a work of fiction. Names, characters, places, and incidents either are the
product of the author's imagination or are used fictitiously, and any resemblance
to actual persons, living or dead, events, or locales is entirely coincidental.

BOOKS ARE AVAILABLE AT QUANTITY DISCOUNTS WHEN USED TO PROMOTE PROD-
UCTS OR SERVICES. FOR INFORMATION PLEASE WRITE TO PREMIUM MARKETING DIVI-
SION, PENGUIN BOOKS USA INC., 375 HUDSON STREET, NEW YORK, NEW YORK 10014.

For Theodora,
who taught me
a new kind
of love.

## ACKNOWLEDGMENTS

Thanks are due my editor, Peter K. Borland, a bright, steady hand at the helm; my friend and agent, Jane Gelfman, who launched the series—and a career; my liaison, Donald von Wicdenman, coxswain to the West Hollywood galley; and Stanley Silverman, who mans the watch for slips that pass in the type.

# 1

# Rayford Goodman

I can't believe I let myself get talked into it.

Five o'clock in the afternoon, and there I was in the back seat of a limo. In a tux, yet.

All right, people in Hollywood do that. They go to the Oscars, or the Grammies, or the Golden Globules. At some snazzy spot big enough to take that kind of crowd. Like the Dorothy Chandler Pavilion. Or Aaron Spelling's house.

The reason everybody has to go at five o'clock, looking pretty silly all tricked out in broad daylight, because it's going to be on TV at six. Which makes it nine in New York. And everything's geared to make life comfy in New York. Except the actual city. Another story.

Only the thing is, it wasn't going to be on TV. Not being one of the seventy-seven major awards. Plus which, black tie optional—never a good sign. No, they just plain scheduled farmer-early because it was going to be tacky—I felt surer by the minute.

What it was, it was the "Lammies." Awards given out by the Lambda Literary Society, for—oh boy—"Gay and Lesbian Literary Excellence." And my partner and I had been nominated for "Best Achievement in Gay Biography"—can you stand it?

Better do a fast rewind here.

I'm Ray Goodman (Rayford to ex-wives, and whoever else finds fault). My partner's this kid Mark Bradley (who doesn't have ex-wives, for reasons it won't take long to dawn on you). He's one of those "as told to" writers I first met when he put down the words for my autobiography. Me being—there's no way I can be totally modest about this—Private Eye to the Stars.

My autobiography'd involved the two of us going back over my most famous case. Back in the Sixties. During which he found out there'd been an understandable mix-up on my nabbing the actual killer. Which, no need to go into all over again.

At any rate, once past that little complication, the commercial part'd worked out so good we teamed up a couple times more, me solving, him doing a larger part of the writing.

As it happened, one of the cases we'd worked on it turned out the murder victim was a studio head who'd led his life under cover (manner of speaking) and only got exposed when it looked like some rough trade he'd picked up did him in instead of up.

But what old supersleuth here found, that wasn't the case after all. In terms of killing. In terms of what all else, it didn't matter. My terrific detecting nailed the actual, straight, bad guy who'd simply killed the studio boss for one of the many reasons studio bosses tend to deserve killing. And then together (well, mostly Bradley) we'd produced us a book on the subject turned out a semi-bestseller (*The Face on the Closet Floor*).

Which gets us to being in the limo, betuxed, and headed not toward the Dorothy Chandler Pavilion in downtown L.A. and network interviews, but the Anaheim Hilton, next to Disneyland, and probably some guy with a handcuff for an earring and a condom-covered mike doing color for *West Hollywood After Dark*.

I'd wanted to bring a ladyfriend to head off anybody getting the idea I was into encounters of the third kind. But Bradley put the kibosh on that. Even when I suggested we could make it half business by inviting Francie, our researcher, and my one-time semi-flame.

"The invitation was specifically just for the two of us," he said. "Seating's at a premium."

Which I guess made it more popular than I would've expected. Sort of a hard ticket. And now, the more I thought about it and the closer we got, the less enthusiastic I got.

"So what is this thing again? The Dickies?"

"The Lammies, as you well know."

"I should of sprung for a gown."

"I'm beginning to get subtle hints that I'm going to regret this," said Bradley. Who, I must say, took kidding pretty good.

But anybody'd have to agree the old ball was certainly taking some funny bounces. To help get through which I meanwhile found the felt-covered compartment where they'd stashed the vodka decanter and decided to do a few warm-up exercises. There wasn't any club soda, the mixes running to cans of orange crush and fake grape, plus only a handful of ice cubes. Iranian driver, culture gap. I had a quick vodka on a rock. Didn't do much for my spirit.

"I still wish I'd brought a date," I said. "Everybody's going to think I'm with *you*."

"Not in a million years," said Bradley, no smile at all. "Why would I pick an old bozo like you for a lover?"

Made me feel a lot better.

It was Friday night, holiday weekend (Memorial Day), and traffic on the Santa Ana Freeway was slower than our publisher reaching for the check.

I'd wanted to drive. Especially after it turned out the aforementioned publisher (aptly named Dick Penny) wouldn't spring for the limo.

But I had to admit Bradley'd been right to push for it. Being bumper to bumper when you were driving was a stressful, aggravating, crotch-wrinkling business. Which could've seriously cut into my general even-tempered mood. And chance of being a genial winner. Whereas lounging in a cozy Caddy stretch, sipping vodka out of a crystal goblet—your basic horse of a different hue.

Being we weren't going anywhere at the moment (except maybe to good times with the vodka), I thought we might make use of the chance to get a little work done.

I personally hadn't been doing much of anything since we weren't into any new writing job. My P.I. ticket had been suspended by the California Department of Professional and Vocational Standards, pending an investigation into my alleged misbehavior on jury duty in another case. Which would all work out eventually, since I *did* solve that, too—saving a miscarriage of justice. (I told you I was good.) But meanwhile the no work left me a little high and dry.

Only now, second drink down, I was a little high and *not* so dry.

"I been kicking around some ideas," I began. "Thinking we might get started another project."

"Oh, well—you know I'm pretty much involved with finally doing *my* book," he said.

Bradley'd been on and off working on a novel of his own about his misspent youth, which I had a feeling was going to be a very long book about a lot of things I'd really rather not know.

"Yeah, but I figured even so, you could maybe do that part-time, and maybe something else, too. To make us some money. Capitalize our fame."

"What'd you have in mind?" he said.

"Well, I thought we might check out some famous Hollywood scandals and follow up how it affected the family. You know, like did Fatty Arbuckle have kids?"

"You mean, a Chubby Arbuckle somewhere?"

"Right. And say, maybe follow up on some stars' illegitimate kids. Sort of, 'Where Are They Now?' and what names are they using."

"And in case any of them managed to have a halfway okay life see if we can ruin that, too?"

"You're going to take that attitude, there wouldn't of been any Watergate."

"Goodman—it's a terrible idea."

"I don't see why. People are always interested in the movies and scandal and famous people falling on their ass."

"Forget it, it's awful. Bad enough when you're dealing with the person in question themselves. But to harass the children . . ."

"Who said harass? Did I say harass? And there might be some did all right. Anyway, it was just a place to jump off. Something to kick around."

"Run up the pole?"

"I'm perfectly willing to listen any your ideas," I said, keeping my eye on the ball.

"My *idea*," he went on with that homeroom-teacher

tone I'd come to really hate, "was to utilize this time to write my book—which is exactly what I'm doing—after waiting years for the opportunity." Right, teach. "I am not looking to commit another Hollywood biography."

I tried pouting. "Sure, just think of yourself."

He sighed. Which I admit was a little more mature than pouting. "At the moment," he added. "Why don't you take another case, meanwhile?"

"I can't take another case. I'm on suspension," I reminded him.

"Well, who would know if you had a license or not? What's the difference?"

"You just don't understand the integrity of the profession."

"The private eye profession?!"

"We have standards, ethics."

"Right, you need a code of ethics to peek into motel windows."

"I can see you're in one of your moods, just forget it."

Which I guess he was. Because we did. Forget it. For the time being.

The traffic kept being a bitch. And I kept putting away the sauce. One of us had to give. Turned out it was the traffic, and we finally got to Anaheim. Or, basically—America.

And, my god, what *happened* to America?

You live in or around Beverly Hills, the women are closing in on perfection. Walking Clairol ads. Gorgeous. Huge numbers of fantastic girls (I know not to say "girls" out loud), slim, tall, shapely, sexy, more and more of them more and more incredible looking by the minute.

These days, Betty Grable would have to play best friend. *Goofy* best friend.

Guys, too—actually.

Outside Beverly Hills—and Anaheim was *way* outside—you got the Disney/McDonald's group. Exact opposite. Real exact. Three-hundred pounders (buns included)—guys and gals—in baggy shorts, funny T-shirts, and one-size-fits-all caps (wasn't *that* an improvement).

Whatever happened to "average"? Didn't we used to

have a basically good-looking country? Now it's all super-unbelievably gorgeous or super-unbelievably grungy. With nothing in between.

Just a bit of observation, there.

We pulled up to the Anaheim Hilton and waded through the mountains of flesh (see above), fighting our way to the mezzanine. And past various convention meeting rooms (in California usually with Conquistadory names, which must please the hell out of the Mexican help) and at the farthest end, right on the mezzanine, *The Advocate* (a major "alternate-lifestyle" publication, Bradley'd informed me) was throwing this big invitation-only cocktail bash.

With a no-host bar!

They actually checked our invitation. To get to a no-host bar!

Anaheim.

America.

Above the fruited plain.

Add insult to stingy, four seventy-five for a shot of vodka and soda, with the quaint notion a shot was one ounce. Anaheim! (In Beverly Hills, about the same price, you got a *tureen* of vodka you could hardly find *room* to put soda in.) Plus on the rent-a-bar, a glass full of dollar bills as a hint for tips—for serving yourself.

I felt my basic good humor slipping a little.

I rubbed elbows (and carefully avoided other parts) with a lot of strange-looking people. About half you'd think they dressed for Mardi Gras—and the rest for a schoolyard pickup game.

Bradley seemed to know a lot of the folks there and introduced me to several "very important" people in "the movement." I think I showed a lot of class not mentioning what *I* considered a movement.

The place was packed, but if possible even more packed in one corner. There, what looked like half the party surrounded two guys. One was a chubby, thirtyish fellow with a hairline receded past the middle of his head, and hair real long in back in a ponytail. A look always seemed to me like a semibald cheerleader about to lose her fall. The other guy (getting most of the attention) was this tall, thin, Asian gent, apparently some kind of celebrity.

"Who's the Jap?" I asked Bradley.

"The *Jap* is Chinese, for one thing."

"OK, who's the Chink?" I corrected. "One of your overseas reps?"

"That's Jeffrey Hong, our councilman. And, no, I don't know if he's gay. There's a Mrs. Hong."

"Ah," I said inscrutably.

"But we know that doesn't mean anything."

We do?

At any rate, a lot of people seemed very interested in whatever it was Mr. Hong had to say. Especially the ponytail guy.

"Big wheel? This Hong guy?"

"Yes. He's supposedly going to run for mayor."

I had heard his name. "And who's the other guy, the one *really* looks like a horse's ass?"

Bradley told me he was Marvin Fischer, worked in the current mayor's office and was either a spy for the mayor, or a counterspy for the councilman—nobody knew which. But always wherever the Hong guy was. Representing the city, which was possible. Or seeing Hong didn't get too far in front of the present mayor, which he seemed to think more probably the case.

I liked politics about as much as prohibition.

At that point a photographer approached the popular twosome. Fischer smiled and put his arm around Hong. Hong smiled back. Looking about as comfortable as Nixon getting hugged by Sammy Davis, Jr.

And it right away got to be seven o'clock, and on the dot we all got herded into the ballroom.

Once inside the Inquisition Room (or whatever, but bigger than the mezzanine) we got a better view of the group. And we were, turned out, two out of about only seven guys in tuxedos. Though there were a fair number of ladies with big watchbands and large asses favoring the same sartorial mode. Like to kill Bradley. (Who had been right about bringing a guest, though—it was packed, not a single empty seat.)

Whoever produced evidently hadn't watched too many

other awards shows because there wasn't much of a show. Or any. Well, there was one sort of tailored woman who was into some political satire. I guess. She said a couple of nasty things about Bush and Quayle, which got some cheap chuckles. Considering B and Q weren't exactly a moving target. Or even close to current. Some guy with a minicam was capturing it all for posterity. Or indictment.

As part of the "festivities" the councilman was invited up to share a few words. He was so shy if his name had two syllables he'd of been at the mike before they finished the intro.

Councilman Hong looked over this sea of shining faces and told us how pleased he was that all these people had come out tonight. Which got him a laugh he didn't understand. Then he went on to say how much he supported his constituency, regardless of orientation—another laugh—and how happy he was to be included in this distinguished cultural event. And, finally, to reassure everyone his hand was always out and his door always open. (No flies on this guy.) Which got him another laugh went over his head and annoyed hell out of the emcee.

From there they went straight to the awards. This may have been part to conserve time and to distract us from dinner, which, being for several hundred people wasn't any worse, really, than any hotel. Like, say, the Mogadishu Hilton.

The awards themselves seemed to me dominated by the lesbian contingency. Who were very organized and united and loud. And pretty much known to one another. Several old parties who looked like they'd done their share of close-order drill got honored, and one got a standing ovation when she said lesbians were clearly superior to everyone else. Just what we needed, a Nazi lesbian. (I would of thought, "Please don't hurt us," might be a good place to start.) But the gay guys stood up and cheered, too.

I'd always been a little surprised they were allies when it seemed to me gays and lesbians weren't a natural combo. Since one bunch didn't like women and the other didn't like men. (Not totally accurate. Lesbians didn't seem to like men much, whereas gays often did like women, and a lot—just not for the usual reasons.) But I guess, "My enemy's enemy is my friend" still has its following.

By now the salad was out of the way. Which I had to admit was pretty tasty. You couldn't get drinks at the table (wine, but I don't consider wine drinks) but the no-host bar had moved from the mezzanine into the ballroom itself. I suppose for my convenience. And to see how much actual cash I had. I was loving every minute of it.

Bradley had very little to say, I would guess less he was overwhelmed by the festivities than he didn't want me punching him in the arm.

Up on stage they finally finished the lesbian awards and went to the gay ones.

They started right in entertaining us by a reading. To do this, they didn't have someone was an actor might be good at it but another writer (not usually your best public speakers). To keep it light, the reading was about eighty pages from the diary of a guy dying of AIDS. Though he really did have my sympathy ("Michael couldn't be with us this evening") I thought this might be a good time to go to the bathroom so I'd have no distraction from whatever came next.

This had man-height urinals and child-height urinals, and I was really relieved there weren't any Mickey Mouse-height urinals. I'm also happy to report nobody did anything out of line while I was there.

When I got back to our table, someone else was getting an award for Gay Poetry, which managed to combine *two* of my favorite things. And a lot more about "absent friends"—touching, but not your best party material. It was turning into a pretty long night.

Mind wandering, I checked the room. Fischer had been seated at a table two tables away from us, and the same from Hong. When a girl next to Hong I understood was his secretary got up to powder her nose I saw Fischer get up from his table and move over to Hong's. Hong didn't seem all that glad to see him, but Fischer sat down on the secretary's empty chair next to him anyway.

I made another trip to the no-host bar—which I was starting to think of as me-hosting, and I guess they did, too, since it'd been moved even closer. I got back to our table and back to the subject of Gay Awards. And finally to the category of Best Gay Biography. The nominees included books on fellows who'd contributed greatly to society in one way or another, without being recognized. And us. Who had, I felt, a fat chance, being to my way of thinking we should never of been nominated in the first place.

What we'd written wasn't a gay biography; it was a Hollywood celebrity murder happened to include some gays.

Not that I gave a damn about the Silly Twit Award, but I have to admit I did feel some kind of interest when they announced our book and Bradley and me as writers.

"And," said the lady, "the winner of this year's Lambda Award for Best Gay Biography goes to . . ." which then got teased more when, true to tradition, she had trouble opening the envelope they always seem to glue together with the stuff they hang locomotives in the air. Bradley leaned forward. I felt myself holding my breath, too—to my own surprise.

But a hell of a lot bigger surprise was when we all heard this huge incredible crash. And turned. And saw the bartender had pushed over his bar with all the bottles and glasses.

To give himself a clear field of fire when he raised the machine gun and started pumping about eleven thousand bullets into the room.

# 2

# Mark Bradley

This was *not* my idea of a good time.

Bullets were flying, people were screaming, crockery was disintegrating. There wasn't going to be much of a hassle over who got to take home the centerpiece.

It was definitely beyond anything in my experience. Or fantasy. I don't think I was even terribly frightened.

Inured by decades of action films and special effects, the real thing *had* no special effect at first, but seemed simply a technical upgrade of all the fake violence we'd assimilated subliminally. (A thousand-foot fall does not hurt the Roadrunner, nor bombs much bother Sylvester Stallone.)

Until I saw the Hong/Fischer table, and watched the marching progression of bullets change table wood to splinters, glassware to shards, and finally life itself to death as Hong tried to push Fischer to safety but himself went down and I saw Fischer's chest suddenly blossom with a dozen bloody roses.

There was such an unbelievably deafening amount of noise between the explosion of the shots themselves and the breakage they caused and the shrieking, yelling, screaming of the now-panic-driven crowd that it took several moments before I realized that one element was abating—the shots. A few additional spurts—but then none.

I had instinctively dropped to the floor—in very good and majority company—at the first deadly realization that this wasn't some grisly guerrilla theater but serious shit.

Goodman, on the other hand, I realized in retrospect—contrary to that same instinct and all the known laws of

self-preservation—must have left my side and, reacting
with spontaneous courage and amazing heroism, fought
his way through the screaming, wailing, terror-filled
crowd, and leaped on the bartender/assassin, in an attempt to smother the threat. They had evidently grappled
for a few moments—hence the additional bursts of fire—
before he was able totally to subdue the assailant. In this
it appeared he had been aided by a number of like-
minded citizens as by the time I raised myself up he was
atop the shooter, and gaggles of gays and loads of lesbians were atop Goodman. It was, in the vernacular, about
a fifteen-way.

What followed was fairly predictable. Hotel Security,
now that there was no immediate danger, took charge
with military efficiency. Which is to say, formed a protective circle about the incapacitated crazy—no doubt informed by Hotel Legal to be certain nothing untoward
happened that might be actionable. Prior to this the at-
tacker had been pretty much roughed-up, but nothing
life-threatening. There'd been a superficial argument
over whether he ought to be tied up, but he seemed
fairly well subdued and neutralized by the presence of
at least a dozen heavyweight armed guards.

Others of the hotel security force, those whose uni-
forms were of the gray slacks, blue blazer sort (the visible
plainclothes), organized the survivors, herding us against
a far wall. "For your own protection."

Being in a group sounded like a good and protective
move to me. Goodman, whether because of his actions
or professional courtesy, seemed excused from these precautions, lingering with the troops.

Next came a corps of paramedics, who sprang into
action, caring for the many many wounded. However,
once the moaning and general hysteria abated, it turned
out, incredibly, that most of the injuries were relatively
superficial. My impression was a few flesh wounds, a
good number of cuts from flying glass and plates, perhaps
two or three others who'd taken bullets or fragments in
nonstrategic areas. Astonishingly, among their number
Jeffrey Hong seemed to have escaped with only an upper

arm or shoulder wound, not so severe as to deprive him of the political sense to manfully suggest they "take care of the others first."

Next, notedly anticlimactic, a SWAT team arrived, precipitating a near-confrontation with the private hotel army over asserting authority and assuming custody.

Adding to the confusion, the regular cops chose this moment to invade in force, and insist on their jurisdiction. For a moment as the three autonomous forces faced each other, it looked like the bloodshed wasn't quite all over.

However, the discovery at that instant of an obviously dead Marvin Fischer brought things into something closer to a reasonable perspective.

The senior regular P.D. officer, considering the massive contamination of the crime scene, elected to have the mayor's aide immediately removed, as little investigative advantage remained to keeping him on site. The paramedics responded to this order.

The sight of the team toting the body-bagged city rep quieted and sobered the crowd.

However, once accomplished, none of the three forces yet seemed agreeable to quitting the scene, and actual custody of the assassin wasn't formally taken (he remained surrounded by the hotel's security force, in turn circled by the SWAT team, themselves flanked by the regular cops).

To one side, the wounded Hong stood stoically beside the paramedics, waiting his turn at the tourniquet. And then I saw why the whole jurisdictional hassle had occurred, and mutely continued, as the TV crews started arriving, to tape a record of the dramatic events and its participants.

If sensationalism were to ensue (count on it!), the hotel was going to be sure it was positively represented, the SWAT team likewise, the local cops ditto, and it certainly seemed reasonable to assume it had entered the councilman's mind.

There were, it appeared, enough talking heads to assure everybody a place in the sun and a piece of the action.

As established by Tiffany Stevens, KNUS-TV's roving anchor (a neat little oxymoron), the officer in charge was a Lt. Billy Baylor.

"Now, your attention please, ladies and gentlemen," he commenced, once he got his hand on the public address system, as a half-dozen media mikes were also thrust under his face. "I'm going to ask your cooperation while we sort things out. I don't want anybody to leave until he or her—or whatever—has been interviewed by one of my officers. First off, stay back against the wall, and let's let the paramedics take care of the wounded and get them all evacuated."

Which was accomplished with relative efficiency. Paramedics tend to be pretty good. And besides, that's what they had been doing right along. The single delay was caused by Councilman Hong, who insisted on being on camera as he was treated (having delayed it till the last minute). Minor celebrity that he was, the media acceded, recording his statement. His statement was that this violent breakdown of law and order was exactly the sort of thing that had so engaged his sense of civic outrage that therefore he was taking this opportunity to announce his candidacy for mayor and promise that if elected—once he was assured he would recover enough from his wounds not to impair his ability to serve—he would personally see this sort of thing didn't happen again to any of the decent people of this fair city. And he sort of stumbled, apparently weakened by loss of blood, or glare of publicity—and was led away.

"Now, then," continued the lieutenant, "we're going to be removing the prisoner. I want everybody to stay standing back. We're going to protect him, and nobody's going to do any of that Jack Ruby stuff."

At which the media all broke into demands they be allowed to interview the shooter, and hurled a dozen questions at him.

"Wait, wait," said the lieutenant. "First off, this might be a real good time for me to publicly read him his rights." Which he did, loud and clear, and accurately.

"Now, I'm sure you all understand the best way to proceed with this case and not see it fuh ... snafued is to not have him making any public statements till he's got a lawyer and all that."

The press didn't care for "all that"—and didn't pay much attention, either, continuing to bombard the prisoner with questions.

Which prompted him to take charge, himself. Somewhat roughed up, scratched, and superficially bleeding, he raised a hand for silence, and said the following.

"My name is William Hobart Kiskessler." (Don't they always have three names?) "K-I-S-K-E-S-S-L-E-R. I have a prepared statement."

At which all cameras zoomed in tight as a dozen tape recorders were thrust into his face.

He said, "The statement goes like so: 'This will show the radical commie fag dyke AIDS Jew nigger Jap Korean bastards how America *really* feels.'" (He didn't seem to have any beef with fluoridization.)

"End of statement," he said. "No questions." And he was escorted off, most of the TV and other newsfolks following.

Which prompted a quick resolution of the jurisdictional dispute as the SWAT team accepted relief by the investigative and custodial group of more or less regulars, and anticlimactically ambled away, their equipment noisily rattling and creaking in the sudden quiet.

Now, going on two and a half hours later, Goodman and I were still ensconced in the cocktail lounge adjacent to the lobby, which Goodman insisted on calling the Torquemada Room, based on his dissatisfaction with the quality and pricing of the drinks, but I felt sure was something more innocuous (and less inventive)—Hacienda Room? Cantina? One of those.

The reason we were still there ("Pissing away a fortune while the limo meter ticks") was the Anaheim P.D. had not yet finished taking statements from the hundreds of witnesses to the attack.

Plus, of course, with Goodman a principal in the capture, his statement was especially valued.

"Then why the fuck don't they take me first?" he groused, whilst downing yet another "double double" vodka with some reference to basketball, which totally eluded me.

The Awards Ball itself had, of course, been aborted, with the word passed around that remaining winners would be notified and Lammies delivered by Federal Express.

A few discreet inquiries had informed me that we would not be among those so favored. We had lost. Which was, in reality, as we had expected.

No doubt I should have waited for a more opportune moment to so inform my collaborator, but under the stress of events I was not thinking all that clearly.

While at first I thought he took the disappointment fairly calmly, in reality, it was merely that his reflexes had been slowed by alcohol, as I soon enough discovered.

"So we came to this fucking fruit bowl for no good fucking reason at all," was his measured reaction to the news.

"I wouldn't say that," I responded. "You got to be a hero, saving no doubt countless lives. Publicity will accrue; medals may be awarded. Book sales could be helped."

Then to my amazement and chagrin, he suddenly deteriorated even farther.

"I have—pre-pared a spee-ch," he announced, in that careful not to trip over your tongue way the extremely inebriated often employ. With which to add fuel to my fears of impending humiliation he rose to his feet and asked for attention. This he accompanied by clanging a cocktail mixer against his glass. However, since the cocktail mixer was made of plastic, and the glass some similar compound, his demand was mostly mime and mostly unnoticed. Undaunted, he upped the decibels.

"La-dies an' gemn," he shouted, which did get the attention of those nearest. I started sinking down in my seat.

But there is a God, or at least someone watching to see inebriates don't make as total enormous asses of themselves as they are determined to try. This was exemplified by the fact at that exact moment the electronic mariachi band elected to play its extremely amplified version of "Besame Mucho."

Well into his cups, ten or twelve sheets to the wind, this went largely unremarked by Goodman who continued reading from his prepared notes—totally unnoticed by the shocked survivors and/or revellers.

It was only when the band had completed its rendition that anyone at all would have been able to hear Goodman say, "and in 'clusion, as I stan' 'fore you gays and lesbi'ns t'night, I am grateful for two things. One, you've seen fit to give me this won'ful award—and, two, my mother's dead and I don't have to s'plain it to her." With which he sat down.

On the floor.

# 3

# Rayford Goodman

The good news—I wasn't totally paralyzed. It was just too painful to move.

We weren't talking the aches and bruises wrestling with a killer and a dozen people on your side. This was more in the area of self-inflicted. Morning after. Though you could make a strong case it wasn't totally my fault.

So—clang clang clang went the trolley. And the 1812 Overture. And Krakatoa.

Toss in special effects a dozen barking dogs next door went bananas every time their mistress—a word not total poetic license—waltzed off to "work" the various luxury hotels in the Greater Los Angeles area, and you start getting the idea.

True, aftereffects of last night's forty-four fingers of vodka might of made me a smidge less tolerant of your basic ungodly howling banshees. It was a pain in the ass any time. Some kind of death given the mother of all hangovers.

Add in the weight and heat of my cat, Phantom of the Garage—which didn't sleep in the garage anymore but my lap—and I'm sure the picture's fairly clear: not the best morning I ever faced.

The Phantom yowled like blue murder when I tossed him off, and I did pretty much the same sitting up when every nerve in my body checked in to report massive hideous pain.

I eased my legs around, put my feet on the floor and pushed off, grunting and groaning about on a par with your average terminal ward.

I managed a stiff-legged walk to the kitchen, Phantom weaving in and out of my legs just to complicate matters, where I dumped some cat food in a dish, put it on the floor and got back up without actually passing out. Moving right along.

The trick was not to stop. So I put it on automatic—showered, shaved, stypticked, dressed, and staggered to the door.

The Phantom was parked by the litter box with a definite cranky look on his lopsided face (result of biting a live electric wire before moving in with me from the semipro lady living above, I was pretty sure) but I definitely wasn't up for cleaning animal toilets at the moment. Take the damn things in out of the cold and next thing you know they're making demands.

I kept from eye contact and dodged his taking a swipe at me as I popped through the kitchen and out the door.

I set the house alarm, pushed the button raised the garage door and got into my classic '64 Cadillac convertible. All of which seemed to clue the motherfucking dogs next door to try for even louder howling and barking. I got the hell out of there.

With a song in my heart.

I popped down the hill, duked right, right again, then looped into the sharp left that cut into Doheny Drive heading down to Sunset.

I hit Sunset, turned left, past the famous old Scandia restaurant (mismanaged by new owners into empty), then the block they were about to tear down to put up another empty mall. (I don't know beans about business, but it doesn't take a rocket scientist to figure when they can't rent forty, fifty percent of the ones they already have, putting up more's not the greatest idea.)

Then by Carolco, across from Tower Records, by Horn—up which is Spago, doing so good they'd begun cramming the tables back to back close enough you could catch dandruff—and turned into Mirabelle.

My partner Bradley, among other faults a morning person, was naturally already waiting. He'd no doubt also already been up for hours and Nautilused himself half to death. Young people today sure have twisted values.

He knew enough to get a table toward the back (away from the sunny street, with my place set facing in) at which he was sipping an orange juice and reading the paper, which I could see was all about last night.

"Hey, hi," I managed.

"And a good morning to you," he said. "I took the liberty of ordering you a Bloody Mary, double Mary, easy on the blood," he added with a slightly superior smile. Which I generously decided to overlook since he seemed to have the priorities right.

"You're a gentleman, a scholar, and a pederast," I answered, covering thanks and smartassery.

He took a moment when I thought he'd let it pass, opted for a GPCP (Gay Pride Counter Punch). "It strikes me," he said, "that by now you'd *begin* to catch on I'm not totally thrilled with homophobic zingers."

"I begin," I said. "It's just I'm a weak person, and a victim of my conditioning. So where's the fucking drink?"

I turned around—still no easy move—to check for the waitress. And there she was, Julia Roberts—one of the terrific beauties they staff the place with.

They were equal opportunity employers—all the girls had an equal opportunity to show their body. Julia had on a skirt a bit higher than the table and only a little lower than paydirt, tight enough not to get snagged on anything—besides teeth. Safety first!

Spite of my condition, I was able to appreciate all this as she smoothly made her way over with my celery float and put it and herself down in front of me, a combination close to actual foreplay.

I surely do love living in a town you could cast a major movie from the help.

"There you go, sir," she said, with a smile big enough to figure maybe life's going to work out after all. "May I bring you a menu?"

"I know what I want," said Bradley.

"I know what I want, too," I said. "But I'm going to have breakfast."

Now, just in passing—believe me, the woman was not insulted to hear she was desirable and hadn't done all that working out and orthodontia for nothing. (I find most of the ones who say flattery's just a male chauvinist ploy tend to be on the doggy side and not apt to get victimized by it a whole lot.)

We both ordered—me, another Mary first.

When Bradley called this morning I was glad to hear we were off the hook on going back to Anaheim to give our statements. He said the one I gave wasn't particularly helpful (I didn't exactly remember giving it, tell you the truth) but they had so many witnesses they didn't feel any need for more of the same.

"So what do the papers have to say?" I asked, finding out chewing on the lemon from the bottom of the glass wasn't the best idea first thing in the morning.

"Basically, this Kiskessler guy's some kind of conspiracy freak the FBI—and Secret Service, for that matter—have a file on. He's tried to join the CIA, and FBI and Treasury, and it seems actually did join a number of hate groups—he says as undercover agent."

"Undercover agent? Who for?"

"He says if he tells that he blows his cover."

"That's all in the paper?"

"Some. Some I got from Francine, earlier."

Francine was our crack researcher, and my ex-girlfriend. She had a longer track record as researcher, sorry to say. I somehow had botched up a very meaningful relationship, but for the life of me, I didn't know how or why. Which, given the complicated rules today, may have been the reason.

"And what do you figure?" I asked Bradley, getting back to business.

"I figure he's your basic homophobe."

"If I remember from last night, he didn't totally specialize in that."

"Target of opportunity."

"Fischer?"

"No, my guess is he was merely attracted to a large gathering of gays and lesbians."

"So Fischer just by accident?"

"I don't actually know, but I can't see why anybody'd want to take out somebody as innocuous and unimportant as Fischer. Who I don't think was even gay."

"But the shooter guy named everybody and everything. He might of also been against bald guys with ponytails."

"Might have at that, you could be right."

The food showed up, and I went to work on a stack of hotcakes, bacon, eggs, and wheat toast. I always found the best way to get over a hangover was to eat your way out. If you weren't too nauseous.

"You don't pay any attention whatsoever to your cholesterol," said Bradley.

"Is that a question?"

"You are a man with a heart condition. You have had attacks. Two angioplasties."

"So that I could enjoy a nice breakfast. Though the doctor did say I should cut down on the aggravation."

"I'll say no more."

"I doubt that all to hell."

Kathleen Turner asked did I want more coffee (Julia was on a break, looked like). I nodded yes, though I'd of preferred another blast. Just didn't seem like the time to give Bradley any more ammo. And she poured. Real nicely.

"So we're off the hook for Anaheim. Then why'd you want to see me?" I asked.

"I've grown accustomed to your charms." For sure. "No, I thought you'd like to assume some of the duties of cowriter and help me with the proofs on *Jaeger*."

"Can't you have some secretary do that?"

"Not if you want to guard your prose and make sure they don't 'correct' all your punch lines."

"Why would they do that?"

"It's one of the mysteries of the ages."

"Well, sure, I guess. And we could discuss maybe doing some other project? Make us a few dollars."

"I don't see why not. Something perhaps you could get started on while I finish *my* book."

There was a certain note of insincerity there I didn't feel up to dealing with this morning. I finished the coffee, put down the cup. Gaining.

Bradley looked up, spotted the maitresse d' (Michelle Pfeiffer), made a writing move with his hand (they should really make a holding up a credit-card move) and mouthed the word, "Check."

"Expense account?" I asked.

"I don't know."

"Continuation of a business function," I suggested. "About to proof ourselves."

"Long reach. I think our publisher's a little slicker than that."

"Give it a shot," I said, as still another stunner came with the check and I watched as he gave you'd swear Kim Basinger his card.

New York can talk theater and museums all they want, I love L.A.

I followed his BMW in my Cad as we circled on back of Holloway and around to Sunset, right to Sunset Plaza (where we had to wait three lights—lots of construction up ahead) and on up to Rising Glen. Then to Thrasher, Tanager, and the other bird streets. And my house.

He parked out front. I pulled into the garage.

I always parked and entered through the back door because first of all it didn't have steps leading up (darling, we are growing old-er), and it was the only flat surface on the steep hill, so I didn't have to worry about old brakes letting go—which visiting cars had happen time to time.

He followed me into the kitchen where I tried to not pay any attention to the pointed dump the Phantom'd taken alongside the litter box to clue me we weren't in total sync on the litter-changing schedule. And moved on into the living room.

Bradley took out the proofs of our latest book, *Jaeger, a House Divided,* which was about when I was on the jury for Carey Jaeger's murder trial. Well, actually I got thrown off it, but I did prove the kid was innocent and big old Stacy Jaeger could go back to making movies— and taking on fat.

"I thought what we might do," said Bradley, spreading out the pages. "I'd take a half-dozen chapters and you take the same and check for typos and omissions or whatever."

Just then the dogs next door, which had been barking and howling all along suddenly got even more frantic.

"What *is* that?" said Bradley. "I don't know how you can work with all that going on."

"Can't too good," I said. "Which is maybe why I haven't come up with a perfect idea for the next book."

"Does it go on often?" he said, ignoring the hint.

"Mostly weekends. When Teri leaves them alone."

"Teri."

"Teri Dart."

"Sounds familiar. Would I know her?"

"Sure. She's the original babe kept baring her tits at the Cannes film festival."

"Right, I think I remember reading about that. It's some sort of an annual event? 'The Boobs of Spring.' She's an actress, right? What am I saying—no, she's a neurosurgeon."

"Originally a dancer. Tap dancer. Came along just about when they decided not to make musicals anymore."

" 'Timing is everything.' Seth Thomas."

"Actually, she had her moment in the sun when they started doing some soft porn in the late fifties, early sixties. Her biggie was *Bimbos on Broadway*."

"Hard act to follow."

"For some reason she thought taking her clothes off was going to make her a star. So she kept doing it. First Cannes, then Monte Carlo, and through the years ... Cairo, Crakow, till now it's sort of like, down to Compton."

"That's sad."

"And sadder she still thinks she's going to make it."

"You seem to know a lot about her."

"Well, we once had a little fling."

"Ah, tender feelings?"

"Nothing penicillin didn't handle."

Actually, I was being a little more flippant than truthful. Must be close to twenty years ago, Teri and I'd had a thing for a while. That was almost pretty good. I knew she was a tramp, but then again, so was I. Problem was, I had the notion she'd put it on hold while we were together. She never understood why I couldn't see one thing had nothing to do with the other. I knew that, but I also knew that only worked if you were both pros—in the same business.

But in those days she was at least also more fun than crazy.

"She lived here long?" Bradley was saying, as the barking lightened up a bit.

"About a year and a half. We went out a couple times again when she first moved in but the old magic wasn't there." Especially since the old attitude was. "We haven't talked now in, oh, the better part of a year."

And there went the dogs again, with another burst of barking.

"What's with all the dogs?" said Bradley.

"She kind of picks up strays."

"So I gather."

"All kinds. She's got a whole menagerie up there. Dogs, cats, too; once a snake, I think. She does love animals. Beyond reasonable."

"She doesn't mind the barking?"

"Doesn't hear it. Usually means she's away. On 'dates.' "

"Making ends meet by making ends meet?"

"That's about it. Let me check it out," I said, reaching for my address book.

I dialed, let it ring four times, and a machine kicked in.

"Hiiii," it said in the throaty voice of the devil we'd been speaking of. "I'm not here at the moment, but I dooo want to talk to you, so puleese, at the ... tooone, leave your name and number and I'll ... get ... back to you. 'Byeeee."

"It's me, uhm, Ray, uhm, neighbor Ray? Goodman," I said to the machine. "Never mind, I'll call again." And hung up. What was I going to say, sorry we almost fell in love but it was a long time ago and by the way, there's a lot of barking you're not here to hear? (And a lot of loving you're not here to get.)

And right on cue the dogs starting howling even more, if that was possible.

"This is ridiculous," said Bradley. "I can't work with this."

"It's worse than usual, even for her."

"Don't you think you ought to go check on it? Maybe she's been murdered in her bed."

"My recollection, she could take care of herself in bed."

"Suit yourself, but this is not working for me."

So I agreed to take a look.

I wasn't surprised nobody answered the door. Nobody'd answered the phone.

I climbed over the short front fence. Right away challenged by six or eight snarling, hysterical dogs. With crazy eyes and bad vibes.

I inched my way around the side of the house (which, like mine, was hung on the hill and didn't give you a lot of spots to put your feet). Then climbed to the pathway led around back. The dogs alternated running at me and away, front, then back—definitely spooked. As I grabbed handfuls of bushes and made my way up to the patio.

And the back.

And right on the money no big surprise, floating in the heart-shaped pool, the no-longer-any-shaped Teri.

Hate when that happens.

# 4

# Mark Bradley

It seemed to me the dogs were barking a bit less and howling a great deal more. Which didn't constitute a major improvement, and either way was entirely too distracting for any serious work. Ergo I go.

To that end I'd commenced packing the proof pages back into my tote (absolutely no use pretending Goodman would do any of it left to his own devious devices) preparatory to taking my leave. At which juncture the door burst open and himself hurtled in, all asweat and disarrayed with a blood-pressure-driven complexion seven shades past ruddy to the far side of aubergine.

"Calm down," I cautioned, in deference to his medical history. "Easy does it. Take a couple of deep breaths."

He calmed, he easy did it, he deep breathed.

"So," I said in that talk-nice-to-the-crazy-man-with-the-bomb way, smooth-smiling, toothily reassuring. "What's up?"

"Pshew!" he said uninformatively, dashing past me and sliding to a halt before his desk. There he frantically pulled open drawers and rummaged through till he found a camera; then another frenetic search to produce a mini-tape recorder, and a folded plastic bag.

" 'Pshew' doesn't quite cover it for me," I said, hoping for a little exposition. But instead he merely grabbed me roughly by the arm, and said, "C'mon!"

"C'mon where? What's up?"

"Out back. In the pool." He pointed vaguely north-easterly. "I had to climb around," he further indicated with a cant of his head, squeezing my arm for a non sequiturial emphasis. "She's dead," he finally added, belatedly identifying the subject of this rambling discourse.

Possessed of a pretty fair idea we weren't talking about one of the dogs I said, "Well, wait. Shouldn't we be calling the police, or something?"

"Sure. In about five minutes. Ten, tops."

Which was the obvious limit of his patience as he gave me an explanation-ending yank and dragged me back through the kitchen where I ricocheted against a closet door, sending an already alarmed Phantom dashing behind the washing machine. Then to a lurching synchronized pileup at the door, a live homage to two-thirds of the Three Stooges, before he opened the back door and we were out, through the garage and into the street. And without further comedic choreography quickly up the hill and to the house next door.

Typically Californian, the dwelling bore no stylistic relationship to any of the others around it. Actually, it didn't appear to have been designed so much as simply built, a sort of Fifties Eisenhower-bland generic "ranch style" one-floor structure.

Goodman had unlocked the front door on his way out, so we didn't have to duplicate his original precarious climb around back, for which I was grateful. The man didn't look up to another reverse rappel at the moment (or most moments, given his condition, and disdain for getting into any).

The interior was either an eclectic, if you were generous, or bizarre, if you were objective, mix of decorator styles. Or lack thereof. It looked like a defunct storage facility in Neosho—with accessories from Woodstock. Whatever oddball charm or attraction it might have once projected under certain circumstances (drunk and horny came to mind) was qualified by the fact it appeared to have gone uncleaned, dusted, or even aired in any remotely measurable past.

Additionally, the place had obviously been ransacked—every drawer was dislodged, pillows torn up, pictures ripped from the walls—which could have been vandalism but looked more to be the result of an intensive search for something.

To top that off, or more accurately bottom it off, the dogs had apparently expressed their distress in various unseemly digestive ways willy-nilly helter-skelter and with incredible frequency.

At the moment what looked to be at least a half-dozen overweight and frenzied mongrels dashed about in lathery confusion and urinary panic. Adding to the monumental disarray was an occasional flurry of fur as a cat or two scurried hither and yon, mostly yon. It was extraordinarily disorienting.

"She's in the pool," said Goodman, as I stood rapt in shock. "You might want to take a look."

"Why would I want to do that?"

"Experience. For one thing, even a quick look, it wasn't simple drowning. She was badly worked over."

"I'm really quite willing to take your word for it."

Even in the midst of all this chaos and disorder I couldn't help reflect on the frightening turn my life had taken since associating with Goodman. While it certainly wasn't his fault, the fact remains before I knew him there'd been no violent deaths in my life or even proximity. And now two in two days! Not what Mother had in mind for her little boy.

Meanwhile he was striding through the various rooms, shooting lots of film—for what reason I couldn't imagine—me now tagging along, for a very definite reason—the clear recollection of a lot of scary movies where people senselessly separate and make it easy for the mad killer.

"What *are* we doing here?" I finally asked, when he stopped for a moment.

"Looking for clues."

"How about the possibility the perpetrator's still around?"

"No, no—long gone."

"How do you know?"

"The dogs. They'd be chasing him instead of only us. See if you can find her answerphone." And he tossed me the mini-recorder. Then he stood for a moment, obviously pondering a decision.

"What?" I finally asked.

"Trying to think should I have you erase my call."

"Why? It was perfectly legitimate. You wanted to complain about the noise."

"Yeah, I guess."

I couldn't see why he'd want to tamper with evidence for no reason at all. I know I didn't feel inclined to. Although it was possible he was so conditioned to being hassled by his former police nemesis, Chief Broward, that he was simply reflexively evasive.

"You know, you don't have to worry about that kind of stuff anymore," I reminded him. The chief had long since retired to some offshore unextradictable haven—to luxuriate in his ill-gotten gains—replaced by the eminently more reasonable and honest Lieutenant Lewis Ellard (with whom we had worked on a previous occasion to our mutual benefit).

"You're right. Okay, leave whatever you find on the tape, but dub it for us, just in case there's something we can use."

"What, use? What're you talking about?"

"Go," he urged me. Adding, with Nikelike insistence, "Just do it."

So I went, found the answerphone in the master (mistress?) bedroom on a night table, next to a fax machine. I set Goodman's mini-tape to "record," and using its edge to depress the "play" key on the answering machine—to avoid leaving fingerprints (lo, what evil companions had reduced me to)—placed it alongside the answerphone speaker. I didn't pay any special attention to the calls (there were several) since we'd have plenty of time to listen later at our leisure, for reasons that remained obscure to me at the moment anyway.

As the messages played on, I checked out the rest of the room. On the walls and the floor when they'd been dislodged from the walls were several large photos of Teri in better days (one had to feel *any* days were better) and I could see she had been quite attractive in a fairly obvious way. From what I'd learned about her, subtlety hadn't been a strong point. This was pretty well corroborated by the fact all the photos were of Teri undressed and varied in refinement from nude to naked to gynecological. (With the sole exception of a life-size teenage portrait in top hat, tails, tights, black stockings, and bow-decorated taps, which I found, in its determined lack of originality, to be singularly touching.)

Additionally, I found it interesting that there were no photos in which other parties had even a subsidiary role—they were Teri, period. Clearly her primary love interest.

There was one other photo technically not of her alone—it included a horse. Teri *was* clothed in that one—though the horse was nude.

This was obviously a relationship of some value to her as the photo was in a silver frame on the bed table, its glass cracked.

Most of her clothes were off their hangers and on the floor of the large walk-in closet, but whether that was part of the rampage or merely a reflection of indifferent housekeeping, I couldn't be sure. Well, I could really. The woman had clearly been a slob. But clearly, too, somebody or bodys had done a pretty thorough job of looking for something. And the odds were hadn't found it since the disorder was universal throughout the house. (One would assume it would have stopped at the point success was achieved.)

While I was in the closet (literally, in this case), the phone playback continued. I caught snatches of various messages. "You know who this is—miss you, where you been? I'll try again tomorrow," was one.

I kept rummaging through her clothing, most of which seemed to have suffered at least one wearing, often stained—very unappetizing. Another message: "... arv, we *must* talk. Call."

Some others.

Almost all the various things she kept in shelves had been swept onto the floor. The shelf above the clothes rack was totally bare.

I noticed on the same level a bracket-supported half-moon sort of shelf, empty. I guess it was for a fan, though it wasn't there now and was a strange place for one. Perhaps it cooled the bed when the heat was on. That must have been it, as I now noticed a screened panel had been put into the closet door. Though why it'd be needed in a house with central air-conditioning I couldn't imagine. Or maybe I could.

Another couple of messages went by I didn't particularly catch. And, finally, Goodman's.

She had apparently kept every pair of shoes she'd ever bought, most in terrible condition. In the midst of this discovery there was a noise, as of something dropping, which gave me a start, but when there was no further sound I relaxed again.

The phone playback concluded and I returned to the room to pick up Goodman's tape. But it was gone!

TV-movie phony curtain! Before I could call for help, a medium smallish dog I hadn't seen before, either a wire haired terrier—or mostly wire haired terrier (a very un-California un-trendy dog)—sidled with suspicious nonchalance from under the bed and left the room with a studied cool. If dogs could whistle, this one would have. (Could Asta, William Powell's dog, be still alive?)

I bent down and took a look under the bed. Not a pretty sight. I felt fairly certain the mess under there was largely a result of the late Teri Dart's own neglect and not a product of the search. At any rate, sure enough, buried beneath a pile of old and, I felt certain, gender-neutrally repugnant yellowed lingerie, the kleptomaniacal canine had hastily stashed Goodman's tape machine. I retrieved it and crawled back out, amid a dozen dust-bunnies.

I again used its edge to reset the phone tape and resumed searching the rest of the room. But between not knowing what I was looking for and considering that whoever'd been there first had been looking for whatever it was (even probably *knowing* what it was), and not found it, and not really wanting to touch and rummage through anything, it wasn't the most comprehensive search.

Nevertheless, satisfied I'd gotten a sense of the mess, if not entirely of why we weren't obeying the law and contacting the law, I decided to go see what my partner was up to and find out if I was, as I suspected, being simultaneously incriminated, too.

I found him circling the patio deck, delving in and

under furniture, inside the grill of a barbecue device, checking between a pile of fire logs.

"How'd you do, find out anything?" he asked.

"Yes—she didn't exactly run a tight ship."

"Yeah, always was a little on the casual side."

He turned over the cushions on a chaise.

"What do you think they were looking for?" I asked.

"Well, just a guess—I haven't come across an address book. You?"

"No."

"Which in her case might have been more like a trick book."

"Meaning her customers? That kind of trick?"

"I'm not talking Doug Henning."

"So what you're suggesting is murder by someone she knew," I said. "Most likely in the biblical sense."

"Or at least by someone who was put up to it by someone in the book."

"And she was killed because she wouldn't give it up?"

"Not likely. In real life people don't resist torture. You torture people, they talk. Quick. It had to be somehow she didn't know where it was. You find the answer-phone?"

"Yep."

"Tape it?"

I nodded, patting my pocket. "What now?"

He took one final look around, sighed. "Now, good-citizen time. We go back to my place and call the cops."

He took a few more shots of film, including the body—which I managed to avoid looking at pretty well—and on sudden inspiration, took a stick and probed a kitty litter box.

"Any luck?" I asked.

"Only if you're looking for some relatively petrified doo-doo. No, I'd have to say the way the place was tossed and our own shot at it, the address book, and/or whatever else, is still missing."

"Now leave?" I asked.

"Now leave," he answered. Though on the way out he did step into the bedroom for a minute, after which we retraced our steps back to his garage, and through to the kitchen and his large combination dining room/living room/bar/family room/den/office.

It was hard to imagine the house had ever been shared by a wife. My impression was since the main room was large, airy, and had a fantastic view, he'd decided to gather his most functional furniture and spend all his time there (except sleeping) rather than allocate partial usage to a succession of several smaller rooms. Not the most unreasonable choice.

Once inside, he seemed to pause for thought.

"911?" I prompted.

"No, let me call Ellard directly."

"But he's Beverly Hills."

"Yeah, but also sort of chief roving celebrity-scandal cop. And I might as well build up my favors bank."

So Goodman put in his call while I ambled into the kitchen to get a glass of water.

The kitchen window faced the hill between the two properties. And the sink was on that wall. While I was running the water, finding a glass, and filling the glass, I looked out and noticed the fence immediately south of Teri's property had a small hole under it at one point. Definitely too small for any of her large and overweight dogs. The only one capable of using it was at the moment doing just that. Asta, the terrier whose acquaintance I'd made in Teri's bedroom, and a thousand crossword puzzles, slithered underneath and made his way down to Goodman's property. There he favored one of the lovely hybrid rosebushes ("Sheer Bliss," I believe) residual from the marriage to Luana ( I couldn't imagine Goodman actually doing any gardening) with a sample of wire-hair pee. Never the fertilizer of choice.

I drank my water, rinsed the glass, and joined Goodman back in the living room/dining room/den, etc. He'd completed his call.

"They'll be right over. We should keep ourselves available for questioning. As a staunch upholder of the law, I said I'd naturally be at their service."

Then he removed the film from the camera, slipped it into the plastic container ("We'll run this down to the one-hour place after we're done with Ellard"), slipped the mini-recorder into the top drawer of his desk ("Give a listen to this later, too") and likewise dumped the plastic bag, now obviously containing something, into the drawer. Some staunch upholder.

"What's in the bag?" one couldn't help asking.

"Picture of Teri with a horse."

"Yeah, I noticed that. How come you took it?"

"It was the only one anybody was in besides her."

"A horse?"

"Struck me."

"Yeah?"

"Might be a clue."

"So? Why are we taking clues, or whatever strikes you and withholding them from the people who might need them to solve the crime and are supposed to have them?"

He gave me a look of enormous self-satisfaction.

"What? What is that shit-eating grin?"

"You know, I never did understand that expression," he said. "Why would anybody eating shit be grinning? Puking, I could understand."

"All right, why the whatever-grin?"

He sighed, then smiled even more broadly.

"Come on, give me a break," he said. "You don't know this is going to be our next book?"

# 5

# Rayford Goodman

Most police forces, the cops have to live in the town where they're cops. Beverly Hills doesn't have that rule. Because nobody on a cop's pay can afford it. And my guess is the new head of Homicide, Lieutenant Lewis Ellard, wouldn't want to anyway. Being black.

There's no law in Beverly Hills against being black. But no law for it, either.

Beverly Hills does have black people. But mostly they either sing, dance, make movies or are anesthesiologists who wear masks.

I would guess Ellard was the sort who'd find it easier to relax elsewhere. And maybe figure he had a duty to live in some area short on role models.

The Sixties would of been another story. Just breaking into the Establishment made you a model. He could of maybe inspected the Daisy, or the Factory, or Pips, or any of the nighttime disco scenes hot at the time. Casually checking cocaine abuse. Which in those days meant not sharing.

But after a dozen years of returning to family values, the chic thing stopped being the integrated thing.

For whatever reason, Ellard wasn't a hanger-outer.

Of course where I lived technically was the Hollywood Hills, a couple blocks shy of B.H. And about a million short.

I mention all this because I knew Ellard was in the neighborhood. There wasn't much chance of missing the three black-and-whites (Chevies) and the plainclothes cop car (Dodge)—to say nothing of the ambulance and the fire engine. (Personally, I never understood using

those big old fire engines for medical emergencies.
Couldn't they put a first-aid kit in a Honda?)

Lieutenant Ellard was no doubt the user of the plain
cop car. Actually a Dodge in Beverly Hills wasn't exactly
low-profiling it. Since it stuck out like a goiter in the face
of all the Mercedeses, Jaguars, and Rollses.

At any rate it took a surprising long time before the
doorbell rang and Lieutenant Ellard asked could he
come in.

"Mi casa, su pad," I told him.

"Thanks for the call," he said.

"Pretty messy up there."

"Keep *me* out of medical school for sure," he said.
Then asked how we fit in the picture and to tell whatever
we thought might help.

So we went through why I went up there (dogs barking), how I found the body (floated and bloated), how
long she'd been living here (year and a bit), kind of
neighbor (dog-barking kind), anything out of the ordinary I might have recently observed (*nada*) and whatever
else I knew or cared to speculate about Teri Dart. I gave
him the broad public knowledge, pun and all.

Turned out he knew some about her, too. From
before.

"There was an obsessed fan," he said.

"Obsessed *fan*?" said Bradley. "From what, the
Fifties?"

"She wasn't all that old," I reminded him. "I dated
her."

"I rest my case," said Bradley.

"You dated her?" said Ellard, picking right up on it.
Where were my brains?

"I didn't—*date*—her. We went out. Long ago."

"How long ago?"

Before wrinkles and gray and a lot of regrets. "Not
hardly since we're neighbors."

"What's 'hardly'?"

"You mean besides a straight line?" said Bradley.

"Are you saying no contact at all since she moved
here?" said Ellard, sticking to the subject.

"I didn't say no contact. I'd see her in the street, say

hello. I didn't have any contact you could catch anything."

"How about this fan guy? See him around?"

"I don't think so," I said. "I can recall. What'd he look like?"

"Nondescript, late thirties. Your basic nerdy drifter."

"I don't think you can be a nerd and a drifter," said Bradley. "It's a contradiction in terms. I think of a nerd as quiet, introspective, bookish. But a drifter as better-built, outdoorsy. Maybe a construction worker."

"Shirt off, tan? We're not talking cruising here," I reminded him.

"For the sake of this conversation," Ellard cut in, getting back to business, "let's define it as a nerd without a purpose—or at least not a wholesome one."

"She filed a complaint?" I asked.

"Yeah," said Ellard.

"The guy's name?"

"Harvard Lawrence Singleton. There was an injunction. He wasn't allowed to come within, I don't know, a hundred yards."

"Harvard?" said Bradley. "A drifter named Harvard?"

"What do you want from me?" said Ellard. "It's countercasting, all right?"

I was trying to remember. "Pickup truck? The guy had a pickup truck?"

"Toyota," said Ellard. "With the 'TO' and 'TA' painted over on the tailgate."

"A 'YO,'" said Bradley. It'd become a fad. Some people's idea of clever.

"You know, maybe I have seen him," I seemed to remember. "Thin, sandy-haired, tall?"

"Uh-huh."

"Well built?" said Bradley. Then, seeing my look, "Just trying to get a description."

"Yeah," I said to Ellard. "On second thought, I think so. I figured he was doing some work around her house. But I don't remember seeing the truck yesterday particularly."

"Well, we've put out a bulletin. Sort of first-choice best bet."

"They always seem to be blond and thin," said Bradley, avoiding my eyes. "And have three names."

"I must say," said Ellard, must saying, "you fellows certainly managed to be around an awful lot of action lately. Two murders in two days."

"What's that supposed to mean?" I said. "Sounds like something Broward would've said. It's our fault there's so much violence you guys can't keep things under control?"

"Just a simple observation," said Ellard calmly.

"You don't think there's any connection, do you?" asked Bradley.

"How could there be any connection?" I answered. "One's a nutcase shooting indiscriminately in Anaheim and the other's an obsessed fan taking out a party girl in Beverly Hills."

"Hollywood Hills," corrected Ellard, nitpicking. "And we're not positive about the obsessed fan. Anyway," checking his notes, "other than what you've said about the truck and the dogs barking, you didn't see or hear anything?"

"Nope."

"You?" he said to Bradley.

"Just the dogs," said Bradley. Which reminded us both it'd got quiet. "What happened to the dogs?"

"Animal Control. Couldn't leave them just running all over the crime scene, destroying evidence."

"So, where are they?" said Bradley.

"They're wherever they take them. The pound, I guess," said Ellard.

"And what happens?" I got sucked in.

"Well, they hold them. A certain time. In case there're relatives, or something."

"Then?"

"They do whatever they do."

"We know what they do," said Bradley.

"If nobody comes forward, and either of you guys're interested in any of them . . ."

We both also knew when to shut up.

"So that's it, huh? You went in, you found the body, you called."

"About covers it," I said.

"And, of course, you didn't disturb anything."

We both shook our heads.

"I don't know why the fact you live next door doesn't fill me with confidence," said Ellard, I thought unnecessarily.

"Your line of work tends to make you a little cynical," said Bradley, taking my side.

"Okay," said Ellard, heading for the back door. Then he stopped, did one of those little second-thought turns, a black Columbo, and said, "Oh, you didn't by any chance come across any address books or anything with phone numbers or like that?"

"No," said Bradley. "Though she did have an answering machine, because Goodman called to complain about the dogs."

"Ah," said Ellard, who I guess already listened to the tape. Bradley was getting cute, admitting before I got accused of anything. Though I did think I could make up my own mind about my own confessing.

"You went through the house."

"Well, yeah, I didn't want to climb all the way around again."

"Ah-hah," said Ellard. Or Columbo. For a minute there I thought he was going to take out one of those little cigar jobs. "Well, if you think of anything else, you know where to reach me," he finally added. "Thanks again for the call."

We said good-bye, and he headed back to leave through the kitchen.

"You don't think we ..." started Bradley, but I held up a hand to cool him. Sure enough, Ellard stuck his cheery face back in.

"Thought you might like to know, your cat left a ..."

"I know, on the floor. Get to it in a minute. Thanks for sharing."

And this time he actually left.

"You were going to say we should of told him about the picture of her with the horse," I said to Bradley.

He nodded. "I don't know why you took it in the first place."

"I don't either." Something about it touched me. "Instinct," I said. "It's what separates the great detectives from the animals."

"Animals have instincts; that's the part that *is* animal. You've never heard of 'animal instinct'?"

I don't know why this particular moment, but he suddenly really got on my nerves. "Hey!" I said. "Put a lid on it. If I liked arguing I could of stayed married."

Since he'd done all those "as told to" books, practically on staff, Bradley kept an office at our publisher's, Pendragon Press. They were located in the Playboy Building on Sunset Boulevard. (Lucky Bradley—got to see all those pretty models coming in and out. Har har.)

I'd dropped off the film at the one-hour place in the mini-mall across the street on our way over. And now we were in Penny's office where we'd made an appointment to pitch a deal on a Teri Dart book.

Dick Penny was the editor/publisher of Pendragon Press and the guy first put Bradley and me together as a writing team. Bradley hated Penny's guts from way back. I only hated him lately. Since I didn't know him way back.

The fact it was Saturday was no big deal. They always kept open Saturdays because Penny said he believed in the work ethic real bad. Actually, I had a feeling he had to work Saturdays to catch up on all the work he never got done because he was always in the hall spying on everybody else.

He also had some kind of strange ego to keep taking bits of hair from someplace else and trying to have it planted in his head. Plus he'd had new caps put in that made him do a lot of smiling. Which was pretty scary by itself.

Add to that, he was no great sport when it came to a dollar. In a town with offices spiffier than Mussolini's, his looked like a temporary H & R Block. Without the trimmings.

He asked did we want a glass of water, to give you an idea.

"Thanks, we had breakfast," said Bradley, not setting the exact tone I was looking for, either.

"So. What can you do for me?" asked Penny, at least honest.

"We have this really fantastic idea for a biography," I said. "Everybody's always doing books about celebrities and famous actors and what not. How about somebody burst out of the blocks, got a lot of publicity, but never really made it?"

"Like the Edsel?" said Penny, not too encouraging.

"Frankly, we're talking about Teri Dart," I said.

"Oh, the girl kept showing her tits."

"The *first* girl showed her tits," I pointed out. "And the only one during a Presidential Debate."

"I don't know. So, she's a girl took her clothes off and got a lot of publicity. There're a million of them."

"*And* got murdered!" I reminded him, the clincher.

"Like Dorothy Stratten?"

"Not like Dorothy Stratten at all. This girl was a pioneer, you have to remember that. She was taking her clothes off when movie stars still kissed with their mouths closed."

"It doesn't grab me, guys."

"Think of the potential. She knew lots of big celebrities. I mean really *knew* them. A lot of skeletons." I was being professional about this and putting my personal feelings aside. Except maybe my personal feelings about making a dollar.

"What do you think, Mark?"

"I think it's viable."

"How about your own book, *My Life at the Y*—or whatever you're calling it?"

"I'll meet my deadline on that, too. And it's *Not So Quiet The Night,* as you well know."

"Look, boys—I know we've done some nice work together. But it was always on projects we all agreed on. I'd really like to go along with you, but it just doesn't grab me. So some small-time over-the-hill semipro ends up as dead as her career. What's the hook?"

"The hook is we solve the murder."

"First, can you be sure? Second, maybe the police will beat you to it. And third, who cares?"

"I do think you're being a little arbitrary," said Bradley, to my surprise, maybe just not wanting to find himself on the same side as Penny. "Why don't you buy an option and we'll do a presentation with a cutoff. If you still don't like it, you're only out the option money."

"This way if I don't like it, and I don't like it, I'm not out anything."

"So, you want to sleep on it, or what?" I threw in before heading for the lifeboats.

"Guys, you want to do it on spec, it's your business."

"Or take it to another publisher," added Bradley, getting more involved.

"Yes, you could. It wouldn't be very loyal, but I suppose you could. Why don't you go as far as you feel comfortable, then give me first look?"

"For which you'd be willing to pay . . . ?" put in Bradley, more savvy to the business aspects than me.

"Whatever it is we agree at the time if I want to publish it."

"Excuse me, Mr. Penny," I said. "I want to ask my partner a question."

"Yeah?" said Bradley.

"Is this where we tell him to go fuck himself?"

"This is where," said Bradley.


We crossed the street and had a cup of coffee at Ben Frank's, waiting for the Sunset Plaza One-Hour Photo store to finish up. Our interview with Penny hadn't taken as long as we'd planned.

We finished the coffee. Still had twenty minutes to go.

So we took a walk. Not something you do in California. Not in cities, anyway. You want to walk, you drive an hour somewhere and walk *there*. For a town this size we probably have fewer pedestrians than any other city. And we'd have fewer yet if you didn't have the health walkers and joggers busy cardiovascularizing the smog.

There was a new store another block down just opened up called the Spy Factory. They sold bugging devices and infrared gizmos—all the stuff it was legal to sell but illegal to use. I'd been meaning to check it out anyway.

It was kind of a switch on pornography, which was legal to have but illegal to make. Whoever it was said the law's an asshole had it right.

They had some cute hardware and sophisticated ways to invade the privacy of your neighbor. Not basically my kind of thing. I thanked the guy and we killed the time.

The pictures were ready. I'd taken the better part of a thirty-six-shot roll. Standing in the parking lot, I gave a batch to Bradley, and thumbed through a batch on my own.

In my experience you just shot everything in every way and every once in a while you got lucky.

"What're these?" asked Bradley. "I don't recognize them."

"Those're the inside of the cabana back of the pool. I don't guess you went in there."

I'd gone through almost two dozen others and nothing jumped out at me.

"Was it air-conditioned?" Bradley asked.

I had to think. "Yeah, it was. I remember now because it was actually cold with all the doors and windows closed. Why?"

"Because it has the same mount for a fan as she had in the bedroom. With no fan. And it looks like this one's in a closet, too."

I took the picture and gave it a look. Took a moment.

"Those aren't mounts for fans," I said, recognizing we'd got lucky. "They're where camcorders used to be."

# 6

# Mark Bradley

We were back at Goodman's house, all the photographs spread out on his dining-room table, old Sherlock poring over them with a large magnifying glass. I could just see the "hold" button flickering on my book. We were definitely involved.

Not that I wanted to be. I was well into writing *Not So Quiet The Night,* my not very disguised autobiographical novel. Which one wouldn't expect of someone with my professional experience, autobiography being the cliché grist for a first-time novelist's mill (to say nothing of lines like that). But given the particularity of my life in mainstream terms, and the incipient backlash currently gaining force, it seemed an appropriate time to do it—personally and politically.

Which is not to say it wasn't painfully poignant to dig up memories and reminiscences of loves lost both figuratively and literally (oh the dreadful toll), and the concurrent distress reflecting on my present solitary existence evoked.

It mattered surprisingly little that I'd enjoyed some financial success and more importantly lucked out in the health department despite an inordinate amount of world-class outrageous behavior during the times that was considered sophisticated. I still had to cope with present loneliness and diminished prospects. Come to me, my melancholy.

While recent years had produced a great deal of enlightenment and heightened awareness in the straight world, most gays, sad to say, still hadn't come to grips with their own sub-bias in superficially overvaluing physical beauty. Which almost automatically included ageism.

It was a young man's market (our hearts are not *old* and gay), with a seemingly inflexible premium on youth. And a world where anybody over thirty bought the drinks.

Coupled with that, however, since I was now both thirty and able easily to afford the drinks, was the reluctance to go where the drinks—and the dangers— colluded.

"See, here's the hole," said Goodman, startling me back to the project at hand. "Where the camera cable went in the wall. She couldn't have it just manually operated. Had to be fairly sophisticated for any kind of remote control."

"You're convinced this was for blackmail? It couldn't be just some Rob Lowe kind of kick?"

"Remember her place? The kind of slob. Was that a person could organize this sort of thing, choose hardware, install it, pick angles?"

"I'd have to say no," I agreed. "So what you're suggesting, not alone was it blackmail but blackmail in concert with a partner?"

"Seems like."

"Then the next question has to be were the tapes actually kept in the house, did the killer or killers get them, and did they kill her for revenge or in the act of trying to find out where they were?"

"I doubt it, I don't know, and maybe neither—they could've killed her merely to shut her up."

"So, what now?"

"Let's listen to the tape."

"The tape? We don't know where the tapes are."

"The answerphone tape," he explained, just a touch impatiently, as he went to his desk, opened the drawer and took out the mini-recorder I'd used to dub Teri's answering machine. I crossed over to join him as he put it atop his desk and pushed "play."

The first message was evidently from a store. "This is Gretchen, of Mary's Melrose. I have to tell you Mary's getting real bent about your check. You said redeposit, and we redeposited. And so far all we're getting is NSF's. Mary said last chance or we'll have to turn it over to the collection agency."

Which informed us that Teri'd been in financial difficulty.

"Or just careless," said Goodman. I love the way nothing pins anything down with him.

The second message went: "Hi. Bill Henford? I don't know if you remember me. I was the guy at the bar at Nicky Blair's about a week ago? I bought you a Kir? And then a Campari? Then a Kaluha?"

"Right, she'd certainly remember talking to a guy she met in a bar a week ago," said Goodman, fast-forwarding.

"She might if she threw up on him," I suggested, considering the mix.

Then a hang-up.

Next one went, "Harry. Finally got through to Howie at TriStar and he passed. Looks like Sid won't let me renew. I'm real sorry, but we haven't been doing all that good for you anyhow. I'll try to help find you another agent. And I hope this doesn't mean we can't still be friends every once in a while some afternoon. I'll call you. 'Bye."

Career not exactly in high. But that wasn't any news.

Another hang up. Busy girl. Or busy body.

Then an intriguing number. "It's Leah again. I'm not going to just go away. It's up to you, if you want money or you want trouble. And I mean a lot of trouble. You know the number." This in a voice totally void of regional accent. Actress? Second language?

"If I had a choice, I'd go for the money," said Goodman.

Next, "Hi, Teri. Been trying for days to get you— heh heh—guess I'll have to just keep at it." Not much clue there.

Followed by: "This is your Taxi Man. Got your message, but you didn't say did you want the green taxi or the white taxi, or how many rides. Check you later." Apparently small-time dope dealers hadn't gotten noticeably more inventive. ("Bring the car with the *white*walls, I want an eighth whitewall.")

Then there was some static, maybe a crimp in the tape,

and a partially obliterated message, which I'd caught before in Teri's bedroom. ". . . arv, we *must* talk. Call."

Next a sobbing voice saying, "Teri, it's Matt. Damn it, oh, I'm so sorry. I couldn't help it. I really tried. Are you all right? Call me, huh? 'Bye. Oh, shit."

"That didn't bode too well," I said.

"Matt," said Goodman, hitting "pause." "Now, who is Matt, and why is he so upset?"

Of course I didn't know. Goodman pressed "play" again, and we monitored the next call. "Fabrisio Sugarman. Why aren't you picking up your calls? Get back to me, it's important."

"Fabrisio Sugarman?" I said. "Of the U.S. Pictures Sugarmans?"

"No, the diabetes Sugarmans. Who else?" said Goodman, really cranky.

"Hey, lighten up. Just asking."

"Well, how many Fabrisio Sugarmans do you think there are?"

"I didn't know there were any. I heard of *Albert* Sugarman, the old movie mogul."

"It's the same family. Albert pensioned off the original Selma or Sylvia or whatever and married Gabriella Allegretto. You remember her?"

"Very vaguely," I said.

"Sure you do, she was the Sicilian Volcano. One of those starlets same time as Gina Lollobrigida."

I remembered her. Thanks to late night TV—and Trivial Pursuit. And Gabriella vaguely, too. "As I recall she just made one or two American pictures and then retired."

"Sugarman's idea. He was a producer. Knew all about actresses and actors, and actresses and directors. And actresses and any warm bodies happened to be around. Plus, by this time he wasn't any spring chicken. So, he figured get her out of the business if he wanted to keep the home fires home."

"Barefoot and pregnant?"

"Well, she was about as barefoot as Imelda Marcos. But you get the general idea."

"They began the begat?"

"Right. I think they had six kids altogether. The ones I remember are Marcello, Lorenzo, and Fabrisio."

"I got a feeling Mama Gabriella got to do the naming. They in the picture business, too?"

"Well, they tried. A lot of development deals, with Papa putting up the development money. An actual picture or two, but no talent. Lord knows he could afford it. Used to do all those swashbuckling *Captain From Capri* kind of things. The whole bunch're filthy rich, last I heard. Another expression I don't understand. Filthy *poor* makes sense."

"That being the case," I couldn't help wondering, "filthy rich—what would Fabuloso be doing with somebody like Teri?"

"Good question," said Goodman, evidently without a ready answer, turning the tape back on.

The final entry went: "It's me, uhm, Ray, uhm, neighbor Ray? Goodman. Never mind, I'll call again."

Well, almost the final. Technically, there was one more—a hang-up. Followed by the long hum that filled out the allotted time, frighteningly reminiscent of a heart monitor flat-lining.

In the past, the books we'd done together had been commissioned by Pendragon. With contracts, and advances, and the sure knowledge that the project was going to go forward. But now we were in a situation where we were sort of going forward on our own not so much out of any great conviction but propelled by petulance and a desire for revenge on Dick Penny. Which suddenly struck me as something less than the best motivation. Additionally, for all his shortcomings (which were so numerous they should have been called longcomings) Penny was not without business acumen. And if he felt so certain there was no book in this idea, why was I interrupting production on my own novel, bought and advanced against, to spec-write something only my partner, not really renowned for his perspicacity anent matters literary, saw great merit in? And how could I get out of it?

These were the thoughts that occupied me as we stood facing the north window in Goodman's kitchen, fashioning sandwiches for ourselves out of the wealth of culinary delights he kept on hand.

When the key broke off the can of sardines, and the electric can opener only managed to mash one corner without making a continuous cut, and Goodman's long-nosed pliers kept slipping off the stub of the key tab as a result of the leaking olive oil that covered his hands, I had a hunch we weren't in for the best luncheon I'd ever had.

"It is the twentieth fucking century," he began. "Not all that far from the twenty-first. Is it really such a stretch to expect the goddamn Norwegians or whoever the fuck it is to go on line with pull-tab cans?"

"Hey, I thought you were the traditionalist who considered the old ways were the best ways. We could go out for lunch."

"We can't go out, Francie's coming." At which point he inserted a screwdriver with definite rust stains into the corner with the slight hole in it and attempted to pry the top back.

"Hey," I said. "You know what sounds good to me? Eggs. Wouldn't eggs go nice? I'll even make them. Why don't you go inside and make yourself a Bloody Mary or something."

"I could still get the damn sardines out. If the batteries weren't down on my portable drill."

Thank God. "Just let me take care of it. Go ahead. Think about the case. Make notes."

And he tacitly agreed, leaving the room. But not before admonishing, "Fried. But not runny. I don't like my eggs runny."

I would try to bear that in mind. I didn't think it was a good idea to tell him I was so kitchen-inept I always either ate at restaurants or had take-out sent in.

I found a pan, the cleanliness of which I didn't want to examine too closely, put some margarine in it, the age of which neither, and after cracking and running two yolks, which I threw away, managed to get four eggs whole and intact into a pan and onto the stove. Neither a hausfrau nor a bachelor, fish nor fowl, there was a message here. I wasn't having a good time.

Assembling the various accouterments—stale bread, steak sauce, whatever might mollify my cranky cohort— I glanced out of the window and noticed Teri's terrier (forever Asta in my mind), slithering through the hole beneath her fence. Then the dog slid down the hill, and once again went to Goodman's rosebush where he sniffed, dug a hole, and did his stuff. So evidently he'd managed to avoid the dogcatcher and the I didn't want to think about it fate of the other animals she'd had.

"Hey, Goodman," I called.

"Yeah?"

"One of Teri's dogs is still around. The terrier. Asta— remember Asta? Maybe you ought to feed it."

"Yeah, right, to encourage it to go away."

"It's probably hungry."

"So am I, how are those eggs coming?"

Ooh, the eggs. Which had begun to burn. (I didn't know eggs could burn.)

"I don't think you're going to have to worry about them being too runny," I said.

We settled down to eat at the coffee table in front of the couch. (The dining room table was covered by the photos, the magnifying glass, the tape recorder, the silver-framed picture of Teri with the horse, and what looked to be a year's worth of unanswered mail and unpaid bills.)

He groused and grumbled and acknowledged my inferior cooking did serve a purpose. Not so much to nourish as to disabuse him of a stereotype concerning those of my ilk. He didn't say it that politely, but I think it was supposed to be a compliment.

And the doorbell rang.

As expected, it was Francine Rizetti, my ace researcher and confidante, ex-lover of Goodman (we all have *something* we don't include in the résumé), and reformed, crankily recovering dope addict.

If that sounds negative, it shouldn't. She was also my best friend, and whatever slight shortcomings she was heir to were akin to my inability to cook—part of her ambient charm. I adored her and she was worth it, as the ad advises.

She carried a battered attaché case, a portable P.C., and a fresh pizza, and as usual offered no greeting (as a matter of non-form—she believed life was continuous and not made up of fits and starts).

"OK," said Goodman. "You guys can eat the attaché case and I get the pizza." Apparently the eggs had left him less than totally satisfied.

"The pizza's for me," said Francine. "I know what kind of pantry this bozo keeps."

"The only reason I don't have a well-stocked freezer is I'm still pining over you," said Goodman, with more than a little truth, I felt certain. "And it's affected my appetite."

"You could have fooled me," said Francine, staring at his middle. "Drilled a few new holes in the old belt, I see."

"Actually, sweetheart, you don't seem to be wasting away yourself," he responded. Which was true. Francine had put on nearly ten pounds since embracing sobriety.

"I don't have the *Vogue* cocaine diet going for me anymore. This is the real me, baby fat restored—isn't that thrilling?" she replied, opening the pizza and removing a slice.

The truth to be known, she'd always tended to be a little overweight by Beverly Hills standards, but her extraordinarily beautiful skin, shining hair, and naturally full lips made for a lush conventional sensuality. I would imagine.

"Anyhow," she continued, digging into her attaché case to remove a large folder of clippings as she finished chewing and swallowing, "I've done a little advance stuff on Teri Dart, just to get a feel."

I didn't even bother asking how she knew we'd be doing a book. Knowing such things and anticipating my needs had always been a mere peripheral aspect of her talents as a researcher.

Goodman quietly helped himself to a slice, his interest obviously divided.

"Most of it's publicity," Francine went on. "The

woman had more publicity per actual movie made than Jayne Mansfield—remember her?"

"Of course I remember her," said Goodman, swallowing a bite. "Wasn't that long ago."

"Final bow—June 1967," she recited, taking another piece of pizza.

"Jesus," said Goodman. "I don't know what's worse, everybody dying all over the place, or the ones left turning into those 'blast from the past' pictures look like Civil War vets."

"Now, let's not get maudlin," said Francine.

"And Karl Malden, you seen him?" Goodman was reminded. "His nose got bigger than his hat."

"So, what else have you come up with?" I asked Francine before Goodman became totally depressed.

"Well, nothing that jumps out at me so far. All the taking off her tops, through the years—and funny that the top stayed in the same place," she added, just a touch of bitchiness. "The woman was a hundred and ten but the boobs were still under warranty."

"Now, now," I said. "Whatever happened to women sticking up for one another?"

"She sticks up, at least I have the decency to sag," she replied.

She didn't, really. As I say, a little *zaftig,* maybe, but with a youthful bounce.

"But I haven't really gotten into it much yet," she continued, back to business. "Though I have a feeling news clips aren't going to help us a whole bunch. Oh, yeah, a nasty divorce—but only one and a long time ago."

"Name?" asked Goodman.

She didn't have to look. "Buzz Baxter."

"That sounds familiar," I said. "Or else it's a comic strip."

"Produced and directed the early soft-porn stuff in the late Fifties, early Sixties. The first time anything like it had gone mainstream, with actual releases in regular theaters. Of course, all pretty tame by current standards, but hot stuff at the time."

"Yes, I remember," said Goodman, having managed

to finish off a slice of the pie. "I may be old, but I still have all my facilities.'

"Faculties," prompted Francine.

"Whatever. Not that a good memory isn't a mixed blessing."

"Come on, don't get into that all over again," I told him.

"Anyway," continued Francine, "a little flurry when the old movies found their way onto cable and our girl tried to get a few dollars out of old Buzz."

"Did she prevail?" I asked.

"I think she got something, yes. Even though technically the Screen Actors' Guild hadn't been able to get residuals before a certain date—I can find out exactly, if you want."

"It doesn't matter," said Goodman. "What matters is if she wangled a settlement."

"No settlement, they actually went to court and she won an award."

"Ah-hah," I said. "So we can add another suspect, the former husband, Buzz Baxter. You're sure it's not Buzz Baxter, Space Cadet—or something?"

"Technically we can add him," said Goodman, ignoring my aside. "But if it happened so long ago, why would he act now, after all these years?"

Maybe because he'd become senile and paranoid nursing a grudge came to mind, but discretion advised me not to mention. Goodman wasn't in a mood for any subjective kidding involving age.

"And what have you guys got?" asked Francine, biting into her second slice.

We covered everybody mentioned on the answerphone tape while she entered all the names and made notes on her portable computer. Then we led her to the dining room table on which were the photos, which we explained to her—and how we found the camcorder mounts but no tapes. That significance. And commented on the certainty there had to be an address book of some sort. And that we hadn't found either the tapes or the address book.

"What's this?" she said, indicating the broken glass

frame in which was mounted the picture of Teri and the horse.

"I took that from the night table by her bed," said Goodman.

"The only picture I can see that wasn't of her alone," observed Francine.

"Yeah. Struck me, too. Why I took it."

"So you think it's her horse?"

"Could very well be," I said.

"And she keeps it where?"

"Don't have a clue."

"But the tapes and address book weren't in the house."

"It wouldn't appear they were."

"So they'd have to be someplace else."

"You think where she keeps the horse," said Goodman, getting the message.

"Good possibility."

"And now you're going to tell us how we find out where that is," I said.

"Well, that could be a job and a half," said Francine, picking up the frame, carefully removing the shards of glass, and taking out the picture.

"There must be God knows how many stables in the Valley, dismissing the additional possibility it could be kept at a private home zoned for it."

She examined the photo, turned it over.

"On the other hand," she said, indicating the writing on the back, "it could be as it says here, 'Warlock, photo by Anton Leimert, taken at Keeny Stables, Chatsworth.' "

Goodman and I exchanged embarrassed looks.

"Anybody want that last piece of pizza?" said Francine, arranging her lush, collagen-free lips into a smug moue.

# 7

# Rayford Goodman

Because it was the weekend and everybody had plans (Francie to see some guy named Marshal Hildebrandt that Bradley'd told me about a while back, Bradley himself to visit his mother, me to mumble a lot) we shut down till Monday morning.

Which was good in a way. It left time for thinking and to figure what next. Well, actually, watch a lot of ball games, wear sweats, and check how gray my beard would be if I stopped shaving.

Sunday I ran out of booze and decided to test my willpower. I really could take it or leave it. Especially napping.

Monday I got up feeling not too terrible (which was my version of raring to go), did the morning things with the animal (food and litter), cleaned my face and body, put on some clothes, and waited for Bradley and Francie.

They came in Bradley's car about a quarter after ten.

This was a very special time (not the quarter after ten, the time in a case), I always felt. The real beginning. It was like you got the jigsaw puzzle, opened the box, and dumped the pieces on the table. Then you sort of fiddled around getting them flat, right side up, before deciding an opening move—like a corner to start.

Well, we had our puzzle—who killed Teri Dart? And some of the pieces already on the table. Plus a tentative move or two—the photos, which'd established it was likely there'd been videotapes; the answerphone messages, giving us some names; and the picture with the horse, a possible place where the tapes and/or the missing address book might be. Now we needed to pick a corner to start.

"What's worked for us in the past," I said, still a little embarrassed I hadn't thought to look back of the photo for an address, "let's divvy up our efforts. I figure Francie, you should keep on researching Teri, taking whatever side trips into whoever she was involved with you think might be helpful."

"Boy, that's real specific," said Francie. "You really nailed it." I don't know why she kept always being snide and sarcastic with me. She wasn't the injured party, I was. (Hereinafter called the dumpee.)

"All right, you want specific—for openers find out who Harry the agent is, see if you can get a current whereabouts on Buzz Baxter, the ex-husband, ditto what Fabrisio Sugarman's up to these days."

And it wouldn't hurt being a little nicer to me. Forgetting our own personal history, even the Intervention when we all bullied her into taking the cure was going on a year already. Why was she still mad? And madder by the minute?

When was the new sober, in-charge-of-herself personality going to turn sweet? Or was the fun and funny person part of her erstwhile evil ways? Didn't want to even think about that.

Anyway, things should be better. She was going steady—with one of those significant-others, or whatever the fuck they call boyfriends these days. The Marshal person. Who was supposed to be a director. Sort of. Since nobody knows he ever directed anything. Beside the point. If we still couldn't be friends she owed me at least civil.

"Bradley," I said, forcing myself back to business, "I think you ought to follow up this Keeny Stables lead. Seems likely her horse would still be there. And at least an outside chance the tapes could be, too."

"What about the address book?" asked Francie.

"That's less likely. An address book a person needs. Should of been around the house. If not, then the killer probably got it."

"In spite of the fact they apparently tortured Teri to death, and the house was totally torn up?" said Bradley.

"In spite of," I said. "That could of been just looking

for the tapes. We don't know. So, everybody got their assignments? Any questions?"

"Yeah. Who made you Indian chief?" said Francie, in case things were getting pleasant.

I took a deep breath.

"This is all just suggestions. You don't want to, I'll just go solve the case all by myself."

"Or not," said Francie.

"Listen, I'm getting a little tired of this, Francie. Correct me if I'm wrong, do you work for us, or what?"

"I work for him," she said, indicating "him."

"Well, then maybe we ought to get somebody who works for both of us, seeing we're a team."

"People, people," said Bradley. "Let's not do this. We work together. We've been working together; we'll continue working together. Francine, you're out of line."

"Then maybe you'd rather I didn't work for you, either," she said, picking up her attaché case and portable P.C. and heading for the door.

Now I happen to have one of those door arrangements where what looks like the logical knob is actually the lock. And there's a twist thingee that frees the catch and a pull thingo you use to open the whole thing. If that wasn't designed stupidly enough, you usually had to first figure out whether accidentally turning what looked like the right knob hadn't actually locked it and turn it again to get back to square one. Basically, it was a three-hand door lock and latch. I'd meant to get it changed since 1975, but kept hoping it'd break first.

So that's why neither of us made any big move to stop her. The storming-out trick wasn't going to come off and we both knew it.

"Oh this goddamn door, I never could get it open!" (Except when she'd semi-lived there it'd been sort of cute quaint.)

"All right, Francine," Bradley said firmly. "Enough is enough. You are officially no longer in withdrawal. Any further rudeness and crankiness will be construed as deficiencies of character. Come back here and settle down."

Which, given the limited option of the balky door, is just what she did.

"Now that we've all reacquired a civilized demeanor," said Bradley, "I, myself, do have one small query."

I thought "query" was a pretty dangerous word for him to choose, but this wasn't the moment to play with it. I settled for, "Oh?"

"Aren't we overlooking the obvious?"

"Which is?"

"The obsessed fan?"

"What makes you think we're overlooking it?" I said. "That's what I'm going to be checking out."

"Well, then I guess it's all more or less OK by me," said Bradley, not exactly brimming with enthusiasm.

"Hey, this is going to be a good case, you'll see."

"I still can't fathom exactly why."

"Because I knew this girl, she was your basic busy-body. A lot of very big names one time or other wrinkled a lot of her sheets."

"You sly old romantic," said Francie.

I let it pass. Today slight sarcasm was practically an apology.

"But the point is," Bradley continued, "does anybody really care about that stuff anymore?"

This from a man made a living out of just that. Boy, was he fighting me.

"Look, by the time Francie does her wonderful research, and you do your incredible word magic, you could make people care if it was about celebrity car-rentals."

Which seemed to damp down the cranky.

"All right, all right," said Bradley. "If you're going to get into blatant flattery I guess I'll have to get with the program. And my mother always said if you're going to do something do it graciously."

"Right."

"Of course, I am an only child."

So Francie this time put her printouts back in her attaché case. Bradley took the picture of Teri and the horse and put it in his tote bag. And to impress my partners about my organization and reliability, I took last night's Chinese take-out carton to the garbage. Actually, to the floor of the kitchen. The Phantom came over to check out the leftovers. He took one sniff, gave me one of those superior cat looks, pointed his tail at the ceiling and flashed his little pink asshole. I guess cold egg roll didn't do much for him, either.

When I went back in the main room, they'd just about packed up and were standing helplessly at my trick door when the phone rang.

"Be right with you, let me get this first," I said, going for the phone.

It was Lieutenant Lewis Ellard, from the BHPD.

"Hi, Lieutenant, just the man I want to talk to."

"Yeah? What do you want?"

"I wondered could you spare me half an hour for a favor?"

"What's that?"

"About the Teri Dart case."

"What about it?"

"I wondered would you fill me in a little about the obsessed fan?"

"And I would get in exchange?"

"Gratitude?"

"Sort of like one hand washing itself."

"What have you got to lose?" I pushed.

"You going to be involved in this?" he picked up.

"Yeah, I think."

"And investigating."

"Likely."

"And sharing whatever you find with me?"

"Lieutenant, that goes without saying. So, what do you say?"

"I'll be on duty till about five, I could see you after then."

"Great. How about Le Dome for a drink? My treat."

"Your treat! I guess middle-age does want to know. Not Le Dome, it's a little too high-profile for a lowly Negro peace officer."

"You name it, anyplace you say." (Spare me—"Negro." The man did like to put me on.)

"Mama Cece's."

"Mama Cece's," I repeated. "Didn't I read something about that in the food section of the *Times*?"

"It's a rib joint on Pico just east of Fairfax."

"And they got a liquor license?"

"No."

"There must be some place midway—"

"But Mama's a good hostess," he went on cheerfully. "She might just fill your cup with a little homebrew could clear your intestines and alter your honky perceptions."

I could see he was determined to do his down-home number, which on him sounded like the man from Yale who didn't inhale.

"Sounds—great. Out of sight," I went along. And was about to say good-bye and hang up when I remembered he'd called *me*. "By the way, what was it you wanted?"

"Some sinister developments. You recall your friend William Hobart Kiskessler—the Anaheim bartender and part-time assassin?"

"The name does strike a familiar note," I said.

"Seems to have had an altercation early this morning with another prisoner."

"Yeah?"

"Killed the son of a bitch."

"The other prisoner?"

"Kiskessler."

What was I supposed to make of that?

"Thought you might like to know," he added.

"Yeah, sure. Thanks, Lieutenant." Silence while we both thought it over. "I am a little surprised they didn't isolate him, major murder like that."

"I am, too. Off the record."

"So, was it retaliation, or what?"

"The official line at Parker Center is a routine jail fight."

"And the guy who did it?"

"Nobody seems to have noticed."

"Gee. Makes a person suspicious."

"Don't it, though." And we both thought some more. "See you between five-fifteen and five-thirty at Mama Cece's."

"Look forward to it. And thanks, Lew."

"You calling me by my first name?"

"No, Loo for Lieutenant," I said. "And you can call me Mr. Goodman—till after the homebrew, bro."

"Who you callin' 'brew'?"

He added a little one-snort laugh and hung up. A hoot and a half.

"So?' said Bradley, still waiting at the door with Francie.

"Oh. That was Ellard. Somebody seems to've knocked off the Kiskessler guy."

I fiddled with the bolt, got it unlocked, grabbed the dingus that turned the latch and the handle that gave you enough leverage to deal with a twelve-foot door (hooray for Hollywood) and opened it.

"And what does that mean in terms of us?" said Bradley, following Francie out.

"Not a damn thing, really," I said. "He was apples and Teri's oranges."

It's possible having lived this long I've been that wrong before.

But I don't think so.

# 8

# Mark Bradley

I headed the Beemer back toward the office, Francine by my side.

From Goodman's house in the hills there were two ways to get down to Sunset. If you were going west, down Doheny. If east, Rising Glen, which merged into Sunset Plaza, and down to Sunset.

Since our offices were in the Playboy Building opposite Londonderry and next to Alta Loma, we naturally headed down Sunset Plaza.

We had to wait for the light to change twice (opposite Chin Chin and the new Tribeca pizzeria) as the traffic was already heavy. They were building a huge new mall complex in the vicinity that somehow or other had passed an environmental impact study which had determined an additional eight or ten thousand cars a day on a street already gridlocked wouldn't seriously impact on one's convenience or air quality. (In other times I understand they used to send basketball players to jail for shaving a few points.)

It would probably be easier on me than most, since I didn't have to keep specific hours at the office, but it looked to be a serious problem for residents up on the hill.

While they were only into excavation at the moment, one lane was already permanently blocked by equipment and storage facilities. And in California, any time one lane is blocked, it's a guaranteed jam.

I was amazed Goodman hadn't reacted more violently about it—so far. Especially since there were rumors of variances and all sorts of dubious accommodations made by the city of West Hollywood to encourage the developers. West Hollywood being my place of abode, in common with multitudinous members of my minority.

Actually, Jeffrey Hong, our councilman (and you can well imagine the butt, so to speak, of many an anatomical pun) who was wounded in the same fusillade that assassinated Marvin Fischer, had been prominently involved at the time the plans were approved. The proposed mall was politically popular among my people since having this huge revenue-producer on our city's northernmost boundary allowed us to get the taxes while the nonresidents above the Strip got to have the inconvenience. A not uncommon tactical maneuver between communities, called border wars.

I got to think all this while waiting for the second light change at Sunset Boulevard and Sunset Plaza Drive. I could just imagine how much additional time I'd have for thinking once the actual construction got underway.

A further inconvenience was studiously trying to avoid a homeless person on the island immediately beside my window. The enterprising fellow had calculatedly staked out this territory a week or so earlier on the not unreasonable premise that he would be harder to ignore the longer you were stalled.

Like most, I wasn't unmoved by their plight and not a little distressed that the super-affluent Eighties had created a corresponding mass of super-deprived unlike anything since and maybe including the Great Depression of the Thirties. I also resented the imposition on my emotions.

The man kept shoving a sign in my face which read, HUNGRY, WILL WORK FOR FOOD. An offer I felt fairly certain he never meant to be actually accepted. I kept thinking I'd have to make one of my own to counterflash in future. When they held up, "Hungry, will work for food," I'd hold up, "Thirsty, will social interface for cocktails."

I gave him a dollar.

And the light finally changed again and Francine and I both made the turn and proceeded to the company parking lot.

We almost got to our office before being hallwaywaylayed by our boss, Dick Penny, forever lingering for *mal*ingerers.

"Ah-hah," he actually said. I sometimes thought he ought to grow mustaches to twirl.

"Ah-hah yourself," said Francine, as ever in no mood to take nothin' fum no-body.

"You, at least, are on the payroll," said Penny, parrying with an accusatory forefinger in her thorax. "And subject to rules and regulations."

"You mean from the secretarial union, with whom I've had the foresight to ally myself? Mark, as an impartial witness would you say that finger he's harassing me with is sexual in nature, or merely gross physical abuse?"

"Don't tuh ... tutz with me, missy," he said, removing the offending digit. "And this is some hour to be coming to work."

"She is not just coming to work," I answered for her. "Ms. Rizetti was in conference, doing research for Mr. Goodman and myself at Mr. Goodman's home office."

"Yes," said Penny, baring his new chicklet-sized caps, and resembling nothing so much as a balding Percheron who'd gone through the Rembrandt tooth-bleaching process, "but Mr. Goodman and you are not working on a Pendragon project. *You* are working on a Pendragon project—presumably—your filthy little autobiography ..."

"Filthy *novel*," I corrected.

"The other thing, the Teri Dart thing, is not authorized, as you well know."

"Listen," said Francine, "much as I'd love to stay and chat with you literary gents, I've got actual work to do, so, unless you want me to wait while you make a written apology ..."

"Just get in your office," said Penny. "And you," to me, "what you do on your own time is one thing, but I don't want you using company employees on *my* time. Is that clear?"

"Just one little question."

"Yes?"

"Doesn't being a publisher involve some actual work?" Which was enough of that crap, albeit not the strongest exit line I've ever devised. Nevertheless, I did exit, marching off and into my office.

I always kept my office totally impersonal. I didn't want to invest it with any sense of permanence. There were no mementos, gimcracks, or serious toys. Just a packed tote bag with a few items of portable value, a change of clothing, passport, bottle of Evian, small first-aid kit, matches, essential items should I suddenly be called to commit major journalism in some far-off corner of the world—or caught in an earthquake.

By the time I settled down and considered what work-evasion props I would need for what remained of the morning, Francine was in with the address of the Keeny Stables in Chatsworth, a Hi-Liter marked section of the Thomas Bros. Guide indicating the route, and a firm suggestion to "Let's get our asses on the road before I set fire to this place."

It seemed a good idea to humor her.

Chatsworth is located north of Canoga Park and west of Northridge and Granada Hills. A lot of places to keep horses. You could easily tell that by the aromatic ammonia-like smell that seemed to permeate the whole district and gave massive evidence to the efficacy of the equine digestive system.

A little is kind of pleasant. It gives you a sense of community with the earth and its creatures. A bit more and it's one of the things you have to put up with in order for nature's balance to be maintained. A lot and you tried to get your business over with as quick as you could.

Keeny's Stables was an impressively affluent, sizable establishment with several dirt avenues lined with stables, exercise spaces, a track, and evidence of some history. This included a life-size representation of a horse which a plaque informed us was named Tax-Shelter and had glued out in the year 1951 after evidently doing impressive things at Hollywood Park and Del Mar, among others. The horse had been owned by Mickey Cohen, a prominent local gangster and evidently named in homage to Mickey's mentor, Al Capone, who'd learned about the wily Internal Revenue folks the hard way.

The place seemed to be doing pretty well. Lots of activity, horses being groomed, horses being fed, horses being tended—horse manure being schlepped.

We were left pretty much to wander around unimpeded, but once you've seen one stable you've pretty much seen them all.

A miniature black person was walking a large horse around a circle, to the center of which it was tethered. It didn't seem to be drawing any water or grinding any wheat, so I guessed the object was exercise.

"Excuse me," I said to the man, who was kid-size, but looked to be about fifty, with that wizened look undersized people often have. He was, perhaps, a failed or over-the-hill jockey—there seemed several such, I guess, exercise boys. (Although I found it interesting that a very fair number of employees seemed to be girls or women—their emotional attachment to horses having been documented at length by Krafft-Ebing.)

"Yeah?"

"Who would I see to find out about one of your, what, clients? A person who keeps horses here."

"The office is over there." Over there seemed to be a house some fifty yards distant.

"I should have brought the Reeboks without the heels," said Francine.

I thanked the little gentleman, not without a guilt-by-association recollection of the pretentious fad some recent years ago when blackamoor jockey statues (to which one presumably tied his Mercedes-Benz) seemed to blossom in front of every new Beverly Hills home. (Which then reflected an awareness transition commencing with white-facing and proceeding to eventual removal.)

"This is a hell of a long drive for someone to make to just ride a horse now and then."

"It's a very handsome horse," said Francine.

It had commenced to drizzle, which I didn't find too thrilling, since the route we were transversing was neither paved nor sod and already fairly muddy and I happened to be wearing a pair of Ferragamo suede loafers. (I think it was the discovery of suede that put rainmakers out of business—all you had to do was don something suede and you could reach for an umbrella.)

The rain intensified, catching us full blast just before we reached the shelter of the office. Which had floors of wood. They'd had some experience with mud, I expect.

A tomboyish, small-busted young woman with a *Northern Exposure* haircut, wearing jeans and boots, and a Levi shirt with the sleeves rolled down and the buttons buttoned up, sat behind a littered desk exuding horsewomanly toughness.

"Yeah?" she said, barely short of drawing a gun.

Francine, never slow to analyze a situation, quickly took over.

"We were wondering if you might help me," she said, I swear sounding like it was "little old helpless me."
"We're investigating a murder and we believe the victim was a client of yours."

"You're with the police?"

"Whose name is Teri Dart," continued Francine evasively. "Could you, I wonder, give us some information? For example, I understand she kept a horse here named . . ." and she hesitated.

"Warlock," I prompted, earning a look from the horse lady that seemed to imply she wouldn't be surprised if I knew *all* about warlocks.

"I figure the horse is still here," continued Francine. "And I wondered if anyone's made any inquiries about it, or arranged for its disposition, things like that."

"Uhm," said the horse lady. "Maybe you should talk to the owner."

"Sounds good," said Francine. I stayed out; she was doing fine.

"Let me see if Matt's available." With which she rose and crossed the room to knock on a closed door.

Matt?! I mouthed wordlessly to Francine. Maybe the same Matt who was on Teri's answering machine who was so sorry. Who couldn't help it. Who really tried. And who wondered if she was all right.

"OK, you can go on inside," said the horse lady, returning from the office across the room, the door to which now stood open.

We crossed in.

The room didn't hold a lot of surprises. It was wood and leather and brass and smelled of saddles and saddle soap. One surprise.

"You'll forgive me if I don't stand," said the Mickey Rooneyish guy in the wheelchair with his arm in a cast and a big bandage around his head. "I'm Matt McKensie, I own this place. And you're . . . ?"

"Real sorry about whatever it was," said Francine.

The minute he spoke, we recognized his voice from the tape. He was very cooperative, even anxious to help. He'd been fond of Teri and very much upset by her murder, to say nothing of the events that preceded it.

The story was that Teri had stabled her horse there for over two years. She'd first been recommended by another of his clients, one with many horses, seldom fewer than six—although at the moment, peculiarly down to one—by the name of Fabrisio Sugarman. Perhaps we'd heard of him?

We allowed that we did find the name familiar (excited to have another name from the phone tape turn up).

"I called her, on Friday—I guess the day she was murdered," he said. "Or, I don't know, was that Saturday? Anyway, she never got back to me."

"What was it you wanted to tell her?" I asked.

"It was about Warlock." Her horse.

"What about Warlock?"

"They killed him. They just came and—killed that horse." And he choked up.

"Take your time," said Francine.

"Beautiful animal. A sweetheart."

"How exactly did that come about?" I asked.

"These two bent-noses came around. We should have figured they were paid muscle, but we weren't really looking for anything like that, you know how it is."

"Sure."

"Not that it would have helped anyway," he added. "They asked which was Teri's horse. By then I got suspicious. I wouldn't have just let anybody go to somebody else's horse, anyhow, so I said they should ask Teri. Bam, they were all over me. Beat the bejesus out of me. I've got a broken arm, torn cartilage and a concussion. By that time I was getting a little stubborn, you know? I'd be fucked I was going to tell them—pardon me, lady."

"No, I've been fucked myself," allowed Francine.

"Sam—my assistant"—somehow I didn't think it was short for Samantha, more like Samuel—"tried to help me. She said she'd show them, just leave me alone. They would have found out themselves sooner or later anyway. I don't hold her responsible."

"And what exactly happened?"

"They killed the horse. Just like that—killed the horse."

I could see what killing a horse meant to this man. He started to cry. And crying embarrassed him.

"Excuse me," said Sam, at the open door. "Matt's been under a lot of strain and you can see he's been worked over pretty bad. Why don't you leave him alone now?"

"Because we have to get a little more information," I began.

"No, no," said Francine. "Leave him alone. She can help us—Sam, isn't it? I'm Fran." (Fran? I'd never heard her be Fran before.) "I'm sure she will, won't you, Sam?"

I backed off.

We thanked Mr. McKensie, wished him a speedy recovery, and old Fran asked old Sam to take us out to the stables.

By now the rain had stopped, God having decided the mud was of a sufficient consistency to ruin what was left of my suede loafers.

"I knew right away they were trouble," Sam said en route, perhaps having read some Chandler. "But if I didn't go along with them they might have killed Matt."

"Sure," said Francine reassuringly. "The only way to play it."

"Anyway, when we got to the stable they did two

things. They searched the tack box. Seemed to know exactly what they were looking for."

"Wasn't necessary, but I couldn't resist. "Which was?" I said.

"A carton of tapes."

"Videotapes."

"Right, vidcotapes."

"Of the horse?"

"I don't think so."

"What were they of?" I asked.

"Well, I wouldn't really know," said Sam.

"You never looked at them?" said Francine with a little smile of encouragement.

"I wouldn't—I wasn't supposed—they were private property."

"Still, human nature," I prodded.

"I did take a peek at one."

"Pornographic?" cued Francine.

"And how," said Sam.

"Which they carted away," I repeated. She nodded. "And the other thing they did?"

"They shot the horse, like Matt said. Bang, just like that. Didn't bat an eye."

So we knew they had found the tapes. But then why still kill the horse? Sheer meanness?

During all this we'd been sort off ambling around the stable itself and the adjoining tack area. And now I spotted a bit of black plastic half buried. I bent down and picked it up.

"This looks familiar," I said, though I couldn't put my finger on it. (Frankly I didn't want to put my finger on it, considering it'd been on the ground in a stable.)

"It's a piece of a Polaroid pack," said Francine.

"They took pictures?" I asked Sam.

"Yeah, come to think of it."

"*After* they killed the horse," said Francine.

"Right, after."

So they wanted to have some proof of what they'd done and what they were capable of doing. To pressure Teri. Since it wasn't for the tapes, she'd evidently been tortured into telling them that. Then what for?

"Had to be for the trick book," said Francine, sotto voce, reading my mind.

But if she told them about the tapes, why wouldn't she tell them about the address book?

Because she didn't *know* where it was.

We thanked Sam for her help, wished our best to Matt, and headed for the car.

"Oh, Fran," Sam called after us. "If you ever want to—ride—give me a call."

"I'll do that," said Francine with a sly little smile.

"Why you little tease," I said, once we were out of earshot.

"I don't know," she replied. "I thought she was kind of cute—in a k.d. lang-y sort of way."

# 9

## Rayford Goodman

After Bradley and Francie left, the Phantom reminded
me again I was supposed to change the litter box every
once in a while. I thought he went about it a little crude.
But I did get the message.

So that was one thing I did. Cleaned up the message.

I'd started out with an open pan sort of arrangement,
which made changing it easy. But smelling it not so hot.

First I experimented with various places in the house.
Turned out there were prevailing winds, even indoors.
So I eventually found the best spot. Happened to be
under a counter, next to the dryer and washer—which
were largely ornamental since I didn't know how to work
either one. No special distinction, my ax-wife hadn't either. Or maybe wouldn't. Though in fairness Luana had
the mechanical aptitude of a newt. *Did* know how to
direct-dial Marvin Mitchelson, though. Alimony under
the bridge.

Anyway, there was still some eau de pussee, so I
bought one of those litter arrangements with a cover,
like a little cathouse. It was fairly heavy, had a filter
and several "scientifically designed" parts that almost fit
together. And didn't really do much for the problem, but
did give the Phantom a little privacy. Which was an iffy
trade-off for what the extra weight did to my herniated
disc.

Having a cat wasn't all cozy fur and warm kootchy-
coo. On the other hand, they didn't go dial a lawyer
every time things got sticky.

I washed up, slipped a CD on the box and took a
listen to Diane Schuur with the Count Basie orchestra,
recorded in 1987. Which should of been called at least

the Late Count Basie orchestra. I really loved the way everybody kept making movies and records after they died.

And since it was getting on toward lunchtime but I wasn't ready for lunch, I fixed myself a nice Bloody Mary, took it to my easy chair, and made easy.

I listened to Diane do her wonderful thing through "Deedles' Blues," "Caught a Touch of Your Love," and was into "Travelin' Light"—to say nothing of Mary II, the Drink. Freddie Green, the great guitarist, had died three days after they finished the album, joining Basie. So heaven was pretty much set on rhythm.

Diane slipped into "I Just Found Out About Love" and I realized I'd slipped into "where does the time go?" Clear to me I was far from focused on the case yet.

I figured maybe to clear the track by taking care of some personal business that'd been piling up. But after about twenty minutes writing checks and licking stamps I was back to why it kept piling up. I hated it more than soccer.

So I made myself a sandwich, and got lunch out of the way. I was just into cleaning the table up enough to find the list of household things had to be done right away when I was saved by the bell.

It was Bradley on his car phone, heading south from Chatsworth, filling me in on what went down at Keeny's Stables—the tapes gone, the mysterious "Matt" located, the horse killed, Polaroids taken. It was nice work; he was getting good at it. Plus I felt pretty sure enjoyed using his car phone. I noticed people with car phones are always on them. Maybe it wasn't just showing off. (I still had my doubts about most, though. And a sneaking suspicion lots of them were faking actual calls.)

I thanked Bradley and said I'd get back to him later after I'd met with Ellard. And meanwhile he might see what Francie had come up with. Turned out she'd come up with same as him, them being together. He put her on the line.

"This is what we were supposed to avoid," I said. "Duplicating effort."

"We didn't exactly duplicate," she said.

"Yeah? What did you learn that he wouldn't have learned alone?"

"I learned that I'm attractive to members of my own sex," she answered, whatever the hell that meant.

"Can we just say good-bye?" I asked. "Or do we have to say 'over and out and ten four'?"

"How about go fuck yourself?"

I didn't know they could say that over the air.

The Santa Palm is a car wash on the corner of—surprise—Palm and Santa Monica. You could get gas there, too, for only about forty cents more a gallon than anywhere else. Plus your car washed for a total of something near forty dollars. Maybe being the only car wash in about five miles had something to do with it. Why all the car washes and all the gas stations went out of business just when the prices got out of sight, I'll never understand. One of the drags about getting old, as if you needed any more, was remembering things like they used to throw in the wash free if you bought gas—at cut-rate prices. Anyway . . .

I got the gas, turned down the offer of any of three waxes that could push the total over fifty bucks, paid, got the little slip you used to claim your car. Put it with a buck you had to tip after the guy wiped some of the water off the car, in order to get your keys, which they'd learned to put in their pocket instead of leaving in the ignition. Or learning English.

I walked through the long corridor on one side of which you could watch your car being washed. Almost everybody did that, though it really wasn't very entertaining. On the other side was a series of autographed pictures of all the famous actors got their car washed there. A scary number of which were dead. And all of which had their retouching oxidized by the sun and showed where their real cheeks were and how wide their noses would be without the shading.

Halfway down the hall was a short, chubby, pockmarked guy in tennis togs—white Fila shorts and one of those tennis shirts with a lot of uneven pattern on one side, like they'd been painted on somebody standing on a hill.

He had Porsche sunglasses on top of his head, a Rolex on his wrist, and a thin portable phone in his hand. I couldn't help overhearing—since I'd slowed down to make sure—when he said, "Hey, it's the Taxi Man. Can I give you a lift today?"

Number two on Teri's answering machine!

His car (not a taxi to no surprise, a black Corvette) was through the wash ahead of mine. So when he went to claim it, all I had to do was take down the license plate. Which I managed to do without showing him my face, just in case. It was almost like I'd been working.

Fairfax, above Santa Monica is ethnic-neutral. Going south, it starts sliding into Jewish, first with a King David Convalescent Home that kind of clues you, a bakery or two could be anything, a fake Gucci/Vuitton sidewalk store, then a poultry shop, more food things, kosher this and kosher that, till by the time you're passing Canter's Delicatessen you could swear they're beaming out pickled garlic as a sales pitch.

Heading down it eases off, sort of ending at Wallenberg Square with a movie and a bank, then south with fast-food chains, mixed shops, stationery stores, TV repair, and other businesses that were ethnic-neutral again.

At Pico, heading east, it starts moving in another direction, getting grimmer and edgier and by the time I got to Mama Cece's, it was a whole other story. If there were any Jews in the restaurant, they were Ethiopian. In fact, I was the only white person of any persuasion. No Beverly Hills-type Buppies (Black Urban Professionals) with a friendly smile, either. It was more like a bunch of Mau Mau with a migraine.

Lieutenant Ellard was late, adding to the fun.

A very fat woman in her sixties wearing an apron that years of detective experience clued me was Mama Cece saw me standing at the door checking other exits and came over.

"You Goodman?"

I nodded.

"Lewis going be a little late. Come sit down, I'll get you a cup of tea." And she led me to a table, while I got a sense of the room-changing attitudes, now that I'd been accounted for. I didn't get hate, I didn't get welcome. I got ignore. Which I guess is an improvement, but doesn't make for exactly comfortable, either. Though, if I was going to be fair about it, must be what being black in a room full of whites has to feel like.

I spent some time checking out stains on the table-cloth. Then things got a bit brighter when Mama Cece brought me my tea.

"Could I have some milk with it, please?"

"You don't want milk."

Jesus, I had to go through this now?

"Taste it first," she added.

I tasted. Bourbon.

"Right you are, lady," I said. "Tea should be taken neat."

I sipped my "tea" to make it last, and managed to get to the bottom where there would have been leaves if there'd been tea when Ellard finally showed up.

Mama Cece immediately spotted him and he went to give her a big hug, which is the only kind you can give a woman weighs three hundred pounds, and they made a large fuss over each other, part of which had to do with him getting too big for his breeches and not remembering his roots and him kidding back that he was there to thank the little people who'd made him what he is today.

And he low-, medium-, and high-fived several friends and acquaintances and finally made it over to my table, threw a lanky leg over the back of a chair, and settled down.

"Hey, bro—what's happening?" he said cheerfully.

"What, what, what?" I said. "We going to do some tricky handshake now? Give me five and a quarter and back and top. What is this shit?"

"Roots, man."

"What roots?"

"She makes some fine roots," he said, suckering me into it. "Or chitlins, or collard greens."

Right. Mr. Sophistication, here, was going to get down and dirty.

"It's a little early for me," I said. "I think I'll just stick to my tea. You go ahead, though. In fact, I'd like to see it. Chitlins are what, chitterlings, intestines, bowels, like that?"

"Now, now, I don't make fun of the culinary customs of your people."

"What, my people, I'm American. My food is American."

"Yes, that is true, my large pale friend. And more's the pity."

Oh, boy. "What pity's that, again?"

"That you don't afford yourself the virility-enhancing qualities we who are closer to the earth know so well."

Mr. Close to the earth. "You're talking sex life? Not that it's any of your business."

"I'm sure you've heard tales of our legendary prowess."

"Based on soul food?"

"Of course, man—ain't you never heard of an afrodisiac?"

"OK, OK, I'm leaving."

"Sit down, I'm just pulling your leg. Your slow-running leg."

"All right, enough!"

He held up his hand in half surrender, through teasing. "You're not going anywhere until you get the information you came for," he said.

That was true. I sat down.

Actually, I was more and more getting to like Ellard. At first I liked him just because he wasn't Broward, who used to have the job heading up Homicide in Beverly Hills and who used to make my life miserable, just on principle—or lack of it. But also because Ellard'd been really honest with me, and because he'd helped out when we did the Intervention with Francie to get her to rehab (having an ex-wife of his own was an addict).

Still, it was a novelty cooperating with the *po*lice. And it did go against all my instincts.

"So tell me again, how'd you get to be Beverly Hills's first black chief of detectives?"

"Mostly because they were so thrilled I wasn't Eddie Murphy."

Mama Cece brought in two large plates of God knows what, and I was going to have to push stuff around and maybe slip some into my pocket or face insulting her.

Ellard made a bunch of eating noises I know he wouldn't have at Spago, I guess to show he was still just folks—or just folks in an Armani suit.

Finally, after all the "ah's" and "urm's" and "uh's" of appreciation, he stopped for breath, and to sip his "tea."

"So," he said. "You want to know about Harvard Lawrence Singleton." I nodded. "He's written Teri Dart three hundred and seven letters, most of them just skirting the edge of actionable pornography through the mails—with his right hand, by the way, Teri was killed by a right-handed person."

"That really narrows it down."

"He managed to get hold of her phone number and called as often as twenty times a day till she changed it; and got in her proximity enough times to be classified as a stalker—at which point she was able to get an injunction against him. Even though he never really threatened anything. He was not allowed within three hundred feet of her, and if you're willing to testify you saw his truck parked outside her house, we might have the start of a case."

"I'd be willing to testify, but who's to say it was actually his truck and not just the same make and color. What else about the guy?"

"He fits the profile, so far as we've been able to establish one, but the profile has two sides—passive and active. Those who worship and put their subject on a pedestal, and those who fantasize and lose touch enough to believe they've actually got a relationship that the celebrity's somehow denying."

"And he fits the passive profile?"

"Up to now."

"But they can change, right?"

"The book's still being written. You're not eating your greens."

"You noticed that. So what about this guy, what're you doing about him?"

"Besides trying to find him?"

"Ah-ha." I took a little bite. Not bad.

"He's white . . ."

"That's 'Caucasian.' "

". . . Twenty-seven—which makes it somewhat rare, since she had to be closer to your age."

"How did you tell, carbon dating?"

"So we're thinking some sort of misplaced mother-image thing."

"Except Teri was hardly that kind of image."

"Right. But Singleton's actual birth mother—he was brought up mostly in foster homes—was a prostitute who abandoned him. So he could easily both have identified Teri with her and/or built a murderous hatred."

"With incestuous overtones."

"Wholesome, ain't it? You could try the chitlins, it won't kill you."

"How can you be sure? Maybe there's some genetic thing honkys have and it *would* kill me."

"And what have you got for me?"

Fair enough, it was supposed to be a two-way street. Besides, I wanted another favor.

I didn't tell him what Bradley and Francie'd found out up in Chatsworth. I did tell him about running into Taxi Man at the Santa Palm Car Wash and handed him the license number of the Corvette and asked him to run it down.

"So this guy's a dealer and he was Teri's?"

"Uh-huh."

"Which you knew by, what, taking a copy of the tape on her answering machine?"

"Oops."

About when Mama Cece came by to check how everything was and bawl me out for not eating. I said it was too early for me, but from the tastes I'd taken it was out of sight and I'd be real grateful for a doggy bag.

Then all I'd have to do was give it to the first homeless homeboy I ran into.

# 10

## Mark Bradley

Goodman and I were having cocktails at the St. James's Club, where I had an honorary membership, the pleasant residual perquisite of a brief fling with a Certain Party in middle management.

St. James's was a constant esthetic delight, with its Erte sculpture and abundance of Art Deco objets. Following years of disuse and disarray, the former Sunset Tower had changed hands and undergone a total restoration back to what, in its naughty Hollywood heyday, had made it the tryst of the town.

Now luxuriously and extravagantly resonant of the movie capital at its zenith, every corner provided some sort of visual delight—including at the moment the faintly familiar elderly actor hunched on a barstool. The one who always played a disreputable whiner, now looking amazingly distinguished in his old age.

And speaking of old performers, Goodman was recounting his interview with Ellard.

"Well, that doesn't really give us all that much," I said when he paused. "We knew before about the fact of the obsessed fan. What Ellard told you about the profile's interesting, but more or less to be expected. The idea that he's 'probably passive' doesn't exonerate him, in my book—or our book, as the case may be."

"Well, that wasn't all I found out. Give me a little credit," he continued, and speaking of credit flagged a passing waitress for another Tanqueray Sterling on the rocks, which I had a feeling I'd be paying for, being the "member."

"OK, what else?"

"The autopsy found Teri'd been cut something like

twenty-seven times with a small knife before the actual fatal stabbing with a larger one."

"Which was to torture her to disclose where the tapes were, and then, once she'd revealed that—at the stables—probably further torture for the trick book."

"Right, so logically whoever was responsible's a good bet to be in the book. Or at least have an interest in someone who is."

"An address book that nobody has found."

The waitress wasted a sexy smile on me as she brought Goodman his drink. Little did she know eye contact was the only contact we were likely to have. I ordered another Bombay gin and tonic.

"Further," continued Goodman, "the time of death was between three and five in the morning—the night we were being honored by not winning the gay biography awards in Anaheim."

"Three to five sounds awful vague; I thought they could narrow it down more than that."

"Well, being in the water for a day didn't help any. That distorts a lot of the stuff. Besides the pool being heated to about ninety degrees. Two hours is pretty good."

"What else did you learn?"

"I learned I'm not too crazy about soul food. Plus, Ellard was pretty wrapped up in the Fischer murder. Come to think of it, I don't exactly know why, not being his beat."

"That is a little strange. They still don't have any suspects for Kiskessler's murder?"

"No. And my guess is they aren't trying all that hard. It's a good way to wrap things up when there's a political assassination, rather than having to go to trial and risk a fuckup there. That kind of fallout."

"You're not suggesting the authorities had anything to do with it?"

"I'm not suggesting anything—except, dear"—he said to my girlfriend/waitress—"could I have a couple onions?"

She told him how happy she'd be to do that for us,

again looking at me. Or if there was anything else she could do?

I assured her I'd let her know, and resumed our conversation. "You were saying?"

"Well, they've got a fair amount of paper on this Kiskessler guy. Turns out to be your basic Nazi for hire."

"Did they have a chance to question him?"

"Sort of. But only got one answer. 'CIA—enough said.' Nobody taking it very seriously. He had tried to get into the CIA, and the FBI, and the Secret Service. But never got past the psychologicals. About all he seemed to manage was an ad in *Soldier of Fortune* magazine."

"Saying?"

"Something like 'experienced operative, covert-overt, seeks challenging assignment.' "

"And you think someone hired him based on that to kill Marvin Fischer?"

"I don't think anything; I don't know. Besides just happening to be there, it doesn't mean anything for us."

"Well, being there and your disarming him certainly gives our book a little extra pizzazz."

"Not if they're not connected."

"You think they might be?"

"How could they? The only connection I see is us—being next to Fischer and being next to Teri. Nobody could of planned that."

The waitress brought a crystal glass full of onions and olives and one suggestive maraschino cherry. I thanked her.

Goodman popped an onion into his mouth, watched the waitress retreat gracefully, and it wasn't hard to follow the sequence of his train of thought.

"I expected you were going to bring Francie along."

He just would not let it go. He couldn't seem to accept that they had had a brief thing and it was over and wasn't ever going to be reinstated. There never was any logical reason for them to get together in the first place.

"She had a date to meet Marshal for cocktails someplace else."

"And that's more important than work?"

"Of course it is. Well, not more important, it's after hours. She's not obliged to keep working twenty-four hours a day. She's a paid researcher. And in this case, we haven't even established what we're going to do about that, since it's not a Pendragon project. I suppose we'll have to pay her ourselves."

"But she works days for Pendragon."

"Right."

"So if she works days for them, and they pay her, why should we have to pay her when she's doing the work for us on their time and not working nights?"

"You really want me to answer?"

"No."

"Anyway, she is working nights. After her date, she's meeting us for dinner at Olive. About half an hour."

"More like it. Who is this Marshal guy anyway?"

"It's somebody she's been seeing."

"Marshal what again?" As if he didn't know.

"Hildebrandt. Marshal Hildebrandt."

"Sounds like a German general. What's he do?"

"Come on, you know he's a director."

"Yeah, right. But what's he directed?"

"A would-be director," I qualified.

"You mean he's a bum."

"I don't mean anything of the sort and I don't want to talk about it. Francine's my friend and I respect her confidence."

"If she's your friend you ought to protect her from lowlifes and see she doesn't make any serious mistakes."

"Goodman, she's a grown woman, what the hell are you talking about?"

"I'm talking about her making a good choice. If it's not me, at least she should go with someone who has a job and makes a living. What do we know about this turkey, really?"

"I'm just not going to talk about it."

As it happened, I didn't want to talk about it because for the wrong reason Goodman happened to be right. Francine had told me on the ride back from Chatsworth that they were going to break up. Marshal had tended to freeload, which was OK since she was working and he wasn't, but not OK when she spotted him going through her purse, and later found one of her credit cards missing. Which also explained why she'd been so cranky lately—not that I could let on to Goodman. According to the schedule she was supposed to be having one quick drink with Hildebrandt about now, tell him she needed more space, and then catch up with us.

We finished our drinks, watched two waiters help the slumping actor on the corner stool to his feet and prop him up as they made a stiff but dignified exit.

"That's who he is," said Goodman. "There was a picture, two gangsters were taking him for a ride. What's his name?" and he clicked his fingers in frustration. "Oh, I've seen him a million times, the guy who squealed all the time."

I shrugged. I had enough trouble with my own generation, keeping track of the Sheens and the Estevezes.

The smiling waitress asked if I was *sure* there wasn't something else she could do. I promised to be in touch if I could think of it and meanwhile would she be kind enough to bring the check.

Which she did; little folded note attached.

I told Goodman what the total was.

"You're the one getting all the smiles," he said. "My book that makes you the host."

I had a feeling if we were going to go through with this freelance number, I'd better keep track of the expenses.

The note said "Laurie Burns" with a number in the two one three area. Would that life were that simple.

Olive was one of those trendy places that was super in. It was in a weird un-chic location, south Fairfax Avenue, but the young crowd it catered to didn't mind things like that.

It had no sign identifying it, just a simple door with a number. There was no parking lot, though they did have parking attendants who took your car somewhere or other.

Besides no sign over the door, there was no telephone listing, either. Originally. I suppose the idea had been to make it feel like an underground club—as if it just happened to be at that place that night.

But several things compromised the premise. One, the *Los Angeles Times* did an article with a favorable write-up and listed the phone number. And two, it failed to resemble an underground club in almost every significant way—there was no music, no dancing, and no apparent drugs.

What there was—in the totally undecorated room with some sort of harlequin motif on the walls from a previous incarnation—the most noise you ever heard in your life. It seemed a thousand people were all yelling at the top of their lungs, and the hard walls, hard floors, and hard ceilings weren't doing any acoustical favors.

The same misleading article had made reference to an all-black mode of dress being *de rigueur*. The truth was I did see some black T-shirts among the white with funny sayings. But even calling the dress casual was overstating. They were correct that Olive was a sort of retro hip place where the drug of choice was booze and everybody smoked. The *help* smoked.

David, the maitre d', carried a cordless phone so as not to miss a reservation. Though why they would take any I couldn't imagine since it wasn't possible to get two more people into the place. Perhaps the phone was for a tip-off when the fire department got ready to raid. He collared a waiter to help clear a way to squeeze us into a spot where we could stand in the aisle, five deep from the bar, and assured me we would get the very next table. Whether this was because the almost exclusively under twenty-five crowd were less lavish tippers or because Goodman was the oldest person ever there and he feared for his health in the crush, I couldn't be sure.

Fortunately, the excruciating din prevented me from hearing most of Goodman's complaints at the time, but I knew I wouldn't be getting off that light. And we had no choice but to wait for Francine.

After Goodman had used his large body and accumulated anger to force a way through the throng to the actual bar to get us a couple of watered-down drinks, and we were jostled and yelled at as stress-hysterical waitpersons tried to push through the aisle, we were, to my surprise, actually rather quickly seated. Though not before my toes had been mashed half a dozen times and Goodman had nearly come to blows with an elbow-tossing college type in beery high spirits.

Our booth afforded relief from the press of the thousand sweating bodies (could there really be a maximum occupancy sign somewhere?), and from the noisiest area. But it was a minimal improvement.

Goodman just shook his head, drank and smoked. Half an hour went by and no Francine.

Goodman's mood wasn't improving any, due in part to the fact the drinks were so light he was actually sobering up. Though younger, less-experienced types were achieving remarkable levels of boisterousness on the thin stimuli.

"Why don't we order?" I finally suggested.

"I'm going to get you for this," he promised, blowing a lethal fog of smoke my way. I'd been under the impression he'd quit, but didn't feel this was a good time to call him on it.

We ordered.

And one more drink.

The food came in remarkably short order, and it was rather better than one would have expected.

But no Francine.

We ate.

We lingered.

We lingered some more.

The maitre d' looked covetously at the table.

The waitress returned. Would there be anything else? There wouldn't be.

Would we like an after-dinner drink?

"We would like the check," I decided. "Francine's not coming," I explained to Goodman.

"That's this modern generation; you just can't depend on them," said Goodman.

The fact that Francine was in her late thirties and hardly qualified as anybody's modern generation wasn't something I was going to challenge him with at the moment, either.

The check came. Goodman reached (admittedly not with any urgency) for his wallet.

"I'll get it," I yelled over the din. "It's the least I can do."

"You're right," he yelled back. "It is the least you can do."

It took five minutes just to fight our way out. You give the public what it wants ...

We'd come together in Goodman's big old Cadillac convertible, so I had the dubious pleasure of watching him hassle the parking attendant for a quarter change from the $2.75 charge.

"They just do that, you know. They count on nobody asking it back. I wouldn't mind they just made it a straight three dollars, but if they say two-seventy-five they ought to give you back change."

The attendant ostentatiously gave Goodman his quarter just as a probably professional homeless man with a nice flair for a retro Annie Hall look made his pitch.

Good sport Goodman offered him the quarter (see, it's the principle of the thing) which the man refused with an airy, "Sorry, I can't made change."

"Smartass," Goodman mumbled as I tried to make myself as inconspicuous as I could getting into the passenger side.

He U-turned on Fairfax, up to Willoughby, turned left, and stopped just west of Kings Road, the site of my costly condo, where I egressed.

"Thanks for the ride, we'll talk tomorrow," I said.

"And tell Francine, when you see her, she better get her act together. If we're going to be paying her, she better start being more reliable."

I didn't answer. Sometimes even he was right.

A poodle-walking local passed, commenting, "Nice car." Goodman quickly put the pedal to the metal (it was a '64 car and still *had* metal).

"Was it something I said?" asked the canine cruiser.

"Poodlephobia," I explained, heading to the lobby.

I collected my mail, and went upstairs.

The apartment was appallingly empty.

A bad time of night. Too early for sleep, too late to do anything.

No one to do it with.

The time of casual affairs was over. There was no dancing in the dark, waiting for the light of your life.

I gave Francine a call.

The machine clicked on.

"You can leave a message if you want," her recorded voice said.

"Are you there? Hello. Francine?"

Nothing.

I hung up. Whistled.

In the dark.

It felt a lot like the blues.

# 11

## Rayford Goodman

There was something to be said for spending your evenings at juvenile hot spots—you didn't wake up with a hangover. Drinks were too weak for that.

I don't say I exactly felt like surfing, but it was relatively good. The sun was shining. The birds were chirping. And the cat was using the litter box according to the truce we'd worked out.

I thought maybe I'd get an early jump on the day by eating breakfast home. Which meant I made a cup of instant coffee.

Through the kitchen window I could see Teri's wire-haired dog (really did look like Asta) laying an axe on my rosebush. Not exactly adding to property values. It dug a hole trying to cover the muck, which showed a little more class. Then it suddenly looked up, spotted me and started whining. Dogs do that something pitiful.

I borrowed a can of cat food from the Phantom and put it out back for him. I knew that was a mistake, but it had to be pretty hungry unless someone else was feeding it. I sure didn't want it dropping dead on my land somewhere and making a big problem for me.

While I was out back the phone rang, wouldn't you know. I managed to unstick the rear door only throwing my back out a little, stumble over the garbage cans, and run back through the garage and into the house just in time for the hum after somebody's finished their message on your answerphone. I did a short Andy Rooney—" 'Jever wonder why the phone always rings the minute you step out?"—and pressed "play" on the machine.

"Hi, Mark here. I guess you're still sleeping." Don't you hate that, the way everybody always assumes you're sleeping when they can't reach you, like you didn't do a thing all day but sleep? (Once you get on Andy Rooney it's hard to stop.)

"Anyway," he went on, "I'm on my way to the gym and then I'll be in the office trying to get things a little organized. I spoke to Francine who's going to work at home today building some files for the project. She's sorry about last night, she got hung up." I really love that one. Oh, right—excused. "She also reminded me we still haven't made a deal with her so I guess you and I will have to figure what's fair pretty soon. That's all for now. Call me when you wake up."

"Damn it, I *am* up," I yelled at the machine. Or maybe the ghost of my mother. (I just realized that's what Andy Rooney's job is, a national nagging mother.)

Back to life. I replayed Teri's phone tape. The store message of the overdue bill didn't bear further investigating. Bill Henford, the guy who'd picked her up or talked to her at Nicky Blair's was a longshot possibility ("Crazed Suitor Slays Starlet") but it felt like something on the bottom of the list unless something else tied him in.

Harry whoever, the agent, was a stronger possibility, but didn't feel like a high priority, either.

The Leah lady who was going to give Teri either money or trouble definitely registered higher, since there was no denying Teri'd found maximum trouble.

The hang-ups, of course—no help. Plus the voice didn't identify itself. Hated when people did that. Someone calls and just starts talking and you spend the first five minutes trying to figure out who it is and somehow it works out *you* did something wrong, not recognizing them. (Wonder if Andy paid for ideas.)

Ellard was working on nailing down the Taxi Man dope dealer.

"Arv"—I didn't know who the hell Arv was.

Matt turned out to be Matt McKensie, the guy at the stable she kept her horse. Since he was all crippled up from being beaten, and with a witness to vouch, he was certainly clear.

That left Fabrisio Sugarman, who I definitely wanted to look into. And one more unidentified hang-up.

I didn't think I should tackle Sugarman without Francie first doing a little data-basing or whatever the hell it was to get some sort of fix in front. Since he wasn't just another shnook.

So it was mostly pass on the phone tape for now. That left Harvard Lawrence Singleton, the obsessed fan, which there was nothing I could do about till the law latched onto him or he surfaced some other way. And Buzz Baxter, Teri's ex-husband and soft-porn impresario.

He wasn't all that hard to find. Buzz Baxter—nee Bernie Baxt—was on the first page of the Unfair List of both the Writers' and Screen Actors' guilds.

That meant he'd contracted for work from writers and actors he hadn't paid for. It also meant he wasn't currently in business. He'd have to make good in order to get off the Unfairs or nobody'd be allowed to work for him.

Baxter Productions, a.k.a. Erosfilm, and Hard Times Pictures, had its Unfair location listed at an address on McFarlane, just west of Pass Avenue in Burbank.

The phone company said I had reached a number that was no longer in service and I should check the directory and be sure I was dialing correctly. Like I'm an idiot.

I knew damn well I was dialing correctly (I've been doing it for years) but the odds were Buzz Baxter, nee Bernie Baxt, wasn't going to be in his office on McFarlane, phone or no phone. There wasn't even going to be an office on McFarlane. But I had nothing better to do and figured to take a shot.

I gave Bradley a call, got his machine. "I guess you must be taking a *nap,*" I said. "When you wake up I just wanted you to know I'm off to the Valley to check on Teri's ex-old man. Catch you later."

It was a lovely day and I put the top down on my convertible, backed the big guy carefully out the garage (you had to ease it or the tailpipe tended to scrape on the hill) slipped an Oscar Peterson cassette in the slot and boogied on down the road to the tune of "Easy

Listenin' Blues"—Joe Pass on guitar, Niels Pedersen on bass.

*   *   *

Whatever the overs and unders made up the average mean price of a house in California, the one on McFarlane was definitely an under. In a side street not too far from Warner Brothers it had probably been built for less than twenty thousand in the Forties—under ten if the Thirties.

It didn't look like they'd thrown a lot of money into maintenance, either.

And of course, it wasn't a business at all, it was the mailing address for the ghost of one.

I was surprised to see an old Mercedes 190SL parked outside, together with a recent Jetta. The ragtop on the Mercedes was just that, shredded rags, and the most recent paint was Rustoleum. Even so, I would guess it had some collector value.

I parked the Eldorado, walked up the littered walk, almost fell through a hole in the porch step.

I could hear music from somewhere inside—The Doors ("Riders of the Storm"). One of those groups that's hard to kill. Even when they're already dead. I pushed the doorbell. No one came. I knocked. No one came. Pounded. Ditto.

I walked around the side of the house on some almost-grass where a driveway would have been if the house had a garage and that got me to the patio—or backyardo.

There, around what had to be about the smallest, dirtiest pool I'd ever seen, were a couple of drug-skinny girls, slug-white, almost no muscle tone, in kind of sagging bikinis. They still had a few minutes left on the teen clock, which accounted for being anywhere remotely attractive. But it wouldn't be long. They were with the most unhealthy-looking person I'd ever seen actually standing up.

Buzz Baxter was, I guess, in his early sixties. One of those skinny guys with a belly—potato on a stick. Which just now he was treating me to the sight of by leaving a very old silk bathrobe untied. Under the belly was a pair of stained Speedo's nobody very real about himself would have still worn.

He had the kind of pattern baldness where it's OK on the sides, real receded over the eyebrows, but comes to a point in the middle like Fred Whatsisname, from *Hunter*. Which for some reason he'd dyed canary yellow. So we wouldn't notice.

The final touch was bigger bags under his eyes than Duke Ellington after a year of one-nighters.

The man had seen better days.

He told me to get out.

I told him I just wanted to ask a few questions.

He told me to get the *fuck* out.

It occurred to me he'd figure anybody wanted to talk to him was a bill collector or at least some kind of trouble. I tried to explain I wasn't any of the above.

"Look, I'm casting, here," he said. "I'm in the middle of a project. If you want to see me, call my office and make an appointment."

I didn't think embarrassing him in front of the starlets was going to accomplish anything. On the other hand, I knew there wasn't any office, or any working telephone to call it on if there was.

"I'll only take a minute of your time, I promise," I said.

"Hey, do you want me to call Security?" he said. I really would've liked to see how he'd manage that.

"Of course not, Mr. Baxter. Please, just a moment. No trouble. I'm here in reference to the death of Teri Dart."

At which whatever little light he had left in his face seemed to dim out. He slowly nodded.

"Go inside, girls. I'm going to have to take a meeting here."

"We just came ouuuut," whined one of the teeny-boppers.

"Can't we just hang arouuuund?" said the other.

He fumbled to find the pocket of his torn silk bathrobe.

"Here, darlings," he said, then glanced at me. I turned away while he dug in the pocket for a bottle of coke and the spoon rattling against it. "Go inside. This won't take long. I have to talk to Mr. . . . ?"

"Ray Goodman," I prompted. (I keep seeing on TV where P.I.s are all the time giving out their card. It was the one refinement I'd overlooked.)

"Mr. Goodman," he repeated. "Go on, now," he said to the girls, shooing them off like the children they were. We both watched their little asses sulk off toward the back of the house.

"You want something to drink, Ray?" he said, going right to the Hollywood first-person familiar.

"No, thank you," I said. It wasn't a house you'd want to eat, drink, or even touch anything.

He helped himself from a cracked and filthy styrofoam cooler beside the umbrella-covered patio table. The umbrella was tattered, too, and one of the three table legs was bent. It was all so overdone bad it looked designed.

Pulling the pop top from a can of generic beer, he pointed to a chair.

"Take that one, that's a good one," he said, looking at a chair with a board covering the torn-through seat.

"In the middle of refurbishing, as you can see." Which even he thought was funny enough to prompt a smoker's hack took more than a minute to get over.

"OK—what can I do for you?" he said when he could finally talk again.

"I'm writing a book on Teri and Hollywood and all that and I wanted to interview you, since you're naturally an important part of her life."

"Well, was once. I discovered her, you know."

I nodded. Everybody in show business gets "discovered"—as if they didn't exist before. Like America.

"We made six films together," he went on. "Really shook everybody up." He laughed that awful phlegmy laugh, settled down. Ran his hand over the stubble of a gray beard missed matching the blond hair by about fifty shades. "A lot of teasing shit. Jiggling—tits and asses. Nothing, really. But at the time . . . the churches, the censors went out of their mind."

"I guess you made some good money, too."

"Yeah."

I tried not to let him see me look around. But he did.

"Yeah, right. It's Hollywood. Who ever thinks it'll ever stop?"

I knew a little about that.

"So, you spend it," he went on. "And it's Bel Air, and partying and doing deals."

"Yeah." Not exactly breaking new ground.

"And then one day, the third wife's gone, and the movers and shakers aren't taking your calls, and it's Burbank and walking distance to a studio where you can't even get past the gate."

"Tell me about it. We all know that story. I was hoping you might give me something about you and Teri. You were married, right?"

"Yep. Pygmalion always gets the girl."

I thought it was Henry Higgins, but who's arguing?

"And?"

"Pygmalion was a sculptor, you know." (Didn't really.) "King of Cyprus. He created a statue he fell in love with."

This, I didn't expect.

"Sure."

"Only statues are cold and lifeless."

"Yeah, I guess."

"But then Aphrodite brought the statue to life."

"Hey, great."

"And I brought Teri to life."

"Teri was cold and lifeless?"

"No, Teri was a hot bitch who fucked anything in pants."

That part sounded familiar.

"Then I guess I don't understand the comparison."

"The point is," he said, lighting a Sherman cigarillo with a very shaky hand. "You can't make a pumpkin out of a sow's ear."

Huh?

"Expecially once the pumpkin splits."

Now you're talking. "Not one of the friendlier divorces, I understand."

Suddenly he broke into a broad smile and started that

awful cough again. Then, over that, he said, "You think I killed her!"

"I didn't say that."

"Yeah, but you're thinking."

"All right, I do think it's possible. You're one of the better candidates. Why not? Didn't I read where you sold your old movies to cable or something and didn't she sue you for a big bunch of residuals not too long ago?"

"Yeah, I did and she did. Though it wasn't that big a bunch."

"And didn't she win?"

"Uh-huh."

"So wouldn't that piss you off a little?"

"Nah, that's just Hollywood. You hold off paying till you have to."

"But I would think it would make for bad feelings at least."

"Nah-nah, everybody sues in Hollywood. It's just part of doing business. And didn't make that much difference, most of mine was attached, anyhow."

"And you're saying she had no hard feelings, either?"

"Absolutely. Look, we went out. She called me. I was at her house."

Oh?

"When was this?"

"Week or ten days ago."

"And why was that? I mean, you hadn't been friends."

"Yeah, I'm telling you we were. There were no bad feelings."

"You're saying she just out of the blue said come on over, we'll talk about old times?"

"Well, actually, she was a little spooked. There'd been this guy stalking her, it was in the paper."

"The one she got an injunction against."

"Yeah, but he was still hanging around, and it was getting to her."

"So you went over to protect her?"

"Yeah. Keep her company a day or two."

"Did you actually spot the guy?"

"I think so, the truck anyhow. Toyota. I wouldn't guess stalkers would be into Mercedeses."

"Then what?"

"Well, ironically, I had to leave because of the investment thing."

"What was that?"

"As a favor, and for old times' sake and all that, she wanted to let me in on a good investment."

Investment? Him? Who couldn't invest in paying his phone bill?

"I know what you're thinking. But according to Teri, this was one of those once-in-a-lifetime things."

"Yeah, what exactly?"

"It's a big shopping center going up on Sunset she had the inside track on, that some heavy hitters were involved in. But she had a connection with them and I should get every cent I possibly could together and put it into this Sunset Center project."

"The Sunset Center."

"You know, the Sunset Center Supermall they're building near Sunset Plaza."

Did I ever, with the dirt and the noise and the traffic.

"Yeah? Who's building?" I said, anyway.

"Just everybody who's anybody in Hollywood."

"That's a little vague."

"Well, I'm talking investors. I don't know who's doing the actual building. The largest block, something like forty million, comes from the Sugarman Family Trust."

"Sugarman?" I said. "That wouldn't be Fabrisio Sugarman?"

"Well it's the whole family, but he's the head honcho—president."

"Forty million."

"And another forty or so by a syndicate of personal managers for some major actors and producers and directors."

"And you? You didn't think she was conning you?"

"Nah, why would she? I'm small potatoes. She just wanted to do me a favor, help me get a piece of something could bail me out. All real confidential."

"But didn't they already have the money? They're building."

"She said there was some still open."

"And this inside information came from Teri Dart?"

"Right."

"Why would she know, or be in a position to know? What was her connection?"

"I suppose, knowing Teri, she had some kind of 'intimate knowledge.' "

That sounded right.

"Did you actually invest?"

"Every cent I could beg, borrow, or steal. It's last-chanceville for me. I went for third mortgage, shylocks, the works."

"That confident?"

"From what she told me, and what I know. Hey, the swallows go back to Capistrano, and the big money goes back to the big money."

Then he suddenly had tears in his eyes.

"What?" I said.

"Well, that's why I had to leave—to go scrounge up the money. I mean, not that I could have stayed there indefinitely. But it wasn't too long after that the son of a bitch must've returned and done her in."

"The stalker, Singleton guy."

"Motherfucker."

The torn screen backdoor squeaked open. "Can we come out, nowwwww?" whined one of the white dust twins. Baxter looked at me. I nodded.

"Thank you for your time," I said. "Appreciate it."

He flicked away the tears with a nicotine-stained finger. "Teri was—something else. She had that thing. That camera thing. Could have really made it. But she was crazy. If she'd listened to me she could have ended up another Marilyn."

I was beginning to wonder if that wasn't exactly how she did end up.

# 12

# Mark Bradley

I watered the twenty-two large plants that Goodman said made my apartment look like a cross between Guadalcanal and the Astrodome, splitting the difference between the half of the world that thought I used too much water and the half not enough. I did have a green thumb—would that it were so in the human interpersonal area. Still, nice to see something flourish.

Francine had called earlier to say she was going to work at home, which was okay, she had computers, modems, and faxes—all the tools she'd need. It was just that it reminded me too much of the difficult times when she was on drugs, and all those evasive cop-outs. Especially since she'd also called me at eight in the morning, not a time she's normally up—unless she'd been up all night. But I really shouldn't have such negative thoughts. I felt a twinge of guilt at my lack of confidence.

Goodman hadn't answered his phone, but we'd earlier agreed to go our separate ways so as to maximize the gathering of preliminary information.

I put off having breakfast as this was one of my gym days and previous experience had taught me it was best to get it over with first thing in the morning. There were too many distractions later in the day, for one thing. Sloth was another.

I dressed in my gray sweats, left my gray apartment, elevatored down to the subterranean garage where I got into my gray BMW. The thought occurred to me I might consider a color breakout.

I headed north up Kings Road to Santa Monica Boulevard, left to just beyond the West Hollywood city hall—which looked like a city mall (stores on the ground floor, city business on the second), U-turned back to the Sports Connection on the south side of the street.

The parking structure was jammed (everybody seemed to get the guilts on the same days) and I had to park on the roof. I startled a fellow passenger by a sudden laugh when I realized we were riding down the elevator of an exercise facility full of Stairmasters and avoiding the natural exercise afforded by the actual stairs. I explained it to him—he didn't find it funny. In fact, the minute we reached the ground floor he dashed out the door and put immediate distance between us.

Though this was an entirely new structure, the original building had housed the Beverly Hills Health Club, which was bought out by the Sports Connection. In order to do that, they had to honor the many lifetime memberships various people had in the old BHHC. That turned out to be a lot of old Middle European Jews who now coexisted with the preponderantly young gay members. So there was a lot of youthful pec flexing ("Eat your heart out, Arnold") and elderly wattle waggling ("Free Russian jowlery") side by side. Well, not totally side by side. The gay contingency sweated over the various muscle-enhancing machines; the *alter kakkers* took a *shvitz*.

Not surprisingly there wasn't a lot of social interfacing between them. But then again, no overt hostility, either. Live and let live—which gave the gay members an inevitable demographic edge, they weren't ninety years old.

There were of course many women members as well— also of varying persuasions.

At any rate, I flashed my card, signed in, stamped my parking ticket and headed to the second floor and the cardiovascular pit for my opening exercise on the Trackmasters.

I'd tried to get Goodman to join. But he continued to regard his several myocardial infarctions as temporary aberrations not worth inconveniencing himself about. While naturally his physician had prescribed vigorous exercise, his only response to that was an occasional two-mile mosey down Sunset Boulevard in Beverly Hills, snorting smog. There's an opposite to "a word to the wise."

The CV section of the gym was heavily patronized and often required a wait to get one of the fifteen treadmills.

Today, however, there were two available side by side and I quickly crossed the floor to claim one. Simultaneously, someone else claimed the other.

Adonis.

His earthly name was Christopher Winfield. He was about my age, which if there was a God and this turned out to be the Start of Something Big, would make it a rarity for me, my height, six-one, in noticeably better condition (though he modestly claimed otherwise), a real estate broker (considering a change now that real estate was in a holding pattern), apparently affluent, definitely charming, engagingly witty, not easily winded (I learned all this during the exercise), uninvolved, HIV negative— and free for dinner.

I always knew working out was good for you.

I went home after gym to shower and change for reasons both hygienic and aesthetic, and in mood both optimistic and elated. Chris had preceded me—not home, alas, but leaving the Sports Connection. Having an appointment to show a house, he'd only done the cardios and a few leg and arm exercises. I did mostly eye-popping and jaw-slacking exercises.

Now, in pressed jeans and a white dress shirt open at the neck and turned over at the cuffs, brown Magli loafers (I would, of course, change later for dinner) I said good-bye to my flourishing plants (which obviously knew I was giving them the *exact* amount of water), considered seriously whether the place wouldn't be the better for a new coat of paint—something cheerful, maybe a light yellow—at least white (enough gray!) and found I still remembered a lot of upbeat lyrics.

I popped up to Sunset and stopped at Greenblatt's to pick up some deli. I was going to surprise Francine with brunch. I had a feeling she could use a little cheering up. My gut instinct was things hadn't gone all that well in the "need some space" confrontation with Marshal. Plus I had to tell *some*body about Chris!

I must say Goodman had really turned me on to deli.

I could still remember his disdain when I'd ordered a liverwurst on white the first time he took me. Now, under his skillful tutelage, I was a regular regular. I had to take his word for the fact the *old* Greenblatt's was much better, with sweaty, harried countermen who still managed to chew the fat as they trimmed the fat, telling corny jokes, and noshing odd bits of whatever they were dishing. There are no anorexics in delicatessens.

The new Greenblatt's suited me just fine. I was in a remarkably good mood. I felt terrific! Obviously, I'd missed being Significantly-Othered a lot more than I realized.

I filled my order, paid the bill, climbed back up the stairs, gave the attendant my validated ticket ("You have a nice day, too!"), popped into the Beemer, a really nice car, exited, and eased back across Sunset heading south.

Francine lived on Fountain near Crescent Heights in an early Hollywood medieval castle replete with turrets and gargoyles (and palm trees and birds-of-paradise). They'd had to pass on the moat—too much traffic in and out of the underground garage.

They tell you to take time to smell the flowers along life's way. But they have no idea how overwhelming it is to smell the kosher pickles in the bag along the way. I was actually salivating.

After I got to Francine's and parked in the jousting area out front, I took the bag and crossed to the door. In a further compromise with tradition a bell system had been installed, perhaps from the outset, an armed watch on armored steed being a touch impractical. I rang her bell and got no answer. I waited, rang again. Riding the wake of another tenant, I entered (so much for security) and went up to her door where I listened and found she really wasn't home. I decided to give her a chance and wait outside.

I returned to my car. However, I wasn't able to resist eating a corned beef and Swiss on corn rye while I waited. And a pickle, boy oh boy. Us *goyim* didn't know what we'd been missing!

I was certainly glad I'd waited because it wasn't more than ten or fifteen minutes before I saw her familiar hunter green classic '64 Mustang pull up to the garage gate—or perhaps portcullis. She dialed her access code, the gate slid back, and the car disappeared inside. Apparently she'd just been out on an errand.

I got out of the Beemer and walked toward the garage, bag of fragrant goodies in hand.

Her spot was about midway and she had just finished parking. I was about to call out to her when she got out of the car, stumbled, and dropped her bag. I watched as if in a slow-motion dream the bag fell open, and in the acoustically exaggerating way of garages heard as well as saw the small white-filled vial roll across the aisle that instantly took all the joy out of my day.

Wasn't it Shakespeare's elfin Puck who first observed, "What assholes we mortals be?"

I wasn't going to think about it. I couldn't think about it. To think about it was to be forced to do something about it—or at least about her. Help, abandon, detach, give up on? Scarlett O'Hara knew what she was doing.

I backed quietly out and, intent on retreating to my car, stepped into a partially dug hole in which was a bone, on which I turned my ankle.

I limped back to the Beemer, almost thankful for the pain that diverted my attention. But then, every movement having a meaning all its own and every piece a place in the grand mosaic, it gave me an idea, which I proceeded immediately to act upon, not alone to protect myself from psychic pain, the responsibilities of friendship et al., but because it was a very hot idea.

I instantly departed Francine's now suddenly drab and ridiculous castle and headed north to Sunset Boulevard. I turned left, going west. And tried not to think. Or not about item one, just item two—the new idea.

En route, at the first bus stop bench on which a homeless person had staked his territory, I pulled over and popped out with the bag of delicatessen. This I casually, and I thought unobtrusively, placed on the ground near his head. He opened an eye.

"Get outta, motherfuckin' bastard bitch pisser, son of a goddamn fucking asshole shit."

Clearly the man was either a victim of Tourette's syndrome or had a lot to learn about gratitude.

Surprisingly, for a city dweller, I was momentarily nonplussed and didn't immediately retreat. This seemed to further enrage him. He reached into the bag, got hold of something, and was about to fling it in my direction when he got a whiff of garlic, with all its compelling propaganda. This distracted him momentarily enough for my motor skills to return. I left him cautiously unwrapping a sandwich, albeit still eyeing me malevolently.

Back in the car, I continued west on Sunset, crossed La Cienega (and the dusty traffic jam at the excavation site), passed my office in the Playboy Building and turned right at Sunset Plaza.

I bore left on Rising Glen, then left again on Thrasher and over to Goodman's street and up the hill.

Even as I parked outside his house I felt pretty sure he wouldn't be home. And a quick ring of his bell confirmed as much.

However, it wasn't Goodman I had come to see.

I went around the north side of his garage, through the unlocked gate that allowed the various meter readers onto the property and over to the Sheer Bliss rosebush on a line with the kitchen window.

This was the spot so favored by Asta for doing his business. What I had suddenly remembered was how the wirehair had behaved when I was in Teri's bedroom. It had snatched the mini-tape recorder and "buried" it under the bed in a bundle of dirty laundry. He was a snatch and bury-er. And since we were convinced Teri had died in part because she didn't know what had become of her address book, could it be he had done the same with her book?

Also suddenly further remembering he also buried a great deal of shit in the same spot, I retreated to Goodman's garage where I found a shovel and a pair of work gloves. (Which I figured some workman must have left, it was a cinch Goodman would never have used them.)

Thus armed and protected I went back to the rosebush and started gingerly to dig around its base.

Sure enough, there was a goodly supply of doggy

waste. As expected. I persisted. If I were correct, I wouldn't have to dig very deep.

It was only another minute or two before I struck something definitely more substantial.

Carefully removing the dirt (and doggy doo) all around it, and damn happy for the gloves, I did find a book.

Tremendously excited (Goodman was right, not only doing the puzzle but finding the pieces was a real adrenaline rush) I picked it up, dusted off the bits and pieces of dirt and offal, discovered I'd been holding my breath, breathed, and took a look.

It wasn't Teri's address book after all.

It was only her diary.

# 13

## Rayford Goodman

When I finished with Baxter in Burbank, I stopped at the Smoke House to make a call—on the phone. And answer a call—of nature.

The big restaurant, opposite Warner's, was busy setting up for the huge lunch crowd that'd be arriving any minute. They had a terrific calf's liver and bacon I was tempted to go for, but it was just a touch early.

So I did my business and made the call. The business was a great relief, but the call was a bust. Bradley wasn't at his condo or his office.

I decided maybe while I was there and before the bar got all busy for lunch, I ought to just have a quick blast to settle my nerves and top off my bladder.

I ordered a bullshot and decided to check my messages. I never used to carry the gizmo to call my answerphone. In fact, I've never been much of a fan of answerphones altogether. I always felt if someone called you and you weren't there, they'd know they hadn't reached you and try again. With an answer machine the onus got shifted to you. They called, now you owed them.

But then again I used to work solo and when you had a partner you had to make adjustments. And compromises. Plus, he was good with all that shit and showed me how to use it.

There was only one message. From Bradley.

"I'm sitting in my car, top down, with a number fifteen sunblock on top of a light application of Quick Tan, letting nature and chemistry fight it out while waiting for you in front of your house. I think you ought to ..."

and there was a beep ending the message. My answerphone was old and you could only leave a short message.

There was another beep. "... and get yourself a god-damn machine that a civilized person would have," said Bradley. "I was saying, you ought to get back here as soon as you possibly can because you will be very much interested in some reading material I have literally un-earthed." Another beep, ending the message. And one more starting a third. "... eally ridiculous and I can't understand how you expect to function in the final dec-ade of the twentieth century. Get your ass in gear—I've got Teri Dart's diary."

That sounded really promising. A lot better than bitchy comments about my electronic equipment. Which happened to be state of the art. For 1972.

So I hurried back to the bar, gulped down the rest of my bullshot, got back in the Cad Classic and headed for home.

Except—a funny thing happened on the way to the rest of my life.

I was just this side of the Hollywood Freeway overpass to get to Cahuenga, which I usually took to go home from Barham. That's the one runs parallel to the freeway and then by the Hollywood Bowl, around to Franklin, and so forth.

But just before the overpass there's an on-ramp, and just before I got there, I spotted a Toyota pickup making a very fast, skidding turn into the freeway.

And it hit me Singleton could of either been following me (less likely), or plain found out where the ex-husband of the woman he was obsessed with lived, and started stalking him—for whatever reasons made sense to weirdos like that.

For all I knew, he could have knocked off poor old Buzz while I was knocking off my bullshot.

Any rate, I zipped on over to the far right lane, getting two horns and a finger, and managed to make the turn just as I saw the truck leave the ramp and make it to the freeway.

I didn't know whether he'd spotted me, but the guy was definitely moving out.

I called on the extra hundred horses really well-kept old American cars had to spare, and zoomed after him.

We were pushing seventy-five by the time I closed the gap, and heading into the wilds of the Valley. I could see the car wasn't exactly the same color as when I'd made it back on my street, and didn't have the "TO" and the "TA" blanked out, but he'd had time to do a repaint. I also couldn't tell much on his looks at the distance and speed, but he was the right color and the right sex.

He definitely spotted me chasing him, and got us up to eighty-five. I finally pulled up parallel and got a look at his hate-filled crazy face. He had a mustache, which of course he could of got fake, and darker hair, which he could of dyed. The guy was after all on the run. Now we were zooming side by side and I was trying to figure should I try running him off the road. On the one hand, it was just about the only option I had. On the other was my old sweet car getting a big bunch of dents at best. We kept up like that for I would guess about two and a half miles, neck and neck, only a few inches between us. I was waving him to pull over, not that I thought for a minute he would. And he was making the kind of faces gave me a strong feeling we weren't going to wind up friends. Finally, with some thicker traffic looming up ahead, he slowed back to about seventy. I did the same, and eased slightly away.

And that's when he lifted the gun and fired at least two shots at me.

Even before I was sure I hadn't been hit, just lost at least my side window, and who knows what to my door, I cut back on the speed. After all, if he had a gun, and I didn't, I didn't think I'd get to dictate the terms of surrender. I drifted over to the right, cutting somebody else off who gave me a horn and a finger, and coasted to a stop.

It took a couple minutes to get my breath back. Another to check the damage (bullet hole in door, shattered side window), and no time at all to wish I had a car phone.

I got back in, eased back onto the freeway, got the next off-ramp, circled to the opposite on-ramp, and headed back, breathing okay, heart still racing a little scary.

When I got to my house, as usual, I parked in the garage. Out front, Bradley's car was, as they say, nowhere to be seen. But he'd left a note on the door. "Decided we ought to get copies of that certain document to save time and preserve the original. Gone to Xerox; back in a flash."

I went inside, ignored lunch-face, alias the Phantom, rubbing against my leg—I knew these Hollywood types.

I considered whether I should call the cops and tell them about my sighting. But since they were always getting those kinds of calls, and since there was an APB out already anyhow, I didn't see much point wasting a lot of time explaining how I managed to get myself shot at by someone wouldn't be there anymore anyway.

Then I cleared away the dining-room table, got us a couple of legal pads and click pens to take notes. In case something interesting showed up in the diary. Wherever the hell he got that. And sent out for some pizza. Even if we were pretty sure now who the murderer was, we still had a book to do.

The pizza came in a dead heat with Bradley (who could of gone to Xerox before, instead of getting a suntan—for such a smart guy).

I paid the delivery kid, pocketed the change.

Bradley stepped in, said, "I got it," and tipped him two bucks. I think he just does those things to aggravate me.

The kid split.

"The guy is on salary," I said. "His job is to deliver pizza. It's what he gets paid for."

"Minimum wage."

"Well, he's not a rocket scientist. Minimum wage for minimum kind of work."

"What difference does it make? A couple of bucks is nothing to us, it could be dinner to him."

"It's people like you ruin it for everybody else," I said. "What's someone supposed to do on a fixed income?"

"Are you on a fixed income?"

"I'm talking theoretically."

"Then those people, I guess, would tip less."

"Ah-hah! Those people shouldn't be ordering out," I added, at least making a part point.

We ate the pizza, plus I had a cup of coffee. Bradley didn't drink caffeine. Wouldn't you know.

He told me how he came by the diary—pretty nifty. I filled him in on my morning with Buzz Baxter including Teri's tip for him to invest in this Sunset Center thing.

"Which doesn't make him much of a candidate as a suspect," he pointed out.

"There's another reason," I said, and told him about my hassle on the freeway with Singleton, which of course made him the primo suspect.

"Certainly looks that way," he agreed, looking a little down in the mouth.

"What's the trouble."

"Just that I'd like it a lot better if it weren't that simple."

"You mean because of the book."

"I suppose we can still do her story, where she came from, how she got here, how someone like her winds up a murder victim in bad old Hollywood. But . . ."

"Yeah, I see what you mean."

"Well, we've got the diary. Let's take a look. We're not that heavily committed that we can't still bail out if it doesn't look more promising."

Which don't ask me why, even then somehow I knew we weren't going to.

He opened the bag with the two sets of Xeroxes of Teri's diary, which looked a lot longer than I'd expected.

"What I think," I said, "we ought to each take a look at the last parts first. That's when it's most likely to have come together."

"I think you're right."

And he gave me like the back third. Which was still a lot of pages. It turned out Teri was one of those Sixties-type people who wrote everything down as if nobody but them ever thought those thoughts before.

"There are a lot of birds up here on the hill," was one of her sharp, insightful observations. That didn't include connecting that the streets were named Thrasher, Warbler, Tanager, Oriole, and Skylark for example.

"I like the morning. When the dew is on the leafs. And it's still foggy out before the sun burns away the smog. Fucked F.P.'s brains out yesterday. Which wasn't too hard, since he has very few brains. Ha ha. Real close thing, just got rid of him only a minute before Mogul showed up. Swore mine was the most perfect body in the whole world. So we did it, too. Watching me in the mirror. Dance class or gym?"

I wanted a drink. Even dead old loves can hurt.

"You like something?" I asked Bradley, pointing to the bar.

"No thanks. Hey, listen to this: 'Wednesday'—she doesn't say which—'the sunset was so beautiful with the poisonous smog providing a deceptual filter for nature's murder. Called B.B. for T.M.'s number. He was funny. Came by, fixed a glitch in the tape. Fixed *his* glitch, too. Outside by the pool, in the stigey darkness.' "

" 'Stigey'?"

"I think she meant Stygian. B.B. and T.M."

"I'm getting that, too. I got an F.P. and a Mogul—the initials and nicknames bit. She's not going to make it easy for us."

"Well, one doesn't sound too hard. B.B. for Buzz Baxter?"

"Could be. And T.M. for Taxi Man—since Baxter seems to be a doper. But no clue on F.P. or Mogul." Just a thirst. But it was too early. I didn't feel up to a whole day drinking, and if I didn't hold off now till at least cocktail hour, that's what I'd be doing.

"Maybe I'll have one, too," said Bradley. "Fix me a gin and tonic."

On the other hand there's no cause to be rude and let a man drink alone.

We got good at skipping Teri on life and philosophy—not a lot of which was original or interesting. And concentrated on the juicy stuff—the trick-book kind of entries. "C.B. fixed me up with L.L., who's into some S & M, which is all right except C.B. wanted me to really twist the guy. It wasn't too hard, though he really hurt my hair with the leather face thing. But C.B. says he's big bucks for the project and promised to get me a real nice outfit if I just played along. Plus, of course, I have my own agender. Ha ha. We got him on tape, so at least that part's covered."

"I got an L.L. who's into S & M, courtesy of C.B."

"I've got several C.B.'s, too," said Bradley.

"One thing, it's definite they were taping. And if B.B.'s Baxter it doesn't seem too far-fetched he'd know something about cameras."

"Good," said Bradley. "Then he's a possible for the partner in the blackmail scheme?"

"Well, that I have my doubts. The guy's got a lifestyle costs about a dollar and a half."

"For that matter, Teri didn't seem to be exactly rolling in money, either—from the looks of her place."

"Yes and no," I said. "When she bought the house it had to be in the high six figures. If she just paid the mortgage we're talking big bucks. Plus pool; plus gardener. Utilities, taxes."

He nodded. "It's kind of weird, isn't it? Reading the diary of someone murdered."

He didn't know the half of it.

We went back to reading. Teri may have liked the sunset and world peace, but so did every candidate for Miss Anything. She'd had an offbeat and interesting life in some ways, but not all that unique enough. Which was why if I was right about the Singleton guy, we'd probably lost the main drive for the book. Or "thrust" as they say in pub biz.

Major personal conflict. I wanted to be right as a detective. Yet wanted to be wrong as a writer.

The phone rang. It was Francie.

"You watching TV?" she said. Francie wasn't big on hello.

"Oh, hi, there," I said. "How you doing?"

"Stop with that shit, just turn on Channel Five," she said charmingly and hung up.

I crossed over to the set. "Francie," I explained. "What's with her, anyway?"

"Nothing, just a little moody," said Bradley.

"When wasn't she?"

"What'd she want?" he asked, I notice not meeting my eyes. Maybe there was something up with the boyfriend.

"She just said turn on Channel Five," I explained, turning it on.

They showed a picture of one of the canyons, a tow truck, two police cars, and a torn-up spot through the brush where a car'd obviously gone through.

In front of all that was a black guy in a trench coat (I wonder if they came in summer-weight for L.A. reporters), saying, ". . . and down the bank two hundred yards below before exploding in what eyewitnesses described as a 'ball of fire.' " (There's a fresh phrase.)

"Firefighters and police recovered one body from the Toyota pickup," he went on as Bradley and I exchanged raised eyebrows, "which has been identified as that of Harvard Lawrence Singleton, a white male," (slight sigh of relief?) "twenty-nine years of age, whose last known address was in Compton."

The scene then shifted back to the studio, where a fellow of what they call Hispanic origin took over. (The Asian lady didn't come on till five—so far the Asians were all ladies, don't ask me why.)

"That was a little over an hour and a half ago, when Chuck Washington gave us that on-the-spot report from Coldwater Canyon," the Mexican guy went on. "Since then Channel Five has had an update on the story. According to sources at the Beverly Hills Police Department, the coroner's office has already determined that Singleton did not die of injuries sustained in the crash. A preliminary examination revealed the unemployed handyman had been stabbed repeatedly before his car went off the road and down the slope where it exploded in a ball of fire." (They were going to stick with the "ball of fire.") "Stay tuned for full details and further developments on the News at Five on Five. We now return you to our regular programming."

They hadn't yet connected him with Teri.

So. Some murders don't stay solved very long.

"Then my question is," I said, "who was that guy shooting at me, and why?"

"Well, it is California," said Bradley. "It could have been just a basic freeway crazy who didn't like your attitude."

Usually people have to know me better than that before they hate me.

# 14

## Mark Bradley

"Look on the bright side," said Goodman. "We can cross Harvard Lawrence Singleton off the list."

"I don't see why. Singleton could have killed Teri and someone else killed him for revenge."

"Nah, murder of a murderer? I don't buy that. Especially not when the guy's already a number one suspect, being sought by the police. Why wouldn't anybody just let nature take its course?"

"So, what, then, back to square one?"

"Well, square one and a quarter, maybe. Listen, it's really good news. We've still got a good mystery, we got rid of an obvious suspect so it's still a good puzzle. I think we have us a definite go on the book. Right?"

"Well, we won't close it out yet, anyway," I allowed.

Goodman nodded, a touch eagerly, also forcing a little smile.

"I'm telling you, you should look on this as a very positive development. You yourself didn't want it to be Singleton, and now it looks like not. I'd say definitely not. Terrific, huh? What do you say, doesn't that call for another little drink?" he added, crossing to his bar, obviously rhetorical. "Bombay gin and tonic still?"

I nodded. Whatever brain damage he'd suffered didn't extend to forgetting what everybody drank. Happily engaged in the chase, I could hear him opening the freezer and singing (to "Matchmaker") "Ice maker, ice maker, make me a drink—lemon, lime?"

"Either."

"You say 'either' and I say lemon," he added, in higher spirits than I'd seen in quite some time.

"Boy, it doesn't take much to cheer you up—a grisly murder or two and you're practically euphoric."

"Well, it is kind of proof the old instincts haven't rotted out."

I didn't feel it politic to point out "the old instincts" had only a moment before been convinced the latest victim was himself the killer.

But maybe he was right, more than likely this did mean Singleton hadn't killed Teri. Which would eliminate the obvious and enhance the chances of coming up with a good book.

Confirmation wasn't long in coming.

"For you," said Goodman, handing me the phone and my Bombay.

"I thought I might track you bloodhounds there," came the voice of Dick Penny, our I felt certain would-be publisher.

"Heard the news, I take it," I replied, restraining an urge to gloat, now that he, himself, was resolving my doubts.

"The news?"

"About the murder of the obsessed fan who was supposed to have killed our little girl next door?"

"Oh, that news—yeah. Funny you should mention that. I've been rethinking your little project and I must say I begin to see you could be right, there might be a book in it."

"Uh-huh." I covered the mouthpiece. "Penny," I said to Goodman. "Wants to play catch-up with our project."

Goodman gave me a thumbs down. Not that I needed one.

"Yes, those of us with faith in our judgment felt so all along."

"Ah-hah," said Penny. "So, you want me to draw up papers?"

"Well, gee, Dick—since you turned it down we've talked to one or two other publishers ..."

"No, you haven't, you really haven't." I don't recall ever hearing a voice sweat before.

"Can't fool you, Dick—you're right. There wasn't time for anything substantive."

"Good, good, so we'll just make our usual . . ."

"No, we won't. When you write on spec and take all the gamble, you get to have a bigger payoff if you win."

"All right, we could sweeten . . ."

"Please. Tell you what, you just hang tight. We're going to continue as we are. And when we're done, we'll give you a shot. Even if we decide to go the auction route, you'll certainly have an opportunity to partic-ipate."

"You're going to really bleed me," he said.

"That's right, Dick," I said, enjoying myself enor-mously. "We'll be in touch." And I hung up, laughed, clinked glasses in a toast with Goodman and took a good long swig. Life was good!

Then we returned to the table to get back to work when I had another thought. "Shouldn't we be getting the diary to the authorities?"

"In good time," said Goodman.

"Withholding evidence," I reminded him.

"They have no way of knowing when we found it."

"But we don't need to, we have our own copies," I reminded him. "What are we waiting for?"

"We're waiting for me to figure out what I'm going to trade Ellard for it," said Goodman, picking up a section of the diary and resuming his reading.

I picked up my own batch of pages. There was a long series of entries that had to do with a kiwi, broccoli, and asparagus regimen apparently designed to reduce water retention and enhance psychic awareness (from the Cali-fornia school of Zenistry), a skin problem that resisted more conventional treatment, and a yeast infection with a life of its own. Hard times in the easy-living de-partment.

C.B. was often on her mind, the subject of repeated entries. "We are both going to the top. He may not know it, but *I* do." "I will be at his side all the way."

And again, by way of self-assurance: "He doesn't love his wife—they don't even do it anymore." (Amazing that even the most experienced women still bought that. Not only women, come to think of it.)

In any event C.B.'s wife apparently wasn't missing all

that much since Teri described him as "the fastest gun in the West. Ha ha."

"Evidently C.B. leaves a lot to be desired in the sack," I commented to Goodman.

"Yeah, I guess that's what 'noodle dick' means," he replied, pointing to another confirming passage.

"Lord, I hope nobody ever keeps a diary on me and critiques my performance."

"Listen, kid," said Goodman, taking a sip of his drink that evidently fueled Dutch uncle impulses, "one thing you ought to remember. Everybody's a bad lay to somebody. What the somebody doesn't realize, it's even money it's their own fault, and the other person could be world's champ boffer with someone else."

In addition to the wisdom of this observation, I thought it showed a lot of sensitivity for Goodman to refrain from identifying the sex of the somebodys and everybodys doing the boffing.

To which he added, "I think it was Dan Jenkins—my all-time favorite writer—once said something like, 'Next time you run into the prettiest girl in the world just remember somewhere someone's tired of her.' "

Well, I couldn't expect him to maintain gender sensitivity indefinitely. (I had a feeling Dan Jenkins wasn't for me.)

Pages, pages. The skin condition got worse, the bills were piling up, and D.F. was starting to hint around. Then, a page later, she slipped up. "It'll be a cold day in hell when I let old Derma Face in the door." Not exactly a breakthrough, but I felt it was safe to say Derma Face was her skin doctor. And not too cute. The bad news was she sometimes used initials for nicknames! Good God, we were talking codes within codes. I told Goodman as much.

"Right," he said. "Which means F.P., for example, might not be someone's initials. Oh, boy."

"Only sometimes. I'm pretty sure we're right that B.B. is Buzz Baxter and T.M. is Taxi Man. Though Taxi Man is not a name."

"No, but he calls himself that. There's another one, T.B., turns out Toy Boy—I guess a younger lover. N.S.H.

younger lover—not so hot, looks like." Then he pointed
to another spot. "Here's one I'd like to know for sure.
'C.B. says M.F. is really pressing him, and he might have
to let him in on it.' Whatever 'it' is."

" 'M.F.'—mother fucker?"

Goodman just shrugged, kept reading.

"Another one," he said. "M.F.'s threatening to go to
the mayor."

"There's an M.F. somewhere ringing some kind of
bell," I said.

"Wait," said Goodman. "Later—last week, for a
change it's dated, Wednesday, the seventh—'C.B. says
M.F. pushing. In or out? Permanently out!' "

"Permanently out. Who's permanently out? M.F.,
M.F.—'Arv—Marv—Marvin Fischer, the mayor's aide!"

"Murdered at the gay guys ball."

"R-ight." I let it pass. "Assassinated by Kiskessler."

"Which means it wasn't just a random shoot-'em-up
thing. He was aiming at the politicians—Jeffrey Hong
and Marvin Fischer!"

"And he wounded the one and killed the other."

"Fucking fantastic," said Goodman, grinning from ear
to ear.

"You like that? That pleases you?" I said.

"Yeah, it does," he replied. "Because now look what
we've got—instead of a random murder Friday in Anaheim, then the two others we know were connected,
we've now got three murders, Fischer, Teri, and Singleton *all* tied together, all part of the same something—
all three!"

"Four, if you count Kiskessler."

"Right!"

"So what does that mean?!"

"Haven't a clue!!"

Well, that wasn't exactly true. We had made some progress. The first and most obvious, that all the murders
were connected and of a piece. Therefore connected to
Teri. Which vindicated Goodman's instinct, and Ellard's
for that matter. And our best chance of finding what the

connection was and what it was all about lay in solving Teri's murder. Solve one, solve all!

To that end, we had some players in place, others with code names.

Marvin Fischer, the mayor's aide and Jeffrey Hong's dinner guest the night of the Lambda Awards, was dead. Killed by William Hobart Kiskessler, free-lance (or else part of a larger conspiracy involving the government, CIA, that kind of stuff—heaven help us), an apparently expert assassin, but, according to Goodman, indifferent bartender.

Kiskessler himself murdered while in prison—by party or parties unknown (getting us back into the government, covert whatever stuff that's too scary and complicated to even contemplate—except perhaps by Oliver Stone).

Jeffrey Hong, West Hollywood councilman and himself wounded in the shooting, apparently a co-target. The connection between him and Fischer known but unclear—whether allies or competitors in politics.

Teri, of course, the party girl, involved on the fringe (or by her fringe) with an agent named Harry, a stable-owner named Matt McKensie (who'd been roughed up by someone looking for and finding incriminating tapes), and Fabrisio Sugarman, an apparent acquaintance and head man on a commercial venture involving some major real estate.

To that we add Buzz Baxter, ex-husband, tied to it all by a desperate investment of assets and IOUs in the venture; Taxi Man, who is probably simply her dope connection; and another victim who at first looked like Teri's killer, her obsessed fan, Harvard Lawrence Singleton, who by all accounts was just what he appeared to be— a looney hooked on Teri.

On the phone tape we have a couple more unaccounted-for men, one who picked her up at Nicky Blair's, plus a disgruntled woman (gruntled ones are hard to come by).

The diary, with still a lot to be read, gives us an "F.P.," a "Mogul," a dermatologist, and an "L.L." into sadomasochism at the behest of the obviously central "C.B."

And—we're still missing an address book.

Given the above, plus the sun's progression toward

the west gently reminding me of other important events pending—my dinner date with Christopher—I thought it time to suggest we call it a day.

"But we're just starting to get hot," Goodman protested.

That, too, I thought. "I find I work better if I walk away from it for a while and come back later, refreshed."

"You've got a date," said Goodman.

The man *is* a detective.

"Some of us do have a life, you know," I answered, admittedly a touch defensive.

"Well, I'm glad for you."

That was a switch.

"Just be careful."

"Hey, we're not going to actually be together. We'll just go to two latex-lined telephone booths and *call* each other."

"Now you're being sensible."

After shave, shower, shampoo, talc and balming, I taped my turned ankle that was a bit tender. I put on my silk art deco boxer shorts from Sulka, cashmere socks from the Burlington Arcade in London, a blue-striped Charvet Egyptian cotton shirt, under the perfectly met spread collar of which I affixed my shorts-matching Sulka foulard in a modified half Windsor. Then I donned the seventeen-hundred-dollar Oggie midnight blue double-breasted suit from Ron Ross on which I splurged after our last paperback sale that I told Goodman only cost four-fifty ("That's your generation, easy come, easy go"), and finally stepped into a pair of black leather low-cut Salvatore Ferragamo loafers so soft you'd think Gucci was in the galosh business.

Even after the five full minutes I spent admiring my sartorial elegance in the gray muted full-length mirror discreetly adjacent to my bed, and the further minute or so I spent in indecisive consideration of a breast-pocket silk, I was still early.

I retreated to the living room, checked the lights, turned the champagne gently chilling in the silver bucket, settled on an airy Madonna album (*Dick Tracy*) to affect a noncommittal mood that belied my intentions and responded to the slightly premature ringing of my doorbell. (One hopes not a portent.)

Unusual, since there was a security system of buzzer codes and video checks downstairs. But sometimes someone just followed someone else through unchecked.

Such was surely the case in point as I opened the door. To Francine.

"Hi, sorry to barge in like this, can I come in, you don't mind, what's that, champagne, expecting company, you look good, really good, that's a new suit, huh, wow, you are dressed up, listen, there's something I'd like to ask you, a favor, really, but not really, if you look at it another way."

"C-c-c-come in," I said, referring to an old joke, originally about Swiss watchmakers and impatient fast-talking Americans, not research workers on speed.

"I won't take much of your time—" she went on.

"You bet!" I interrupted.

"But I need an advance on our deal."

"We haven't made a deal, yet."

"But we will."

"That was before. I'm not sure we want to have our usual working arrangement."

"Oh stop the shit, I need money. I have to get something."

"Yeah, I'll bet."

"Some medical thing—that I don't want to go through the company plan."

"Right," I said.

She gave me a long look, stopping the manic rush. "You think I'm back on dope."

What was I going to say, "I've *seen* you back on dope?" At least, *with* the dope.

"What's the problem, what do you need?" I said, instead.

"I don't want to go into it. You going to help me or not?"

"What do you want?"

"Five hundred."

"Can't we at least talk? I'm your friend . . ."

"OK, friend, give me the five. We'll talk another time. I know you're waiting for someone."

"I can make time for you."

"This isn't the moment for it, all right?"

"Was it Marshal? Breaking up with Marshal?"

"I don't want to fucking talk about it."

"When, then? When you've got yourself all fucked-up again? Just because you fell off the wagon doesn't mean you have to go hog-wild. OK, you slipped. Get right back on, it'll be easier—no big disgrace. You're not going for the world's consecutive record."

"Listen, asshole, I'm telling you, I haven't slipped up, I'm not back on dope."

Denial, denial, oh boy, denial. "Francine . . ."

With which she went over to the silver bucket, took out the champagne bottle, held it up.

"Give me the five hundred dollars or I'll break your mirror."

We glared at each other for a very long time. I blinked.

"Boy, I've seen tough negotiators," I said, reaching for my alligator-skin Hermes wallet.

# 15

## Rayford Goodman

The kid was right, of course, we did have to turn the diary over. And since we had Xeroxes there wasn't any point in waiting.

I called the BHPD. But Lieutenant Ellard was out. I left word for him to call back and said it was important.

It was now legitimately cocktail hour so I made myself a legitimate cocktail. Highball, really. Though nobody called highballs highballs anymore, for whatever reason. Now when I ordered vodka and Perrier they always brought two glasses, one with vodka, one for the Perrier. When they had highballs, that didn't happen. It's enough to drive you to drink.

I dug back into the diary, still concentrating on the most recent part.

C.B. kept on figuring a lot. "C.B. is sure we are all going to get very rich on the project. He promised on a stack of bibles I will get a piece. I am going to get a lot more than a piece, I am going to get C.B.!!!"

And then later: "Mogul came up to the house. And down to the honey pot! Looked pretty funny from a bird's-eye view watching that wig bobbing up and down."

OK, Mogul's bald. That's something. And I guess not that great in the oral department if all she could think was how funny he looked (getting to gnaw you).

"After I recovered from the throws of passion, I got around to asking how come they were building this enormous project when it was supposed to be such a bad time for real estate."

Ah-hah!

"And first all I got was a laugh. And I said, come on.

And then finally a smile and the real reason: 'We have to hide the money somewhere.' "

Laundering? Were we talking dope, maybe? Brought to mind Taxi Man. Who was definitely connected to Teri, probably more ways than one. And if the money the Mogul had to hide came from dope, he was a possible. Still and all, quite a stretch to feature a small-time operator like him even fronting that kind of serious money.

Then Mogul disappeared a couple pages—I guess to give his tongue a rest. C.B. as usual kept popping up.

"C.B. accidentally dropped a note out of his pocket today. I picked it up, but he caught me. It turned out to be a phone number. He said it was his new home number that he had to get changed because too many people knew the old one, and he hadn't had a chance to memorize it yet. All I needed was one glimpse to remember. Maybe because I am an actress and used to memorizing lines. He said never call him there. Like I didn't know. 2734."

But did she write the rest of it down? Remember the prefix? Is it in her address book? That nobody can find. Maybe she called, after all. If only to check. That case there'd be a record in her phone company file. Though not on the bill if it was local. It was one thing I could trade Ellard for.

"L.L. again, with the kinky stuff. Since he is not really the main money I do not see why he is so necessary. But C.B. says he is and a lot of the money follows him and what do I know about it. So I have to do it. I do not really care since he is the one getting hurt, not me. I am not the horse. Ha ha. And I look *so* hot in leather. (The D.B. with the pizza almost popped his eyeballs!!!)"

I wondered did Bradley spot any of the outfits in the bedroom closet?

I did a quick check through the photos I'd taken. Nothing there. So that was another thing looked like missing—leathers and whips and what-all. (How did someone first find out they liked things like that?)

"C.B. is so smart. And really handsome once you think about it. He is my dream man all right. I sure am glad he is tall, too. And with my blond hair we will look so great together. I can hardly wait."

Silly stupid schoolgirl stuff. Maybe he'll take her to the prom. Then again, I have a feeling I wouldn't be too impressed with Marilyn Monroe's diary, either.

The phone finally rang, but it wasn't Ellard.

"Councilman Jeffrey Hong for Rayford Goodman," came the sweet-voiced lady.

"Rayford Goodman undecided about Councilman Hong," I said back.

Which got no laughs, just a little confused pause. Then, "Will you hold for the councilman?"

It was too good a straight line to waste on someone with no sense of humor. "Sure," I said, dropping another cube in my glass.

Which was about as long as it took.

"Rayford—Jeff Hong, here. How are you?"

"Oh, feeling no pain."

"Good. I still have a bit from the bullet, but that's why I'm calling. I haven't had a chance to thank you for your heroic efforts at the Hilton the other night."

"Well, you're welcome, Councilman," I said.

"I've proposed a civilian medal for heroism on your behalf, and the mayor has indicated he will look on it favorably, I'm happy to say."

"That's very nice of you, I'm sure, Councilman."

"Call me Jeff, Rayford."

"And you can call me anything but Rayford. Ray's good."

"Fine, Ray. Listen, I had another thought. Why don't we get together for a drink—I understand you are a drinking man. Tanqueray Sterling and Perrier, right?" (I could see his assistant handing him a three-by-five card. Attention to detail is good, but dossiers get me a little nervous.)

"Why would we want to do that, Councilman—outside the fact we're both nice guys and all?"

"Heh heh," he forced laugh. "Not to beat about the bush, I was hoping I could convince you to endorse my candidacy. Always nice to have a hero on your side."

"I see."

"And I don't think the publicity would hurt your book sales any. As a matter of actual fact, I'd be happy to have your partner on board as well."

"Possible, I guess. He's Bombay gin and tonic."

"Ah ha ha, thanks for the input. As you can imagine, Mr. Bradley's endorsement would serve to remind some of my potential constituents of my service in West Hollywood."

"I'm sure he'd enjoy that."

"Although yours could do me more good, in a general sense, off the record. A lot of people already say I'm too much in bed with the gays. Ha ha."

"Ha ha."

"Well, why don't you talk to your partner and I'll have Mei Ling get back to you and fix a date when we can all get together. 'Kydoky?"

" 'Kydoky," I said, which sounded vaguely Japanese to me now that I thought of it. And we hung up.

Before I could refresh my drink, the phone rang again. Ellard this time.

"Sorry it took me so long to get back to you, I was waiting for the M.E. to finish Singleton."

"Any more surprises?"

"Just that anybody would be dumb enough to think burning up the car was going to keep us from finding all those knife wounds. What can I do for you?"

"Ask not what you you can do for me—though we'll get to that—ask what I can do for you."

"OK, what can you do for me?" he asked.

"I can give you Teri Dart's diary," I said.

There was what they call a pregnant pause. While Ellard tried to figure out how casual he ought to sound.

"Where and how soon?" was the best he could come up with.

"Into Italian?" I said.

"Sure."

"How about Madeo's and soon as you can."

"Last one there's a rotten linguine," he said. And we said good-bye and hung up.

At the word "linguine" I suddenly flashed on what put

the Dodgers in the dumpster. Lasorda should of never gone on that diet.

Madeo's is one of the classier restaurants around where the dress code is so relaxed you see everything from tuxes to T-shirts. The place is real pretty European-style with a lot of brass and wood and beveled glass, a few steps down a sort of half basement of the ICM Building on Beverly Boulevard.

Just now, early evening, the bar was getting a lot of cocktail action from would-be actresses on the make for jobs and ICM would-be humpers on the make for the actresses.

The smart money was on the agents.

Since Ellard would be coming from downtown (Beverly Hills didn't have its own coroner) I knew I wasn't going to be the rotten linguine. But I didn't think I'd mind being early since actress-watching isn't the hardest way to spend your time.

I wedged my way to the bar alongside a giggle of girls wearing skirts so tight and short they made tennis togs look like nun-wear.

I ordered my vodka and small Perrier, knowing like most Italian restaurants the Perrier would turn out San Pellegrino or Ramlossa. The main idea anyway was just to avoid club soda out of a hose.

The giggler on my left was telling the jiggler on my far left, "The guy tries to give me a hundred-dollar bill. What does he take me for?"

Seemed pretty clear to me.

"A hundred dollars?" said the jiggler. "I don't believe it."

"So I go, what's this for? And he goes, it's for taxi fare. So I go, get this, I only travel by limo."

"Oh, great. So like what happened?"

I suddenly found I didn't care much what happened. And girl-watching was losing its appeal—mostly when it included girl-listening. Was it just getting older? Or was it all dumber than I remembered and with a lot less meaning?

True, there'd been plenty times all I wanted out of life

was just get laid. But at least it was a lighthearted thing between us, not a contest where one or the other tried for an edge. I think. Could be wrong. (I do remember a barroom sage once saying perspective was just how something seemed after the passion died. But since passion was or used to be *part* of the something, which was the real truth?)

The bartender brought me my vodka on the rocks and a second glass full of ice, together with a bottle of Ramlossa a lot larger than I considered small. (I didn't realize they made magnums of club soda.)

On my other side, two guys in their early twenties wearing designer knockoffs were seriously trying to decide between Meryl and Demi for "the project." My gut feeling they should be worrying if everybody using fax machines wasn't going to cost their jobs in the mail room.

Not every happy hour works.

"I told him where he could put his two-hundred-and-fifty," Girl One was saying, I guess about the negotiations.

While the designer knockoff guy on my right said, "Did you read the memo on the Allegretto deal?"

"Yeah. Unbelievable," said the second.

I really didn't much care whether it was believable or not. I still hadn't decided whether to go for Meryl or Demi. But leaned toward Meryl, partly based on not caring a whole lot for Bruce.

"I understand it's something like forty million dollars," said the second guy. Which I guess wasn't the movie, but the Allegretto deal. Whatever that was. (Though the name struck a familiar note.)

"More, I heard," said the first.

At which point they decided money wasn't everything and moved around the other side of me, trying to get next to the girls. I made room.

I could have saved them some time and embarrassment—they'd never get to take off with that pair of frequent flyers. But it wasn't my game to lose, as they say. And I had my own things to be dumb about.

Anyway, Ellard showed up and I carried my drink over to join him at a little table near the front side of the bar.

Allegretto. In music it meant light and lively. And then I remembered. In life it was the maiden name of Albert Sugarman's wife.

Ellard was on the slender side for a cop. I doubted he was more than six feet tall and built like a tennis player. Not too much chest and shoulders, but strong legs and what even nice girls these days call perky buns. I think it was Sammy Davis once said blacks had protruding buttocks from carrying bales of cotton on their heads as slaves. (Or was it William Shockley?)

Just now Ellard was resting the aforementioned butt on a comfortable Madeo's chair, having given the waiter his order.

"I'll have a Jubilacum akvavit, with a Beck's chaser." (Weren't we getting trendy.) And now he was making gimme gestures at me.

"All right, what've you got?"

"All in good time," I said.

"Let's don't start withholding evidence now that I know you have it."

"I'm gonna give it to you. I just want a favor or two in exchange."

"You're going to give it to me anyway," he said, just a little stiff.

"Sure I am. Let me have some fun here."

"What do you want?"

"Could use the phone company printout of all Teri's calls last month."

"I've got it, and I'll let you see it—I can't give it to you, you know that—but take my word, there's nothing there that's going to tell you anything." (I'll be the judge of that.) "Now what's in the diary?"

"Lieutenant, you aren't suggesting I looked at it?"

He gave me the old fish eye. Or the middle-aged fish eye.

"Well, I may have taken a quick look or two."

And I summed up what we'd found so far. About the code names and the nicknames and the abbreviations.

"But you'll see all that for yourself."

Which was when the waiter came with his drink. I had

to wait for further negotiations on my trade while he went through the ritual knocking back of the akvavit, then the long sigh, the "Ahhhhh," and finally the beer chaser. At least he didn't have a Viking helmet and a ram's horn.

Then I handed him the stained and dirty diary, which I'd, of course, put in a baggy.

"And you came about this how again?" he said.

"The dog. One of Teri's dogs didn't get picked up by the animal control folks. And it was the one liked to bury things. Bradley found that out."

"How?"

By seeing him do it when we were copying the phone messages off her machine, not a good idea to remind him.

"Uhm, you know—saw him, uhm, do it before. Anyway, the dog has a spot on my property, by one of the rosebushes my ex-old lady planted, where he stashes things. And, on a hunch, my partner dug it up. And there it was."

He thought for a moment.

"You know, the terrible thing is Teri might have been killed over this."

"I thought of that. They could of been torturing her to tell where it was and she couldn't 'cause she didn't know."

"Exactly."

At which point Ellard caught the waiter's eye and signaled another round (I guess he didn't figure he had to ask me).

"I appreciate this, Ray," he said.

"Hey, just doing my civic duty."

"Right. And of course you understand whatever evidence is in here is confidential."

"Lieutenant, I am bound by the same rules as any other journalist."

"Journalist! What is this journalist shit?"

"I do write books, you know. First amendment; all that. Let's not get into it. Whatever I'd be using, the way it takes twelve years to get a book into print you'll either have the case knocked or Robert Stack'll do it for you on *Unsolved Mysteries*."

"I suppose you're right," he answered agreeably. Took a gulp of beer. Then said, "Have you noticed when you sit down here you really get quite a view up these ladies' skirts?"

"Yes, but not having your primitive urges, I'm a little more able to control myself."

"Hey, I'm not doing the flaunting here. No law against looking."

"You're excluding Alabama. Listen, you know anything about an Allegretto deal?"

"What's an Allegretto deal—some sort of birth-control device?"

"I don't think so. If we can change the subject? I would guess it's something to do with show business."

"Close." Then he thought a moment, shook his head. "No, I really don't."

I'd have to look into that myself.

"How about the Singleton thing, anything new on that?" I asked. "Besides the autopsy."

"No. Well, did you know he had called in and confessed?"

"Confessed? To Teri Dart?"

"Yeah."

"But if he confessed, then I don't get it—someone killed him knowing he killed Teri?" (The one complication I didn't want.)

"Not necessarily. Lots of weirdos confess to things they didn't do, for various psychiatric reasons—guilt, desire for attention, who knows. Just crazy's another way to put it."

"Yeah?"

"But in this case, my take is he confessed under duress. The tape reveals stress, which of course might be even if it were true. But given the way he died, the scenario I lean toward is somebody got him—probably the one who actually killed Teri—and forced him to call."

"Could have been, if he was hanging around."

"Which he was—you said as much."

True.

"Maybe he even saw the killers. Possible. Say they're pressing Teri for this diary, now I know there was one. Before I thought it was probably the address book. But maybe they even got that—we sure never found it."

"By press you mean torture."

"Exactly. But she doesn't know where it is. If she did she'd have given it up. People don't die over diaries. So, if you're right and the dog snatched it and buried it, she didn't know and they kept on torturing her till—goodbye and she's dead."

"So then they needed a patsy," I chimed in.

"Exactly. And Singleton's right there. They get him to confess over the phone—that call *is* on the list from Teri's, by the way—and take him out for what they expect to make look like a suicide."

"They load up his car with gas . . ."

"Way too much gas. Stab him to death, push the car over Benedict Canyon, it either bursts into flame or they go down and set it off, and hope to clear the books with the confession and the suicide."

"Only you know it's not suicide."

"Exactly. You want to order? Should we eat here?"

"It's good; not totally cheap."

"You mean you're not taking me out on an expense account?" said Ellard.

"I'm sure going to try," I said, signaling the waiter for menus.

"So one other thing it tells us, it was kind of amateur night in Dixie."

"No pros. Unlike, say, Fischer."

"What the hell's Fischer got to do with it? The book's closed on that number. I mean, a little on-going over the killer's being offed in jail. There's a connection?"

I was getting careless. It's hard to lie and withhold from someone you like and trust.

"No, no, go ahead," I said.

"Go ahead what?"

"Well—what about the Taxi Man thing—you follow up on that?"

"Naturally. What about Fischer, come on."

"Nothing, nothing. The Taxi Man," I prompted.

"Well, no big surprises. Small-time cocaine and marijuana dealer; did six months once; probation twice—seems to be well enough connected to get good representation."

"Lawyers have been known to use cocaine, too."

"Apparently."

"And his tie with Teri?"

"To the best of my knowledge, just sold her an eighth or a quarter now and then."

The waiter came and we picked up the menus for the first time.

"I come back," said the waiter.

"They do a great veal," I offered. "What's the fellow's name, by the way—this Taxi Man?"

He kept looking at the menu. "The Marsala, or scaloppini? Or chops? I do like chops. Fellow's name. Bolton. Charles no middle initial Bolton."

And speaking of initials, Charles Bolton equals C.B.

Terrific restaurant.

# 16

# Mark Bradley

I was horribly depressed by Francine's visit. After all she had gone through to get sober. The Intervention, the horrendous detox. Why didn't it stick? Was it really all a lost cause? And nobody really made it except the owners of rehab clinics? Oh, shit, man.

She had to know I, of all people, wasn't taking a moral position. Why lie to me?

She was so bright and intelligent—how could she let this happen all over again? Not peer pressure—half the people we knew didn't even drink anymore. Maybe that was the problem, they should have let her at least still drink. I'm really not at all convinced "addicts are addicts" is true. I think for sure cocaine addicts are cocaine addicts, and alcoholics are alcoholics. But maybe the generalization is overworked. It might be it's just as simple as giving up the one you like most. (With that kind of logic I'd have to get married.)

What in God's name was I going to do about it? She'd never denied it before. But I'd seen the vial.

I shouldn't have given her the money. But short of locking her up, she was going to get drugs somewhere.

The depression wasn't so pervasive that I failed to recognize and be embarrassed to find myself thinking I don't need this—as if it were really happening to me. ("And then along came World War II, I didn't have enough on my mind.")

All of which (thankfully) was interrupted by a pay phone call from Goodman at Madeo's, with a brief report on his meeting with Lieutenant Ellard. He told me about overhearing an agent's allusion to some sort of show business "Allegretto deal," which I found footnote-interesting since she was related to one of our principals, as Fabrisio Sugarman's mother; and the more exciting news that he was on the trail of and intended to pursue nailing down the identity of the oft-mentioned C.B. in Teri's diary.

I appreciated his enthusiasm and immediate sharing of this intelligence.

"Meanwhile, is there anything you want to tell me?" he concluded.

And I bit my tongue. On the one hand I wanted company to share the burdensome knowledge of Francine's backsliding. On the other I was afraid of what his reaction might be. If there was something I/we should do, I wanted first to decide what it was and what his involvement might be and whether it would require some lobbying—and I didn't want to get into the whole fucking thing at this particular juncture. Which is longform for: "No, but thanks for asking."

We said our good-byes, planned to touch base either later or in the morning, and the downstairs buzzer put a hiatus on the whole ugly business.

"It's Christopher" came through the intercom somewhat on the level of scratchy fidelity I expect "Watson, come here—I want you" must have sounded. But to me, bells were ringing.

"Come on up," I replied, resisting any attempt at badinage via the decrepit equipment (in itself remarkable in a building less than a decade old) and pushed the buzzer releasing the lock.

Christopher was resplendent in a blue flannel blazer suit that by the oddest coincidence was the exact deep blue of his eyes, his skin a retro-golden tan, his hair the lightest shade of blond found in nature, the whites of his eyes in perfect concord with the identical shade of his even teeth, all of which—eyes, teeth, the entire perfect person—now shone upon me in a generous display of happy greeting.

Life was not *all* bad.

We'd shared the Dom Pérignon '72 in my mother's finest crystal begrudgingly bequeathed to me in lieu of the daughter she never had (or, really, *thought* she never had), covered the conventional expositional requirements. He had a brother, straight, a sister, not—parents commuting between gay pride and fundamentalist despair—had actually married the banker's cheerleader daughter after captaining the state championship football team, and only after all this exemplary and apparently successful concurrence with parental mores and societal expectations discovered himself to be a bench warmer on the heterosexual team of life.

Disillusionment had been so rapid, and self-realization so immediate that an annulment was hastily colluded, happily before issue could be forthcoming and lifelong commitments established.

"And I've been cruising ever since!" he concluded, tongue in cheek.

What had actually ensued, though, was an otherwise relatively conventional life—completion of college, and a career in real estate investment, plus effecting a working truce with his parents that I envied.

"Not exactly perfect, I don't want you to think," he went on. "I don't bring my lovers home for the weekend. But then again, in my family my brother doesn't bring his girlfriends home, either. So, they're better able to maintain a facade to whatever extent they want."

"At least you're honest and still together."

"You're not?"

"Well, my parents are divorced, for one thing. My father's a lieutenant-colonel in the army, there never was any chance of openness with him."

"Which is odd since I have a feeling the military's recruited more of their children into our ranks than their own."

"Plus, he's away most of the time, and manages to close his eyes to the obvious on the few occasions we have a lunch together."

"And your mother?"

"My mother, being somewhat to the right of Anita Bryant, I simply lie to."

"Oh, really?"

Which I hoped didn't indicate respect eroding. Even militants have to pick their spots.

"Not too proud, but it's the only possible way to go. I've examined this very carefully and at great length and I can truly say I do it more for her sake than my own. She just plain couldn't handle it. Hell, she was barely able to handle heterosexuality."

We each had a final sip of the Dom, and I rose.

"Our reservation is for eight-thirty at Chaya Brasserie."

He rose, too. We stood a foot apart, thunderbolts ablaze.

"You know," he said. "One thing I sort of like about the heterosexuals—there's some doubt about whether they're going to go to bed with each other. It adds a note of drama."

"This is about as dramatic as I care for," I said, amid thunder and lightning crackling.

Chaya Brasserie said they could accommodate us as well at nine-thirty.

Leaning on an art nouveau cane I just happened to have in stock, I limped into the restaurant, favoring my sore ankle (having been swept off my foot).

We had a table in the front part, on the left, which was quieter—in a restaurant not notable for its acoustics—an excellent choice in the circumstances. There was at once so much to be said and so little need to.

Our appetizer was the Chef's Medley for two, in some small part for the celebratory fact that it was the most expensive on the menu (thirty bucks—on a bill of fare that only priced shark-fin soup at seven-fifty).

For our entrées Christopher opted for sautéed scallops rolled in John Dory with shallot butter, and I went for the lobster tail stuffed with spinach and bell pepper rolled in shiitake mushrooms—forgive us, Somalia.

But on top of everything else, for the first time being with a contemporary and intellectual equal who would know what and where Somalia *was,* unlike my usual choice of companions. To get blond, beautiful, and *smart* I knew I had to be incurring some serious karmic debt.

However, stopping barely short of selecting our silver pattern, we got to talking about my case and the book I was working on with Goodman. And Goodman himself.

"Sounds like Truman Capote meets Archie Bunker," said Christopher. "Must be very difficult to work with that kind of person."

"Yes and no. While he's not exactly Mr. Sensitivity— or Geniality, come to think of it—he has his moments."

"There may be someone who would say the same about Saddam Hussein."

"No, once you get to know him, you do realize he's a stand-up guy."

"Oh?"

"Heaven forfend. Really, he's loyal, honorable, and, uh, a Neanderthal. But he's *my* Neanderthal."

"But to collaborate, day by day . . ."

"Well, we don't really work that way. We tend to divide the chores rather than duplicate them. And while esthetically he may leave something to be desired he's good at what he does and has an intuitive instinct that is sometimes astounding."

"Sounds pretty good. What's the downside?"

"Wears a lot of brown."

"Writing is so fascinating. I always wondered how you get your ideas?"

I guess he wasn't going to be perfect.

"The same way businessmen get them, you sit down and work at it. The notion that we walk down the street and a bolt of lightning says 'Write *Gone With The Wind*' is one of the most persistent fantasies. There is no methodology for thinking up. You address yourself to it and plod, and panic, and after all sorts of hell and doubts there comes a moment when something seems promising and you *decide* to go with it. And you build on it. The way you might design a house. Not with a complete total vision, but bit by bit."

"This isn't the first time anybody's asked you this question, is it?" he said, partially redeeming himself.

"And you? Real estate, right?"

"I can see you thinking, God, how can I sound like I'm interested in that, it's so boring! And a lot of it is.

But putting together a deal—especially if you've conceived of a project in the first place—can be very exciting and creative."

"I'm sure," I said.

"No, you're not, but take my word for it. The problem, of course, is you're a victim of market conditions."

"Which for a number of years in California were terrific."

"You bet. It took talent not to make money during the boom. Every divorced woman who didn't become a decorator or a psychologist became a real estate agent. In Beverly Hills, anyway. And since a lot of house sales— especially in upper brackets—involved connections with that society, it worked while the working was good."

"But now, not? Yet it seems there are still so many rich people out here."

"Yes, but even the rich rich, who would have gone for an eight-million-dollar house, now want to pay five. Besides not being willing to sell the house they paid five for for three. So there're a lot of houses on the market and very little market for houses."

"And commercial?"

"Well, commercial was a different story. The malls and office buildings weren't built so much on a basis of need as a basis of investment in a rising market. So there was an incredible amount of overbuilding. Especially when there were tax shelters and incentives to do that and savings-and-loans pushing to get the money working."

"But now it's just sitting there."

"Pretty much."

"So why," I said, maybe at last being able to get some informed insight, "would anybody put up an eighty- or a hundred-million-dollar mall now?"

"They wouldn't, if they had any sense."

"But somebody is. Maybe you know something about it. You must have heard of the Sunset Center Supermall."

"Oh, sure."

"Well?"

"Death wish?"

"Even assuming someone was dumb enough to do it, why would the banks lend them the money?"

"I don't know that any banks have."

"What do you mean?"

"I mean it's no local bank, or consortium of banks."

"You know that for a fact?"

"Yeah."

"Then where did the money come from?"

"You mean originally?"

"Originally, lately, whenever."

"Well, lately it came from the BCCI."

"That sounds familiar, isn't that the one with all the scandal?"

"Right, the Bank for Credit and Commerce International."

"The dope and dictator money."

"Right," said Christopher. "And CIA and whatever didn't want to be too closely looked into. The Iran-contra money was laundered there."

"So do you think the center's being built because they have to spend the money—I never really understood that whole laundering concept, that it was okay to have money if it came from somewhere else, then you didn't have to explain it, but if it came from here you did."

"No, it's not being built exactly for those reasons, but I suspect laundering plays a big part in it. The principal backer is the Allegretto Fund."

"Wow, I just heard something about that not two hours ago. What is it, exactly?"

"It's originally a legal tax-avoidance setup named after Gabriella Allegretto."

"The Italian starlet Albert Sugarman married."

"Uh-huh, you know your trivia. And the fund is where all the Sugarman family money got stashed."

"Earned from making movies?"

"One would imagine."

"But then why would it have to be laundered?"

"Because, further industry inside gossip has it, when the film library of U.S. Pictures—Sugarman's company— was sold for worldwide TV and whatever, it went through the BCCI via the Allegretto Company so no one who was entitled to a piece of the original picture profits would get it."

"The usual Hollywood."

"The usual Hollywood," he agreed.

"And in order for laundered money to be clean, it has to be invested in something legit."

"Generally, generally, but in this case hastened by the collapse of the BCCI. They had to get the money out, and had to put it somewhere. Ergo, the Sunset Center," said Christopher.

Which, it wasn't hard to imagine, had something to do with the Allegretto deal Goodman alluded to. Christopher was a font of knowledge.

And other things. I found myself pleasured just by the quiet sight of him eating.

"My scallops are superb," he noted.

"Your biceps aren't bad, either," I replied.

# 17

# Rayford Goodman

We finished our meal, and true to his word, Ellard let me pay. Even honest cops don't make a habit of picking up tabs. Or going Dutch, for that matter. I could see I better keep track of the old expense account so I could put the bite on Penny when and if our deal went through. And Bradley, if not.

I had a funny relationship with Ellard. Big change from the outright enemies I was with old Chief Broward—that son of a bitch. But we still weren't basically buddies. I didn't feel like we ought to take in a game together, or go pub-crawling. But I did like the guy. And it wasn't till after my divorce I noticed how much my ax-wife had disconnected me from most of my men friends. Boy, the weird losses you never even realized. So, if you were going to build something new somebody had to make the first move.

Which was about a nanosecond before Ellard said, "Listen, I got to split," and saved me making an asshole of myself.

"Yeah, right, I'm busy, too," I said back.

Quite possible the guy didn't happen to be in the market for new friends. You couldn't really tell from the signals. Though he did seem to be in touch with me more than real business needed. I sure liked life a lot better when you just lived it without analyzing everybody's attitudes and body language and all that interpersonal shit.

The thought passed my mind I might not exactly be a man for the Nineties. Being I still wasn't real comfortable with the Seventies.

"Listen," said Ellard once we were outside and waiting for our cars. "I appreciate this exchange of info."

I nodded. I did, too. And he seemed like maybe he was going to say something, I don't know, personal? After all, he was divorced, too. What did a cop do when he wasn't working—cop out?

But then his car came and the guy held the door open. "Thanks for dinner," Ellard said.

I nodded.

He got in the car. The kid didn't move. Ellard reached in his pocket, pulled out his wallet. And flashed his badge. The kid shrugged and headed off. Maybe he was my kind of guy after all.

"Hey," he called the boy back. "Just kidding." And handed him a deuce. Maybe he wasn't my kind of guy after all.

I got in my own car, still crunching bits of glass from the shot-out window underfoot (fuck!), gave the kid two bucks.

"Two-seventy-five," he said, probably the only English he knew.

I handed him another dollar. (Two bucks for police, two-seventy-five for me?) And what the hell, drove off— keep the damn quarter. Some battles are beneath me.

Ellard had given me an address on Charles Bolton (C.B.), the Taxi Man, and a home phone. I'd already tried it and got his machine. "Out on a call; leave your number if you want a cab and I'll get back to you." He'd managed to record it without actually laughing. I hung up.

The mistake I'd made was not getting his cellular number from Ellard, if he even knew it.

And while I had a contact at the phone company (Martina Gonsalves), she worked days and would be gone by now. And anyway was starting to pressure me for at least one of the "dinner and all that" I kept promising whenever I asked a favor. Martina was an overage police groupie—what I called a cop-ulator—in which she kind of included me; which was all right though not exactly an ego builder. Plus as a looker, on a scale of one to ten, five was semigenerous. There had to be a better way.

*       *       *

I waited a while parked on Crescent Heights near Fountain, trying to decide did I just want to see Francie or was it really legitimate.

For one thing I really did have to get on with my life. It just wasn't going to work out with this girl. Who after all was too young for openers. And had all those problems, with the dope and whatnot. I mean, who needed it?

It was partly work.

At that, considering how crabby she'd been lately, I was surprised when she buzzed me through. And was waiting by the door when I showed up on her floor.

"I would of phoned, but since I was in the neighborhood anyway, thought I'd take a shot," I explained.

"Whatever," she said. "Come on in."

I did. It'd been a while.

Francie lived in one of those Thirties buildings when construction was cheap and they built some really great apartments. This one had a two-story living room long before condos reinvented them. And not like the new ones which feel like you're sitting in the bottom of a well, this was nicer proportioned with the room at least as long as it was high.

The place had come furnished, which meant the bamboo-y furniture with the overstuffed floral-pattern pillows weren't quite her taste. I sort of liked it. I could imagine, say, Linda Darnell sitting there in a kind of strapless clingy rayon number.

There was also some more modern things that didn't quite fit, I guess bought when the original broke. A desk in "Danish Modern," a plywood knockoff of the kind of Dansk stuff they used to have in the old days of Van Keppel-Green. But done cheap, it didn't really come off. Next to it was a standing lamp had two of those twisted metal extensions you could adjust the lights. Not crazy about that, either. And a baby-blue terry cloth loveseat seemed totally out of place.

Basically, though, the room was dominated by electronic equipment. Maybe three or four different computers with several printers, a modem—all kinds of that stuff.

I told her what I wanted—the Taxi Man's portable number.

"Well, it's probably either Pac Tel or L.A. Cellular," she said. "But there's no phone book listings."

"Hey, there's a great idea the phone company's missing." I said. "They ought to put out a special cellular phone book. Then they could charge you not to be listed in that, too, like they do with the regular ones."

She laughed. Then sat down at one of her computers, typed something, programmed something and I think wound up sending a fax. Egad, this kept up people were going to lose the power of speech.

Nothing happened for a few minutes. While she hung around nervously drumming her fingers on the keyboard.

" 'Scuse me," she said suddenly, and got up and went out the room.

Which, of course, was when the fax started faxing.

"Incoming," I yelled.

"Minute," she yelled back.

And I watched a longhand sheet that gave a 310–701 number work its way through the machine.

And back popped Francie, suspiciously full of p-and-v. "Oh, good, I was hoping, wasn't too long a shot, thought I'd take a try, first out of the chute, great, got it!" she said, energized.

"Got what?"

"Charlie Bolton's cellular."

"Wow, that's incredible. How'd you do that?"

"I asked a friend of mine with similar interests if he had the number for a dope dealer named Taxi Man," she said.

Which was good results but didn't sit all that well with me.

"Connections," she explained, smiling, letting me work out the two meanings. "Or networking, if you prefer."

"No, at least I understand connections. Networking I'll never be comfortable with."

"So what now?" she asked.

"Well, I have to talk to him. Sound him out. If it turns out he's really C.B., I certainly got to feel we'd have a big leg up on at least identifying all the suspects in the case."

"Then why don't we get in touch with the man?" she said.

The dope dealer man.

"I will," I said.

"I think it'd probably go better if we did it together, since I speak the language, you might say."

Didn't I know.

"I don't want to put you to any trouble," I said, meaning in the way of temptation.

"Hey, I'm cool," she said, meaning, I hope, everything's under control.


Francie's plan that she would represent herself as wanting to score some cocaine didn't exactly feel all that marvelous to me.

But when she asked what other plan I'd suggest, I had to admit she had me.

Now as we waited in the parking lot back of Citibank on Doheny and Sunset, up the street from where Gazzarri's used to be, I was having serious second thoughts.

"Boy, this guy really doesn't go out of his way to be inconspicuous," I said.

"Hey, his first choice was to meet at the Rainbow."

"It's amazing he's ever out of jail."

"He explained the theory is if you go where everybody looks like a doper you don't stand out."

"I suppose he has a point."

We had got there by proceeding from her house up to Sunset, then west, past the Roxy, which had a line of kids unbelievably long probably been there for a day and a half. Didn't any of them work, or go to school? I knew better than to ask who was playing. It'd turn out to be some group I'd never heard of named Cleft Palate, or Liver Bile.

Then past the aforementioned Rainbow (Bar & Grill) where I'd actually once had a pretty good steak, before it became whatever it became for the Madonnas and Chers and the Woodies and Bagel Boys and Sarah Bernhardt or whatever the hell her name was.

I guess it isn't I really mind that everybody's young and gorgeous (the Bernhardt person excepted), but do they have to be so damn rich, too? Christ, you could make a fortune on the tattoo and ear-piercing concessions. (I guess I do mind.)

And past ex-Gazzarri's and then Citibank, turn up Doheny and into the lot. Citibank was, of course, closed (which in terms of service wasn't very noticeable—another story) but the lot was hot. With cars parked for the Sunset action.

And in a far corner, catty cornered in a right-angle spot wasn't officially a location, a familiar black Corvette.

I double-parked nearby.

"That's the car," I told Francie. "You wait here and let me . . ."

"Bad idea," she interrupted. "I never saw a coke dealer wasn't paranoid for openers. He sees a big cop type like you and he's off like a shot. Let me go sound him first."

It made sense. (There was a remote possibility he might have spotted me at the car wash, though I doubted it.) But . . .

"Suppose he wants you to try it?"

"I'll fake it, don't worry."

"Promise."

"I promise—not that you should trust an addict."

"Then let's not."

"But I'm an ex-addict, current definition to the contrary notwithstanding. Relax." And she eased out of the car and ambled up to the Corvy. I could see by the tilt of his head he was watching through the rearview mirror. I guess satisfied, besides being semi-blocked by my car, he got out.

I watched the short chubby guy in his black leathers cross to Francie and they exchanged a few words. She went with him back to his car and they sat in the front seat. I right away got very nervous seeing her take something from him and I sure hope pretend to be sniffing it. Because if not, I didn't think it was going to turn out Neo-Synephrine.

Then they both got out and came over to my car and got in.

"Ray, this is Charlie; Charlie, Ray," she said, while I looked for white rings on her nostrils. She smiled and winked.

"Hi," I said.

"Hi. Francine tells me you're this hotshot book writer."

"That's me; old hotshot Ray."

"Wow, that's neat. You wanna snort?"

I was about to tell him what he could do with his snort when I saw Francie nodding to me.

"Sure, sure, great, out of sight, and all that shit," I said.

"Lemme," said Francie, taking his little bottle and dipping his little spoon in it (with his little AIDS?) and sticking it under my nose, while miming inhaling. I didn't know enough how to fake it; inhaled.

She dipped the spoon again, and again put it under my nose—this time the other nostril. (I'd get her for this.) But, in for a penny, in for a gram, I snorted again.

She took the whole thing from me and while I felt my hair start to grow, went ahead with our undercover act by some very convincing fake snorting herself. Jesus, Francie, what have I done?

"I never met a real writer before," Charlie was saying. "I mean, plenty wrote for TV, but not a real writer. Books, boy. That's something. You used to be some kind of private eye, right?"

"I used to be. Now I'm a celebrity. A celebrity reporter investigative type," I added.

He shook his head, numb with admiration.

"So, like, you're on a case, right?"

"Right," get to work. "We're looking into who killed Teri Dart."

"Aw, Teri, damn. What a bummer. Nice old chick."

"You seem to come up a lot in her diary."

"Really? Far out. What'd she say? She wasn't even that good a customer, tell you the truth."

"She said she thought you made a cute couple."

"Go on; no shit?"

"Well, assuming you're C.B."

"That's my initials. Not that anybody calls me that."

True.

"Listen, who else did you know up there?" I asked.

"Oh, I can't like tell you that. It's, you know, like a priest."

"You mean a connection keeps everything confidential?"

Charlie took the bottle from Francie, poured some of the cocaine onto the back of his fist and brought it up to his face. Never even looked down as he vacuumed it up.

"I didn't that often hang out, really. Usually it was just business."

"But you must have seen different people from time to time."

"Well, yeah," he said, moving his fist under the other nostril and snorting.

Francie reached over and spooned me some more. I started to shake my head, but inhaled instead. My hair grew another half inch.

"I don't know what I could tell you that'd help. I sometimes saw the Sugarman guy, Fabrisio—he hung around a lot."

We knew that.

"Then there was this other old actor, I don't know his name—he showed up time to time. I seen him in some old movies on TV."

"You don't remember a name?"

"Nnno—wait. One time, after he left, I do kind of remember—Teri and Fabrisio were kidding about him. And that time she did call him something."

"Something."

"I mean, couldn't be anybody's name, I don't think."

"What?" said Francie, who'd been busy maintaining our cover by keeping on pretending to snort, it seemed a lot.

"Lash LaRue? Is there such a person?"

"There *was* a Lash LaRue," I said. "But I'm sure he's long dead." L.L.? In the diary L.L.—the S & M freak?

"Maybe it wasn't Lash LaRue," said Charlie. "But I do remember an actor. Used to be in all those cowboy pictures. A lot younger."

"I don't think the real Lash LaRue."

"That's it, babe; best I remember. Listen, I got to work. People are waiting. Parties are on hold."

In service to mankind.

"Real nice meeting you and everything. Oh"—to Francie—"here's the rest of your gram." And he handed her back the little mostly empty bottle.

She shrugged. (I think this happened before.)

He didn't move.

Francie punched my arm. "Give him the hundred," she said.

I gave him the hundred. (Wonder how Penny would react to that on the expense account.)

"So look, anytime you want to, like, do it up, you got my number. You can call direct," Charlie said, I guess meaning I passed the hipness test.

"Got it," I said, wondering why my own voice sounded so loud and sort of hurt in back of my eyes. Uh-oh.

Meantime he got out of the car and stood up—this short, chubby, pockmarked guy it hit me definitely couldn't possibly be the C.B. Teri wrote in the diary was "tall, handsome once you think about it."

He was just opening the Corvy door when he suddenly flashed on something, turned back.

"I don't suppose it means anything," he said. "But I thought of someone else I seen up there couple times."

"Yeah?"

"The one Teri called 'Big K.' "

"Ah-hah—tell me about him."

"Or Harry K, that was it—Harry K. Older stud, white hair; horn rims."

"Harry *Kakonis,* maybe?" said Francie.

Couldn't be—*the* head of *the* biggest studio? At Teri's?

"Yeah, Kakonis, that's the dude," said old Charlie, the Taxi Man. Hitting me right between the eyes and the ears and the top of the head. Which was rapidly expanding.

# 18

# Mark Bradley

"So then Taxi Man or Charlie Bolton, it turns out, drops this bomb about Harry Kakonis, Hollywood's Gray Eminence," Goodman was saying, totally oblivious to the fact that he'd interrupted some seriously sophisticated and expositionally significant verbal foreplay.

"All very interesting, you know Christopher Winfield?" I said, I thought pointedly.

"I don't believe I've had the pleasure," responded Goodman who I'm sure would have remembered had he had.

"My partner, Ray Goodman?"

"How do you do?" said Christopher.

"How do. So, well, Jesus, I can't believe it. What possible connection would Kakonis have with a group like that?"

"I'm sure I don't know."

"And, wait, then he goes on to tell me—the Charlie Taxi guy—he also saw this old Italian broad with humongous knockers made a couple pictures playing like Sophia Loren's sister during the war. Naturally not hard to figure that has to be Gabriella Sugarman."

"Very interesting, I admit," I said. "But can't it wait till morning?"

"Why?"

"Why? I'm busy; I have company." I inclined my head in his direction. "Christopher?"

"Oh, hey, I'm sorry," said Goodman, his eyes narrowing as it dimly and belatedly registered that the presence of a woman might not be required to make it "company."

"Gabriella Sugarman," said Christopher, into the

breach. "That's the Allegretto person, if I'm not mistaken."

"You know her?" Goodman asked.

"He knows *of* her. And in an interesting context. We can discuss it in great and exhaustive detail—another time. On which occasion I'll be happy to tell you all about it," I added, but clearly failed to make my point. "By a fortuitous coincidence, Christopher has actually been quite helpful."

"Yeah?" said Goodman, still not totally responding to the obvious.

"And I would like to reward him, in our own special way."

That registered. "Well, look, yeah that's great," said Goodman, with that glazed eye way he had of "not dealing with it." "But the Kakonis and Gabriella links aren't actually the main reason I'm here."

"Look, I guess . . ." began Christopher.

"No, wait. Goodman, we can discuss all that tomorrow."

"Of course we can, but 'all that' is not the problem, I'm trying to tell you."

"What *is* the problem?" I said, murderously calm.

"Francie. See, we wanted to talk to this Taxi Man guy, I got some further information from Ellard, that's another story, who's a dope dealer—Taxi Man, not Ellard, he's a cop," he explained for Christopher's benefit.

"I really should . . ." Christopher began again.

"No, not yet, please!" I said.

"Ellard got his home number but not his cellular so I went to Francie for that and she got it. And then came up with the idea she ought to go with me when I met up with the guy because he'd be more apt to open up with her than me. Which was in a way right."

"Yes? Quickly, to the point, go on, yes, what?"

"But she meanwhile, to make it look good, was supposed to act like she was snorting some coke—all right to talk in front of him?" he added, nodding toward Chris.

"If it wasn't, this would be a hell of a time to think of it," I replied a bit testily.

"Look, it's clear you fellows have things ..." said Christopher.

"Down, sit down. This won't take a minute," I said, about as pointedly as I could. "Not one more minute!"

"Just let me finish," said Goodman.

"Please."

"I went along with her. The plan. Fact, I even took an actual sniff or two my own self, to gain his confidence. That part's not really the problem, more or less."

"Would you, for God sakes, get to it?"

"I am. That's what I'm doing. So we finish up with Charlie boy and I take her home—Francie, not Charlie. He had other stuff to do, customers, I don't know. Well, probably yes."

Which was partly when it struck me Goodman was still stoned and I would just have to wait out this burst of logorrhea, there was simply not going to be any way I could shorten the narrative.

"O-kay," I said, calmly encouraging.

"So you with me so far?"

"I'm really with you."

"Good. Got to her place on Fountain and Crescent, you know, the castle and all that. Weird way to build an apartment, you'd think it should look like an apartment. But kind of interesting in its own way."

"Uh-huh," I said, frozen smile and all.

"Mark, really, I understand," said Christopher. "It's clear you have some sort of urgent business or personal problem."

I gestured for him to sit back down in a way that brooked no argument.

"I wanted to take her to her door. But you know, she's a little standoffish with me," continued Goodman.

"I'm aware of the fact."

"At least walk her to the front door."

"But she didn't want you to," I prompted.

"Right. But I sure was going to wait to see she got safely at least through the front door."

"Ah-hah."

"But when she was about ten feet from the door, out pops some guy from the bushes and jumps at her. She lets out a bloodcurdling scream. Even before, I'm out of my car like a shot. The guy spots me, lets her go, and turns to take me on. I rush him, but he slips it, gives me a chop kick in the side of my thigh—that tai chi, or koo chi, or something—and takes off. I try to get up, but I'm, like, crippled, and anyway, he's long gone. Meanwhile, Francie's screaming to high heaven, even though nothing really happened. But anyway I try to comfort her."

Which, of course, did engage my interest.

"I couldn't seem to calm her down, she just kept wailing and screaming and carrying on and ranting and raving. Total hysterical. So I took her key and unlocked the door. There were a few neighbors by now sticking their heads out, thought maybe *I* was the problem, but I managed to convince them not so. And finally got her up to her place."

"Did you call the police?"

He shook his head. "And I guess nobody else did, either. There didn't seem much point by then. The guy'd be in another county, and I had my hands full with Francie. Who wouldn't be any better off for being bothered by the cops. Especially she was still the most hysterical for the longest while. I just kind of stayed with her and shushed her and finally, finally, must have been ten minutes, she eventually calmed down to only being very upset. And I thought, you know, it'd been a bit out of line for not that big a scare, especially someone like Francie who's fairly gutsy."

"But she's all right now?"

He held up a hand. "Wait. I thought so. She said so, and told me to go. Only the minute I'm out the door, I hear screaming and wailing and things breaking and she won't let me back in."

"Well ..."

"Wait. And then I found out the bottle of coke I thought was in my pocket, wasn't anymore."

"Ah."

"And I feel so guilty because if I didn't take her with me to meet that Taxi guy she wouldn't of backslid like that. If she actually did. Which I think."

And he collapsed in a chair, suddenly spent.

"In the first place, don't blame yourself," I said. "You didn't singly put her in the way of temptation. She's been back on drugs for at least a couple of days, I *think,* too. She says no, and I can't really challenge her. But there's certainly been a mood change."

Which didn't seem to be much comfort as he slumped even deeper into the chair, literally as if the wind had gone out of his sails.

"Why would she do that?" he asked sadly. "If she did."

"God only knows. And she did."

He took a deep breath, seemed to will himself to regather his strength. "Well, look, one way or another, she's major crazy at the moment. She's got this . . . resistance to me so I can't help. I can see you had plans here in mind with Chris, but she really shouldn't be alone."

"An opinion with which, as a newly interested bystanding outsider, I concur," said Christopher. "And on which mutually disappointing note I really am going to say good night."

I raised my arms, took a breath, but . . .

"We'll see each other again; there'll be other times," he added, rising.

The man was right. At best, the rest of the evening was in shambles.

Goodman and Christopher exchanged nods.

"Let me at least walk you to the door," I said, and Goodman got very busy going over to the window and staring out.

And I apologized and was assured there was nothing to apologize for and I said what a wonderful time I'd had and was assured it was mutual and Christopher left, showing the back of his jacket was just as perfectly tailored.

I returned to Goodman, trying to remember it wasn't his fault and I wasn't really mad at him, though it was difficult not to be, the messenger and all that, and literally dreadfully fatigued, took a fortifying breath and said, "OK, let me get my gear together and I'll go see what I can do for Francine."

\* \* \*

She didn't answer the downstairs buzzer.

I went back to my car and called her. She didn't pick up, but I informed the answering machine I was going to be the one pushing her buzzer for the next six or seven hours.

"Who is it?" she finally said.

"United Parcel," I answered, secure in the knowledge there wasn't a woman alive who wouldn't open the door to Jack the Ripper if she thought he was delivering something mail-order. And of course, she knew it was me.

The door to her apartment was slightly ajar, not the greatest breach in security since she knew I was on my way up. And I wasn't about to start with a criticism.

I tossed my tote bag with its toilet articles and an extra pair of shorts and socks on the couch, and headed for the kitchen.

"I have a feeling we're drinking," I said, getting out a tray of ice.

"We're doing whatever we can to get us through the night. Are you going to be a pain in the ass?"

"That wasn't my intention," I said, fixing myself a gin and tonic.

"Anyway, I've come up with a whole new plan for us substance abusers. It's got the basic twelve steps, but a few more. You abstain all the time except on national holidays, which I've expanded and amended to include Vice-Presidents' Day, Martin Luther King's Dog's Day, and three Personal Major Trauma Days. Otherwise, clean as a whistle."

"From the forthcoming biography, *Throwing Up In America*."

"I'm glad to see we're going to be approaching this in a spirit of fun."

"We're going to do whatever it takes for your friends to do," I responded.

"Right now it just means be here and be quiet. Well, a hug wouldn't be bad."

And I did hug her. And she did hug for quite a while.

I knew Francine well enough to know she was going to tell me what it was all about. In her own good time.

Which I also sensed wasn't going to be all that long from now.

She drank and drank and wept and wept. And I knew we were several steps away from dealing with the recidivism, even if it were only alcoholic. First we'd have to play out one of the Personal Major Trauma exemptions she'd added to the addict's bill of rights.

And it got to be two-thirty or so, and I fell asleep on the couch. And I woke up to find her just staring out the window, and went to the bathroom and came back to discover her curled up on the couch, fitting herself to the residual warmth of my outline.

Then I went in and lay down on her bed and fell asleep again.

And when I woke next at seven-thirty or so, Francine was sitting in a chair beside the bed, her head back, staring at the ceiling, tears silently coursing down her cheeks. Could all this be merely connected to the breakup with Marshal? Seemed extravagant, but pain's pain.

"Ah, darling," I said, struggling to rise. "I know it must have been very painful. But to go back on coke . . ."

"I didn't go back on coke. How could you have so little faith in me that you'd think I'd go back?"

"Well, I did see you in the garage with a vial of cocaine."

"Yeah. And did you see me use it?"

"No, but you bought it."

"Well?"

"Well, that's sort of a first step, isn't it?"

"I suppose it might look suspicious." And she laughed, a wan little laugh. "Yeah, I did intend to. But I got myself back together, I wasn't going to let the son of a bitch do that to me, too."

"What son of a bitch, do what?"

"Marshal Hildebrandt—that's why I flipped out last night, I thought he'd come back."

"To fight some more?"

"No, to rape me again."

# 19

## Rayford Goodman

The thing to do was not concentrate on Francie. First place, she wasn't my girl. The time she'd been was something as they say very special (I love the way everything's special these days—they have special classes for special students, meaning dumbos, unless they're so special they're hopeless, in which case they're exceptional). So maybe in those terms, our relationship had been exceptional. Or truth be known, maybe meant more to me than her. No question meant more to me than her.

So that was my first order of business, forget it. Yeah, right.

But also the dope thing. I really didn't take a moral position. I mean, hell, I had the booze. I didn't kid myself I was some kind of social drinker. Well, I was, but I was very very social.

Still, somehow, it was different. Legal, for one thing. And it took longer to kill yourself and everyone around you. Usually. OK, there wasn't a hell of a lot of difference. Any more than, say, jazz and heavy metal. Could I help it I just plain didn't like heavy metal?

Or new haircuts, or new clothes, or new a lot of things. Which meant I was getting old and becoming just like all old people, not liking anything new. Well—I liked the new bodies on girls.

After I left Bradley's I was so sad I didn't even stop off for a drink but just went home.

Asta was hanging around back, acting like he lived there. So I fed him leftovers from some Thai take-out, which he seemed to find OK. I notice dogs don't tend to be that fussy eaters. I knew it wasn't a good idea to encourage him by feeding him. But, for one thing, he had helped by finding the diary. And second it didn't seem right he'd have to die just because his owner did. I mean, what the hell, are we a bunch of Hindus or something, the main guy goes everybody goes?

I guess the trick was to find him a good home. Or any home. Meantime, he was good for the ecology, ate up the garbage and fertilized the land.

Inside, the Phantom wasn't too thrilled by both the attention I was paying Asta or the delay in feeding him. What the hell was happening to me? What happened to the lone wolf independent guy went his own way did what he wanted?

Or the dodo bird?

I undressed, got into bed, flashed on a time when I'd shower and shave before getting into bed. O, Romeo, wherefore art thou Romeo?

Present. Underneath these wrinkles and this flab. It's fucking Juliet flew the coop.

Watched a little TV.

I didn't like any the new guys. True, I was tired of Johnny. But I didn't like any the new guys.

And went to sleep.

It was too early to call Bradley and check what went down with Francie. I had too much of a hangover to keep sleeping. One of these days, one of these days. Everybody waited too late. They stopped and died, or the spirit died in them. Or it never did work sober—for some of us. Shit. Ask the question again around cocktail hour.

So after the long long hot shower (fuck the drought, maybe it would drive enough people away from California it'd become the heaven it used to be), and the shaky shave, I sat down to breakfast.

Well, not exactly. There was nothing in the fridge.

In the freezer, left over from Francie's time, were frozen the following: an orange-like flavored drink, toy eggs called Scramblers ("egg whites, nonfat milk, soybean and/or corn oil, calcium caseinate, modified corn starch, artificial flavors, monosodium glutamate, disodium guanylate, disodium inosimate, salt, lecithin, aluminum sulfate, mono- and digylcerides, lactoesters of prophylene glycol, vitamins (D) calcium pantothenate, a palmitate, riboflavin ($B_1$), thiamine mononitrate ($B_1$), pyridoxine hydrochloride ($B_4$, $B_{12}$), iron (as ferric oathophosphate), zinc sulfate, artificial color (beta carotene); toy bacon (defatted soy flour, partially hydrogenated vegetable oil [soybean and/or cottonseed], salt, natural and artificial flavor, sugar, artificial color"); toy butter (margarine), a sugar-removed jamlike "spread," decaffeinated coffee, with Mocha Mix nondairy "creamer," Nutrasweet sugar substitute, and a piece of toy Danish—granola. (Didn't we invade that?)

This was called health food. By a lady junkie yet.

I popped in my car and zoomed down to the International House of Cholesterol, where I had the special special—fresh orange juice, pancakes with butter and syrup, eggs, bacon, sausage and fried potatoes, coffee and Danish Danish. If that was going to kill me, it was the way I wanted to go.


OK, personal problems aside, what I needed now was everything there was to know about Harry Kakonis. There was something so freaking unbelievable about putting Hollywood's number-one studio executive and Elder Statesman to the Industry and Teri in the same sentence, much less her house. Why, what possible connection?

For sex? If he was at all still interested he could have the pick of the pros. Or ambitious young actresses half her age and twice as pretty.

And if he was, or it had something to do with old times' sakes, it wouldn't be on some bird street in the Hollywood hills, it'd be a discreet bungalow at the Bel Air Hotel.

So what'd that leave? It couldn't be blackmail. There was nothing she could possibly have on him he wouldn't have the juice to get taken care of.

Or have *her* taken care of.

Hmm.

It would have to be something monumental for him to have her killed. She was just a fly on Hollywood's fly.

And to be there when the Taxi Man made a delivery?

Well, I suppose that could be an accident. It could even be he didn't know what or who Taxi Man was.

Job for Francie. But was it? Were we going to be using her? Or was it time to face facts as they were and get on with our own lives?

It was a job for Francie. Who was I kidding, we weren't about to dump her no matter what.

I couldn't reach Bradley. He wasn't home, he wasn't at the office. Probably still at Francie's, my guess.

I called Francie. Answerphone. How do I hate thee? Eighty four thousand ways.

I could continue on my own; it wasn't like I'd never done any investigating before having a "researcher." It was she was so much better and more efficient at the part I hated most. You couldn't beat doing legwork by fingerwork on a computer.

I went over there.

Francie's car was in the garage. Bradley's on the street. With a ticket on it.

Which didn't mean they answered the buzzer. To get in I had to wait for somebody to leave—the sissy way to get around basic security. But since it was morning and people went to work, it didn't take very long.

She opened the door. "I warned you not to call him; I told you not to call him," she said to Bradley.

"I didn't call him," he said.

"He didn't call me," I said. Then since it clearly wasn't about the dope, since I was the one called *him,* "About what shouldn't he call me?" I asked.

"Not a good time," said Bradley.

"Listen, you guys—I can't put my life on hold. We've got work to do. You've got problems, I can help with the problems, glad to. Otherwise, let's get on with our shit and get going."

"The man makes perfect sense to me," said Francie. "Since if we told him it would only make him crazy."

"Right," I said, being made crazy.

Then, just to show how above it all I was, I went through what I wanted her to do about Kakonis. I needed the book on him. Not just his usual studio things and how Harry had gone from being the top agent at the top agency to forming the biggest studio conglomerate.

Agent?! "Could he possibly be 'Harry the F.P.'?"

"As in Flesh Peddler?" suggested Francie.

"Ooh, I like it," said Bradley.

And we made an outline of the avenues she would investigate about Harry. There remained the tantalizing mystery of why someone so elegant and above it all would be in cahoots with someone so down and dirty. Even remotely.

And she excused herself.

"The dope?" I said to Bradley.

"No."

"What do you mean no? I saw it myself yesterday."

"You think you saw."

"You said you knew from before."

"I was wrong."

"So what's she doing in the bathroom?"

"I imagine some bodily function common to us all."

"You're telling me . . ."

"I'm telling you forget it. It's not the problem."

"What's the problem?" I asked.

"I can't tell you."

"You can tell me, I'm your partner."

"Stop it, I can't tell you. She specifically doesn't want you to know."

Oh, boy.

And she came back, and there didn't appear to be any noticeable difference, so maybe he was right. Hope, I hope, I hope.

"OK. Now in addition, what I think we need to do is get into the Sugarmans. For openers, Gabriella. I think maybe I should handle that."

"And I could look into Fabrisio, in a manner of speaking," said Bradley.

"Right. So, we all set here? Francie's going to do Harry Kakonis, you Fabrisio, and me Gabriella."

"Fair enough," said Bradley. "I think we ought to settle the matter of Francine's employment, too, while we're at it."

"All right," I agreed.

"How does five hundred a week sound?"

"Sounds pretty high to me," I couldn't help answering. "Seeing she's still drawing her salary down at Pendragon."

"It's not high," said Bradley.

"Let me think about it," I said.

At which point Francie again left the room.

"You're telling me she's going to the bathroom again?"

"I'm not telling you anything."

"I *know* that—what's going on?"

But he hemmed and hawed, and still wouldn't tell me. So when she came back, I took a shot at it. "I know, you had a fight with Marshal."

Which made her bust into tears.

"I guess I hit that on the nose," I said. "An affair of the heart."

"You asshole," screamed Francie, "he raped me!"

"Marshal?"

"Who're we talking about? Yes, Marshal."

"But you were going with him. You're not going to tell me you weren't sleeping with him."

"Of course I was sleeping with him. But I stopped going with him."

"Yeah?"

"And then he forced me."

"Which is why naturally you didn't go to the police," I said.

"I didn't go to the police because they would think like you, what's the difference, instead of eighty-five times it was eighty-six."

Eighty-six?

"Well, I guess it really isn't like a stranger."

"No, it's not like a stranger. You want details what it's like? He was a spermicidal maniac."

"Francine," said Bradley.

"He was super-duper, no stopping him. In, out, up, down—the man Gomorrah'd me," said Francie.

"Honey," said Bradley.

"He tied me up, he did me in—he wanted his friends . . ."

"Please, don't," I said. "I can tell you're upset."

"Upset, upset?! Oh, boy. See, I told you," she said to Bradley. "I shouldn't have said anything. But I thought it was because I wanted to spare him the pain."

"I have pain. Listen, I hate it." I did. I hated her even dating anybody else. Then, another thought. "That was him last night, right, waiting for you?"

"No, that wasn't him. I don't know who that was. Other than not someone with my best interests at heart."

She could really be some sarcastic. I didn't say that. I said, "That was not your boyfriend?"

"No, it was not my boyfriend—who's *not* my boyfriend, can't you get that through your head? I don't know who this particular bastard was," and she burst out crying again.

"I don't know what's the matter with you," said Bradley. To me.

"What, you think I'm not sympathetic? I'm sympathetic. I just don't think it's quite the same as some guy in an alley you never met."

"It is, worse in some ways; it's a complete betrayal. And murder on your self-confidence to make such a mistake in judgment."

"Well, I guess I'm wrong. But if you feel that way you should of gone to the police."

"Yeah, right." And she burst into tears again. Bradley went over and comforted her.

"I'm wrong, I'm wrong, I admit I'm wrong," I said, feeling helpless.

"Look, fuck it; let's not talk about it anymore," said Francie, breaking away from Bradley and wiping her nose with the sleeve of her sweatshirt. "Let's get on with our business."

"Oh, boy, what a ploy to get sympathy for a good deal," said Bradley.

"Are we going to make a deal, or not?" she said.

"OK, I give," I said.

"All right," said Francie. "It's five hundred a week plus you have to kill Marshal. The money I'm flexible on."

I sort of smiled.

They didn't.

# 20

# Mark Bradley

After a night of heavy drinking and only intermittent snatches of sleep I felt about the way Keith Richards looks. But if he could face another day, why not me?

We left Francine getting ready to go to the office. (The five hundred she'd borrowed was to cover charges on the stolen credit card, by the way, which made me feel like a total jerk.) She could have built a file on Harry Kakonis every bit as easily at home, but because she was on salary to Pendragon Press, and because Pendragon Press was Richard Penny, she would have to do it at the office. And, of course, we were stealing time from him. But he wouldn't know that, so long as she observed the superficial but inflexible rule—in at ten, out at six. A lot like being a writer at the old Warner Brothers, I'm told, where your effectiveness was measured not by literary quality, but by how many pages you turned out in each structured day, written *at* the studio. (They tell the story of Jack Warner, also a notorious hall-lurker, coming upon a writer taking a snap on his office couch. The wary writer, sensing a presence, snapped his fingers, leaped up and yelled, "I got it!" Warner patted him on the shoulder.)

Goodman and I were in the elevator, one of those tiny affairs that resemble a standing MRI machine. Definitely too close for claustrophobes.

"She's really upset about this rape business," he was saying while I quietly gasped for air.

"No kidding," I managed.

"I first didn't see how it was exactly all that bad. Being she knew him and had had a thing with him. But the more I think about it, the more I understand and the more I begin to feel I have to go have some words with this Hildebrandt bird."

"Don't you do anything," I cautioned him. "That's one of the reasons she didn't want to tell you, so you wouldn't go off half-cocked."

He gave me a look. "Impulsively," I amended. "Really. Just cool it. We'll think of something."

"The woman's talking about killing him."

"Well . . ."

"Yeah, right; heat of the moment. She wouldn't, right?"

"To the best of my knowledge, she never has," I answered truthfully.

"But a guy like that really does deserve to die."

"Yes, he does. But *you* don't deserve to die for killing him. A distinct possibility under the law. Which is one of those little rules that sort of helps civilization keep on hip-hopping."

"And helps creeps like that keep doing their shit."

"That, too."

The elevator, which besides being small, was also Guinness-class slow, finally lumbered its way to the ground floor and we delifted.

Outside the front door I spotted the little depression where the dog had tried to bury a bone and into which I had stepped the other day. The power of suggestion sent a twinge through my still tender ankle.

Goodman saw me falter, caught my arm.

"OK?" he said.

"Yeah, I tripped in that hole recently," I explained. "They ought to do something about it, fill it in."

He gave it a glance, stopped, bent down and picked up something.

"What's that?" I asked.

"Looks like somebody else tripped over it, too. Maybe the guy waiting for Francie last night."

"What is it?"

"A knife."

"Oh, my god, you think someone wanted to kill her?"

"Not with this."

And then he handed it to me, a very small, obviously

expensive penknife. At first I thought the handle was
fashioned out of a buffed pearl or nacre. But a closer
look revealed it to be some kind of horn with a dash
and a zero carved into one side.

"Who carries penknives, these days?" I asked.

"I don't know. But someone who did, doesn't anymore," said Goodman, not adding a great deal to our
store of knowledge.

Thank heaven for the Hollywood ego. All it took to get
an appointment with Fabrisio Sugarman was a little mis-
representation by me that I was doing an article for *Vanity Fair* on the new generation of Hollywood movers and
shakers whose parents were the old generation of movers
and shakers.

I not only got an appointment, I got lunch and I got
it that day at the Bistro Garden. (Originally decorated
by Barbara Windom, daughter of social mover and shaker
Edie Goetz, herself daughter of Louis B. Mayer, one of
the founding inventors of the move and shake. Isn't it a
small Hollywood?)

The Bistro Garden, a good half of which was a disguised yard with patio tables and umbrellas, which, together with the now-defunct (or reborn as a hotel) Ma
Maison was one of the forerunners of the no-building
superchic luncheon meccas, was jammed to its nonexis-
tent rafters when I arrived interviewer-punctually for our
one o'clock appointment.

I asked for my reservation and was directed to "Mr.
Sugarman's table." You can reserve and you can pay,
but that still doesn't get you top billing in this town.

Fabrisio Sugarman was, I'd guess, closer to sixty than
fifty and closer to his third "martini" than his first (Beef-
eater, straight up, no vermouth) and either glowing with
bonhomie or pre-strokal.

He appeared to have inherited his mother's luxuriant
hair, which he wore theatrically long and wavy, but that
seemed the sum and substance of the Fabrisio part. The
Sugarman genes seemed to have prevailed elsewhere. He
had his father's nearsighted squint, which even solid gold
eyeglasses didn't obscure. He was small and chubby and

exquisitely dressed in cashmere and suede. But for the
hair, he looked like a Latin teacher in a Middle European country who'd won the lottery.

At that, we exchanged unexpectedly strong forehands
when we introduced ourselves.

"Yes," he said, "you're the writer does those celebrity
mysteries with that P.I. person," he said, with a hint of
Oxbridge accent.

And a number of solo biographies prior to that, and
innumerable articles and ...

"That's me," I said instead. Umbrage wouldn't get me
far in this world of names above the title.

"What can I tell you?" he said.

"You can tell me what's good for lunch, for openers,"
I riposted.

"When I went to the lavatory I thought I heard the
chap at the next urinal singing, 'Hang down your head,
John Dory.' But then again, he may have been merely
discouraging an overzealous private part."

Definitely third "martini."

"Junk fish, by the way, you know. Used to throw them
away," he continued in his pedantic manner. "They only
achieved popularity when the whole cholesterol business
got everybody crazy and started depopulating the seven
seas."

"You've spent some time abroad," I said.

"By a strange and non-nepotic coincidence, I was se-
lected to be in charge of Daddy's London office for
eight years."

"That would be two-hundred-and-eight fortnights?"

Got a chuckle. And a small opening in the curtain
of rapport.

"So what is this article you're doing; what're we talking about?"

"As I mentioned over the phone, what this generation's up to; what it's accomplished. Advantages,
handicaps."

Life being the rippling of smooth waters that it is, the
waiter chose this moment to intrude and inquire after
our aperitif desires.

"I'll have a Bombay and tonic," I said. "Mr Sugarman?"

"Fabrisio, please."

"He'll have a Fabrisio."

Got another laugh.

"The same, Mr. Sugarman?"

He nodded and the waiter departed.

"It's better than when they say, 'The usual?' which stamps one as a definite juicehead," Fabrisio noted.

"And you believe in moderation?"

He laughed again. "I believe in whatever gets you through the morning."

"So what was it like, growing up in such a prominent Hollywood family?"

"What was it like growing up wherever you grew up?"

"You're right; dumb question. To be specific, were you aware you were different, that you moved in a privileged, more rarefied world?"

"When you were a clumsy, socially backward kid and they called Jackie Cooper and Mickey Rooney over to play ball with you—and they *lost*—you began to get a sense of your importance, even refracted."

And then, one or two "martinis" later, plus a toyed-with seafood salad ("where they really unload the junk fish") and an extended biographical sketch (two wives, no children, costly divorces, sporadic career attempts) I got to the meat of the interview.

"So you've really more or less given up on the movie business," I said.

"Well, I wouldn't say 'given up' so much as found other equally rewarding fields of endeavor."

"Real estate."

"How'd you guess?"

"Just a hunch. I'm kidding. It's certainly no great secret the principal investor in the Sunset Center is Allegretto."

"And Allegretto is, of course, the company named after my mother."

"Wherein reside the residual assets of your father's company, U.S. Pictures."

"Is that a fact?"

"It's my understanding. Correct me if I'm wrong, aren't you the chief executive officer of Allegretto?"

"No, no, not really. I am the chief executive officer of the Sunset Center Project, I'll grant you that."

"How did you get into that?"

"Luck and breeding," he said, with a self-deprecating smile. "My family's owned that land since the early Forties."

"And you or they never saw fit to build on it before?"

"There was no particular need; plus it was an evolving, growing market. Keeping it was better than selling and trying to make comparable money by investing in other things."

"But haven't you waited too long? Isn't now a bad time to build so huge a project?"

"We'll find out, won't we?"

"Or weren't you compelled by the breakup of BCCI to conspire immediately to launder the money you and your family got from the sale of the U.S. Pictures library without accounting to several entities who allegedly had a stake in the company's profits into something large and legitimate and vastly complicated?"

"Boy, this turned nasty in a hurry. You sounded like a senatorial fact-finding commission there for a minute. What happened to did you have a dog when you were a boy?"

"Why the Sunset Center?"

"Why not? You're acting as if nobody's building anything anymore. Though I will admit we might have moved to more advantage had we moved earlier."

"Is there another reason, possibly?"

"OK, you got me. My father was a contemporary of Joe Kennedy and Bugsy Siegel. Both of whom were silent partners in the original property. It's been common knowledge in my family for decades that Joe buried bullion by the billions and Bugsy buried bodies—that's a lot like Peter Pepper, isn't it—somewhere on the property. When we finish excavating, we'll find out one or the other or both."

"You're putting me on."

"You bet your ass."

But he didn't walk out. Try again.

"How come Sunset Center got such major variances in the building code? I was under the impression you couldn't build more than forty-five feet in height there, by West Hollywood standards."

"The plans have been approved. There were open meetings. Councilmen counseled. Consultants consulted. And lawyers lawyered."

"So you're saying there were restrictions, but the restrictions were got around."

"Am I? I thought I was saying everything has proceeded according to law and custom to the satisfaction of the city and our other investors."

"And who are your other investors?"

"I'm sure an enterprising investigator like yourself could find all that out."

"Have we become adversarial?"

"Well, I don't seem to be enjoying my lunch as much as I was. All right. There are a couple of syndicates headed by business managers. A few prominent actors, producers, two directors."

I noticed no writers. Alas.

"And may I have a name?"

"You may. The principal outside investor is H. 'Wrangler' Morangis. The 'H' is for Herman, incidentally. Thus the cognomen 'Wrangler,' by which handle he has become known and beloved to millions of fans and buckeroos and bankers."

"Wrangler Morangis, the cowboy movie star. And he is the principal investor—or you?"

"He, in the medium of Bar None Enterprises and I, in the medium of Allegretto Ventures, are copartnered. More than that I do not believe it is necessary for you to know. Plus I must add I'm beginning to lose faith in the *Vanity Fair* article bit on Hollywood's kids."

"Fabrisio . . ."

"I think maybe we should go back to Mr. Sugarman. Or maybe we should get the check and call it a day."

"No, no, I'm sorry if I misrepresented myself. You're right. I'm not writing an article on this generation. I'm investigating the death of Teri Dart."

At which I could swear I detected an almost imperceptible sagging of features.

"Well, you've certainly gone very far afield," he said.

That was true.

What was also true, he had scratched his head, either in confusion, remorse, or simple distress, pushing back the luxuriant hair at his temple. That revealed, in the truest Hollywood tradition of illusion, the fine hair-netting that was the basic foundation of all wigs.

Even, according to a certain diary, the one "Mogul" wore in the performance of some indifferent cunnilingus on the person of the late Teri Dart.

# 21

## Rayford Goodman

There were thirteen Sugarmans in the Beverly Hills directory. Possibly only eleven since three of them were Ronalds, two with the same address.

I didn't really expect Gabriella to be listed. It was just if you didn't rule that out and it turned out she was, you'd feel like such a horse's ass (or a Pinto's gas tank). And of course, she might not even live in Beverly Hills.

She had, I was told confidentially, given up her membership in the Screen Actors' Guild (a penny saved and all that). So I couldn't get a listing from them.

The driver's license approach wasn't promising. She'd probably use a chauffeur and even if she had a license it'd likely list her business manager's office as an address. Although business manager wasn't too bad a way to go.

I called Francie at the office. Not there. Found that out by pressing seven—another of my favorites. And only five more options before I could leave a message.

"Goodman here. I need a current address and phone number on Gabriella Sugarman. Check back later."

No doubt Francie could do that easy as pie. (However easy pie is.) Actually, I've always been impressed how the politicians and super-show business people could just pick up a phone and tell their secretary, "Call Barbra Streisand. Get me Rodney King. I want Tipper Gore's cousin." And their people always found the numbers.

"Too late for Boris Yeltsin? Get me Desmond Tutu."

Francie was one of those people could do that.

You just never do get used to staring into the barrel of a gun.

"Whoa ho. Una momento," I said, holding my hands

in front of me, palms out, no harm from me—to the tough-looking Asian number pointing what looked to be a Heckler & Koch 9mm. Parabellum. (I could be wrong, I was a little shook up and the angle was bad.)

"Look, lady, I don't mean any harm. No one answered the door and it was open so I just stuck my head in, I could go right away, in a flash." I always felt if you were talking you weren't dead, and if you kept talking you might keep living.

"What are you doing here?" she asked.

"I just came to see Mrs. Marvin Fischer."

"No, you didn't."

"Yeah, really."

"You didn't have an appointment."

"Right, I didn't have an appointment. I didn't say I had an appointment, I just wanted to talk to her."

"I know you," she said suddenly. "How do I know you?"

"Can I put my hands down?"

"No. Who are you?"

"My name's Ray Goodman. Rayford Goodman? I was with Mr. Fischer at the Lambda awards. Well, I wasn't *with* him, exactly . . ."

"Right!" she said. "You captured the man who shot him."

"That's right. That's me."

"And what do you want with Mrs. Fischer?"

"Uh, well, to tell you the truth, it's kind of personal. You want to put the gun down?"

"OK."

And she did.

"So, can I see her?"

"Yeah, I said OK."

"I wasn't sure whether it was OK just to put the gun down or OK put the gun down and I can see her."

"All of the above."

But she didn't move.

"So—she home?"

"Home and here. I'm Mrs. Fischer."

I thought of the mousy, chubby guy with the receding hairline and the long silly ponytail. And I couldn't imagine how he'd ever lucked out to marry this exotic Asian beauty.

Now that I didn't look to be in danger of immediate death, I took a more relaxed look. She was dynamite. That great black hair, of course, the smooth, almost gold skin, the great eyes (how could any of them be so dumb they had them surgically changed?), the long, slim body, with super legs (probably not Japanese), really nice boobs (probably not Chinese) and an "attitude" (probably Korean). Call me a cynic but it was hard to imagine this was exactly a total love match—at least on her side. And of course, Oriental women have been known to be every bit as "practical" as their western sisters. (All right, Asian—at least I didn't say wily.)

The weird thing, though, since we had Marvin ('Arv) on Teri's tape, he seems to have been dumb enough to cheat on her. Go figure. I'd take the missus Fischer over Teri any day in the week and twice on Sundays. As they used to say when I was a boy. (When Hector was a pup.)

"May I come in?" I asked, now that we'd moved onto better terms.

"Yes, excuse me," she said, stepping aside to let me by. "I'm a little jumpy, I guess you noticed. Having your husband murdered will do that to you."

"I can understand that."

She checked the door was locked this time and then led me into a small parlor. Well, maybe den? It was an old house in Hancock Park, probably dating back to the Thirties, and fairly small. Well made, but with the little windows and little rooms typical of the times. When they still had parlors, or were on the parlor cusp, on the way to dens. For a short time after parlors they had living rooms, but once people spent all their money fixing up their living rooms they didn't want to wear them out by using them, so they found some other small room and made it into a den, where everybody did their living.

Since I hadn't connected with Francie and didn't know where to reach Gabriella, I'd decided to make use of the afternoon to get this one out of the way. We'd included her on our list to interview. Not that she was a suspect, but because I'd found people connected to the people in a case knew other people who often wound up knowing whoever did the killing. Sometimes called fishing.

The room was what they call richly furnished with mostly Asian stuff, even to my eye real costly goods. Yet the house was pretty modest. Especially for the neighborhood. Which, while it wasn't any longer fashionable as it used to be before the trend-setters moved west, had mostly substantial houses. (They'd staged a comeback and been a real buy during the early go-go Eighties when real estate went totally crazy in L.A.)

It was a smart kind of place for someone political to live in comfort without the splash that looked like he might be on the take.

"Well, I certainly appreciate your trying."

"Trying . . ."

"To save my husband."

"Oh, yeah. Well, too bad I didn't spot the guy in time."

"Still, it was very brave of you."

I gave her a brave smile. Actually, when I thought back on it, I jumped the guy just in case he had any idea of turning around and taking a pop in my direction. I think. Who really knew?

"The least I can do is offer you something to drink."

I smiled my brave smile again.

"May I—offer you something?" she repeated, wetting her lips with a pink tongue in a way she knew damn well made me think of more than drinks.

"That would be nice," I said.

"How about a Singapore Sling?" she said, squaring her shoulders and taking a breath that couldn't help featuring her nifty nibs.

Which seemed to be the real decoy and made me feel definitely sure she wasn't Chinese. Among other things.

So what was the Singapore shtik? Did she really take me for a rube who thought all Asians were alike? And/or what was she taking me for altogether?

"That would be nice," I said.

It was a slow weekday afternoon.

Let the games commence.

When I was a young man (starting to say a lot of

things like that—shit) there used to be a drink called a Zombie. It was made up of different rums and liqueurs and I don't know what all. The idea was if you could get your date to drink one of these there was a fair chance you could get her into the sack.

The downside was she wouldn't do a lot of moving.

Singapore Slings have a lot in common. And if it wasn't for the fact I'm in such great shape, booze-train-ingwise, I might have had trouble holding up my end, as they say.

The trick was enjoying this sudden bonanza of the most incredibly smooth flesh I'd run into in a dog's age, while feasting my eyes on a really world-class set of hills and valleys, and still keeping my inner eye on the main idea of the whole encounter.

What I did, I decided to do it in sections. Section one was have a really marvelous time. This I managed despite a nagging sense the lady was a bit too wonderful to be entirely a gifted amateur. And the thought went fleet-ingly through my mind that the late Marvin Fischer seemed to know his pros and cons, and I wasn't sure about the cons.

My opinion was reinforced as she discouraged any real active participation by me and kept pushing me back to a passive position.

"Just, you lay back there," she said. "And let me give you a real hero's reward."

"Well, that's sure nice of you, but . . ."

"Shhh," she said, first letting her fingers do the walk-ing, then leaning her head over my body and tickling me and mine with her long black hair as she rocked her head back and forth and up and down and which she then parted with her long tapered fingers (on the down side). She looked up once to favor me with a wondrous eastern smile, then turned her head back toward the job in hand, lowered her gorgeous face and took my mind off the case.

So there was that section.

Then there was the cigarette we shared because that was the one you could never give up under any circumstances.

But the truth of the matter was "A" for technique, "F" for sincerity. And while it was wonderful, it wasn't wonderful. Jesus, was I getting sensitive, or something? (Even the cigarette didn't taste all that great.)

Her head was on my shoulder, her body turned toward me, hand resting lightly on my stomach, which I was glad to note not too prominent since I was laying on my back. Sincere or not I wanted to make a good impression.

"So how did you and old Marv get together?" I asked conversationally.

"He came to Korea on a fact-finding mission for the mayor's office."

I could believe that. Politicians always had so many facts to find in so many foreign places. Although there might have been something to that one, being he was only an aide, since the facts they wanted to find in Cannes or Monte Carlo always took the mayor's personal attention.

"And I was his liaison and translator in Seoul."

Which she would be pretty good at. Her English was flawless. She had absolutely no accent whatsoever.

"Your folks from there?"

"Well, my mother. But she died. Always claimed my father was Korean and was killed in the war. But I'm sure he was a G.I. I'm tall."

She was tall.

"And you worked for the government?"

"Yes. I had a benefactor who—helped me get the job."

"I guess it wasn't an easy place to grow up in. I just barely missed that war, myself."

"I don't think you missed anything."

"Oh, I don't know—judging from you."

She smiled at the compliment. Small smile. She was used to them.

"So, you met Marvin and fell in love and he took you back and married you?"

"Married me first, actually. Easier that way."

"And you stayed in politics yourself?"

"Well, not in any major way. I worked with Marvin."

The assistant's assistant. It didn't seem quite enough. She didn't appear overwhelmed by grief, either, I noticed. But in fairness, maybe they didn't show it the same in their culture. ("In my sorrow do I know what I'm doing?" Old Jewish joke: new widower found with the maid.)

"But here I'm doing all the talking. Why did you come to see me?"

"I'm investigating the murder of a woman named Teri Dart."

There was a reaction. She was inscrutable, but she was *more* inscrutable.

"And what's that got to do with me?"

"Nothing, I'm sure. Except, it seems your husband knew her."

"My husband was a politician. He knew lots and lots of people."

"You never heard him mention her?"

"This was that party girl up in the Hollywood Hills?"

I nodded.

"What would he possibly have to do with her?" she said, her eyes lowering just enough to have me look at her body again. As if to say, "When he has this at home."

"I suppose it could have something to do with business. Just as a wild, far-out shot in the dark, your husband ever mention being involved in something called the Sunset Center?"

"That would be the supermall they're building on Sunset Boulevard?"

"That would be the one."

"Well, what do you mean 'involved in'?"

"Have a connection with; be interested in. I don't know, you tell me."

"It wouldn't involve him. That's a West Hollywood deal."

"Doesn't it have to go through Los Angeles?"

"Peripherally. There are environmental-impact studies, county considerations, state, for that matter. Everyone has some hand in it, but it's basically up to West Hollywood."

"And your husband had no connection with that."

"Not that I know of."

"Even though he was with Councilman Hong, when they were both shot."

"I really—I'm afraid I can't help you much. I don't even know what all that has to do with this woman, Teri what's her name?"

"Dart. It just all seems to be interconnected. But you say you didn't know your husband knew her?"

"That's right."

"And *you* didn't know her."

"I didn't even know her name."

"And speaking of which, do you know I don't even know *your* name? I feel a little awkward calling you Mrs. Fischer."

"It's Li Ah. L - i, A - h."

Which was new to me and yet struck a familiar note. Teri's phone tape. The "Leah" who left a message, the one with no regional accent whatsoever. Who posed the musical question, "You want money, or you want trouble?"

And who now denied even knowing her. Li Ah, not Leah.

It put a whole new slant on things.

# 22

## Mark Bradley

"Remember Anna May Wong?" Goodman was saying.

"Anna May Wong," I repeated. Vaguely familiar.

"The actress," Goodman prompted.

"Ah, trivia."

"It's not trivia—it's part of my history. My life is not trivia."

"You're right. I apologize. You knew Anna May Wong?"

"No, she was before my time."

Cymbal crash.

"So let's try this again—what?"

"I'm trying to tell you, this Li Ah lady yesterday was something out of a sex fantasy. Your basic Shanghai Lil Asian vamp. The parts Anna May Wong used to play in the way old days."

I guess my smile wasn't too convincing.

"Never mind," he said. "Not the point."

"I understand," I said, which is something I say when I don't but it's not worth pursuing.

He had given me more than a slight hint as to yesterday afternoon's activities. Almost a blow-by-blow account, one might say. Which I took to be a vote of confidence and a broadening, so to speak, of his area of tolerance—that he would man to man it with me.

"But the significant thing I'm hearing is you're convinced she's our 'Leah' from the tape."

"Without a doubt. I actually recognized the voice," he said. "So why would she deny knowing Teri?"

"I would. 'For the last time, you want money or you want trouble? And I mean a lot of trouble.' She threatens Teri and Teri gets murdered, that's a pretty good reason to deny it."

"Yeah, I guess."

"Though I admit it is incredibly dumb to put that kind of threat on tape."

"Maybe she has one that erases itself after you listen to it and didn't realize Teri's doesn't. Because otherwise, I promise you, she's not dumb."

"Then the next question has to be what is she threatening Teri about? Is it the Sunset Center deal, somehow—or her husband?"

"Well, I sure figured it was her husband," said Goodman.

"But think about it."

"I'm thinking. We don't actually even know Teri had anything tangible to do with the deal. She was just involved with people who were involved in it. My vote it's because of the husband."

"Goodman—her husband was a shnook. You're describing a beautiful, worldly, intelligent woman—she's worried over losing him to this chippy?"

"I wouldn't call Teri a chippy."

"Bimbo?"

"I dated the girl!"

I wasn't going to touch that.

"But I get your drift," he concluded. I hadn't had my drift got in a long time. Well, till recently.

We were in the Beemer, Goodman's Caddy in the shop getting a new window and a bullet-hole patch in the door (which he insisted we ought to split as "expenses doing research"). It was ten-thirty in the morning as we made our way downtown to the mayor's official memorial service in honor of the late Marvin Fischer, his (by now) vital right-hand Man Friday, aide-de-camp, plenipotentiary extraordinaire, and minister without portfolio (or breath).

Since he hadn't been an official part of the government there had been no rotunda-type lying in state. The funeral itself had been private. Or as private as five local, three net plus CNN TV coverage would allow.

But for the big memorial "celebration of life" deal we

were going to at the Sheraton, which involved a lot of rented space, food, hosted bar (at least for the press), servers, parkers et al, a special "committee" had been established. Which meant various enterprises and enterprising individuals with an interest in pleasing the mayor and establishing community-concern public relations contributed toward covering the costs and, I wouldn't be surprised, creating a little "miscellaneous funds" surplus. (A partial list, under the Freedom of Information and Fear of Later Disclosure acts, had been made available and Francine had accessed it. Sunset Center was a donor—in the nebulous, "over one thousand" category that suggested it was substantially more.)

Goodman, honored as a hero of the occasion, had been invited to speak, but my guess was he'd settle for a bow. (A qualified prediction based on how long the bar was open before he was asked.)

I had been permitted entry as "and guest" of Goodman, a category that did little to enhance my prestige or bolster my self-esteem. However (I kept telling myself), an invisible reporter is an effective reporter. And our mission here was information gathering.

Well, our first mission was getting in. The entrance was mobbed. And there appeared to be a virtual gridlock caused by, of course, the enormous turnout, the intrusive presence of several remote-TV teams, and the extraordinary security precautions calculated to avoid a repeat of the event that had brought us all here in the first place.

That preliminary goal had almost been achieved when we were intercepted by TV Reporter Tiffany Stevens, of KNUS, who recognized Goodman.

"Mr. Goodman, Mr. Goodman!" she cried, as two of her linebackers physically restrained him.

"Can we have a word with you?" she said, as if offering him a choice. "Ladies and gentlemen, this is Mr. Rayford Goodman, the man who so courageously threw himself on the late assassin, William Hobart Kiskessler, before he could kill more people. Mr. Goodman, is it true the mayor is planning to give you a special award?"

"I really don't know."

"I've heard they're planning a Citizen's Heroism Medal."

"Well, then I guess your hearing's better than mine."

A mite taken aback, she took a breath, and a new tack. "Can you share with us your thoughts when you saw Mr. Kiskessler begin to open fire?"

"My thoughts were I knew the bastard couldn't make a living as a bartender."

"Heh heh. You're referring to the fact Mr. Kiskessler had gained access to the Awards Dinner by overpowering and taking the place of the original bartender."

"I am? I guess that's what I am."

"But specifically, at the moment the bullets started flying, tell us about that."

"I said to myself, darling—I always call myself darling—better nail that son of a bitch before he turns the gun on you."

"Well, er," said the nonplussed reporter, "thank you for sharing your thoughts with us."

*My* thoughts were Tiffany Stevens didn't know how lucky she was to have interviewed him before he hit the bar.

"So, am I correct in summing up that you aren't aware of being presented with a medal and are here, really, simply, as with so many of us, to pay your last respects to Mr. Martin Fischer, the tragic victim of the late assassin, William Hobart Kiskessler?"

"And get a free lunch," said Goodman with malicious pleasure at her obvious discomfort.

At which point Ms. Stevens's attention was caught with relief by the arrival of the official mayoralty cortege, and Rayford was unceremoniously dropped like the proverbial *pomme chaud*.

"That's it? No more hello, hero?"

"Well," I commiserated, "it looks like you've had your fifteen minutes of fame. Everybody gets fifteen minutes, as Andy Warhol said."

"Who?"

See?

And we took advantage of the diversion to press forward, get our color-coded name tags at the reception desk, move through the security check and finally get inside.

There is something about business hotels, no matter how lavish their construction, that continues to say—we mean business. Not fun. An impression, I must say, despite personal proclivities, that is made more pronounced by the relative absence of women. I think basically, and generally, women *are* more fun.

And, as if to lend substance to my assertion, an attractive young Asian woman, surrounded by several men, directly to our left, gave off a tinkling laugh that seemed to set off harmonic (or hormonic) vibrations in her immediate group.

"No, it's true," she was saying, evidently elaborating on the subject under discussion, "Chinese women can't hold liquor."

"Come on, Mei Ling," pursued one of her pursuers, "where's your spirit of adventure?"

"Not up in your room, that's for sure," she answered, gaining another round of chuckles and setting off the odd bicep-punch between the guys.

"Mei Ling, Mei Ling," Goodman mumbled. "Where've I heard that name?"

I hadn't the foggiest.

He snapped his fingers. What're you going to do, he was one of those guys who snapped fingers.

"Got it—Jeffrey Hong's secretary. Or maybe associate."

"Right. I remember now, I didn't know her name, but I remember the face, she was at the awards. The same table as Fischer and Hong."

"Some lucky she wasn't hit," observed Goodman.

I couldn't help thinking how trendily Pacific Rim this case was becoming, what with the Li Ah woman, Jeffrey Hong, and now Mei Ling.

"Listen," Goodman said, "I think what we ought to do is split up and mix and mingle."

"What exactly are we looking for?"

"I'm looking for the bar, tell you the truth."

"Besides that."

"We're looking for a handle. We're looking for how

all this shit went down, and how it all connects. And maybe why, if we get real lucky."

"And you expect to find that here?"

"I haven't a clue where we'll find it. But here's as good a chance as any. And there," he said pointing to a bar, "is an excellent place to start."

"It's eleven-twenty in the morning."

"Are we synchronizing our watches?"

I yielded. "Meet you in the auditorium?"

He nodded.

"Look for me on the left side, toward the rear. I'll save you a seat for the formalities."

And he was off, making the proverbial beeline.

I had a feeling "toward the rear" was a good idea; to discourage any impulses he might have to go onstage and make a speech—or a spectacle.

There was a light tap on my arm, and I turned to confront the tapper, who turned out to be Lieutenant Ellard of the BHPD.

"Hi, Lieutenant."

"How you doing, Mark."

"Good. A little outside your bailiwick, aren't you?"

"It's what's known as hot pursuit, in the vernacular. Maybe in this case more cold pursuit. And you guys? I presume Ray's here, too."

"Lukewarm pursuit. Plus we—he, anyway—were invited."

I noted, over Ellard's shoulder, that Councilman Hong had joined Mei Ling and the other studs.

"Let me ask you something, Lieutenant."

"All right."

"This Kiskessler guy had a record as a paramilitary kook, right?"

"Right."

"Who would know that?"

"Well, as a matter of routine, of course, all police organizations. Politicians, or their offices, might be informed, would be informed, if there'd been any known threats."

"To them specifically?"

"Well, that, of course. But a broader spectrum if, say,

someone had made a threat against the mayor, we'd routinely alert those most closely allied or in contact."

"I just can't help wondering how someone recruits a guy like that."

"Well, there's no indication he *was* recruited."

"Right. And there's no indication he wasn't murdered by design in jail, either, huh?"

"Well, not officially. But I go along, off the record, it's not too likely to be that coincidental."

"OK. Which then brings us to how does one recruit someone *in* jail to murder a fellow inmate?"

"That I would guess, and it is a guess, would take someone either in law enforcement who knew specifically the sort of inmate who could be recruited."

"Or someone with influence with someone in law enforcement."

"Right. Which could be anybody with enough money to spend. Helpful?"

"Well, pleasant. Nice talking to you."

"Nice talking to you, Mark."

And Ellard wandered off.

Meanwhile the group hanging around Mei Ling had broken up and she was alone with her boss, Councilman Hong. He smiled and beckoned me over.

"Mark Bradley?"

"Yes." Surprised he knew me.

"Jeffrey Hong, how do you do?"

"Hi. How're you?"

"Recovering," he said, indicating his arm, still in a sling.

"Yeah, that was something. I guess you can't help feeling you got off light, considering."

"You know it. I've been in touch with your partner."

"So I understand." That was probably how.

"I've been sort of hoping you fellows might come aboard with an endorsement—of my candidacy?"

"Uh-hah. I don't imagine my endorsement would amount to all that much."

"Don't be modest. You're well known; a member of the 'community' . . ."

Or he had a file on me.

"I do live in West Hollywood."

"Why don't you and Mr. Goodman be my guest for lunch one of these days?"

"Maybe."

"Mei Ling?" he called. She was alert, actually within earshot.

"Yes, Jeff. Councilman."

"You know Mr. Bradley, here?"

"How do you do? Well, I certainly know *of* him."

Flattery, too.

"Hi."

"Why don't you take Mr. Bradley's number and we'll get back to make an appointment with him and his partner for lunch real soon."

"Sure," she said, opening her purse and removing a notebook. As if they didn't already have my number.

"If you'll excuse me," said Hong, spotting someone else he wanted to haul on board his campaign train.

I waved him off.

"Yes, Mr. Bradley," said Mei Ling, pen in hand.

I gave her my number, which she wrote down.

"You know, we were at adjacent tables at the Lambda Awards," I told her.

"Really?"

"You were incredibly lucky to be away from your table when the shooting started."

"I sure was. Ground zero."

"But it just occurred to me, I don't recall seeing an empty seat. At the table."

"That was because when I got up, Marvin Fischer sat down in my chair."

"I don't understand, wasn't he already seated at your table?"

"Oh, no—he was two tables over. He just came by to say hello."

Just moments before the assassin opened fire!

"Talk about wrong place at the wrong time."

"Or in my case, right place at the right time," she said. "Thank heaven for a shiny nose."

# 23

## Rayford Goodman

Hotel bars, or I should say portable temporary bars, no matter where, always seem to be how the name "quick buck" got invented. The drinks were always stingy, glasses full of chipped ice instead, and that awful soda that doesn't fizz made from gas and tap water. In a town where nobody even drank plain water came from the tap.

And you had to stand in line and fight your way to get there. For a no-host bar. On top of everything, there seemed to be some kind of double standard. The main big permanent bar was a host bar, but you needed some kind of VIP ID for that. Which, turned out, I actually had. Being a hero.

I didn't know that. (Would I be paying scalper prices for vodka-flavored water if I did?) But the short, chubby chap holding two martinis (in plastic glasses, by the way) clued me.

"You're actually entitled to the freebies," he said, pointing to my name tag. "The reds are officially guests."

He was a red tag, too.

"So are you then."

"Yeah, well, bad as this is, that's even more crowded. The media, alone ..."

"Not my idea of a fun morning," I said, leaning in to read his name on the tag. "Mr. F. Sugarman." Hmm. "F. like in Fabrisio?" Be still my P.I. heart.

"Guilty," he said (thank you, Jesus), then squinted in at mine, through his thick gold-rim glasses.

"Ray Goodman," I said, helping him out.

"Oh, hi. You'll forgive me if I don't shake," he said, holding up the two martinis. "I figured I'd need two to get through the wait for the next ones."

"My kind of guy. I guess you're a better planner than me. This is really the pits, isn't it?"

"Necessary evil."

"How so?"

"Well, politics."

"Oh, you weren't a personal friend?"

"Hell, no. I'm more in the sponsor line."

"Because?"

"Because my business needs me to be on good terms with the powers that be. Surprise, surprise."

"They put the screws to you, huh?"

"No need. One just wants to avoid all the potential negative interpretations of existing laws. When you're a builder, or involved in a project, you find out just how many such laws there are. I assume you don't have any vested reportorial interest in this kind of information and I'm not making an ass of myself because of the two martinis that preceded this one."

"Absolutely."

"Although it's a little late to cease the volubility that's characterized my liquor-lubricated life. In any event, I'm not really saying anything I didn't more or less say to your partner when we had lunch the other day."

"Ah, so you know who I am."

"You're the famous Rayford Goodman, hero du jour and chronicler of the Hollywood crime scene."

"With, of course, my partner," I added modestly. "Except for the hero part."

"And as I understand it, your current project is a book on Teri Dart?"

"That's right."

"Actually, if it weren't so incredibly crowded in here I might be suspicious we didn't bump into each other by accident."

"Because we know you were a friend of Teri's?"

"Well, yes. But Teri had a lot of friends, as I'm sure you're aware. Extremely popular."

"Yeah, I know." I didn't say "first hand." We both took a sip while I searched for a segue, reached. "And speaking of friends, you could do me a friendly favor."

"What's that?"

"Well, I've been wanting to interview your mother. And I haven't been able to connect just yet."

"Ah."

"Would you give me her number?"

"You could leave a message at Allegretto Enterprises."

"Yeah, but that's so impersonal."

He gulped down what was left of one of his drinks and slipped the full one in the empty and handed it to me. Then he reached in his jacket pocket, and took out a small notebook and a gold Cross pen.

He wrote down a number, tore off the sheet, and gave me that. And I gave him back his two-glass drink.

"Thanks," I said.

"If I were you, I wouldn't tell her where you got it."

"Whatever you say. I thought it might help break the ice."

"More likely break the connection—my mother and I are not on speaking terms."

"Oh."

"And now, if you'll excuse me, I've got about twenty-five hundred dollars' worth of hors d'oeuvres to eat," he said. And left.

But he was going to have to eat awful fast. Because they sounded one of those chime things, like at the theater when the curtain's about to rise. (Maybe he could get a doggy bag.)

Any rate, I started making my way toward the auditorium. Which was an idea only occurred to about three thousand other people at the same time. There were so many of us pressed together it felt like a Moonie mass marriage.

I was beginning to wonder had the whole trip been necessary just to find out Junior wasn't speaking to Mommy. Though that didn't seem to hinder them doing business together, her as the big wheel of Allegretto Enterprises, and him as head honcho of the Sunset Center enchilada.

We inched along. It got hotter and stuffier and more uncomfortable. If I could of backed out, I would of. And just when I thought it couldn't possibly get any more uncomfortable somebody stomped real hard on the back of my heel. Not the shoe part, the part just above the shoe part. Achilles. Where it hurts like crazy.

"Ow, shit!" I said, maybe not the best sport about it—and turned around. "Whyn't you watch what you're doing?" And stopped just short of saying, "Whyn't you watch what you're doing, *fuckface*?"

What stopped me, he was a police captain in uniform. I seldom call police captains fuckface.

"He din do it, Ahm the one," said the chap next to him. An old cowboy. With an old cowboy boot; well, the boot of an old cowboy. The boot was new, very pointy and made out of pack of rare desert animals. The point was silver over steel.

"Sorry, podner," said the old cowboy, not offering any surprises, speechwise. "Got a mite pressed for a moment. You know Cap'n Kilmer, here?" I nodded to Cap'n Kilmer.

"You really mashed the hell out of my heel," I said, not willing to let it go all that easy, even considering Captain Kilmer and that this wasn't just any old cowboy, either.

"Ah tell you, friend, I'm about as sorry as a passel of rabbis on the Day of Atonement."

"That sorry," I said, and couldn't help smiling.

"Howdy," he said, smiling through caps the size of buffalo horns and offering a well-manicured but callused hand. "Wrangler Morangis's my handle, what's yourn?"

"Well, I don't actually have a handle. Especially on my heel. But the name's Ray Goodman, and I think your boot's a lethal weapon."

"Been a few thought as much," he allowed, or hankered, or one of those cowboy things. He certainly looked familiar. But why wouldn't he, after starring in about a hundred movies. Where his specialty was kicking bad guys.

"Yeah," he said. "I heard o' you. You're the feller jumped on that there killer and taught him some country manners."

I nodded modestly. (Kicking. Almost karate-like kicking.)

"Hear that, buddy?" he said to the other gent next to

him. Who I reckoned wasn't a sidekick because he was dressed like someone who lived in the city. And the century.

"Yeah, good going," said the buddy, a tall, thin man in his midthirties, with a kind of stuntman outdoor look. More hunter than camper. And a dramatic pair of scars on one cheek that looked less Heidelberg than bar-room brawl.

"Well, go ahead, shake his hand," Wrangler said. "You don't get to meet an honest-to-God hero ever' day."

Buddy stuck out his hand.

"Rayf'd Goodman—say hello to my real good pal, this here's Marshal Hildebrandt."

And before I knew it, I was shaking hands with the man who raped Francine Rizetti.

I was finally inside, and to my surprise actually found Bradley, who'd actually saved me a seat.

I told him my news, that Fabrisio and his mom weren't on speaking terms—whatever that meant. And that I'd met Marshal the shit Hildebrandt, who I'd managed not to kill for the time being. And that Hildebrandt seemed to have some connection with Wrangler Morangis, who was connected to the Sunset Center and Teri. And by the way, right off the bat, got my vote for Lash LaRue.

We were in the left section, toward the rear, near the aisle when the mayor made his way down, going toward the stage.

With him was none other than the grieving widow, Li Ah Fischer. We locked eyes. That is, I locked eyes—she locked on a point three feet past my shoulder, looking right through me.

I guess we weren't in for a lasting relationship.

The mayor took a long while to get to the dais. Not surprisingly, he knew a lot of people. Almost all of which seemed to want to shake hands. Make me rich; make me famous. At least do me a favor.

The widow Fischer got a lot of attention, too. People wanted to touch her, too. Some probably out of real sympathy.

"A good-looking woman," Bradley said, watching her inscrut her way down.

"She is that."

We were in a good spot for people-watching, and there were lots to watch.

And finally everybody who was supposed to be on the dais was on the dais and everyone who was going to find a seat had found a seat.

There was, no surprise, a microphone in the middle of the stage, and walking up to the microphone was none other than Whoopi Goldberg. Who looked to be mistress of master of ceremonies. Why Whoopi Goldberg, I have no idea. Except it was always Whoopi Goldberg. (The idea passed my mind she might be the reincarnation of Georgie Jessel.)

Whoopi said she was not going to be making any jokes today. And then told us about seven. "Because that's the way Marvin would have wanted it."

She then introduced eighty-four-thousand people. (In case you were wondering, nobody had followed up on asking me to speak. Which didn't break my heart.) All of which were crazy about the guy.

"It's beginning to look like Marvin Fischer was a combination Albert Schweitzer and Albert Einstein," said Bradley.

"And Prince Albert in the can," I added.

"Huh?" said Bradley. A generation gap is a pain in the ass.

A bunch more people talked. They all thought real highly of Marvin, too. Most going on for a lot longer than they should of, catching open-mike fever—or Airline Pilots' Disease.

And then, just when the audience was getting noticeably restless, they got into the relatively heavier hitters. Whoopi Goldberg returned to the stage (not having actually combed her hair meanwhile, sorry to report) and said, "Ladies and gentlemen, please welcome to say a few words, the distinguished Mr. Harry Kakonis."

And a very tall gentleman (who really was distinguished looking), in his late sixties, with heavy horn-rim glasses (as Taxi Man said), got up. And wearing what looked like Gary Cooper's best wardrobe proceeded over to the microphone.

For someone who wasn't actually a performer or politician, but just head of the biggest entertainment conglomerate in Hollywood, his face was as familiar as Lee Iacocca or the guy owns Wendy's. And he didn't even do commercials.

"Thank you, Whoopi," he said. "I first met Marvin Fischer's father in the year 1943," he began. Oh, boy. This was not going to be a few words.

"Why don't we get out of here?" I said to Bradley.

"You can't walk out on Harry Kakonis. It's like leaving when the President's talking."

"I often leave when the President's talking."

"Soon. Maybe right after."

Well, it wasn't soon. It turned out Mr. Kakonis not only knew Marvin's father, he knew his mother, too, and his sister and brother and all his friends in the National Guard.

But it did finally end. I got up to go, but Bradley put a hand on my arm.

"Wait," he said. "I just want to hear Jeff Hong."

Whoopi did several minutes thanking Mr. Kakonis for taking time out of his incredibly busy day, and for all he'd done in the past and the even more he would do in the future maybe even including something for "little bitty black lady actors with funny haircuts." (I guess Marvin would have wanted that, too.) And then introduced the distinguished councilman from West Hollywood, Jeffrey Hong.

Hong was seated next to Mei Ling, who led a standing (and mild) ovation as he went to the microphone, before quietly slinking back down.

His right arm still in a sling, he awkwardly raised the mike (from the little bitty black lady) and began his eulogy.

The man wasn't short on platitudes—hanging out a lot of "sorely misseds," and "losses to us all," and my mind began to wander.

There was Li Ah up there, as naturally she would be. Was she sorely missing Marvin? And mourning his loss?

Far as I could tell, she wasn't even keeping a stiff upper lip.

And all those other important people. Why was everybody making such a big, big fuss over a guy like Fischer, who wasn't that major a deal in the city. A lot of big players, the Wranglers, the Kakonises, the Sugarmans—there had to be a common thread that made Fischer more important than he'd seemed.

"Though we didn't always see eye to eye on politics," Hong was saying (when I regained consciousness), "I think his honor the mayor will agree, our arguments were never personal. But it is especially ironic that we, who were so often on opposite sides of the fence, found ourselves that fateful Friday ten days ago side by side when a madman, with some imagined grievance, which we'll now never know, tried to silence us both. And, tragically, partially succeeded."

At which Mei Ling mistakenly thought that was somehow something called for spontaneous applause. No one agreed. (Maybe Chinese *can't* hold their liquor.)

"By the way, thought you might be interested to know," Bradley whispered to me. "I had a little chat with your Miss Mei Ling."

My Miss Mei Ling? What, am I suddenly in charge of Asians?

"Yeah?"

"Turns out Fischer wasn't supposed to be at Hong's table in the first place. It was full. When she got up to go to the bathroom, he came over from his own table and sat down in her seat to have a few words with Hong."

"Yeah?"

"So, don't you see? He might not even have been one of the targets. It might have been just Hong they were after."

Hong, meanwhile, continued the exciting way of "paying our last respects," to "one who gave his all in the service of his city." If he ever got elected mayor he better get himself some new eulogy material.

Since obviously we weren't about to learn anything more, I got Bradley up and we headed quickly up the aisle. (We weren't walking out on the President, after all.)

We got through the lobby, paid the cashier, and were outside waiting for his car when I had another thought.

"Let me try this. I say Fischer still was the target. And when he got up from his table and walked over to Hong's, the shooter simply pointed his gun in the new direction."

"You know, I really hate when you do that," said Bradley. "Every time we seem to make a breakthrough of some kind, you point out how it just might not be so and therefore we haven't gained an inch."

"It's not like that," I said back. "It's just touching all the bases."

"Yeah, right, touching all the bases, what does that mean, really?"

"It's a baseball term, covering all the bags, whatever."

"I know it's a baseball term. I mean what's the point of putting every possible permutation on the table?"

I didn't know I was a permutation-putter.

"I think now we know Fischer wasn't supposed to be at the table it's obvious Hong was the target and Fischer simply bumbled into it," Bradley said. "And I say let's just stick to one theory and go with it. Otherwise it's total chaos."

I thought it was figuring things out.

I also thought it was a good idea not to answer.

The car came.

I guess he was still sore, I wasn't exactly sure why (but I had several permutations).

"I got it," I said, and tipped the parker guy a dollar.

Bradley reached in his pocket and whipped out another two.

On top of what we paid the cashier.

I think you could call that overcompensating.

# 24

## Mark Bradley

I dropped Goodman off at the office, where he picked up his loaner. He was going to "follow up a few leads"—which could mean follow up a few leads, or spend the afternoon at Le Dome following one vodka after another. But hey, I wasn't his baby-sitter, and I had work of my own to do.

When I got upstairs and to my sumptuously appointed cell, Francine was sitting behind my desk, feet up, reading a copy of Sue Grafton's *'I' Is For Innocent.* This didn't strike me as particularly productive for our cause, either, but I'd been tiptoeing around her ever since the awful "it," as you can well imagine. So I figured to open with a little light vamping to test the waters and mix the metaphors.

"I'm worried about her," I said conversationally, pointing at the book.

"Sue Grafton? Why's that?"

"Well, what's she going to do in another fifteen or sixteen years when she runs out of letters for titles?"

"Oh, hey, that's easy," Francine replied. "She'll simply go, *AA Is For Alcoholics Anonymous, BB Is For A Small Caliber Gun,* and *CC Is For A Spanish Sycophant.*"

I gave her a blandly pained smile, and having ascertained she wasn't feeling snappish decided to take a chance on getting some actual work done.

So the next thing I did was suggest she get busy making a file on Wrangler Morangis, alias Lash La Rue. Well, next to the next thing, actually.

First I had to tell her there was an apparent association between the country singer/horse opera star/investor,

Wrangler Morangis, and the director/rapist/shitheel Marshal Hildebrandt.

"That motherfucker, I'm going to nail his ass to the wall. If I don't kill him, which I haven't ruled out by a long shot. And if that old shit-kicking cowboy has any connection, I'll bust his saddle sores, too."

"I knew I could count on you," I said, reclaiming my desk and dusting off the spot where she'd put her shoes.

Actually, I was a lot happier seeing anger instead of apathy and depression. We could channel that.

What I had in mind was the creation of what used to be called a dossier, before the term fell into disfavor following a lot of serious abuse by sundry fascists, communists, and independent despots.

So people didn't have dossiers, now. Now all we had was a monster data bank, consisting of everything you always wanted to keep private about yourself—on computer.

Case in point: after the recent elections, the media broke down the votes by categories such as race, religion, and sex. Gender is usually apparent by name. But how did they know who's black or Hispanic or Jewish, or Catholic, or gay or lesbian? Make you a little nervous? (59 percent of Native American lacrosse players voted for Governor Clinton.)

At any rate, there was a great deal of information that was public knowledge about old Wrangler—movie star, musician (Goodman would give you an argument about that), and multifaceted entrepreneurial investor.

As Francine left to do her research thing I busied myself reading the rest of Teri's diary.

There continued to be more references to C.B. than anyone else. And yet, to my knowledge, despite tentatively identifying nearly everyone mentioned, we hadn't been able to place him.

I reread the one where she had written that he was kind of handsome, "once you think about it."

That seemed to suggest a qualification. That there was something about C.B. that would at first make you think he *wasn't* handsome. What could that be?

Baldness? Height? Weight?

How about scars? Most people would consider scars disfiguring. Certainly a bar to traditional handsomeness.

Marshal Hildebrandt had scars. (Goodman had pointed him out.) And he was handsome, "once you think about it."

And I could certainly see Teri being attracted to someone like Hildebrandt.

What I couldn't see was him masterminding a big business coup and guaranteeing huge profits and riches. Although, if he were in a partnership with Wrangler, who was a billionaire, there was an outside possibility.

"Harry and the F.P. both in the same day." But I'd just begun to think Harry *was* F.P.—the flesh peddler—and make the case that it was an ironic reference to Kakonis's origin, before he became capo di tutti capo of Hollywood.

"But for different reasons," she went on. "F.P. the usual. Ho hum. But Harry ready with big bucks if I will set up Mogul. Good luck—C.B. would kill me."

Oh, boy.

"Told C.B. After all, we're going to be life partners. He just smiled, told me not to worry, that he knew all about it. We could *use* it, he said. What a mind!"

I was having trouble dealing with all this, the sort of stuff that drives me crazy. Could use what? Against whom? Well, Mogul, whoever that is. But to what purpose?

The one thing that stood out, over and over again, was that Teri was definitely hot for this C.B.—in an acquisitive sense. And had serious plans for their future together. Now it could be that those plans were realistic and ones he shared. But she'd indicated he was married, and pressure tactics could have backfired.

If only we could find her address book with the phone numbers. At least to find out who all the players were.

I forced myself to return to the diary, finishing it. If there was more to be gleaned, I wasn't the right gleaner. Or this wasn't the right time.

I took out the penknife Goodman had found outside Francine's apartment and started whittling a pencil. But

I didn't show any marked talent for that, either. At any rate, I was done with the diary.

Actually, the whole concept of diary-keeping amazed me. I mean, if you happen to be President, you have an inkling the history of your day might have a scholarly value. Even Madonna, apparently. But for the average person, I found it weird. Although, of course, the average person didn't think of themself as average. (Me, neither.)

Francine burst back into the room riding a manic surge of energy. Having a purpose seemed to agree with her.

"OK, OK," she said, dumping a ream of computer paper on my desk. "Mosey Productions, begat long after Republic Pictures ceased to have use for ol' Wrangler as a performer, but a corporation with varied and highly profitable offshoots. Rawhide Realty, for one. Lots and lots of lots, and buildings. And a western clothing chain, 'Dude Duds'—I imagine using 'dude' in the original ofay way. Owns the Portland Ponies baseball team. A sizable interest in a Las Vegas hotel. This is just surface. Should I mention a major major shareholder in the projected Sunset Center Supermall?"

"I think that's worth mentioning."

"You don't suppose this is somebody who could be called a mogul?"

"Certainly in terms of money, which is I guess how you measure moguldom. Mogulness?"

"You didn't happen to notice if he wears a wig?"

"No," I had to admit.

"Didn't notice, or he didn't wear one?"

"Didn't notice. What else you got?"

"Well, it's a lot of more of the same. You might be interested in some of the writeoffs, that's often helpful."

"Did he write off a certain Teri Dart up in the hills?"

"Not that transparently. The biggest I saw that popped out at me was the Bar None ranch."

"Isn't Bar None like the Knott's Berry Farm, or something?"

"In terms of size I think it's even bigger. But it's actually just old Lash's little bitty homestead."

"I think I've seen pictures of it from time to time."

"I'm sure you have. Bar None is sort of like a

Country-Western version of the Playboy Mansion. You like the show so far?"

"Terrific. You're the best—bar none." (The good executive bolsters the confidence of his employees.)

"Betcher boots, honey," she agreed. Then took a moment; a breather. "All right," she said, "what's this thing with Marshal?"

And I took a moment; and a breath. "Only that Marshal and Wrangler were together at Fischer's memorial service. Could be something, could be nothing."

"Yeah?"

"But it is odd, I admit. And would be a hell of a coincidence if they just met, or something."

"What could they possibly have in common?"

"I was hoping you might find that out for us."

"Well, nothing in anything I've run across so far. But I've only just started. What's that?"

"What's what?"

"In your hand."

I'd been idly playing with the penknife.

"Oh, this. Goodman found it in the hole where I turned my ankle. Outside your apartment."

"Might have been dropped by whoever was waiting to jump me?"

"Might have."

"Let me see it."

I handed it over.

"This couldn't be anything like a murder weapon?"

"Only if someone was cuticled to death. Teri was killed with a much larger knife."

She turned it over, examined the workmanship. Pointed to the dash, zero inlay.

"And what's that?"

"Dash, zero."

"Dash, zero. Asshole—how about Bar None?"

Dum de dum dum.


When Goodman called to tell me he'd located the second Harry, the one on the phone tape and did I want to go with him on the interview I said yes. I'd had enough embarrassment about my poor detection for the day.

And since, given Francine's delicate psyche at the moment I couldn't tease back in kind, I was positively delighted to escape the office.

"After this morning, and listening to Harry Kakonis do the eulogy," Goodman was saying as we headed down La Cienega toward Third in his tinny loaner, "I knew there had to be two Harrys. The guy on the tape was just too low class for Kakonis."

"I'd about come to the same conclusion," I agreed.

"So I looked Teri up in the casting books. Would you believe not even listed as Leading Lady, but *Ingenue*? What they really ought to have is a listing Over the Hill."

"And lo and behold ..."

"I found Teri, of course. And between the two twenty-year-old pictures, the name of her agent, Harry Sanford. Of Sanford and Bright."

"Don't think I've heard of them."

"That may be because their office is on Third Street, around La Brea. Not exactly the heart of show business."

Not exactly the heart of show business turned out to be a two-story building of the barracks school of architecture. The ground floor consisted of industrial tenants like a sump pump retailer, whatever a sump pump is, a screen and storm-window outlet, a vault, safe, locksmith store, and a restaurant garbage disposal and grease-trap wholesaler. (And what do you want to be when you grow up, sonny?)

The second floor, with worn linoleum as its literal second floor, had a few private offices—Ace Vending Machines (Aces and Acmes are almost always oxymoronic, I've noted), Moscowitz and Washington, Attorneys at Law (which sounded like a Steve Bochco TV series), two empties, and a large office with shared space. That door had names of a CPA, a realtor, something that had to do with mail-forwarding or post-office boxes, a direct-phone salesman, and the Harry Sanford and Sid Bright Talent Agency. We were not talking about good times here.

Once inside we quickly found Harry Sanford and Sid Bright—they were the ones packing up.

"You got us at our peak business time," said Sid, the

tumulter of the two, taking stuff out of his desk and throwing it into a large plastic trash can.

"Wait, wait, don't you want to save that?" said the other, obviously Harry.

"Save what? Our treasured momentoes?"

"Mementoes. You always said momentoes, it's *meh*mentoes."

"I could care less."

"That's another thing. If you could care less, it means you care some. Should be you *couldn't* care less; you care so little, couldn't be less."

"I care enough to punch you in the nose, you keep that up."

"Looks like we got the Sunshine Boys, here," observed Goodman.

"You folks moving?" I asked politely.

"We're moving to the poorhouse," said Sid.

"That's another thing, they don't have poorhouses anymore. That's why homeless. Times are so bad they can't afford poorhouses anymore."

"Listen, I wonder if we could have a little of your time?" said Goodman.

"Sure, why not? We got till five P.M. to get out before the landlord files a lawsuit for twenty million dollars' damages to this Taj Mahal."

"Which we don't have to worry, we got Moscowitz and Washington on the case."

"I'm sorry," I said. "I know we came at a bad time."

"How can you tell?" said the bitter one. "It's always a bad time."

"I gather then you're going out of business?" I persisted.

Meanwhile Sid opened another drawer, dumped its contents into the trash barrel.

"Our records, our records, you can't just throw away our records," wailed his partner.

"Yeah, watch. What're you going to do with them? You're going to keep from when we had Dane Clark for four months in Fifty-three?"

"It was almost the whole year. And it was a good year.

We split a commission on Lloyd Nolan . . ." He picked a large hunting knife from his drawer.

"What's that?"

"Zachary Scott we got that from."

"Throw it the fuck out!" yelled Sid. "What the hell, it's over. The William Morrises, the CIAs . . ."

"CAA," corrected Harry. "Scott liked to hunt. Remember, Sid, the weekend we went hunting? And you dropped the beef jerky and picked up the deer shit?"

And the two of them started laughing. They laughed and laughed till the tears came.

"You had to be there," explained Sid. I took his word for it.

"See, there was some good times," said Harry finally.

Sid wiped his eyes, nodded. Goodman and I exchanged looks. He quietly took hold of the knife, examined it. There were no evident bloodstains. I could see his mind working. Murder weapon? Such a long shot. He put it down. Sid packed it in a box with other mementoes— with an "e."

"I understand you had other famous actors," said Goodman.

"Oh, yeah. We had Bela Lugosi, he was a funny guy."

"We didn't *have*. We had—for the one picture."

"So what? For that picture we were his representatives."

"Bela Lugosi was funny?" I said.

"Well, not Bob Hope funny, but in his way. He was Hungarian."

"He was more than Hungarian, he was a junkie."

"That's another story. He once said there was an old Hungarian saying if you want a good old age you better like playing bridge and oral sex."

"Because he was a junkie!"

"You're missing the point."

"Right, I'm the one don't get it."

"I understand," said Goodman, forcefully, to get back some kind of control; then, much softer, gently, "you had Teri Dart, too."

"Yeah, ah, that poor girl," said Harry.

"Yeah, yeah, you mean poor Harry," said Sid.

"I admit, I had a crush the woman. She had qualities."

"She had tits and couldn't say no," said Sid.

"Not so, not so," said Sid. "I think she had possibilities."

"I would think so, too, if I spent my Thursday afternoons shtupping her."

"Listen, Sid, for heaven sakes, the woman's dead. And didn't she get me into a good thing, that Sunset Center?"

"Good, we'll see. Expensive, we know."

Harry took a breath—let it pass. Then, to us, "You fellows, what are you, reporters, police?"

"We're not actors, that's a step," said Goodman.

"We're writers, doing a book on Teri. And naturally, since you were friends ..." I said.

"Naturally. Listen, writers, you want to talk, carry some boxes down to the car. Sid, you coming?"

"No, I got more garbage to throw away."

"He wants to look around a last time," Harry whispered. "He's the sentimental one."

"I heard that, you fuck," said the sentimental one.

"Come on, pick up the boxes," said Harry.

We picked up the boxes and carried them down the stairs and to the back parking space reserved for Sanford & Bright.

Harry opened the trunk of a fifteen-year-old Chrysler in royal blue and rust.

"The New Yorker," he said. "I always favored the New Yorker."

And we helped load files and pictures of actors taken twenty years ago he couldn't possibly have any use for.

"I know—I'll throw them out later," he said. "What's the hurry?"

"Right," said Goodman. "Listen, just a thought. Anybody else, you represent anybody else besides actors?"

"Well, we had a few. No writers."

"I don't mean really for us."

"A couple. A cameraman; whatsisname, the assistant director on the *Francis the Mule* pictures?"

"The name just went out of my mind," I said.

"And one we still got, I'll have to tell him he needs a new agent."

"Who's that?"

"Marshal Hildebrandt, you know him? Supposed to be a hotshot director."

"I think I've heard of him," I said, my heart somewhere in my neck.

"We took him because he was supposed to be doing a TV series didn't happen. But also, he promised us Wrangler Morangis."

Goodman didn't drop the box he was putting into the backseat, but did bump his head backing out.

"Wrangler Morangis," Goodman said.

"And did you get him?" I had to ask, knowing full well he didn't.

"Nah, brought him over one day. I'll say that, he actually knew him. But Wrangler Morangis, he don't work no more."

"If you had his money you wouldn't, either," said Goodman.

"I *don't* have his money and I'm not working," said Harry Sanford.

There wasn't much we could add to that.

# 25

## Rayford Goodman

After we left Sanford and Bright I asked Bradley if he wanted to stop somewhere for a pick-me-up. He said in his world pick-me-up meant something else. Cute.

"Thanks, really, but I'm meeting Christopher for cocktails."

"Dinner then?"

He made a hand turning over and back move.

"You don't know what's going to happen," I said.

"That's the one," he said.

Well, I could understand that.

I guess.

My own personal romantic life could get me short-listed for Cardinal. Except for the quickie with Li Ah, which was sort of work-connected (if I had a boss, maybe I could call it harassment), there were a lot of reasons for that.

Start off with the one-two punch of my ax-wife Luana, and then Francie. My wife got so good at fighting, after a while I didn't even have to join in, she just carried both ends herself. ("Oh, you can criticize, I know that look. I know you'd like to say it was my fault, I should have done it differently, but I had good reason. Sure, you could say no reason's good enough, but let me tell you, you don't know all the answers.") (Or even the questions.)

And Francie to this day I don't understand. She got me back into hot and heavy after I'd given up on, well, love—or even semifunctioning—and then had to go and get herself pregnant (ladies, I'm kidding). But when she got rid of the baby, why'd she have to get rid of me, too? I'd of gone either way, really, she only asked me.

But now, at my age, go play the game? With all the diseases and all that?

And that I don't that much feel like it?

Booze, medication, age—banking of the fucking fires, so to speak. Wonderful.

"But you could check with me later, I suppose," Bradley was saying. "Christopher mentioned he might have to do something later on."

Keeping his options?

"Oh, yeah, well, I guess not," I said. "I'll make it an early evening, watch a little TV."

And I dropped him off back at the office where he'd left his car, pulled back out Alta Loma, turned left—a bitch of a turn (don't be so literal, ladies)—and into Sunset. Then the quick right at Sunset Plaza and on up home.

The critters were waiting. Asta outside, barking and piss-on-the-ground glad to see me. The Phantom inside, still sort of generally outraged there *was* an Asta. And anyway considered it bad form to show any emotion. Not that I was going to keep Asta. Go tell a cat that.

But just so he'd at least know who rated number one, I opened a Sheba pâté for him, which he liked a lot, maybe knowing it was top-of-the-line expensive (look at me).

Then I got an Alpo number for the guest outside (who I'd have to find a home for pretty soon) because I knew he liked that best and he was all over me with happiness and dog love. Which I didn't find that hard to take.

I petted him a lot and fake-wrestled. And sort of made enough fuss he wasn't mad I'd been gone so long (dogs forgive a lot easier than cats).

And I had the thought I've come to treat animals better than some of the women who gave me their love. Shame on me. (On the one hand.)

I'd originally thought I wouldn't have a drink tonight. It really wasn't a whole lot of fun to wake up at two-thirty with your heart pounding and waiting to see if this was the one that turned into a massive heart attack. Or just the usual.

\*　　\*　　\*

I woke up on the couch *wishing* I'd had a heart attack. It was a bad time for Stan Kenton and ten thousand trumpets to be screaming A's above high C. That can happen with CDs when you get about eight hours on a six-disk magazine. I'd slept through the time travel of Earl ("Fatha") Hines and the cutes of Fats Waller and the gentle here and now of Moe Koffman's "Music for the Night."

On the other hand, it was just as well Stan and the brass did wake me. It let me get to the bathroom before throwing up.

There was other good and bad news. The car was ready—new side window, done-over bullet hole and re-painted door. Bad news, wouldn't jack up the cost to cover a kickback on the five hundred deductible.

The message I'd left at Gabriella Sugarman's house was that I would like to chat with the namesake person in reference to her involvement in the Sunset Center Supermall and the gang at Teri Dart's.

It was a long shot, but I hadn't been feeling creative enough to come up with a lie that'd get me face-to-face. And since I'd used the truth, if it didn't work it left me with something fake and sneaky to try later.

It worked.

I got a call from her home went: "This is Mitchell Bowers, Miss Allegretto's personal secretary. I've been instructed to ask you if one o'clock today for luncheon at Sugaralla will be agreeable?" (Sugaralla wasn't too hard to guess as their own version of Pickfair.)

"Tell Miss Allegretto Mr. Goodman will be delighted to see her for luncheon."

"She would further like to know if Cobb salad is to your liking."

"It's large in my likingness," I said. Which I guess threw him just a smidge.

There was an extra beat, then: "You know the location?"

"Doesn't everyone?"

Which about ended the pleasantries. (I figured I'd find it on my Map of the Stars Homes.)

"Oh," I said just before Mr. Bowers rang off. "Would you tell Miss Allegretto that my partner will be joining us."

"Well, I'm not sure I . . ."

"She won't mind," I interrupted. Taking a shot.

"I, let me ca . . ." continued Mr. Bowers.

"No, no, I promise you, she won't mind. Trust me, pal." And I said good-bye and hung up.

If he didn't call right back I'd know how nervous she was and anxious to see me to find out what I knew. I didn't know all that much, but knowing she was nervous would be a start.

It was in Pasadena. Bought at a time, I told Bradley, "when a Sugarman in Pasadena was about as welcome as a rabbi in Berchtesgaden." So we were talking real covenant-breaking money.

We'd come in Bradley's BMW since he was taking a stand against my having no seat belts in the old Cad (which we'd picked up).

"First, it's against the law."

"Yeah, right."

"Second, I see no reason to risk my life for no reason."

"There is a reason. Seat belts break the purity of my classic car; it's not a part of original equipment."

"Neither is the color you painted it. It didn't come in Anthracite Gray."

"That's a different story, it's a slight eccentricity. Personality. Like Sugar Ray Robinson used to have his painted borscht color."

"The Olympic champion?"

"No, the *real* champion. Are you going to get in my car or not?"

"I am not."

"OK, we'll go in yours, but you're not making this scene over seat belts."

"Oh, you know better?"

"Yeah, you had a fight with Christopher."

"I guess you do know better. We'll still take mine."

(Hey, let *his* car get shot.)

So now we were at the humongous wrought-iron gates

with the S on a coat of arms on top. (For the Earl of Sugarman from Gdansk.)

There was a gateman. And as soon as we both produced suitable ID he pushed the button that opened the gate and told us we would be met at the top of the drive.

The drive was so long they could of used a refreshment stand in the middle.

We were met on top by a middle-aged Asian guy in the kind of white cotton jacket that doubles for doctors or ice cream salesmen or butlers. He told us we were "Welcome to Sugaralla," and managed his "l's" about as good as Tom Brokaw.

The car park itself was next to a twelve-car garage, over which were quarters for enough servants for a small hotel. Which I guess was what they needed.

The front door was another good seventy yards away past gardens and fish ponds and a lily pond Esther Williams could of made a movie in.

The butler guy walked us to the door that was opened by another guy in a black suit who had the kind of build suggested his main work was security.

And took us through hallways and walkways and through a breakfast room to French doors that opened out to a pool area. There were large awnings around the whole back of the building, shading an area that was full of matching canvas-covered tables with dozens of patio chairs around them. To one side was a bar and just past that, in a big chaise, sporting big dark glasses, a Garbo kind of big brim hat, and wearing a chiffony print dress, was Gabriella Allegretto Sugarman (which suddenly occurred to me why we wouldn't be seeing a whole lot of monograms around).

The butler said, "Mr. Rayford Goodman and Mr. Mark Bradley—Miss Allegretto."

She offered a lace-gloved hand in a way that said you should kiss it. I slipped mine underneath and gave her a shake. Bradley dealt with it by a quick touch of fingertips.

"So good of you to come," she said, like we'd been summoned. "Won't you sit down?" She pointed to the chairs stagily placed together to one side (I wouldn't be at all surprised if it was her "good side") just a little up from her feet.

She actually looked pretty good, I had a feeling more playing the fading screen legend than was the case (especially since she hadn't exactly been a legend). Sort of like TV casting. ("Robert Redford." "Right, Marty Milner.")

"Arthur," she said to the butler fellow.

"May we offer you gentlemen some refreshment," he said on cue.

"What are you having?" Bradley asked Gabriella.

"I usually have a health drink of steamed broccoli, whatever vegetables strike my fancy, and Dr. Jensen's powder in a blender."

"OK, I'm game," said Bradley. "I'll have one of those, too."

"I think I'd like a straight vodka over crushed ice and two onions in a tall glass," I said.

"You know, that does sound tempting," allowed the widow Sugarman. "Except, Arthur, instead of vodka made mine gin, and not so much ice, and no onions."

"Well, gee," said Bradley. "I hate to have him go to all the trouble to make the health drink just for me."

"It's no trouble, sir," said Arthur.

It was turning into fun.

"Gentlemen," said Gabriella, once Arthur'd been sent his merry way, "what exactly is it I can do for you?"

But Bradley was hip to the investigative reporter shtik and didn't want to dive right in.

"You know, it's such an honor meeting you at last," he said. "I'm a real fan."

"How nice of you," she said. (They never get enough.) "Which of my pictures did you especially like?"

"Well, my sentimental favorite was, *The Attack of the Giant Scampi,* from your Italian period."

She laughed. "I'm impressed. At least you've done your homework."

"Then there were six in America, right?"

"Eight," she corrected. "Six produced by Albert."

"You were some sex kitten," said Bradley. "And you're still a very handsome woman."

"Sure, pal," she said.

"And the other two?" I said, not wanting her to go off on an actor getting old self-pity riff.

"*Murder, Sicilian Style,* and *Wit's End*—both personally produced by dear old Harry Kakonis. Actually I did them first, then the others for Albert, and then Albert didn't want me to have a career."

"For which he owes us an apology."

"Well, I wasn't exactly uncompensated," she said, pointing around and I got a look at the large lawn back of the pool with the croquet stuff on it, and beyond that a tennis court, and beyond that the Black Forest.

"I really didn't realize you'd worked with Mr. Kakonis," said Bradley.

"Oh, yes. He discovered me in Turin, can you believe it? I was the assistant in a knife-throwing act."

I bit my tongue not to ask to count the knives if one was missing.

"And through Harry you met Albert?" said Bradley.

"Yes, that's about the way it went," she said as Arthur brought us our drinks and let us get off that line of reminiscing on the good old days, ambling down Abbe Lane.

"But I really have no idea why you gentlemen are here."

"We're doing a book," I said. "A biography."

"Not of me, I don't think."

"Not at this time," said Bradley, staring at his drink and trying to be a good sport about what looked like pea soup in a glass. "But in our preliminary interviews we've come across your name once or twice."

She took a swig of gin, swung her feet around to the other side of the chaise and hopped off.

It didn't look too hard; she was in good shape. And with the sun back of her, I could see she still had a pretty great body. The thought occurred to me she would know about backlighting, and might therefore be flirting.

But when she turned around, and took off her glasses, and looked me in the eye, it wasn't hard to tell we weren't dealing with any kitten, but a tough survivor. Definitely *not* flirting.

"OK, guys, let's level here. What are we talking about—whose biography?"

"Teri Dart."

"Who I knew just very slightly, so?"

"And all the people around her in the Sunset Center Supermall setup."

"Yes? You mean, what, my son Fabrisio?"

"Among others."

"And Harry."

"Kakonis and Sanford," I put in.

"I don't personally know Sanford," she said. "But you're right, these people arc investors in the Sunset project. But I don't see their connection with Teri."

"Well, there *is* a connection, between all of you."

"All of us in the syndicate you mean? That Buzz Baxter fellow was her husband, right?"

"Right," said Bradley.

"But there are loads of investors. I don't even know who all."

"Still, you are the principal one."

"Well, not exactly I," she said.

"Your company. Allegretto."

"My company."

"Which consists of the residual assets of Sugarman's U.S. Pictures, late of BCCI—in the trade referred to as the Allegretto Deal."

"I don't think I care for the direction this conversation is taking," said Gabriella, apparently starting to sweat, since she took off her hat. I could see little streaks of it cutting through the pancake makeup on her face.

"It's very warm out here," she said.

"Not for piano players," I said—old joke.

"Tell us about your situation with Fabrisio. Aren't you estranged?" said Bradley. "Didn't he get his cut of the offshore loot? A little skimming, perhaps?"

"What is this shit?" said Gabriella, waving a hand at someone offstage. I was hoping it'd be Arthur instead of the muscular number let us in.

"Or was it Teri who was raining on your parade?" I said to my embarrassment. Not for asking but for saying rain on your parade.

"The main problem with Teri, besides an enormous greed, was her tendency to talk too much."

"Well, she's not talking now, is she?" said Bradley, really learning his trade.

"Look, I don't know what you fellows are up to, but I'm not enjoying this. And you may have noticed, I don't have to do things I don't enjoy. Arthur?"

Arthur had materialized. Together with the hitter.

"Gentlemen? If you will follow me?"

"Listen," I said. "I don't suppose I could have some of that Cobb salad in a doggy bag?"

But she just turned her back. And the last glimpse I got of her was sweating in the sun, scratching her head. Which is when I noticed her hair. Which wasn't her hair, but a wig.

"You may not have been aware of it," I said to Bradley when we'd got our car and driven back down the driveway and had the gates opened, and been booted out. "But there was absolutely no chemistry between that woman and me."

"And you are irresistible," said Bradley.

"No, but I am a man—we both are—and she is an actress, of the old school, known for her sex appeal. And she never once turned the least bit of it on for either of us. If only to control the interview."

"Which means?" he said.

"Well, let me put it this way. What does being the moneybags in back of the scheme make you?"

"A mogul?" said Bradley, right with me.

"And what was Mogul doing last time we heard the name?"

"As I recall, losing a wig while munching Miss Teri's muff," said Bradley.

"Which reminds me, shall we go have lunch?"

"I'm easy," said Bradley.

I knew that.

# 26

# Mark Bradley

As we drove back from Pasadena Goodman had begun to regret we'd had the showdown before the Cobb salad was served.

"Of course, it was the Brown Derby made Cobb salad famous—and they made the best you ever tasted."

Hoping to avert a maudlin tirade about everything worthwhile in Hollywood being gone (as was the Derby), I quickly served up an alternative. "How about fish, you like fish? There's a great place on Pico, Hymie's Fish."

"I don't want to go all the way down there."

We were at the Forest Lawn off-ramp in Burbank.

"We could go to Art's, on Ventura, that's a great deli."

"Don't feel like deli."

"Or Chadney's, by NBC?"

"Neah."

"Or we could go wherever the fuck you want to," I concluded. Enough already.

I guess he got the message.

"All right, take a right on Barham. I stopped to make a call at the Smoke House the other day and remembered I like the place. OK?"

"Whatever you say."

"No, whatever *you* say."

"Look, we'll go where you want to go and you won't owe me any favors, that's as far as I'm willing to go. I mean, I won't go where you want to go and have you act like you're doing *me* a favor."

"Left here," he said, after I'd made the right on Barham and driven down to the light just at the beginning of Warner's, which immediately turned red. I banged my palm on the steering wheel in frustration.

"What's the matter, you got the rag on or something?" said Goodman in his winning way. "Just how bad was the fight with Christopher?"

I opened my mouth to say something snide, took a breath instead. For Goodman this was friendship, actually. And what passed for sensitivity. Worse yet, astuteness.

"Ah, the son of a bitch had another date for dinner."

"Whyn't you call me?"

"By the time I found out, I wasn't actually in a sociable mood."

The light changed and I made the turn. About a hundred feet down was the driveway to the Smoke House, and beyond that the posh Lakeside Country Club, which, shades of early Pasadena, didn't have a big rabbi problem, either.

"Pull up over there. They'll park it."

"Oh, really? I thought the chaps in red vests were a road company of *Guys and Dolls.*"

"So what if he had a date? You only just met, he must have other friends," Goodman said, ignoring my testicity.

"No, no, not supposed to work that way," I said, as we got out of the car. "This is the point when you're supposed to be blind to anybody but each other."

"Maybe it was a previous engagement."

"If it was he'd have been able to tell me. And/or get out of it. Not just the vague cop-out that he might have something to do later."

"Well, then maybe it's your basic early-warning system this is not the right person."

"There's that," I agreed, as we entered and were immediately greeted and taken to a pleasant table near the bar (which I had a feeling an intuitive maitre d' sensed would be Goodman's location of choice), seated, and given menus. "What's good here?"

"Practically everything. But I really like the calf's liver and onions."

"Liver, bleh."

"I don't know why liver gets such a bad rap, it's a delicious thing," said Goodman.

"Maybe it's generational," I allowed, since I'd never known anyone my age who liked it.

"All the sitcoms make such a big joke about it. Liver, liver, oh barf," and he made the finger in the mouth gesture so favored by the folks at Fox.

"Well, maybe the sitcoms are hard-pressed for material."

"I suppose you sometime or other must of considered the benefits of another sort of, uhm, sexual orientation," said Goodman, not losing track of the subject.

"Up to now I've admired so much that that's the one thing you've never brought up."

"Okey dokey," said Goodman, putting his hands palms out in a gesture of half surrender.

"I didn't mean to be short with you. But it's so offensive that so many people think it's something we can be 'cured of'—or want to."

"Hey—your business. I didn't mean to be out of line."

Progress.

"But speaking of business, and that sort of business, kind of a shock about Gabriella, don't you think?"

"Yeah. Strong lady."

"Strong enough to stab a lady lover she had a tiff with a whole lot of times with a great big knife."

"With which she had some experience back in the old days in Italy, as I recall," I recalled.

The waiter stopped by and asked what our pleasure was and we both managed to resist being a smartass. I ordered an iced coffee and Goodman an iced vodka on the iced rocks. And I let him persuade me to try the liver and onions, too.

"Of course," I continued, "it's hard to see her doing in the Singleton guy, especially since it involved physically transporting him to Benedict Canyon and fire-bombing his car."

"Maybe so; maybe not. First place, he could of still been alive, then. Moving by himself. Or maybe we're just being prejudiced underestimating women. Say she really had big hots for Teri, and say she found out there was something else in Teri's life—more than for professional reasons. Someone really personally important."

"C.B.," I offered.

"C.B. And if on top of that maybe she'd given Teri some business inside information or something that she might have betrayed for more money—remember the 'greed' crack?—then we have a couple of pretty good motives."

"And under the one murderer fits all theory . . ."

"Exactly," he said.

"And it works for Fischer, too, since we know he was having his innings with Teri as well. That was some busy body."

"Plus," Goodman continued, "now that I think of it, she could have had help with Singleton. She's got that muscle working around her place. She's not exactly Princess Grace, either. Even with all the money there's still a lot of street in her left."

"Better and better. But how do we prove it?"

"How do you prove what?" said a voice behind me. I turned around. It was the dapper detective, Lewis Ellard.

"Ah, Lieutenant," Goodman said. "What brings you to this neck of the woods? Sit down, take a load off."

"I don't want to sit down."

"Come on, join us. You're more than welcome," I urged.

"I'll sit for a minute." Which he did. Sit. "What were you saying? What would be hard to prove?"

I opened my mouth, but Goodman beat me to it. "Whether the liver and onions beat the liver and bacon."

"Right," said Ellard, his face hardening, not without justification considering Goodman's lame ad-lib. "Beautiful."

"Iced coffee for you," said the waiter, suddenly and in a very timely fashion materializing and putting the tall glass before me. "And vodka on the rocks for you," for our elder statesman.

"Would you like a little libation, Lewis?" said Goodman out of the side of his mouth, doing what I guess was a W.C. Fields impression, but not garnering any laughs that I could notice.

"No, I wouldn't. I don't want to drink with you and I don't much want to talk with you anymore."

"What'd I do?" said Goodman.

"You didn't live up to the deal."

"Sure. You're mad about Buzz, you've been to see Buzz, right?"

"Absolutely right."

"Buzz Baxter lives around the corner," Goodman explained to me.

"You didn't tell me you went to see him. You didn't tell me there *was* a Buzz Baxter."

"Lewis . . ."

"Lieutenant."

"Hey, you're a cop. I sure knew you were going to find out she was married to Baxter, and find him and go talk to him. Besides, I didn't get anything out of him, what'd you learn?"

"What I learned is police business. This partners shit is over. The two-way street is now officially one-way. But it *is* one-way, so don't you forget it. Withholding evidence is still a felony, in case it slipped your mind."

"Just because I didn't get around to telling you I'd seen Baxter?"

"Or any damn thing else you've done till now. I'm sick and tired of you getting everything from me and me getting fuck-all from you."

"That's not true."

"It is true."

"A little."

"And I wouldn't put it past you to have the address book, too."

"No, I don't, man. Scout's honor."

"Well, it's over, scout. I've had it. You, too, Bradley. You interviewed Fabrisio Sugarman at the Bistro Garden, did I get a report? Shit, you guys."

"You're getting awful upset, Lieutenant, over a little maybe shortchange . . ."

Ellard got up.

"That's it. You got it? From now on, no informal cooperation. You find out something, you tell me. You withhold something, it'll be your ass." And he stormed off.

"Try the liver and onions," Goodman called after him.

I could see Ellard's shoulders stiffen, but he didn't turn around, continuing around a corner to another room.

"So what do you make of that?" I asked when the wind had settled down.

"Somebody's putting a lot of pressure on him. Major pressure. And since Teri Dart was hardly some big celebrity victim the public's demanding action over, I have to figure it's political somehow."

"And what does that do for us?"

"It gives us something else to chew on besides this tasty treat," he said, as the waiter placed our heaping entrées on the table.

It was a good thing I checked with the office after we finished eating because Francine had gotten a call from Sam, the other tough lady, out at Keeny Stables. She'd come across a tape the muscle boys had missed when they'd beat up her boss, killed the horse, and stolen all the other tapes. It'd fallen behind some tack and been overlooked. I said since we were already in the Valley at the Smoke House, we'd pop up and collect it.

"I think Sam's going to be a little disappointed if old Fran, here, doesn't show up. She might have just withheld the tape in hopes of seeing me again," said Francine.

"You have to do something about that inferiority complex of yours."

"Hey, I can't help it if you're the only one who doesn't appreciate my charms."

"Well, actually, it might be easier for you to get her to open up, you should pardon the expression. Hurry up, we'll wait for you. But make it fast or Goodman'll get smashed and it'll be a very long day."

"I'm on my way."

And we said good-bye and hung up.

Goodman didn't get smashed, I'm happy to say. He, in fact, drank nothing more than coffee while we waited, and in about twenty minutes or so Francine joined us.

We left her car parked at the Smoke House and took mine. First thing she did was light a cigarette, which was a habit she'd picked up at AA—which I thought was supposed to discourage habits. Given her fragile situation, I put up with it, though none too subtly lowering all the windows. Fortunately, with minimal traffic for a change, we got to Chatsworth a lot faster this time.

We turned in at the by-now familiar wagon-wheel-framed driveway (there may be a law mandating horsey places have wagon wheels half buried at their entry) and up the long road to the stable area on top.

The same wizened black exercise "boy" (which I think is generic for the trade rather than racial in this case) who on second look had to be in his sixties was doing his thing with a wonderful-looking horse.

"Hi, there," I said. "Remember us?"

He didn't answer.

"Beautiful horse."

He grunted.

"What's his name?"

"Sugarfoot."

"Let me guess, belongs to Fabrisio Sugarman?"

"Ain't supposed to talk about particular horses. Since we had us a incident, here."

"I understand," I said. Knowing the "incident." "Is Ms. Sam up at the office?"

"Ms. Sam, she'd like that," he said. "Yeah, Sam's up there."

And we made the trek once again. This time it hadn't rained and the Santa Ana winds had blown everything dry, so there was no mud. And, of course, now I wasn't wearing my suede loafers. So is there a God, or what?

Matt McKensie was sitting in his wheelchair on the deck in front of the office, taking his ease in the sun. He still looked pretty badly banged up, the bandages still in place, face still swollen. If anything, the change in color from black and blue to yellow and green tended to obscure the fact that healing was actually underway.

"Good afternoon, Mr. McKensie," I said. "Do you remember us?"

He nodded.

"This is my associate, Ray Goodman. Ray, this is Matt McKensie, I may have mentioned him?" Of course we had discussed Matt, as one of the voices on Teri's phone tape but I didn't want to do a lot of explaining here.

They exchanged "how do's."

"Sam around?" said Francine.

"Yeah, she's in the office," answered McKensie.

"Uhm," said Goodman, "Mr. McKensie, I was wondering if that horse that was destroyed, Teri Dart's horse?"

"Yeah?"

"Would there have been any substantial insurance on that sort of thing?"

"I don't think it's any of my business," said Mr. McKensie, clearly implying nor ours, "but I wouldn't think there'd be a lot. It wasn't a thoroughbred racehorse, just a great beautiful brute." And his eyes filled with tears as they had first time we'd met. I had a feeling Mr. McKensie would be some time in recovering from his trauma.

We went into the building and from the far door leading into McKensie's private office Sam came out to meet us.

She was still dressed in boots and Levis and it might have been a different checked man's shirt with every button buttoned. At that she was kind of cute in a raw-hidey way.

I deferred to Francine, all things considered.

"Hi, Sam, brought some friends with me, hope you don't mind."

"Uh-huh," said Sam, I think minding.

"You know Mark Bradley, my sort of boss, and this is his partner, Ray Goodman."

"Her other sort of boss," said Goodman. And before Francine could take umbrage popped back in with, "Kidding, really, we're all associates. Francie tells me you may be able to help us."

"Well, I don't know. I just promised if anything came up I'd call, and I found this tape everyone seems to have overlooked, so I thought I'd give you a call," she said, handing it to Francine.

"And I'm glad you did," said our girl.

"I sort of thought *we'd* watch it together," said Sam,

indicating that she wasn't too thrilled to have to share a potentially erotic moment with an additional pair of other-oriented persons.

"Well, if that would make you uncomfortable," I said, "we could perhaps just take it and view it someplace else."

"Well, I don't think so. I've been told by a Lieutenant Ellard if I thought of anything, or found anything, I was supposed to contact him."

I had a feeling Goodman was shortly going to regret old Chief Droward was no longer the officer in charge. He may have been an enemy, but at least he was incompetent.

"Or we could watch it without you," said Goodman.

"No, I think I ought to protect the tape and see no harm comes to it."

"I think you're dead right," said Francine, handing it back. "So, why don't we all take a gander at this thing. You got a VCR around here?"

"In Matt's office," she said, leading us in to the old wood and brass and leather and tobacco room, with its macho warmth. We found chairs, and she slipped in the tape.

"I did kind of peek, but I haven't really watched more than a few minutes," Sam allowed. "It's pretty raw," she added, mindful of our sensibilities.

"Roll 'em," said Goodman, "we can take it."

She turned on the tape, and I could tell immediately that it'd been shot from the camera mount in Teri's closet.

Teri, who of course had to know it was being shot, not only did nothing to disguise herself, she actually played to the camera. And not as a joke, either, but acting the part of an aroused woman in the heat of passion, wantonly (albeit carefully not messing up her hair) succumbing to a lust that had to be large enough to compensate for being only a medium shot instead of a close-up. It was clear, as I'd suspected from the first, that the only thing that aroused Teri was Teri.

The second interesting thing was her partner—the late

Marvin Fischer. (Doing what I'd rate as about a 4 on peformance and style.)

"Looks like Li Ah knew what she was talking about," said Goodman.

We watched this rather dismal undertaking for about ten or twelve minutes. I was about to ask for a flesh forward when another figure settled on the bed, fully clothed.

You couldn't see his face, and he wasn't exactly a participant. He was sort of arranging the players, directing them, and apparently his principal kick was voyeuristic, for when they'd assumed a position more to his liking, he removed himself from the picture.

Then we watched the uninspired antics of Mr. Fischer and Miss Dart for another four or five minutes, till the jacketed arm intruded again, to reposition them, and then, for just a flash we saw the side of a face.

"Stop it," Goodman said. "Can you go back there?"

Sam rewound the tape a few frames, pushed play.

"Now, freeze it!" said Goodman.

Which she did, but it turned out to be just a blur. Very dark hair, but could have been a disguise.

We backed up and played it twice more, but couldn't nail anyone down. Then we played the tape till it went to black—or that spotted, streaked tape equivalent.

"Well, I guess that's it," said Francine, rising. We all did. Sam went to the machine, had her hand on the off button when something else came on.

"Hold it!" said Goodman again. "Let it run."

And apparently, the Fischer/Teri tape had been recorded over a previous performance, which we now saw, in a manner of speaking, the tail of.

The featured female performer remained Teri. As to her partner?

"Oh, I know him," said Sam, evidently not too surprised. I guess she would. The man stabled his horse there.

It was Fabrisio Sugarman. (Back in the ball game.)

# 27

# Rayford Goodman

Driving back from Keeny's Stables in Bradley's BMW. Me with the safety belt on. ("Is that the spirit took men to the moon?" "They didn't blast off unbuckled.") Francie was puffing cigarettes like crazy, the thirteenth AA step. It was getting so it even bothered me who still sneaked one now and then.

"Well?" said Bradley. "Gabriella?"

"Sure had at least one of the better motives, jealousy. The tape confirms Teri was making it with Fischer, and Fischer's dead. And making it with Fabrisio, and maybe only he's Gabriella's son kept him alive. But mad enough she's not talking to him."

"Assuming she knew."

"Assuming she knew."

"How about opportunity?" said Francie. "Do we know where Gabriella was Friday night, Memorial Day weekend?"

"Doesn't matter," I said. "She wasn't the triggerman; that was Kiskessler. She could of been anywhere."

"Right, dummy," said Francie, not the nicest way of making her point. "One of the places she could have been at or about the same time was murdering Teri."

"Actually," I said, "and I'll thank you to show a little respect, if not for your elders at least your employer, Teri was killed several hours later than Fischer. So it's not whether Gabriella was in Anaheim that counts, it's whether she was someplace besides the Hollywood Hills, later."

"We'll have to look into that," agreed Bradley. "She's certainly made it to the short list."

"I don't know whether you chappies happened to notice," said Francie, lighting a fresh cigarette from a butt, "but the tape was a professional dupe."

"So?" said Bradley.

"Means there's another one somewhere," I explained. Then, to her, "You didn't happen to catch the name on the label?"

"It didn't register at the time, but I suppose I could call old Sambo and find out," she said. "Wouldn't hurt to know who had it copied."

"You betcha," I said.

"Gimme the phone."

I pulled it out of the cradle and handed it back. She was leaning over the front seat since the cord wasn't all that long.

As she called Sam, Bradley said, "I find a lot of material for Greek tragedy with Fabrisio and his mother both competing for the same woman's affections. Especially given Mom's history as a short-tempered egocentric ex-knife juggler from Lesbos."

"It's a wonder he's still alive," I agreed. "But of course she might not of seen the tape."

Then Francie's call went through and she talked to Sam, who read her the name and number of the shop made the dupe.

"Sad to say, they'll respond to fake male authority better than fake female authority. I'll dial."

She dialed, got the shop and handed me the phone.

I told the fellow at the other end I was Detective Steve Carella of the 87th Precinct, investigating a homicide and asked his cooperation. He said he was always glad to support his local police so long as it wasn't with a bribe, ha ha, got hold of his records and found the transaction.

"That dupe was made back in August, Officer, signed for by an Arthur Tsu, T-s-u," said the supporting good citizen, invading somebody's privacy.

Then Detective Carella asked did he remember what the guy looked like? And he did. "Oh, sure. He looked like a Chinaman."

I thanked him and told him if he needed a favor to call me at the 87th, and hung up.

"So, now," I said to Bradley and Francie, "it shouldn't

be hard to find out if Arthur Tsu is Gabriella's Arthur, or some other Arthur."

"And I'll put my money on it being Gabriella's Arthur," said Bradley. "Which certainly adds weight to the likelihood that she did see the tape and she is the killer. Just that she chose Teri instead of Fabrisio."

"Sounds right to me," said Francie, taking out another cigarette. I grabbed it and threw it out the window.

"Oh—mind if I smoke?" she said calm and collected.

"I'm sorry, I shouldn't of done that," I said.

"I think the expression is 'fucking A.' "

"But what is this crap with smoking like it's going back in style?" put in Bradley.

"I believe the technical term is oral gratification, and you can thank me for passing up an obvious straight line."

"You ought to be able to get that just talking," I said.

By which time we were at the Smoke House where she'd left her car.

"One other thing," I said, as she got out. And lit another cigarette, burning me.

Bradley put a hand on my arm. "She can't help it, she's a Leo," he said. She kept this up, I wouldn't care she was Frederick the Great, I was going to belt her one.

"You were saying?" she asked, legs apart, fists on hips, about as unthreatening as Madonna.

Not my table.

"Don't lose sight of Harry K. I still want the book on him. Even it turns out Gabriella's our killer, we'll need all the information we can get to prove it. And he fits somewhere."

"He might even be the orgy master of ceremonies," said Bradley.

We were coming down Cahuenga, passing the Hollywood Bowl, evening rush hour traffic beginning to build up. It was getting too late to go back to the office, so the plan was he'd drop me off to pick up my car and we'd call it a day.

Just to be on the safe side, Bradley called in to check our messages at the office. Buzz Baxter wanted to talk to me. Maybe something to do with Ellard's going to see him. Could wait. And Councilman Jeffrey Hong wanted to know would we both be interested joining him for a drink around ten-thirty at the Roxbury.

"That's that place where the Imperial Gardens used to be," I said.

"Yes," agreed Bradley. "Very trendy now. All the young Hollywood hot and heavies. Or hot and skinnys, mostly."

"Sounds like I'd love it."

"What do you think he wants?"

"What does any politician want? Love, money, and your vote. And in this case, our endorsement."

"Right, he did mention something about that," said Bradley, pulling into the parking lot. "Well, since I don't seem to have anything else on for tonight" (a touch of bitterness), "shall we give it a whirl?"

I figured it wasn't a good time to tell him I didn't do "whirl."

"All right," I said. "But just one fast drink."

"That'll be the day," he said. Go be nice to some people.

The first thing got my eye, the valet parking had a sign, five dollars. Which you paid in advance. So you could still give them a tip, yet, later. Not a good beginning.

The noise was as bad as Olive, decor no better. In fact, amazingly ordinary. And if anything the patrons were even more unruly. Not that I expected any members of the younger generation to be ruly these days. What I didn't understand was with all the din how they communicated with each other. But I suppose you get used to it if you're brought up listening to screaming Rolling Stones. Check that. To this crowd it's "*Papa* Was a Rolling Stone." And by now Papa has a *kidney* stone.

"He's over there," Bradley screamed in my ear, pointing. I started bulling my way through the crowd, along the way bumping into a girl looked to be about twelve years old dressed in a pair of handkerchiefs and a tattoo.

"Yo," she said. "Watch it."

"Yo," I said. "Sorry."

Which got me a look. "You're a big one, aren't you? What, a new bouncer?"

"Truant officer," I said.

"Sexual fucking harassment!" she said, fairly loud. Which nobody could hear anyway.

"Cute," I said. "Can we pass?"

"For what?"

Now I knew why it was so noisy—to keep conversations like this down to a minimum.

I smiled. "Don't make me pull my gat," I said. And she went for playful instead of surly.

"Oh, scary."

"So they tell me. OK we get by?"

And she stepped back and waved us through.

"What was that all about?" said Bradley.

"It was either foreplay or a fight. I'm new in this country."

And we finally got to the councilman's table. He had his aide, Mei Ling, with him and a blond bimbette who also looked about nine years old.

"Mr. Hong."

"Ah," he said, rising. "Mr. Goodman and Mr. Bradley. Thank you for coming." And he offered a left-handed shake, since his right was still in the sling. "Sit down, please."

As there was only one empty chair, Mei Ling took her cue and got up.

"I'll be at the bar," she said.

"Please, don't let us chase you away," said Bradley.

"It's all right. I'm only a beard anyway."

"And a beautiful one at that," I said. "Mr. Hong must have some sex life if you're his alibi."

"Why Mr. Goodman, you old flirt," she said, heading off for the bar. The "old" managed to kill the fun and detumesce me in a hurry. I was more and more getting the feeling what they meant by golden years was rust.

We all sat. (Some of us with a sigh.)

I didn't catch the girl with Hong's name. It was a Tiffany or a Tracy, one of those.

I guess my expression showed I was surprised he'd be seen in public with a girl like that.

"Just mixing with my constituents, responding to their needs and wants."

"I need a blow, and I want to get out of here," said Tiffany/Tracy, getting up.

"The potential for political embarrassment is everywhere," said Hong. "I'm sure I haven't the slightest idea what you mean, young lady, but thank you for sharing your concerns and desires."

"So whatta you mean?"

"See you later, dear. Go play with your friends."

Before she could decide whether it was an insult or not her attention span hit overload and she just wandered off.

"Mrs. Hong doesn't care for these political mixers, Councilman?" said Bradley.

"Exactly so. She's sort of a homebody. Keeps to the old traditions."

"Oh, was she born abroad?"

He nodded. "San Francisco."

Clearly the man didn't believe in keeping a low profile. Maybe following the recent elections the new politics were going to be less "family" and more hip young swinger. Not that I ever thought showing a little sexual fire was such a bad thing in a leader. I always felt the Republicans had a tough act to sell of being fearless and tough and taking no shit from America's enemies, the same time denying they ever got a hard-on.

Still, it didn't look too good if they were teeny-boffers.

The waiter came with a Sterling vodka and Perrier for me and a Bombay gin and tonic for Bradley. Since we hadn't ordered, I had to assume the fine hand of Mei Ling figured in there somewhere.

"Now, then, gentlemen," said Mr. Hong after we thanked him for the drinks. "Have you given some thought to climbing on the bandwagon?"

"I wouldn't mind climbing on something," I said, man to man, pointing my head in the direction of Tiffany/Tracy.

"Is this going to be jock-talk?" said Bradley.

"No, no," assured Hong. "I'm sure you're aware of

my representation in your district," he said to Bradley.
(Hint, hint, I'm gay-okay.) "To each his own."

"And God bless the child that's getting it," I threw in.

"I really would like to have you both aboard," said
our host. "I feel we've at least something in common,
having survived an attack on our lives. And your remarkable courage, Ray" (he remembered I didn't like Rayford), "is, of course, arguably responsible for my being
able to run at all."

I gave a modest little shrug. I didn't say it's no more
than anybody would do, given nobody else had till
after me.

"We are all agog with admiration," said Bradley, making maybe a little *too* light of the occasion. "I wonder,"
he went on, "before we climb aboard and hop on the
bandwagon and march to your music, if we mightn't ask
you a question or two."

"Well, sure," said the councilman. "My life's an
open book."

I doubted that all to hell.

"We're, as you may or may not know, planning to
write a book on the life and death of Teri Dart," continued Bradley.

"That poor unfortunate neighbor of yours, Ray."

I nodded.

"And we're doing a lot of research, looking into people she knew and people she had contact with."

"Yes?"

"And one of the things—you didn't by any chance
know her?"

"I? No."

"One of the things that comes up in our research a
great deal is her involvement, together with many of her
friends, in the Sunset Center Supermall deal."

"Yes. You have enough to drink?"

"We're fine," I said.

He nodded, smiled, and turned his attention back to
Bradley.

"Now we know you were somewhat or maybe consid-
erably influential in guiding that project through the City
Council of West Hollywood."

"For which I take great pride. It will generate a great deal of revenue at a time when our facilities are strained to the maximum. With an infusion of new and substantial tax money, we'll be able to care for our homeless, provide improved services, possibly even endow a hospice for those stricken with AIDS. A very very important project for the city."

"Yes, but one which nevertheless had to get an awful lot of variances. Height, size, square footage. All outside of established limits. Plus an environmental-impact assessment had to be overcome ..."

"I understand we're talking about upwards of eight thousand more cars a day near Sunset Plaza," said Goodman.

"To say nothing of the gridlock during the years it will take to build, and the inconvenience, dirt, noise, and pollution for the neighborhood."

"Don't I know it," he said. "I started out as a construction worker. It's the age-old problem, how to make the omelet without breaking the eggs. Nobody's ever figured a way to do it."

"The lesser evil."

"Exactly. And now that I've answered your questions ..."

"Well, not total," I said. "Since we all agree the whole thing couldn't of happened without your influence and drive and whatnot ..."

"Well, I'm not *solely* responsible."

"But a lot. My question, since the thing is mostly backed by the Allegretto Fund, the Sugarman money that laid offshore in the BCCI since the U.S. Pictures deal ..."

"Now you're getting into areas and details that don't concern me," protested Hong, not too thrilled with the way the wind was blowing.

"Well, but kind of, don't they, really?" I said.

"What we'd sort of like to know," Bradley took the pass and dribbled downcourt, "just as a vague starting point: how big a campaign contribution did you receive from the various Allegretto PACs?"

"Wow, you guys don't pussyfoot around."

"We can, of course, find out, at least those that are a matter of public record. But we'd hate to plow through the layers and evasions . . ."

"Wait a minute."

"Which we are capable of doing."

And that sat there for maybe ten or fifteen seconds.

"OK, you want straight talk?"

I looked away from Bradley. This was no time for a joke.

We both nodded.

"In all its forms, PACs, et cetera, it runs about a hundred and fifty thousand dollars."

"Thank you for your candor," said Bradley.

"You mean thank you for your honesty," corrected Hong.

"Well, we don't know that yet, do we?" said Bradley, rising.

I rose, too.

"Am I going to get an answer? About the endorsement?" said Hong.

"We'll be in touch," said Bradley.

I leaned in. "Thanks for the drinks," I said, patting him on the shoulder.

He winced. And it was his good shoulder.

I guess he didn't like being touched.

Or maybe found out.

# 28

## Mark Bradley

Since we'd come in my car I was able to tip the valet parking attendant despite Goodman's argument "on principle" that we were being not only over but double-overcharged. Which contention wasn't without merit, but I've always found it easier to tilt at windmills when you didn't have a vested interest in the outcome.

Since he'd left his car back at the office parking lot, only a few blocks west, I had merely to endure his fiscal wrath for a relatively short time (albeit the relativity of a minute sitting on a hot stove that equals $mc^2$) before blessed relief would be mine.

Meanwhile, though, I did divert him with considerations of our livelihood instead.

"So what do you make of all that?" I said, referring to our meeting with Hong.

"I get the feeling he's a very ambitious man who'll probably wind up mayor next time."

"I mean in terms of our case."

"In terms of our case it's clear he's smack in the middle of the Sunset Center business, maybe being paid off even more than he lets on."

"Well, our case isn't actually the Sunset Supermall, after all, it's the death of Teri, centrally, and Fisher and Kiskessler and Singleton peripherally."

"Yeah, but the mall deal's a definite big part. It can't be any coincidence everybody that's a possible for murderer has a stake in the thing."

"Everybody we know, you mean."

"True, could be somebody outside we don't know about. But my instinct tells me no, we've already met the killer. One of those, whatever, dozen people."

"Wonderful. That really narrows it down." I hated when he did that, but he always liked a broad playing field.

"I'll grant you some're less likely. I don't think Harry Sanford did it, for one. Though he's still possible. That big knife."

"See?"

"Well, more in the sense he humped Teri once in a while. Over the years. Possible he had deeper feelings."

"Oh, Jesus."

"OK, OK, I'll give you one—I don't think his partner Sid Bright is much of a suspect."

"Great, I can cross him out."

"I wouldn't go that far."

"But if you're going to keep everybody active who knew her you're going to have a very long list."

"I'm not keeping everybody active. Just the ones we know. I told you, it's one of the people we've already met."

I couldn't argue with the man. He'd been in this business a lot longer than I.

"If it means anything to you," he said as I turned into the parking lot behind our building, "I feel we're making nice progress."

"And you're confident we'll solve it?"

"Absolutely."

"And you've never had a case where you didn't solve it?"

"Oh, lots. But I always *believe.*"

I pulled up beside his car and stopped. He opened the door.

"There's nobody else we can eliminate?" I asked.

He pondered a moment.

"I'm pretty sure *you*'re clean," he said. Then turned and walked to his car, and, with a no-look-back finger wave, bade me good night.

The feeling was mutual. I didn't think he was guilty, either. Three down, possibly four, and a dozen or so to go.


It was very quiet in my apartment. It was also very neat, being Thursday. Thursdays what my mother referred to as "the girl" came to clean. Since "the girl" was in her sixties, I had a momentary pang that she'd be retiring one of these days and I'd have to start all over again with someone else.

And then I recognized my potential pique for what it was. I'd become "set in my ways," beginning to emulate one of those "bachelors" of another era—the uncles everybody used to have that no one ever thought were gay, just that they never went out on dates ("Funny he never married").

Sometimes they lived with sisters who also never married, instead dutifully keeping house for them. And/or a surviving mother. My God, was that whole world just a repressed sexual cesspool that'd never been uncloseted?

Count on it.

At any rate, Thursdays were often a little walking on eggsy as my "girl" was of that generation, too, that absolutely refused to acknowledge there was another way to go. As far as she was concerned, and no matter what I said, I was a bachelor, and after seven years she was still demanding to know "when you goin' meet some nice young lady?"

So be it. I couldn't change the world. I was as honest as they let me be as often as I could.

Well, tomorrow morning was Friday, anyway. And nobody'd be there—not maid, or nice young lady. Or nice young man. Sigh.

I got undressed, took a hot shower—I didn't want to be braced, I wanted to be soothed—and was just into my pajamas when the doorbell rang.

Who was going to be petitioning to save the earth at this hour?

I crossed wearily to the door, looked through the peephole. Christopher was lounging against the far wall, legs crossed at the ankles, a bottle of champagne under his arm, and a bouquet of flowers casually over his shoulder. I opened the door.

"Pardon me," he said. "Does Ginger Rogers live here?"

\*     \*     \*

The way Christopher explained it over breakfast actually made sense and was the essence of reason.

"We don't know each other that well. It's not that I'm afraid of commitment, I want commitment. But what value could it have if it was made without due consideration and without being a balanced judgment?"

"So what you're saying is you'd like to test the waters about another hundred times first."

"Wouldn't hurt."

"While simultaneously testing other rivers, other seas? Sounds like a Truman Capote title."

"To a limited extent; I'm not crazy."

"This is just the reason I broke up last time," I told him.

"But the difference here is we aren't together to be broken up. Yet."

"I have to think about it."

"Now. You didn't have to think about it last night."

"There's a simple explanation for that."

"Yes?"

"I'm a tramp."

So the relationship was on hold, with occasional busy signals, coupled with the calls that went through, to belabor a metaphor.

"By the way," Christopher continued, or discontinued, "you got me interested in that Sunset Center deal and the word around the realty world is that while the main backer is Allegretto and the U.S. Pictures residual money, a sizable piece, as much as one-third, came from the Wrangler person."

"How do they know these things?"

"How do they know Larry Fortensky plays this-little-piggy with Elizabeth Taylor's toes? 'Insiders report.' "

"OK."

"Plus, matter of record, some of the smaller parcels that had to be bought up were done in tandem through an entity called Allewrang, if you can believe that."

"Why wouldn't I believe it?"

"I mean the name. So it appears, in the murky world of the superdeal, to get to the bottom of these Machiavellian machinations one must cherchez le cowpoke."

And then, in a serious breach of chicdom, he dumped three spoonfuls of sugar into his coffee.

Francine had called in and left word she'd be late, she had to go to the doctor first.

Goodman never got there much before it was time to go to lunch, so I had a good couple of hours to myself in which to begin plotting an outline for the book.

Since I'd begun working with Goodman this had gotten harder and harder. Before, when I was ghosting celebrity autobiographies, the history, or faux history, was established and it was merely an organizational chore to decide the order in which to relate it. But when you were dealing with murders, especially unsolved ones, you could hardly know what to concentrate on, how to emphasize the parts that led up to the climax before you knew the denouement. So, until the actual story unfolded, a plan for relating it was extraordinarily difficult.

Which was what I told myself in any event as I more or less put off doing any writing.

Instead I made an outline of research still necessary. We would have to investigate the Harry Kakonis connection with Teri and with the others.

We would have to look further into the doings of Wrangler Morangis. Plus those of Marshal Hildebrandt. (For Francine as well as whatever possible connection he had to our project.) And see if he and Wrangler were more than casual acquaintances.

With a final determination on the Taxi Man, Charles Bolton.

And Li Ah Fischer.

And much more likely, Fabrisio Sugarman.

I made a file on each of the above, and listed all we knew about each in general terms. That didn't do any good, but it gave me the feeling of working and allowed me not to write.

At ten forty-five a cloud of smoke came in, followed by Francine.

"Not in here, not in here," I admonished. "You smoke, you do it in your own office."

"This from the Count of Cannabis?"

"At least I don't exhale on people. And anyway, I hardly ever do that anymore, either."

"Because you're getting to be an old fumph."

"No, because I want to *get* to be an old fumph."

"Well, shit, shit, shit!" she exploded in sudden anger.

"What?"

"Never mind."

"Bad as that."

But she'd evidently decided against confiding. Now. I knew her well enough not to push. Since I wasn't forgoing the knowledge anyway, she'd tell me whatever it was sooner or later. I could wait.

So, instead, I got busy with business, and told her what I wanted of her—run down the identity of Arthur Tsu, and see if she can find out what the share splits are on the Sunset Center Supermall setup.

"OK, I ought to be able to do that."

"Plus what Goodman wanted on Harry Kakonis."

"Right."

"So, all set for now?"

"All set for now."

Could have fooled me.

She looked me in the eye, took another puff of her cigarette and disappeared in a cough of smoke.

And at eleven-ten Goodman waltzed in. Or, more accurately, flat-foot-floogied.

"And how are you, this beautiful morning?" I greeted him cheerily.

"You're mighty chipper."

"It's a nice morning. In the main. The air is only moderately unhealthful for those with respiratory problems, the birds are chirping ..."

"Gagging."

"The sun is shining."

"And you had company last night."

"And I had company last night." I kept forgetting the man's a detective.

"Francie working on those Harry K. files I asked for?"

"Yes, she is." I decided not to say anything indicating

the mood she was in. He'd find out himself soon enough. "But I asked her to check out Arthur Tsu first. And some other information on the mall I happened to come upon last night."

"OK. I didn't get back to Baxter yet, I suppose I ought to give Buzz a buzz. Does this sound like a Broadway revue?"

"Off-Broadway, maybe. Jersey City."

"You got the number he left? Because the one for his company's out of service."

"It's on the slip."

"Wherever I left that."

I found a listing in the working data base Francine had already set up.

"You think he might have something?"

"Yeah, could be. He couldn't just be calling me because Ellard dropped by. Let me try it, and you listen in."

He dialed, and after about eight rings, got connected.

"Baxter? Ray Goodman here. You wanted to talk to me?"

"Yeah," said Baxter, I thought rather hesitantly.

"What's up?"

"This is going to cost me, really."

Goodman knew when to wait.

"OK, look," Baxter continued after a moment. "I didn't exactly tell you the truth. This gotta be off the record, just you and me."

"Just you and me," said Goodman, giving me a generation-gap wink (who winks anymore?) as I held onto the extension.

"I told you Teri gave me a tip to get into the deal?"

"Yeah," prompted Goodman dutifully.

"That part was true. The part wasn't, I couldn't raise any money."

Big surprise.

"But I got a little piece, a half point, from Gabriella."

A short beat to take that in. Then Goodman said, really casually, "Oh? And why's that?"

"You gotta promise me."

"I promise, I promise," said Goodman, lying through his teeth.

"For saying we were in a business meeting at my place on Friday the thirtieth—you know, the night of the murder—and because we had too much to drink, she stayed over."

True, from the description I'd got nobody would believe she'd sleep with him.

"So what you're saying ..." Goodman filled in, as required.

"What I'm saying, she wasn't here that night. I don't know where she was. I'm risking my point five percent, but I loved Teri, you know. We were married."

"I know."

"And I can't be part of covering up her murder. Oh, shit, I'm blowing it—I need this money." And he gave a little sob, whether for Teri or the possible lost half point in the Sunset Center I couldn't say. "Remember, man, you promised."

"Look, hey, relax. You did right," said Goodman. "And there's a good chance nobody but me'll ever know." I couldn't meet his eyes this time.

"I loved her," he repeated, slightly slurring.

"She was a good old broad," said Goodman, trying to put a stop to things before they got too maudlin. "Thanks for the call."

"And then Gabby told me yesterday it could all be falling apart and we had a major big problem," Baxter said. And hung up.

I felt pretty sure *he* had a major big problem.

"I'd say we've just about got Gabriella nailed down," I said, as Goodman and I both hung up together.

"Begins to look like," he agreed.

And in another moment, we even added a nail or two as Francine came in with added ammunition.

"Arthur Tsu *is* Gabriella's Man Friday, majordomo, factotum, and aide-de-camp. I don't think he does laundry."

"And he's the one signed for the duplicate tape," I said. "Which means Gabriella did see it. Which, given what Baxter had to say, plus all the other stuff we know, has to make Gabriella our killer."

"She's our man," said Goodman, I thought a bit archly. "And we won't need a whole lot more to be able to prove it, either."

Francine, meanwhile, lit another cigarette (this was really beginning to get on my nerves) and slammed the ashtray down, and kicked a chair, and muttered and generally carried on.

"What's with you?" said Goodman.

"Francine forgot to do her yoga 'Greeting of the sun' this morning."

"Fuck, mother-grabbing bastard."

"You talking to me, by any chance?" said Goodman.

Knowing Francine, she wanted to tell us. It was time for a gentle prompt.

"Francine went to the doctor today," I said.

Goodman knew enough not to say anything. We both just waited attentively for a moment.

"Shitty shit shit shit!"

It was a beginning.

"Son of a bitch gave me the clap. Can you believe this shit?"

"I'm sorry, Jesus." I took her in my arms.

Goodman just looked stricken.

"So, what, did you get a penicillin shot?" I asked, if only to keep Goodman from doing it.

"Yeah, of course. Plus a lecture, yet—on unprotected sex."

"You didn't even tell your doctor?" I asked, still figuring somehow it was better to keep Goodman out of it, more or less.

"No, look. I'm not ashamed, I'm not guilty, I don't for a fucking minute think I contributed to it in any way. I just don't want to be handled, and dealt with, and support-grouped half to death. It's enough of a hassle."

"I know," I said.

"Not really."

"Not really," I agreed.

Then there was quite a long silence.

"So," said Goodman gently.

"So," said Francine. "I thought you might like to know I'm back to going to kill Marshal."

Goodman looked at his shoes.

"And I wondered if you guys would like to help," she added.

# 29

# Rayford Goodman

Oh, boy.

Well, this time I knew she was serious. Francie was a strong lady. Thank God. But that also meant there wasn't going to be any easy talking her out of it. No but-what-about-you, you-want-to-go-to-jail stuff. She'd only say she had to find a way not to get caught. And don't be an asshole, naturally she didn't want to go to jail.

"All right, Francie," I said. "I'll think about it."

"Don't stall me."

"I won't stall you. I'll think about it. And tell you what I decide. Just promise not to do anything meantime 'cause you don't want to do it dumb." (No, asshole, I *want* to do it dumb.)

"That's my technical advisor in matters homicidal," she said to Bradley—instead. "So how about you? You in?"

"Jesus, Francine."

"Hey, I only asked. I can understand if you don't want to; it's not your everyday favor. Though if you could see your way clear I'd be your love slave for a period of time to be negotiated."

"Don't threaten me. Can I think about it, too?"

"Yeah, but only till I get the word from my knight errant, here. I don't really happen to have an enormous amount of faith you'll have the stomach for it."

"Oh, we're going to make a macho deal out of this?"

She took another drag; butted out the damn cigarette.

"Just so you know I'm not kidding," she said.

"We know you're not kidding."

And left the room.

"She's not kidding," said Bradley.

"I got that," I said. "And the truth is she's going to need at least a little input. The last thing we want is for her to get caught."

"The next to last thing. The last thing is for *me* to get caught."

"I don't seem to feel a whole lot of scruples against it."

"Well, I do."

"I don't know if I *could*. Cold blood and everything. But there is something to be said for it. She's entitled to justice."

"There's also a system to obtain it."

"Yeah, well good luck with that."

"If she'd just kept the clothes, and gone for an exam."

"Well, surprise, she was a little upset and wasn't thinking all that clear. Plus like she said, it's a hard prove since she was dating the guy."

"Let me ask you something," said Bradley. "Since we found the knife downstairs from her apartment . . ."

"The Bar None one, Wrangler's."

"Right. And since he, also, in all likelihood was the person you tangled with the night you took her home . . ."

"Was he laying in wait for her, to rape her, too, you want to know?" I said.

"Exactly. Think so?"

"Think so. Especially if it turns out he's best buddies with this Marshal shit, and say Marshal told him about it. We already know he's some kind of sex weird himself."

"Right, so doesn't it follow," said Bradley, "that that's just what Marshal did—tell him to go for it?"

I considered. Now we knew the two men know each other, it certainly would be a strange coincidence for Morangis to decide on his own to pick Francie and be laying in wait.

"I'm beginning to think it's possible I *could* kill the son of a bitch," I said, answering his question.

"So let's say if we did—decide to do this bizarre thing—how would we go about it?" said Bradley, semi-committing.

"Well, not impulsively, for openers. I think we should avoid him for the time being—I wouldn't trust how we'd react. Plus to maintain alibi distance. Let's first nail down where this Wrangler dude fits in. We might want to kill him, too, while we're at it."

He knew I wasn't serious about that.

"The good thing about pursuing that," he said, "it answers the needs of several objectives. We want to know what he intended that night at Francine's."

"And we need to know more where he fits with the Supermall."

"Plus his relationship with Gabriella, and how all that impacted on Teri's murder."

"We know he's the L.L. from Teri's diary, nicknamed Lash La Rue, the kinkajou she had to do numbers on."

"Prompted, aided and abetted by C.B., whoever that is," he wound up.

Which we definitely still had to find out. (Meantime I'd try not to think about the fact we were starting to finish each other's sentences.)

We spent the rest of the morning doing some detail work together. The upside of our closer collaboration, I was glad to see Bradley starting to think of me more as a writing partner and actually asking my opinion how the book should be set up.

"So we could either start with her murder and then flash back to her life, or just do it chronologically. What do you think?"

"Right—either way."

Then for some reason he went back to working alone. So after about forty-five minutes or so I said I thought I would go investigate some more research. And he said he thought that was a good idea.

I didn't actually work. I spent the afternoon running errands.

Most people don't realize, but private investigators have laundry and need to buy toilet paper and cat food and get their lock fixed and put gas in the car and all that stuff just like civilians.

I decided to eat home because I knew if I went to a restaurant I'd have a drink. Or four. And today I decided I wasn't going to drink. Just to prove I could take it or leave it. I spent a lot of energy leaving it. Which told me something I knew but didn't want to dwell on.

So it got to be around twelve-thirty at night and I was in my car, digging a cassette of vintage Ramsey Lewis ("Them Changes"), on the Ventura Freeway on my way to Reseda.

The reason I was on the Ventura Freeway on my way to Reseda was that was where Wrangler Morangis had his ranch. Nobody was rich enough to have one in Bel Air.

It figured, of course, the guy would have a ranch. You didn't expect somebody named Wrangler to live in a penthouse.

The reason I was going so late, I was hoping he'd either be out or asleep.

My map of the stars' homes had the address. Real useful investment, it was like a Yellow Pages for celebrities.

Basically, I wanted to tidy up the loose ends before we took a stab at nailing Gabriella. If Gabriella killed Teri, was it just out of sexual jealousy? Of among others her son Fabrisio? Since she had to know Teri was no hothouse flower—as my mother used to say. So jealousy alone wouldn't explain it—though it could of triggered it.

The likelihood was the motive included another reason. And the best other reason is money. Somehow Teri had become a threat to her business. And where was all the money tied up at the moment? The Supermall. And in that her number one partner was Wrangler Morangis.

If I could find something at Wrangler's that put the money in some danger, and that danger because of Teri, I'd have a stronger motive for the murder.

I knew I was dealing with a very long shot. But I was stuck. I knew, but I couldn't prove. And in my business the proof never came to you, you had to go dig up something.

In this case, the "something" was take a look through Wrangler's files, if I could get in, and see if anything didn't pop out at me.

I figured with Morangis being a freak he'd most likely avoid any on-site live security. To keep down possible blackmail. Or stuff turning up in the *Enquirer.* So after I took out the probable dogs (tranks in ground round) all I'd have to do was cope with the electronic dealies, and I was fairly familiar with that. I'd taken a "course" once with a programmer at one of the major security companies on how to beat most systems—in exchange for proving his wife wasn't guilty of adultery. She was, but it wasn't what he wanted to hear. And she promised to mend her ways—after me. I did turn her down, as a matter of personal integrity—she wasn't that great looking.

The Bar None ranch didn't come with a lot of surprises. There was a forest of log fencing and a couple of half-wrecked buckboards—probably swiped from the studio—and other rusty relics. Some half buried, some just artsy tossed around.

Framing the swinging-gate entry was the Bar None logo, also not breaking any new ground. The most obvious difference from a real 1800s spread was that the whole thing was set back about thirty feet from a high chain link fence and gates with razor wire on top forming a sort of DMZ. It kind of looked like Rancho Rio Checkpoint Charlie.

By the gates was an intercom to the house. Which would have a remote to open the gate. I had a little black box my grateful programmer had given me that would cover it.

First I waited close to half an hour for the tranquilizer-laced hamburger meat to take the work ethic out of the dogs.

Then I punched in my skeleton numbers and watched the gates swing open. I scooted through and reclosed them electronically.

Everything according to plan.

If I was lucky, there'd be nobody home and I could ease myself into the office and just maybe stir up the old paper trail everybody talks about.

Well, I wasn't that kind of lucky. I was the unpredictable kind, where you find someone *is* home. Wrangler. And he had company. Marshal Hildebrandt. Which proved it wasn't just a run-into at the memorial service.

Plus another guest. Li Ah Fischer. Which was an eye-opener—in a way.

I'd lucked out that it was a ranch house with French doors, one of which was open just enough for me to hear pretty good and sneak a peek now and then.

While it might've been more dramatic if Li Ah were stripped naked and tied to a post being beaten, the truth was the three of them were sitting in easy chairs, drinking out of crystal goblets.

Which didn't mean everything was hunky-dory.

"Look," Li Ah was saying. "I could go to Gabriella. Hell, I could even go to the press."

"No, no, little gal, you did the right thing, coming to me," Wrangler was saying.

"I knew my husband was fucking that bimbo, which was bad enough . . ."

"Distressin' as that may be to a woman of your fine sensibilities," Wrangler said. (I knew something of her sensibilities.) "I can't see how that unfortunate marital lapse ties in with us."

"It ties in that Marvin told me we were going to be getting rich pretty soon."

"Well, look at that," said Wrangler, showing an interest. The same time just holding out his glass for Marshal to take and refill without a word. So much for actor-director. Add another hyphen—gofer.

"He even mentioned it was going to be through the Sunset Center Supermall deal."

"Maybe he was going to pony up for some shares."

She shook her head. "I asked. Not that we ever had that kind of money to invest."

"Here you go, Wrang," said Hildebrandt, handing him his drink.

"And what'd he say?" said Wrangler.

"He said someone was going to give us some."

"For the fact?"

"And I figured the someone was you."

"Now why on God's green earth would I do that?"

"Because if there was one thing Marvin knew it was the way around City Hall. It was obvious the fix was in. He knew what it took to override that environmental-impact study, he knew who had to get paid what, and that there was no way the business could possibly be legitimate," she answered.

"And he said I was in charge of seeing to all that?"

"No. That I figured out for myself."

"What else did you figure out?"

"Well, it struck me as quite possible this Kiskessler fellow wasn't acting on his own when he killed Marvin. It struck me he might have been recruited by someone to take care of a Marvin who knew all that stuff."

"And you saw me as doing that? Being *able* to do that?" Wrangler said.

"With your money, and your contacts—you're an honorary member of the FBI, an honorary sheriff, honorary whatever's connected with the law, I know that."

"I'm a great believer in the law."

"I could see you could have the contacts to find out about somebody like Kiskessler. The papers said there were files on him."

"All doggone interesting. Pretty wild, but interesting. But why should I give you anything based on that? Pie-in-the-sky speculation. You do want me to give you something?"

"A small interest. Yes. I think I should have that as compensation for losing my husband."

"But why me, just deep pockets?"

"That and not wanting me to, say, bring these things up—stir the pot. Sort of like a nuisance payment."

At which point Hildebrandt had worked his way behind Li Ah and now grabbed her in a bear hug, lifting her straight out of the chair.

"There're other ways of taking care of a nuisance," said Hildebrandt.

I was figuring I'd have to get into this before a whole lot longer. (I was also starting to think having a portable cellular phone wouldn't of been the worst investment, either.)

"You stupid woman," said old Wrangler. "Didn't it ever enter that pea brain of yourn if you was right I'd most likely have to kill you?"

"There're just so many people you can go around killing," she said, but I thought not quite as ballsy as before. Though ballsy enough for someone in a bear hug.

"Or," said Hildebrandt, "we could at least make her a little sorry—a lot sorry." With which he dropped her to the floor.

"There's that," said Wrangler, moving toward her.

Which is when I decided I'd have to make a move. (The woman had done *me* a favor.)

I flung the French doors all the way open, jumped in, ran straight at Marshal, bouncing him against the wall and on his ass. So far so good.

I turned just in time to anticipate Wrangler trying one of his famous kicks. I was prepared for this; I'd seen it before. I caught the leg, lifted straight up, and put him down hard on his hip.

"Let's go, quick," I said to Li Ah, grabbing for her arm. But Marshal wasn't through. He snatched a poker from the fireplace and took a roundhouse swipe at my head. I ducked under, grabbed it with my left, stepped in, and put all my weight into a short right to the solar plexus. He made a *whoof* sort of noise and then a loud sound like something out of an old Jackie Gleason show as he went down, gasping for breath.

I got hold of Li Ah and dragging her out through the doors, dashed back across the lawn toward the gates.

A glaring bank of lights came on, sirens sounded, and a recorded loudspeaker blared, "Halt! You have intruded on protected property. You have been photographed. Do not move. Do not attempt to escape! Security patrol has you surrounded."

I kept pulling her on.

"They lie," I said, and with a good head start—maybe fifty yards—we got to the gate. I whipped out the little black box and pressed the button.

Zip!

I pressed again.

And again.

And again.

If that fucking little Energizer bunny marched by banging on a drum, he was going to get some kick in the ass—the damn batteries had gone dead!

I turned to face Wrangler and Hildebrandt, coming on like a stampede, the cowboy brandishing a huge handgun. I had thoughtfully left mine at home.

"I was just beginning to wonder what was holding you guys up," I said.

Wrangler just stood there, clutching his hip (at his age they were supposed to break), with the other hand pointing what looked like the sign on a Colt factory at me.

"Kill him, kill the motherfucker!" Marshal wheezed. (Boy, was Francie some bad judge of character.)

"OK, what do we have here?" said Wrangler, ignoring him.

"I think we met—a couple times," I said.

"Yes, I do believe you're right."

"Shoot 'im. He's trespassing," insisted Marshal.

"You don't shoot people 'count of trespassing," said Wrangler.

"That's right," I said. "The man's right."

"You do if they attack you; self-defense," said Marshal.

"Look, look, look," said Wrangler. "I didn't get to be richer'n Gene Autry by being stupid."

He held out his hand. I didn't think it was for shaking, so I gave him the electronic gizmo.

"You heard us say certain threatening things to this little lady," he went on. Then had a second thought. "You don't happen to have a tape, do you?"

"No, I don't have a tape," I said, but Marshal roughly made sure anyway. What happened to trust?

"So you gonna maybe *allege,* your word against ours, we said certain things. On the other hand, I have pictures—you really did get your picture taken—of you illegally on my property, having got there with an illegal device of some kind of electronic type. Seems to me that makes for what in my movies we used to call a Mexican standoff. You don't use nothing against me, I don't use nothing against you. Actually you don't even *have* nothing against me. So I'm being kind of generous."

"That's right, you are. And I appreciate that. So I guess, if there's nothing else, the little lady and I will, as you say in your movies, mosey along."

"You're just going to let him walk?" said Hildebrandt.

"I think it's best under the circumstances."

"So, you want to open the gate, or lend me a battery, or what?"

But the son of a bitch Marshal couldn't let it go at that. He had to come up and blindside me with a vicious punch in the kidneys that'd have me pissing blood for a week.

"Now, I told you not to do that sort of thing, Marshal," said Wrangler. "You can't get good help, these days," he said to me, and shrugged.

I didn't think a smart answer was going to do me a whole lot of good at the moment. Given I was just catching my breath besides. It was enough to know Marshal had just made a career-ending mistake.

Francie, I thought to myself, I decided.

# 30

## Mark Bradley

The three of us were gathered in my office on Saturday morning, one of the only two days a week when they stopped excavating at the Supermall site and the filth, noise, and gridlock abated.

We'd come together in order for Goodman to give us a report on last night's activities involving Marshal, Wrangler, and Li Ah. And elicit our response to it all. Which ranged from my nod to Francine's string of obscenities. Hardly valuable input.

"And Li Ah barely even thanked me," said Goodman. "Definitely not the way I've become accustomed," he added with a surreptitious wink at me.

"I could see why," said Francine, blithely unaware. "As far as she's concerned, you got in the way of her deal."

"I got in the way of her *dead*," Goodman insisted. Maybe.

Another reason we'd assembled was so our crack researcher could relate all she had learned.

Despite everything else on her mind, Francine had done a remarkably thorough job on Harry Kakonis.

Naturally, as head of arguably the biggest studio in Hollywood, there was a lot of print on him, the many many charity drives he'd chaired, the action committees he'd headed, the disputes he'd mediated as unofficial titan emeritus.

Being chairman of the board, his finances vis-à-vis the company were public, to the extent that the law and the SEC required.

The latest report to the stockholders had made note of his continuing confidence in the company as exemplified by extensive stock purchases and exercise of options. His financial stake in the studio—unusual considering his advancing age and impending retirement—had apparently more than doubled over the last eighteen months.

"He must have a lot of confidence in the company to be risking so much additional capital at this late date," I said.

"Not exactly," said Francine. "What I think he was risking was a charge of insider trading."

"Because why?" said Goodman.

"Because his company was considered a prime target for a Japanese takeover."

"So what're you saying, he was loading up on stock, expecting a takeover?"

"Apparently. But since there hadn't been any direct recorded approach it would still be marginally legal."

"I keep hearing past tense—is there going to be a Japanese takeover?"

"Not anymore. That was all before the Nikkei Dow took its dive. But Kakonis had apparently committed—by the ton. Thousands and thousands more shares. And now his stock instead of doubling was in the dumper."

"How do you know all that?" said Goodman.

"It's public record when officers trade in their own company stock. By law."

"Well, all very interesting," I said. "But what does it mean to us?"

"It means in spite of being a very very rich guy, he probably was in serious serious financial trouble."

"How so?"

"It's hard to imagine he just went out and bought a hundred million dollars' worth of stock. So, he had to do one of two things—either borrow the money or buy on margin, which is the same thing, really. The stock goes south and all of a sudden he's minus forty or fifty million."

"I'm going to take your word on this," said Goodman. "Because buying short and selling long and putting your call and all that shit is not exactly my ball of wax."

"Just hold on to the fact he was in a major bind, probably still is. Flashback. When Gabriella made, I'm not sure how many, but the last couple, of her films in Italy, who should be the junior agent assigned to be vice-president of new talent but Harry Kakonis. They 'got on,' as the saying goes. And when Albert Sugarman picked her up to do American pictures she requested and got Harry to be her line producer. They definitely had a thing going."

"How can you know all this?" I asked her. "That's not in any computer."

"Sources, friends, people in the know."

"The old Peter Gunn trick," said Goodman. "The word on the street."

"Are you doubting me?" she challenged.

"Not for a minute," said Goodman, joining me on the stroll over eggs.

"All right, then. Dissolve. Kakonis is now the big gun in Hollywood. He brokers a deal with the Japanese who *are* interested in the U.S. Pictures library, which Gabriella owns—for major money. This—let's say—he plotzes in the BCCI, as far as she knows. But, since there's no talk of big financial distress re his stock, let's take another guess, he uses to cover his margin and his losses."

"Boy, that's a lot of its and buts," I couldn't help noting.

"I could be crazy, this is the way it looks to me. Follow. BCCI collapses; Gabriella wants her money. Since he hasn't got it, he quickly structures another, even bigger deal."

"The Supermall."

"The Supermall. Now he needs some cover money. Wrangler."

"Wait, wait, wait," said Goodman. "What's all this have to do with, say, Teri?"

"Kakonis is Mr. Hollywood. He knows where the bodies are buried, and who buried them. Meaning, he also knows Wrangler's a bit bent. It also follows he knows who to get to take care of odds and ends like that—Teri. How else would you explain his even being near her? She's certainly not in his league. He, personally, is not that kind of guy—anymore. Family values, big in the church."

"They all find God, once they're too old to get it up,"
I couldn't resist noting.

"And just maybe, while he's at it, he also knows about
Gabriella's little eccentricity, too, which Teri can also
handle."

"You're starting to sound like he could be C.B.,"
said Goodman.

"Well, he could, although I don't know what the letters
would stand for. But he's certainly got the clout, the
knowledge of business, and the connections to put it all
together."

"Except," reminded Goodman, "Teri's diary. I sure
don't see him as a love object for her."

"She doesn't say that," I reminded him. "She says she
wants him, she says they'll make a great couple."

"She also says something like really handsome."

" 'Once you think about it'—she qualifies it, 'on second thought.' "

"Wait, wait, wait," said Goodman again. "You're losing me. You got Kakonis dropping a gang of money—
maybe Gabriella's—in his stock. The bank collapses, he
has to cover. To do that he makes a deal to build a
supermall, getting other investors?"

"Right."

"To cover his losses? How?"

"Let me take you by the hand," said Francine. "You
guys don't seem to get it. Even putting together the deal
he'd only get a piece or a fee or something like that.
This is a man who needs a hundred million dollars.
That's what he needs; so that's what he raises."

"I don't understand, either," I said. "You're talking
about the value of the entire project?"

"Uh-huh."

"But," said Goodman, "first it has to be built, then it
has to be leased and successful and rents collected. Even
if it's eventually sold, how can building this huge thing,
which'll take years, bail him out?"

"Because I don't think he ever intended for it to be built."

The new thought, then, was Kakonis had put together
what he considered a doomed venture, to cover the theft

of Gabriella's money. Getting a massive infusion from Wrangler. With odds and ends (a million here, a million there) from other clients and associates. Could this be another *Producers,* that Mel Brooks movie where Zero Mostel got angels to put up more than a hundred percent in the expectation of the show failing and nobody finding out he'd pocketed the extra?

But surely with a real estate venture that didn't go through he'd have to return the capital?

The most likely scenario was that he wanted to use the money during the time it took to find out an environmental-impact study had doomed the project (not realizing his big league associates would shmear their way through that). He probably hoped to recoup his stock losses by getting lucky somewhere else. The classic make-matters-worse house of cards. But that now would fall apart once he had to start paying actual construction bills.

"All well and good. Or bad and not so good," said Goodman. "But let's stick to the facts. While there may be some crooked dealies going on here, or really, monster swindle, what's any of it got to do with murdering Teri?"

"You're right," I agreed. "She couldn't be any major obstacle. Certainly not to Kakonis. He could buy her with one movie job."

"So let's not get sidetracked," said Goodman. "We're concerned with Teri; her life, her times, her murder. And as far as I can see, nothing that happened yesterday and none of the stuff you told me today changes my mind it's Gabriella who's our killer."

"I go along with that," I said.

"Hey, I'm below the line," said Francine. "You guys are the talent."

"So we still agree?" said Goodman. And when we nodded, continued, "Good, because I called Ellard before and told him what we know. And why Gabriella was it. I figured it couldn't hurt to mend a few fences."

"And obey the law," I added.

Which was why, when Ellard called not too long afterward, and said he'd been looking into the valuable tips

that Goodman had given him, and was so appreciative
he wanted to share his gratitude with all of us, we wondered why it was he wanted us to meet him at the Supermall excavation site.

The answer wouldn't be long in coming. The site was
just down the street.

Inasmuch as it wasn't a working day, I didn't expect
there would be much traffic.

Obviously, something was amiss, as there were a couple of police cars and an ambulance. I was surprised we
hadn't heard their arrival from our office.

"Because it wasn't an emergency," explained Ellard,
when we'd connected with him, waiting for our arrival.
That was good, anyway.

We were issued hard hats by some kind of foreman,
or workperson.

"Why do we need hardhats?" asked Goodman.

"It's rules," said the man.

"Yeah, but hats're to keep stuff from falling on your
head. We're going into a hole. Nothing over our head.
Explain me that."

"Rules," said the man.

The universal explanation.

Ellard led the way. And I must say if a person could
walk sarcastically, he was doing it.

"So, where're we going?" I asked.

"Just, come on," said Ellard. "I want to show you
exactly how great a detective this man is. I want you to
see for yourself how much we're all indebted to him."

"Why is it I get the feeling this is not really a tribute?"
said Goodman.

"You ought to just be thankful I didn't take you on
your word and go hog all the credit with my superiors
for having broken the case."

Francine broke the tension by stumbling, momentarily
losing her balance.

"Watch your step," said Ellard.

I didn't point out the futility of people telling you to
watch your step after you'd lost your step. Anyway, I
was busy dodging Francine's hard hat, which had become

dislodged when she stumbled. It fell, after some futile juggling, right on Goodman's toe.

"Ow, God damn it!" he said. "The hard hat. The hard fucking hat. Now we know what it's for. Breaking your damn toe."

"Sorry," said Francine.

"I'm not blaming you," said Goodman unconvincingly. "I don't blame people when they make an innocent mistake."

And we were now at the far end of the excavation, descending about twelve feet on a board ramping down to the bottom.

Ellard got there first and waited patiently by a tarpaulin-covered lump that bore a suspiciously human shape.

"All set, everybody?" said Ellard.

We nodded.

"So now that you've built such a wonderful case and we've caught our killer," added the detective, "would you care to explain this?"

And we all played our parts and waited patiently as he leaned down, took hold of one corner of the canvas and pulled it back—revealing the bloody corpse of Gabriella Allegretto Sugarman.

# 31

## Rayford Goodman

Going good. Take a walk in mud and dust and get stuff in your cuffs. (I like cuffs.) Get a broken toe from a damn hard hat. Have a smug cop lording it over you. Fun day.

"Look at it this way—we've eliminated a suspect," I said.

"Look at it this way," Ellard said, "you're on top of my shit list. I don't want to even cross paths with you, understand? Just stay out of my way."

"Hey, you gotta admit it looked . . ."

"You cost me a lot of points where I work. I even went out of my jurisdiction, courtesy West Hollywood P.D. I'm beginning to think Chief Broward had the right idea."

"The only right idea Chief Broward ever had was leaving before they locked him up for the crook he was."

"Just—stay the fuck away from me."

"OK. This means no problems about withholding evidence or any of that crap, right?"

"Man, will you get out of my face?"

"Hey, come on," said Bradley. "The lieutenant's got work to do."

"To say nothing of us," added Francie, twisting the knife.

So we slogged back out of the hole, my toe throbbing where the damn hard hat clipped it, through the dust and on up to the street.

The foreman or worker or guard collected our tin lids and helped make the day brighter by complaining about the dent in Francine's. (No complaint about the dent in my toe.) That he noticed, but he missed a whole murder, having no doubt kipped out somewhere, which didn't seem to embarrass him a lot.

"Where to now?" said Bradley, moving right along.

"You mean besides back to square one?" I said. "I don't know about you guys, but I got to get out of this dry mouth and into a wet martini."

They exchanged looks. It was too far to go, explaining about Bob Benchley and Dorothy Parker and the Garden of Allah. Or maybe Charles Butterworth, depending. More than a generation gap, there's a wall.

Anyway, I wasn't feeling all that chipper given our case had just collapsed almost completely.

I couldn't help wonder now if I wasn't making a mistake concentrating on Teri's murder on the theory whoever did her did them all. Maybe if I looked for who killed Gabriella?

For which the name Fabrisio loomed large.

"Forget the drink," I said. "Let's go back to work up at the office."

Again a look.

"What, what, you think I have to have a drink whenever something goes wrong?"

"I think you have to have a drink whenever the sun rises, sets, or hides behind a cloud," said Bradley.

"People who sleep in glass beds," said Francie, support from an unexpected quarter.

"She's right," said Bradley. "I apologize. What're we doing fighting with ourselves? OK, we had a setback. What do people do when they have a setback?"

"Pick yourself up, dust yourself off . . ." sang Francie.

"And start all o-ver again!" we finished together.

In Bradley's office he'd put in a large, folding-leg picnic table. And on that was all the printout stuff Francie'd come up with, plus Xeroxes of the diary, plus the snapshots I'd taken at Teri's house.

Just now Bradley was fingering the printouts.

"I don't suppose there's anything here about Gabriella's will, who inherits what?"

"No," said Francie. "Not that I recall."

"We can get it," I said. "Wills are a matter of public

record. Once they're probated. But that won't be a while, since there's a murder."

"Why would that delay it?"

"Well," I explained, "since it's against the law for anyone to profit from a felony, especially murder, they won't be in any hurry to let it go to probate before at least a general idea no suspect's going to cash in."

"But someone will know," said Bradley.

"Oh, sure. It won't be twenty-four hours before Ellard's got a copy and read it."

"Which I'm sure your good friend will be delighted to share with you," added Francie. Like I needed that. What happened to pick yourself up?

"OK, let's just speculate instead," I said. "Fabrisio, Fabrisio, Fabrisio."

"Sure," said Francie. "Though there are other children, in all likelihood he gets a slice of his mother's pie—which we know was huge. Plus, since they shared the same lover—Teri—we have your Greek tragedy thing for an added motive."

"OK," said Bradley, "why don't I give him a call and offer my condolences?"

"And find out where he was between midnight and the wee small hours?"

"Right. Maybe in his grief he won't notice us trying to sit him down in the gas chamber."

It wasn't going to be that easy. (Surprise.) Bradley got the answer machine and left a message saying he'd just heard and how sorry and if there was anything he could do and he'd call back later.

And we were stuck for the time being.

Francie, meanwhile, had been rereading the diary and she reminded us of a loose end.

"When Teri picked up the crumpled note C.B. dropped with his new phone number."

"Yeah, we never found out what the whole number was. Just 2734—but not the prefix."

"No one ever came up with an address book," I said. "It was either destroyed or the killer took it."

"There's also another possibility," she said. "There

might not be one. Teri could have had one of those phones where you program the numbers in."

"But you'd still need to list the code numbers somewhere. 01 equals somebody, 02 somebody else."

"She said in her diary she had a very good memory, from her actress days and learning lines."

"Still, remember everyone you call?"

"Yeah, that is a stretch. Even if you remembered the most frequent calls, there'd still be the Maytag repairman and that kind of stuff. Cancel that."

"Besides, all I remember she just had regular phones."

So we went back to mulling and stewing. Bradley tried Fabrisio again, got the answerphone, hung up without leaving a message.

Francine was going through the photos, seemed to find one she was looking for. "Ah-ha," she said. Then lit a cigarette. Bradley gave me a look. I wasn't about to criticize her.

"You wouldn't by any chance have a key to that house?"

"Teri's? Why would I have a key?"

"Didn't you sort of fuck her or something?"

"Not through the door. And not for a very long time. Way before I met you, love."

"Well, that's not really important."

"It is to me," I said. Why, I don't know. "What're you asking?"

"Can you get in the house?"

"Well, sure. If not the front, I could climb around back. There're twenty-two ways in, between windows and sliding patio doors and doggy doors. Why?"

"I'd like to check it out," she said, putting down a print.

I picked it up, looked at it. Just the end table in Teri's bedroom, with the answerphone, a lamp, fax, and ashtray on it. I didn't get it, but she evidently had some kind of hunch.

"OK," I said. "It's a place to go and a thing to do."

And we started out.

"Oh, one thing else," said Francie. "You got that list

Ellard gave you, calls she made the last couple of months?"

"Yeah, I think it's here somewhere," said Bradley, rummaging around and finding it.

"Take it along," said Francie. Bradley and I exchanged looks. When did we start working for her?

We stopped off first at my place. Francie made a fuss over the Phantom, who surprised me by enduring real patient. In fact, even rubbing up against her leg. (Maybe I could use it for foreplay.) Asta, outside, barked with jealousy.

"You still have that dog?" said Francie.

"Well, I don't *have* him; he hangs around. I sort of feed him. That's about it."

"Can we do this thing, whatever it is?" said Bradley, I guess a combination bored with this domestic scene and losing control.

I went to my desk, opened the bottom drawer where I kept a few tools, took a screwdriver, hammer, pliers, and some masking tape.

"Gee," said Francie, "you mean you don't have one of those heavy tool belts that pull your pants down so the cleavage in your ass shows?"

"It's at the cleaner's," I said. "Let's go."

And we went out my back door, around the garage, and up to Teri's house next door. (Asta meanwhile barking louder when he caught on we weren't gonna play with him. We all live with frustration.)

The front door still had a yellow crime scene tape across it, and they'd added a padlock. Since I was sure they were through looking for clues it must have been to keep out the looters and the morbid. More likely the latter. (They actually have a ghoul tour out here that goes to the sites of celebrity murders. And New Yorkers say we don't have culture.)

We went around the side, that awful steep hill, slipping and sliding. I wasn't doing all that great, either, since my toe still stung where a certain smartass dropped her hard hat. But we finally got around to the back and climbed up to the pool.

"You all right?" said Bradley.

Of course I was all right. What a dopey thing to say, was I all right. And as soon as I caught my breath, I'd tell him. For now I just nodded.

"Why don't we stop a minute and take a breather," he said.

"We—don't—need—to—stop," I said.

"Well maybe *I* do," said Francie. "Some of us are the weaker sex."

Both Bradley and I let that one lay.

"OK, OK," I said after a minute. Maybe two. "Let me try one of these patio doors."

But they weren't only locked, somebody'd put broom handles in the tracks to keep them from being slid open. Windows were locked, too.

"One of you slender teens want to try the doggy door?" I asked. But there was too much evidence of dog around the doggy door and neither one wanted to. So I masking-taped a pane in one of the windows and gave it a little tap with the hammer. Then lifted it out, cleared the shards, unlocked the window, and slid it up. We climbed in.

The place hadn't gotten any less gamey standing empty. For one thing, the electricity'd been turned off. So no air-conditioning or circulation. It was gonna need a real scrub down and face-lift before the real estate folks got to do their thing. Teri hadn't exactly majored in housekeeper to begin with. But now add the trashing murderer, abandoned animal kennel, and cop tracking and it was a real long way from "attractive fixer-upper."

I found myself worrying about what this might do to property values in the neighborhood. (I don't expect the Sharon Tate house was an easy sell.) On the other hand, I wouldn't be bothered with a lot of noise for a while.

Bradley and I just followed Francie as she wandered from room to room. It was interesting getting a fresh look, so neither of us said anything.

Till we were in the kitchen and she had her hand on the refrigerator.

"I wouldn't," said Bradley, the same time I said, "Don't."

The smell was just bearable as it was.

She nodded, catching on. Moved into the dining room, off the kitchen, then turned into the living room. Which like a lot of others didn't get much living in.

"Where's this?" said Francie, holding up the picture with the end table, etc.

"That's in the bedroom," I said.

"Show me."

We did, and she went directly to the table and examined the fax.

"Ah, great, it's got a readout," she said. Then pushed a speed dial number. "Shit. Electricity."

"Right, it's off."

"OK, one of you big strong guys want to unplug this and let's take it back next door."

"That's tampering with evidence," said Bradley, I suppose, to be funny.

"Does that take precedence over stealing?" Francie said, about as much concerned as me.

"I'll get it," I said, leaning down and unplugging both the transformer and the phone line.

"Let me take that," said Bradley. At least not calling me, "sir."

"I got it," I said. "We'll just go through the front door."

"It's got a padlock on it," said Bradley, which I forgot.

"OK, you take it," I said, handing him the machine. "Since my toe's broken."

And we climbed back down from the pool, around the side hill and out to the front. Then down the street, through my garage, and back inside.

Bradley looked around the kitchen. "OK here on the counter?" he said.

"Fine," I said, plugging the transformer in the electric outlet and the modular phone jack into one of my phone jackettes.

"This is one of those faxes, well I guess most, that has a memory system," said Francie. "There are twenty rapid key spots here on the side. You just push the button and whatever number you've programmed in not only gets dialed, but shows up in a readout here on top." And she pushed one and we could see the number.

It didn't ring through because she hadn't picked up the receiver, or put it on speaker. But we could see the number. It was 853-1212.

"That's the time," said Bradley. "The correct time."

And to prove this, she pushed the speaker, then pushed the button. We could hear it dial, then get answered and a recorded voice said, "At the tone, the time will be twelve-twenty-three ... and ten seconds." And there was a tone. We all looked at our watches.

She took out the phone company printout of Teri's bill Ellard had given us, handed it to Bradley, and pushed the second button. The number was for Horton and Converse, Teri's drugstore—and checked out on the list.

Francie went right through all twenty numbers, each one showing up on the display on top. Of the twenty, fifteen were on her bill. We dialed the other five and got nothing special—two were stores, one was a pizza place, one her mechanic, and one an answerphone for a house-cleaning service. (Which I didn't think would get much of a recommendation from us.)

"Another great idea down the tubes," I said, beginning to regret I'd passed on a Bloody Mary for this.

"OK, I guess that's a wrap," said Bradley. "Want to go back to the office, or lunch, or what?"

"Wait," said Francie. "We only dealt with the rapid keys—she might have some speed dial stuff programmed in."

"What's that?" I said.

"After the first twenty numbers are in, you can do another thirty or so on most faxes by number only—21, 22, 23, and so forth. Meaning instead of pushing a designated button for your automatic dial, you push the speed dial button and then whatever number."

We gathered back around the machine and she started with 21, 22, 23, etc., which we were able either to trace on the bill or by calling on my other phone. And then, on 24, we got a screen reference of 273-4881.

It wasn't on Ellard's list. We dialed it and the voice (which I think was the same as the lady gave the time) said we had reached a disconnected number and to consult our directory and be sure we had dialed correctly.

"Why does that number sound familiar?" said Francie. It didn't sound familiar to me. But then I wasn't memorizing any new numbers. I was too busy trying to hold on to the ones I used to know.

"4881?" said Bradley. "Doesn't ring a bell with me, heh heh."

"Don't be cute," said Francie. "That's not the familiar part."

"What, the 273? It's a prefix, not that uncommon," said Bradley. I stayed out of it.

"Do you have a copy of the diary here?" said Francie.

I did, and we went into the living room. She spent two or three minutes leafing through my copy while Bradley and I tried not to be impatient in case she was hot.

"Bingo," Francie finally said, pointing. (She was hot.) "In the diary. It's the number on the piece of paper C.B. drops, 2734. Jesus, we're dumb—we just said it. Not the last four numbers, why not the first four?"

Why not indeed. 273-4881. Now not a working number.

"OK," I said. "I'm up for that." Via my old friend Martina Gonsalves at the phone company. "I think," I added, since I'd stalled her enough times, this time I'd likely have to put out. Martina not being exactly the dream of the universe (as how many cop groupies were?) maybe I could manage one more without compromising my virtue. Of course I could. As this generation says— *not*!

(That's such an improvement over "fat chance"?)

# 32

# Mark Bradley

While a relative tyro at this private-eye stuff, after three other cases with Goodman I was, nevertheless, beginning to develop instincts of my own. I felt that somehow or other we were progressing. And while it seemed, in the vernacular, we didn't have a clue, we *did* have a clue, really—many. Which were adding up, and somehow building to a solution.

Of course that's what Goodman had said just before we all came to the conclusion Gabriella was the villain of the piece. Who still looked guilty on the face of it, but lost a lot of credibility when she got herself murdered.

Nevertheless, if my instincts were improving, we either had enough facts now and weren't perceiving them in a coherent pattern, or we lacked a piece or pieces, which would make the solution apparent. And maybe this phone number would turn out to be that final piece. And, of course, maybe not.

"After I fortify myself with this Bloody Mary, here," Goodman was saying, retreating to the bar, "I guess I'll have to give my old friend at the phone company a shot," evidently thinking along the same lines. "Anybody join me?" he added, with just a touch of a shudder.

We both shook our heads.

"Can't you just call in and do your inspector-wanting-to-speak-to-the-supervisor routine?"

"No, because it's not just an unlisted number, it's a discontinued one. So that's not just push a button on the computer. It's actual work. They'd want a court order or at least delay it for someone else's shift."

"Very cynical of you," I suggested.

"Yeah, right, everybody's just dying to be helpful these days."

The Phantom was rubbing up against Goodman's leg. "No, no," he said. "No drink for you till cocktail hour."

I exchanged a look with Francine. Neither of us wanted to risk the ridicule of taking him seriously. But we weren't absolutely sure he was kidding, either.

"And you?" he asked. "What'll you be doing?"

"I'm a little at loose ends," I said. He gave me a quick look, but as quickly looked away, opting not to provoke me. "I suppose I have to see what I can get out of Fabrisio," I added, this time averting my own eyes.

Goodman finished making his Bloody Mary, took a sip, sighed audibly.

Nobody seemed to want to move.

We were discouraged, I think. While Francine had, of course, come up with the unaccounted-for phone number, I don't think any of us believed in our heart of hearts it was going to wind up being *the* answer. Just the hope it would lead somewhere that led somewhere that ended somewhere. Or maybe we all just needed lunch.

There was a scratching at the back door.

"That would be Asta," said Goodman, hunched over in his at-the-bar mode, unmoving.

"You don't let him in?"

"The Phantom's not crazy about him."

"He could get used to it," suggested Francine.

"He could get killed, too," said Goodman. "Though I understand the dog kills cat thing is mostly dog propaganda. Anyway, I've already been honored by a pet choosing me. I don't think I want a dog, too. Or, either."

"What are you going to do about it?"

"Try to find him a home. Want him?"

"No, I don't want him."

"You?" to Francine.

She shook her head.

"Well, keep it in mind, any your friends."

The scratching changed to whimpering.

"Sooner better than later," Goodman added.

"OK, well I don't think we're going to accomplish anything more here today," I said. "Why don't we just sort of go our separate ways?"

Goodman gave me another of those speculative looks. Resisted. He was getting better at it. (Resisting.) Or more lethargic.

"OK, we'll check later, or tomorrow. Or whenever," he said.

And Francine and I gathered up our things.

"Don't think," she said finally, "just because we're not talking about it I've changed my mind about Marshal."

Goodman and I growled understanding, not wanting to articulate support.

"And since I'm not hearing anything from you stalwarts, I guess I'm going to be doing it on my own."

"'Francine, I really think you ought to seriously reconsider," I began lamely.

"Hey, hey!" she replied sternly, ending that. And she turned to Goodman. "You got something to say?"

"Just it's, uh, the weekend—you don't want to do it on the weekend," he came up with.

"There's a reason?"

"It's, you know, day of rest and all that. Days. Of rest."

She just rolled her eyes, picked up her stuff and stood at the door. Goodman had some sort of silly door that required two hands to open, one of which had to avoid what seemed the obvious knob to turn. No one could open it but Goodman. Who did.

Francine preceded me.

"Well—write if you get work," said Goodman. Which I assumed was some kind of Depression joke.

I went back to my condo. Christopher was away, working, showing residential properties. Weekends were the busiest time for real estate agents. So I wouldn't be seeing him till later.

I sat down at my computer and pulled up the data base I'd been creating and pretty much because I had no place else to start, went back to the beginning. The beginning was the awards show. What information had I entered there?

Descriptions, as I recalled them. Physical premises. Anaheim Hilton. People I'd talked to. The program itself. Speakers. Names of officers on the scene. The assassination. Aftermath. Then, under "references"—the name of the officer taking our statement, the head of hotel security. Nope, nothing.

Which is, of course, when you miss stuff. So I went back, item by item, assassination, aftermath, officer, head of hotel security. And "tape." Which I hadn't noticed before. What was "tape"? What the hell did I mean by that? Tape, tape, tape . . .

I called Goodman. Who was still home, wild guess still at the bar. He told me the bad news was his friend was on duty at the phone company this weekend. I assumed he had his reasons for concluding that was bad news. I asked him what he thought I might have meant by my entry for the awards tape.

"You mean the videotape they were taking of the speeches and everything?"

"Yeah, I guess that's what I do mean. Now that I think of it, there was something to the right of the stage, with a video camera on a tripod. Think there might be something on it?"

"Well, if it didn't get knocked over in the general panic, I'd say there's a good chance there might be. He could of even caught the assassination itself."

"Which of course we also actually saw."

"Right."

"Still, for some reason or other, I have a feeling I'd like to take a look."

"Couldn't hurt; go for it," said Goodman.

"How do I do that?"

"Offhand I'd say unless the local cops were total idiots, they ought to have it. Why don't you check them? I think the guy's name in charge was Billy Baylor. And if not them, maybe L.A., they were the SWAT."

"And I guess, after that, either Lambda or the *Advocate* would, depending on who authorized it. Thanks, I'll look into it."

This kind of detail took some time. I called the Anaheim police where the person who might be authorized to give that sort of information wasn't, of course, on duty. And the one who was didn't find any assistance in the manual concerning the dissemination of material in an ongoing investigation to a simple citizen (a category I wasn't thrilled with). But I was reassured my request would be conveyed to an appropriate command level where a decision might be reached and the outcome conveyed to me if I would try again Monday between the hours . . .

I began to subscribe to the theory that they might be total idiots, at that. With a fair idea Monday wasn't going to bring any great advance in my quest, I tried the *Advocate* meanwhile.

The chap in charge didn't know anything about it but was at least a little more forthcoming. He didn't think if they did have it they'd like to give it out on the premise they weren't looking to help publicize a murder at a mostly gay function.

To be thorough, I gave Lambda a buzz. Fellow named Damon (talk about apt) said he was under the impression someone named Tyler, an amateur, had taken the tape. And yes he had the number. And was I busy later? I thanked him for the number—and his interest—and pleaded an earlier engagement.

My luck held, and Tyler was home. Turned out Tyler was his last name, first name Headley (can you believe it?).

Turned out also he was an avid reader and would-be writer who not only admired writers to the point of adoration (a contention I didn't test) but had actually heard of me, and respected me to death.

He had an especial interest in literature of a gay bent, and annually recorded the Lammy awards. Further he thought it a shame I (we) hadn't won in our category and would be proud and happy to lend me his copy of the tape. I promised him if it proved useful we would mention him in the acknowledgments page of our book and I thought he might expire with happiness.

Which is how, after I sent a messenger service to pick it up, I came to have the tape and review its contents.

\*　　\*　　\*

The phone at Fabrisio Sugarman's still wasn't being answered, but a new message had been recorded saying that Mr. Sugarman and family would be receiving condolence callers at the ancestral manse this Saturday (today) from four to eight.

It didn't say what the address was, presumably to discourage riffraff crashers like me, but I knew from our previous visit.

Goodman, who by the tone of his response evidently had not yet left his bar, was reluctant to join me.

I told him I felt pretty sure it was free drinks and cats.

"Yeah, but they'll probably be wearing a tie. You go on ahead. It might be better for you to try getting a reading from Fabrisio by yourself."

Which I mulled momentarily, testing for objectionability, and found no double entendres.

"And in case you strike out, I can make a separate try another time."

Which also sounded reasonable.

"That way we don't all at once blow our chances."

Six, seven, eight.

"OK," I said, after a beat. "And you?"

"I got a date to see the lovely Martina Gonsalves later."

His contact at the phone company. "Do you know if she's got the number?"

"She says she's got mine. And yeah, she claims to. She better."

"Cheer up, it's just a date."

"Yeah, right. What's that *Tale of Two Cities* thing with Ronald Colman, 'It's a far far better thing I gonna do'?"

"Close."

Huge sigh.

"Is she really that much of a dog?"

"Not really," he said. "Sort of. Just mostly not that much of an inspiration. I'm at the point I need inspiration; just being on a bus doesn't do it anymore."

I had a feeling just being on a bus hadn't done it for about forty years.

"I know what you mean," I said. "Good luck—keep up the good work."

And hung up before we could get any cuter.

And went to see poor bereaved Fabrisio.

Who turned out to be bearing up rather well. A piano player was doing a medley of Cole Porter tunes ("I Get A Kick Out Of You" seemed wildly inappropriate), several waiters dispensed drinks, and a fine spread featuring fish (which I've noted tends to be a staple at wakes, with lox for the hoi polloi and caviar for management). Arthur Tsu appeared to be maitre d', carrying out his duties with characteristic (or stereotypical?) Asian impassivity.

I got to meet another Sugarman, Fabrisio's brother, Lorenzo, but the rest of the family were in other countries and had previous engagements that apparently took priority.

I didn't get the feeling Gabriella was greatly mourned.

I also didn't get to spend much time with Fabrisio, so my impression that he wasn't suffering any great guilt didn't carry much weight.

Harry Kakonis was there. I spent a few minutes with him.

He seemed the most upset at her passing. But wasn't disposed to share his feelings with me in any great detail, which wasn't unreasonable since we were hardly buddies.

I did take the attendance: Buzz Baxter (somewhat of a surprise); Harry Sanford (ditto); Li Ah Fischer, herself demurely bereft (I understood otherwise); Jeffrey Hong, working the crowd with both hands, now that he was out of his sling—with trusty aide Mei Ling; Wrangler Morangis, sans his traditional ten-gallon hat, giving him a strangely naked look, like that of a nearsighted person who's removed his glasses; others probably of the investment group; assorted friends and celebrities; Marshal Hildebrandt, whether an actual member of the inner circle or merely Wrangler's crony (blithely unaware of Francine's plan for his impending demise), toadying up to Morangis and Kakonis. And Charles Bolton, the connection. Antigrief consultant?

On the off chance I could stir something up I calculatedly let slip once or twice my partner and I were on the verge of a solution. The whole exercise seemed largely a waste of my time, but I did learn two things:

Wrangler Morangis, in an animated conversation with a much-publicized deputy commissioner of police and an equally high-profile FBI public relations executive, certainly had substantial law-enforcement contacts (for whatever that was worth).

And second, that Goodman was correct—the gentlemen were wearing ties.

# 33

## Rayford Goodman

What happened was I faced up to my duty. Those in the service had to do what they had to do. And if the uniformed force had to sometimes lay down their life, how bad was it I just had to lay down?

I picked out my jacket—blue blazer. From my three other jackets—blue blazers. This I ensembled with a pair of medium gray pants—opposed to light gray or dark gray—blue oxford shirt, maroon knit tie. Black socks, black loafers.

Oh—new polyester boxer shorts. Do a thing, do it right.

And went to meet Martina Gonsalves.

I'd suggested Hamburger Hamlet; she'd suggested the Belvedere Room at the Peninsula Hotel. I told her last time I was there I found a fly in my vichyssoise.

We settled on the Sunset Marquis on Alta Loma. It was sort of hip, in a lesser rock-band way, as they say, moderately priced, and enough off the beaten path I wouldn't be seen.

Not that Martina was that bad. If you didn't mind twenty or twenty-five pounds overweight. What they call for a blind date "she has nice hair."

Gentleman that I am, I got there first and cozied in at their little bar to the left that sat about two.

I hadn't been sitting more than maybe five minutes when a raven-haired, center-parted (with that half-Gloria Vanderbilt, half-ballerina, half-expensive call-girl look), high-busted, flat-tummied, cute-bunned number tapped me on the shoulder and asked if I'd like to buy a girl a drink.

Is a bear Polish?

It actually took me what seemed about five minutes of instant-arousal silent God-thanking for it to register I was looking at what used to be Martina Gonsalves.

Which I then suavely segued into sputtering and glugging and everything short of spit-takes as she enjoyed the hell out of it, ordered a White Lady direct from the bartender and slid onto the stool next to me.

"Well hi, big guy, what's new with you?" she said.

"Not a damn thing, compared to you. You look absolutely unbelievable; you know that? It's incredible how great you look, it's fantastic, it's I know must be a bore, but what in the world happened?"

"It's not a bore, take my word. You don't think I went through all this not to have it noticed. It started with a bet between two hairdressers."

"Get out."

"Partners. Talking *complete* makeover."

"But the weight . . ."

"Well, naturally it wasn't just cosmetics. It was Golden Door, and private instruction, two-a-day workouts, a nutritionist from Belsen, speech lessons, the whole *Fair Lady.*"

"That must have been some major bet."

"It was, they hate each other—bet the shop. Can you believe it? Hugh took me, one of his regular customers, and Neil took my girlfriend Valencia, who's a pedicurist that works there. Separate judge, before-and-after pictures, the works. Neil promised Valencia a ten percent interest if she won. Hugh promised he'd kill me if I didn't."

"Motivation, motivation—what made America great. I can't get over it, absolutely unbelievable. You're some sight for sore eyes."

"Sore, bloodshot eyes," she said, looking into them.

"I've had a lot on my mind."

"And your tummy, too, I see," she said, patting me there. I suppose a certain amount of attitude was to be expected.

"I didn't have anybody betting on me. Well, well—that is something. Want to finish your drink here or should we go sit down?"

"Let's sit down."

We got up, pushing back our bar stools. I started to take our drinks.

"I'll bring them, sir," said the bartender. Which reminded me, so I left him a five. I debated whether I should lay down five singles so Martina could see for sure, or a fiver, which was neater, but she might possibly think was a one. And decided on the five singles. By which time she was already crossing the lobby to the dining room and didn't give a rat fuck. So I picked three back up. A deuce was certainly plenty for just one drink apiece.

We settled into a booth in the nearly empty dining room. It was always mostly empty. The rockers who smoked grass and got the munchies ordered room service, and those full of coke weren't hungry. Actually, they didn't encourage a dining crowd. They went more for exclusive. Now I was sorry nobody was going to see me with such a knockout.

"Martina, Martina, I just can't get over it," I said.

"You make it sound like I was some dog before."

"No, no, you were always a great-looking girl."

"Then how come I never got to spend any time with you?"

"I was married," I said indignantly.

"Yeah?" I guess the makeover was mainly on the outside.

"The point is we're here, now," I said, ordering us another drink and calling for the menu.

The drink came. We ordered. The food came.

It went very nice. It seemed to me I'd been a little too quick in my judgment, she *was* nicer, more entertaining, wittier. Girls with great bodies do seem wittier, I've noticed.

And we drank some more and ate some more and had a great time.

"I managed to get that information for you," she said when we finally finished and she was wiping her cute mouth with the napkin. (I'd almost forgot there was an ulterior motive behind all this.)

"Oh, yeah, good. I really appreciate it, Marti."

She passed me a note, folded.

"But that's only a small part of why we're here," I said gallantly, putting the note in my pocket without even reading it.

She smiled, wet her lips. I took her hand in mine.

"I want this to be a night to remember," I said.

"It is."

"Well, more, even," I said.

"It's the night that we stopped seeing each other," she said.

"Well, we haven't exactly been *seeing* all that much."

"Right. But the point is, after all these years of being a cop groupie . . ."

"I never really was a cop," I pointed out.

"Whatever. After all the making over I had a little therapy, too."

"Amazing."

"And I discovered my—hanging out with cops was just a symptom. Of insecurity. I didn't have to fuck guys, just to be somebody. I am somebody."

"You certainly are."

"So what I do now . . ."

"Yeah?"

"I don't fuck anybody."

And she wet her lips again. Why I can't imagine.

"Let me ask you something," I said after a while. "Don't you think you ought to get a second opinion?"

She never did answer. Just promised we'd still be friends and I wouldn't have to feel pressured in the future.

I thought it over, and finally decided one thing. As long as she didn't fuck guys, and stayed independent, she might hang on to her job at the phone company. So it wasn't really bad, in terms of I still had the contact.

Only I didn't feel happy about it.

Now it was later, after I'd taken her home and had the good sense not to press. If I hadn't paid her enough attention when she could have used it, why would she want it now she didn't? There aren't many losses you can make back by doubling up.

It was that ten after eleven time when if you went home it was too early and if you went out you were committed to making a night of it. On the other hand, it was Saturday night. And even if you're self-employed Saturday night is not Tuesday.

The bar at Nicky Blair's was more packed than a Detroit unemployment office. And the service was just about as fast. But there was a whole lot better to look at. The girls were so gorgeous you could cast a beer commercial. Or fall in love.

I had a drink while I decided which. Right.

I wasn't about to pick up somebody. First of all, there was the whole health thing to worry about. Second was in this crowd of the young and the hunky I couldn't get arrested.

You know you've reached September when you start wondering whether going out is worth putting your shoes on for.

Fourteen guys wanted my spot at the bar so I finished my drink, went to the bathroom.

I decided to check my calls in case Martina had a late attack of nostalgia. Instead I got a cute message.

"This is a friend," said a heavily disguised voice. First lie. "I know who killed Teri Dart and have the proof. It will cost you five thousand. I left a sample with instructions how to get the money to me where they found Gabriella Allegretto. You have till one A.M."

Oh, wonderful. Hollywood. Boy, does that need a rewrite. How about, "Meet me at the waterfront at midnight. Come alone."

I called the BHPD, on the chance Ellard might be on duty. He wasn't, and I knew better than to leave that kind of message. Especially now we weren't on the best of terms.

I called Bradley. He wasn't home. I left a message on his answerphone of the message on my answerphone. I told him not to worry, I wasn't going.

I fought my way back to the bar, had another drink.

Checked the action on my right. Thought seriously about making a run at the home-wrecker on my left when she backed her ass into my lap. Changed my mind when she apologized. With a "sir," yet. I called it a night.

I went outside, ransomed my car, headed toward Sunset Plaza Drive and the left turn.

My car didn't make the turn. It kept going. On to the site where they were digging the hole to put the Sunset Center in. It parked. All right, I did. Waited for the night guard to come and complain. The night guard didn't come.

I smoked the one cigarette I always carried in case of emergency. This wasn't an emergency. So I lied to myself. I started the engine. This was too stupid. Nobody in their right mind was going to go for this. I turned off the engine.

There wouldn't be anything there. Or anybody. Not even the guard. He'd be kipping out in some cozy nest he fixed himself. Like the other guy did.

There didn't look like any entry from the Sunset Boulevard side. Board fence. And on the side street, there was a similar solid wood fence, except for the driveway the heavy equipment used. That had a chain link gate across it, with a padlock. Locked. But the gate wasn't very high. Anybody could climb it.

I leaned up against the gate. It was simple enough. Either there was a homicidal maniac waiting down there to kill me. In which case I'd be some kind of stupid to go. Or it was a dopey hoax. In which case I'd be stupid to go.

There are times when I lose respect for myself. I climbed the damn fence. My theory was, now that I'd read Martina's note and had a pretty sure idea of the guilty party, I still needed proof. And if that certain party somehow knew I was wise and tried to kill me and I kept it from happening I would at least know for sure.

Another theory was I was fairly drunk by now.

Climbing a chain-link fence makes a certain amount of noise. Especially when you're not your most deft. On the other hand, since I'd been invited, the element of surprise never figured very high.

It was dark. Wouldn't you know.

Still no guard. But no guard body, either. So the jury was out on that. I dropped down on the other side. In.

I'd expected it to be deathly quiet, to coin a phrase. But actually once inside some kind of strange situation happened that all the traffic noises seemed to funnel down into the excavation. It sounded pretty much like you were out in the street. More, maybe. Definitely more than outside the fence. Which took away from defending yourself a little. It wasn't going to be easy hearing someone creep up on you.

On the other hand, it wasn't *as* dark as you'd think, once you were in. That sometimes happened in L.A. The smog or low ceiling over the basin reflected the lights down below and a lot of the time if you were on a hill you could see a definite line of light halfway up the sky. I was able to see enough that I felt pretty sure nobody was in fifty feet of me. Unless maybe behind one of the big pieces of machinery.

I made my way down toward the far end bottom of the hole, found the board that led all the way down. And feeling just a bit of a damn fool, tippy-toed down to the very bottom. Where the body'd been. You couldn't tell now.

There wasn't even a crime-scene tape. Nothing. Just the sudden little puffs of dirt. That clued even a pretty stoned P.I. that he was being shot at.

Make matters worse, there was absolutely no place to hunker down at. I started up the board, but the shots impacted about three feet in front of me, digging up the board itself.

This time I got a glimpse of the flash and put the shooter in the cab of a very big bulldozer. I didn't have a gun with me. I'd really done this right. When you're going to be stupid at least go for consistency.

I took another step; another shot three feet in front.

What it was, someone very good was keeping me pinned down.

OK, I can take a hint. I stopped dead.

Then headlights on the bulldozer came on and the motor turned over and the machine started toward the edge of the pit. That was about when I began thinking the phrase stopped dead took on a whole other meaning. The machine lumbered closer, then the blade dipped, and it began pushing gigantic piles of dirt into the hole. I had to get out.

But the minute I tried the shooting started again. I had to stop. Then the machine pushed another load of dirt down on me. I was being nailed in place till I could be buried alive!

The thought occurred to me that there wasn't all the time in the world. For either of us. If I didn't do something, I'd be buried under tons of earth. On the other hand, with the lights and the noise (even given it hadn't been all that quiet) surely some neighbor was going to complain about them working in the middle of Saturday night.

Then again, if some neighbor didn't complain about chopping up Kitty Genovese, I didn't think I'd better count on that.

The next load put dirt up to my shins. I was barely able to pull my feet out. Minus, of course, one of my good Bally loafers.

Fuck it, I thought, I'd rather be shot than buried. So I just ignored the shots, ran up the board, had to cross practically right under the bulldozer, but that apparently gave me some cover. Maybe the angle was wrong and whoever didn't have a clear field of fire.

I couldn't see who was in the cab, it was the wrong angle for me, too. I just circled around behind the dozer, losing my other loafer along the way—no great loss by this time, unless you were Peg Leg Bates—and made a mad circle dash toward the gate.

There didn't seem to be any shots coming at me from in back. Which surprised the hell out of me.

But I just kept my head down, keeping as low a profile as I could. It wasn't till I was about twenty feet from the gate that I realized there were still shots going off. In the weird echo chamber they seemed to be coming from the wrong direction. Didn't much matter till I looked up and saw the flash of gunfire was coming *at* me. Somehow or other, the son of a bitch had gotten in front of me and I was running right at the gun!

I was a dead man.

I was a shoeless dead man.

And then there was split second when the lights went out and I thought I deserved it for being the biggest asshole ever lived.

# 34

## Mark Bradley

If there was one thing I knew it was that Goodman could handle himself. Make that take care of himself.

And, of course, he had said he wasn't going to walk into what was patently a trap.

On the other hand, he had left me that message. When I couldn't reach him at home I had to consider it might be a cry for help from some little corner of sobriety residual in his vodka-befogged brain. And Christopher hadn't contacted me at all.

(The lady missionary gets carried off into the jungle by a huge, hairy gorilla who ravages her repeatedly. A determined rescue party persists for days till it finally finds and frees her; takes her to the hospital for treatment. Physical wounds healed, she's interviewed by the psychiatrist: "How do you feel about this?" he asks. "How should I feel?" she says. "He doesn't call, he doesn't write . . .")

Christopher wasn't calling and wasn't writing. Just carrying me off into the jungle now and again.

The point being I had nothing *special* to do anyway.

By the time I got there I didn't know who was in the bulldozer, and I didn't really know who was at the bottom of the pit. Though I had a good idea. But I did know it was not a nice thing for whoever was in the bulldozer to be doing. So I fired off a few shots, which I could see spark off the blade of the machine. And after three or four it stopped functioning, and whether whoever was driving stayed inside or exited some other way, I didn't know. I was too busy providing cover fire for the body scampering toward me, which I could see by then was Goodman.

I did call out to him, but he evidently didn't hear me as he ran smack into the iron stanchion supporting the gate and knocked himself out.

As I bent to help him I could see, now that I'd stopped firing, a body leap down from the cab of the bulldozer and head up the hill toward Sunset Boulevard. Evidently there was some sort of an exit up there that wasn't at first readily apparent.

When the figure neared the top there was a sudden enormous burst of sound as a combination claxon/siren exploded, probably a disaster alarm either triggered by the figure's attempt to exit through a wired doorway or perhaps by the guard. In either event, I could see hands go over the ears as the figure actually reeled from the aural assault, which must really have been overwhelming from up that close.

The sound continued, though now modulated to an intermittent pulsation, as I bent to tend to Goodman. Then abruptly ended—producing the cliché deafening silence. I swallowed to clear my ears, and looked back up, but couldn't see anything or anyone.

Goodman regained consciousness but remained disoriented, moaning. I had to make a quick choice, whether to opt for medics and on-site treatment, with which went police and explanations, or get him out of there and find private medical help. Knowing him, I opted for the latter. And, in fact, had managed to half carry half support him and was already in my car and wisely heading south, down to Fountain, as a police car headed down from Sunset and skidded to a stop at the gate I had just left.

I turned left, then right at La Cienega and buzzed down to Beverly Boulevard where I made a right, then a quick left at San Vicente (Hard Rock Cafe still doing wait-in-line business) and into the Cedars-Sinai Emergency Clinic.

An orderly came out and helped me get Goodman inside to the waiting room, and I was beginning to think I'd not only made the wisest choice politically, but also medically. Which was before we'd waited forty-five minutes only to find that "next" meant that was our designation to be interviewed about insurance plans and assurances of credit—medical treatment might be hours yet.

However, a recovery of sorts had been achieved as Goodman regained what passed for his senses and said, "What the fuck are we doing here, let's go!"

And since one of the things we weren't doing was get treatment, I didn't argue.

I took him to my place, which was the closest, got him dosed with a curative vodka on the rocks and listened while he told me his story.

He showed me the folded note Martina had given him with the name of the person who'd had the discontinued phone number.

"But did you see who was in the bulldozer?" I asked.

"No."

"I didn't exactly either," I said, then explained what had transpired while he was unconscious, the person escaping from the bulldozer, the run up the hill, the siren exploding, then my losing track. And as an afterthought, asked, "Did you recognize the voice on your answering machine?"

"No."

"But you're sure you know who did it?"

"Ninety-nine percent."

I shared the belief. The easy part. "But how're we going to prove it?"

Which was when the doorbell rang. Since there'd been no buzzing from the lobby, I assumed it was Christopher, to whom I'd given my spare key. I was wrong.

It was Lieutenant Lewis Ellard.

I must say, I did like Lieutenant Ellard. He didn't pretend to niceties and follow the format. He pushed me aside and marched right past.

"Of course you can come in, Lieutenant," I said. "You're always welcome here."

"What's with the bleeding?" he said to Goodman, immediately spotting the soggy compress, observant detective that he was.

"What's with the questions?" said Goodman, never one to give anything away he didn't have to.

"I tried your house, you weren't there; I took a chance on here," said Ellard.

"Swell."

"Your car has been impounded," he added.

"Oh, shit."

"It was parked in a permit-only area."

"And that's all you have to do on a Saturday night in our crime-filled city, check on illegal parking?"

"An area," Ellard proceeded blithely, "where a guard had been assaulted and an intruder siren had been activated."

"I didn't activate any sirens."

"That's true, Lieutenant, I can vouch for that," I said, implicating myself nicely.

"After which I understand you went to Cedars-Sinai, then ducked out, then apparently came here. Care to tell me what's going down or shall we, as they say, do it downtown—in this case, crosstown?"

"I don't know that it's really any of your ..." Goodman began in that captivating way of his.

"Rayford!" I said (who never call him Rayford, which he hates), "why don't we try to work this out logically and to our mutual advantage?"

"You have a plan?"

"I have a plan. Sort of. Maybe. With a little luck. A lot."

"All right, Philo, shall we get on with it?" said Ellard.

"With your permission," I said with a nod toward Goodman. "I think we're at a point where we might just work things out together that we couldn't independently."

"If you guys have evidence you better just fucking give it to me," said Ellard.

"Lewis, we're negotiating," said Goodman, obviously seeing the advantage to a cooperative approach. "You're going to help us, and we're going to do you a favor."

"Yeah? What favor could you do me?"

"We could let you take credit for the collar, I believe is the expression," I said.

"And who're we gonna collar and how?" said Ellard.

That was the complicated part.

"First, I'm going to tell you what we know."

Which I did.

"And how much of that is evidence?"

And I told him that, too.

"Which is pretty circumstantial."

"True," Goodman agreed.

"I think you're right," said Ellard. "But thinking and proving are two different things."

"That's where trickery comes in."

And I began to tell him the plan I was winging. And Goodman, in the way of all good collaborators, began embellishing and refining as we went along.

"It's sort of like you're pitching a series to the network," said Ellard.

"Not far from it. You're the network, and that's the package," I said.

"Man, if you're wrong," he moaned, "I'm going to be night foot-patrolman on the Fox backlot."

"But if we're right," I countered, "it's miniseries, Joseph Wambaugh time."

"OK, now before we get into the details, I want you to seriously consider—for the *moment* we're not pressing charges on withholding of evidence. *Or* trespassing, *or* conspiracy to commit bodily harm . . ."

"What conspiracy?"

"The guard at the Sunset Center."

"How could I be part of that?" said Goodman.

"Because you were there. Committing all those other breaches of the peace."

"Thin," I ventured.

"Do you doubt I could make both your lives a living hell?"

"Well, if you call that living," said Goodman, his spirits evidently restored. "Come on, stop with the Broward number and the threats—we gonna work together and make you a superstar or not?"

The pause wasn't really all that long. "Just how exactly are we gonna do this?" he asked. "And who do you think would play me?"

To implement the plan we'd worked out it was necessary to assemble all the suspects in one room. To achieve that a crisis had to be manufactured involving the Sunset Center Supermall that would impact on all those with a financial or other interest.

Ellard immediately balked when we told him he had to mislead Harry Kakonis.

When we told him of the huge financial conflict of interest Mr. Kakonis had and documented it with Francine's research, and how it spelled potential ruin for everyone connected with the project, he could see the necessity.

"But we're talking terrible risk!" he said.

"Maybe not just a one-shot, maybe a weekly series," said Goodman.

"I get creative control?"

"Absolutely," I said.

So, utilizing police resources, he got Kakonis's unlisted number. Calling that number and using his official title, he was connected to the main man himself. Whom he told he was tipping off, totally unofficially, as a favor to one who he believed had given so much to the wonderful world of motion pictures and back to the community at large (he was good at this), that an injunction was impending that would halt construction on the project Monday morning, due to the death (false) of a guard on duty there this evening.

An investigation would, in due course, of course follow, but he was confidentially informed that there were certain allegations of misuse and misappropriation of funds in the trust of Mr. Kakonis, through the offices of Fabrisio Sugarman, that the court was anxious to explore. Which could result in a freezing of funds, and accounting thereof. (We knew Kakonis couldn't allow that, he'd "borrowed" enormous sums to finance his disastrous stock purchase.)

What did the lieutenant think Mr. Kakonis should do?

Well, in his position, he thinks he would call a special meeting of all the interested parties tomorrow, say, eleven A.M. at his, Kakonis's house. At which time and place he, the lieutenant, in concert with certain other interested parties, would present a plan of action that could circumvent this prospect.

Mr. Kakonis, not unreasonably, wondered why the two men could not meet *mano a mano,* say in half an hour, and work it out between them? To their mutual financial benefit?

The lieutenant said that wouldn't work because he had to first get to a certain judge and do certain things, and then he'd need the whole board of directors to approve certain actions. It sure sounded tenuous and vague to me, but then I wasn't someone who'd borrowed a hundred million or so of other people's money without their knowing and felt the baying of the hounds on his trail. Evidently that factor proved decisive as Mr. Kakonis agreed to host a Sunday morning meeting at his Bel Air house at eleven A.M.

Ellard hung up. "I'm wrong," he said. "Not the graveyard shift at Fox. If it doesn't work out I'm either a dead man or at least going to jail, forever and ever. But I'm warning you, if it turns out that way, I am not going down alone."

"Now, now, let's not get back into Broward country again," said Goodman.

"It'll work," I said, body-language-herding Ellard to the door. "Believe me, it'll work."

And with a sigh not unreminiscent of anyone who's bet the farm on which shell the pea is under, he was out.

"It will, won't it?" I said to Goodman.

"Think so," he said. "It ought to. And, you know—nothing ventured and all that shit."

# 35

## Rayford Goodman

Sunday morning was not a good time to try to get your car out of the impound. *Never,* was a good time to get your car out of the impound. And this morning we had too much important stuff for me to have to hassle with authorities. Which is why Bradley was driving us to Bel Air in the BMW.

It always killed me anybody could find anybody in Bel Air. You never saw houses, you just saw greenery, which everybody had by the ton, and in there, in the forest, there'd be a castle every now and then, which you could tell when you spotted the gates. Which all looked pretty much like they were built to repel Mongolian hordes, or Visigoths, or Iranian neighbors.

There was, of course, "security" at the gate, with a clipboard. We had star billing, provided by Ellard. Waved on through.

I guess Kakonis hadn't wanted to fuss because there was no valet parking on top of the hill. Just room for a Wal-Mart. We parked and got out. A butler or footman or whatever the hell it was was at the door.

"Mr. Goodman, Mr. Bradley?" he said, clearly in touch with the guy at the bottom of the hill. "This way, please, they're in the screening room."

And we were led to an elevator, directed inside, and a basement button pushed for us. I guess they didn't want to spring for an elevator operator and the greeter had to take care of other greetees.

We went down a long floor and I was surprised to find a screening room had been built in the cellar. It wasn't exactly don't hit your head on the pipes, it had a twelve-foot ceiling, but even so, cellars are pretty rare in California.

Anyway, it looked like it ran the length of the house. Next to the hallway, everything real wood panel, there was a room with a large bar (which did have an attendant) on which they had assorted foods, scrambled eggs, bacon, smoked salmon, bagels, and I suppose a person could get a Bloody Mary if so inclined. I didn't think it was a time to eat or drink.

Also I had a terrible headache that may have had something to do with running into the pole last night, and/or drinking a Saturday night's worth of vodka.

"I wonder, you got a couple of Tylenol?" I asked the flunky on duty.

"Yes, sir. Would you like to wash that down with a spirit of some sort?" he added, I thought a touch of a sneer. Like he knew his customer, or specialized in nose-vein readings.

"Don't be ridiculous, it's eleven o'clock in the morning," I said. "Just give me some water."

Bradley nodded in approval.

I knocked the two Tylenols back and we went through the door into the main screening room. All wood walls again and a lot of nubby wool club chairs and thick glass coffee tables. Plus drapes on the solid walls. For sound, I guess.

Everyone was there. Ellard, of course. And Fabrisio, and his brother Lorenzo, who I hadn't met but Bradley introduced me, Wrangler Morangis and his sidekick the son of a bitch Marshal Hildebrandt, Buzz Baxter, pale and hungover-looking (so what else is new), Li Ah Fischer, out of her widow's weeds and into a skintight catsuit (great), Harry Sanford (who I remembered had a small interest in the project), Arthur Tsu, a surprise entry, left a token taste in Gabriella's will, Charles Bolton, dope connection to the stars, Jeffrey Hong, the celebrity councilman, with his aide, Mei Ling, and of course, our nervous host, Harry Kakonis, who came over to say hello.

"Good morning, gentlemen," he said with a phony

smile and a touch of flop sweat. "Lieutenant Ellard tells me you might be able to help us with our little problem."

"Possible," I said, keeping the edge.

"Well, I'm sure you know we're always appreciative of things done in our behalf," he tacked on, with a trowel.

There was money to be had. Surprise surprise.

Meanwhile Ellard had come over, too.

"See you all got here," he said in a higher than usual voice.

"Not in *my* car," I couldn't help mentioning. "That's neatly being held for ransom by the funny folks in blue."

"Later, huh?" he said. "We have more important things. So, are we all ready? What now?" He was really nervous.

"Well, I suggest we all take our seats," said Bradley. "Then Mr. Goodman and I will have our little say and we'll see what we shall see."

Kakonis gave Ellard a funny look that seemed to say this I don't understand. Ellard gave him a funny little smile back that tried not to say anything.

Fabrisio Sugarman came over. "I'm the chairman of the board here, and I actually run the meetings."

"All right, go for it, Fab," I said.

"But since I don't exactly know what the hell this is all about, the chair waives procedural formalities and recognizes Mr. Goodman and Mr. Bradley, or either. Whatever."

"Thank you," said Bradley. "Everybody cozy?" He was getting to enjoy these things, I could tell.

"I'm somewhat at a loss," said Kakonis—understatement of the year—"how you fellows fit into this . . . problem we're having with the project. I've taken the liberty of informing our participants that we face an injunction on Monday and we're all in agreement that any delay would seriously impair our ability to compete in a narrowing market." Really meaning any investigation would seriously impair his freedom.

"We did kind of notice it's a strange time to build," I said, instead.

"That's a whole other matter," said Kakonis, right away defensive. "Though I would like it on the record that I opposed our going forward at the time." (I would of, too, if I'd stolen all the building money.)

"Somebody taking all this down?" asked Fabrisio.

"Uh, the room is wired," said Kakonis, I guess not having learned much from Richard Nixon. "You'll each be provided with a transcript." (I wondered did you have to send away to Denver and enclose four dollars?)

"Hopefully, that'll become clear before much longer," said Bradley.

"Would you bear with us if we go back over some stuff might not seem to tie in right at first?" I said. Nobody said no.

"Real good," continued Bradley, who occasionally lapsed into Yuppiese. "With your indulgence, then, we'd like to discuss a series of murders that started . . ."

"Wait a minute, wait, wait," said Wrangler. "What in tarnation's all that muck got to do with our business?"

"Because whether you're in tarnation, or anyplace else," I said, "it turns out your business, the building of the mall, the financing, the whole shmear, is all part of the same deal. Or muck, as the case may be."

Which seemed to cause a lot of mumbling.

"You mocking me, boy?" said Wrangler, posing a bit.

"Kinda," I admitted.

"Wait, come on, now," said Ellard. "We're here to help you folks." (Yes and no.) "So, please, hear us out. Just a few minutes of your time. Mr. Bradley, Mr. Goodman?" And he took a deep breath and showed a lot of looking at heaven eye-whites, the way you do when your ass is on the line.

They got quiet.

"There have been a series of murders," Bradley continued. "Which we have substantial reason to believe are tied together and coincidentally are affected by and in part caused by your project. The murder victims are Marvin Fischer, gunned down by William Hobart Kiskessler, an attack that also wounded Councilman Hong, here; Kiskessler, himself, murdered in jail; Teri Dart, with 'loose' ties to many of you; Harvard Lawrence Singleton, an obsessed fan who was at the time of her death stalking

Ms. Dart; and Gabriella Allegretto Sugarman, your colleague and major investor in the project."

Mumble, mumble, mumble.

Kakonis was on his feet. "I fail to see how any of those unfortunate events, with the possible exception of Miss Allegretto, has any bearing on our primary concern here."

"Well, that's what we're trying to tell you," I said. "Now I admit, we, personally, are mostly interested in the murders. But it so happens you solve one, you solve it all."

"Solve one what? What's a murder or murders got to do with an injunction against the Sunset Center Supermall Corporation?"

"Because the injunction is a maybe," said Ellard. "And the murders are a fact."

"Wait a damn minute," said Kakonis. "Then what you're saying is you're here under false pretenses?"

"Yeah, I guess that's what I'm saying," admitted Ellard.

Mumble, mumble, mumble.

"But listen, we *are* here. We do have information. There are ongoing investigations. Give us half an hour of your time—I think it'll be worth your while."

Mumble, mumble, mumble.

"If not," he continued. "Then we get into lawyers and subpoenas, and in-depth corporate probing . . ."

Kakonis, who this wasn't lost on, said, "Listen, all right—the man may be right. We'll give you half an hour. Go."

"OK," I said. "Start with the Lambda Awards thing, Friday night, Memorial Day weekend. Marvin Fischer, the mayor's aide, gunned down by this Kiskessler nut. Now, if it wasn't just some random crazy thing, say *if,* like if somebody put him *up* to it, then why would that somebody want to kill Fischer?"

"His wife, Li Ah Fischer, might," Bradley went on. "She had reasons we know of—Fischer was fooling around with Teri Dart. We know that from mentions in her diary and from Li Ah's own call to Teri, recorded on her answering machine. A direct threat. And a motive for killing both.''

"Listen, if the motive for killing Teri was a jealous wife, there's certainly more than one suspect," said Li Ah.

"I'm sure true," I said. "But you're the one we have on tape." To say nothing, which I wasn't, of her being so awful kind to me when I came visiting.

"So you're suggesting me? You're accusing me?"

"We're examining you. As a candidate. We're equal-opportunity investigators."

"But all right, say I wanted to kill my husband—forgetting for the time being how the hell I would know about or get to hire a maniac like Kiskessler," she said, "and even Teri. But why in the world would I want to kill Gabriella, what's she to me?"

"Because Gabriella, too—we have strong reason to believe—was having a relationship with Teri," said Bradley.

"So? That's no skin off my nose, is it?"

"Well, no. It's more skin off, say, Fabrisio's nose," said Bradley. "Who was also, in the vernacular, enamored of Miss Teri's charms."

"Me? You think I killed my own mother?"

"Not unheard of," said Bradley.

"Over *Teri*?"

"And, say, the enormous amount of money you'd inherit when your mother died," added Ellard, getting into the swing of things.

"No more than Lorenzo, or Marcello," said Fabrisio.

"Ah, but Lorenzo and Marcello weren't in town; weren't involved with Teri; weren't responsible for the money invested in the project."

"Wait, wait, wait," said Fabrisio. "I'm chairman, yeah, but everybody knows it's Harry who actually runs the business."

"Well, I wouldn't say that, exactly, Fabrisio. I have another, larger obligation to the studio, I can't be monitoring the day-to-day operation on an outside investment."

"Nice try," said Fabrisio, who I got the feeling might have suspected the money was funny without knowing what to do about it. "But if there's any money missing, why would I take it? A big part of it was already mine and my family's." Good point. "And what possible thing could I have against Fischer?"

"That would depend on how deeply committed to Teri you were," said Bradley.

"Aw, nonsense," said Fabrisio. "Even if you could make the case I might have wanted to murder Teri and my own mother, how about Kiskessler, and Singleton—you say they're all connected."

"Right, that does give us pause," admitted Bradley, whatever pause was.

"Li Ah brought up a good point, you know," said Kakonis. "How would anybody know about or get to somebody like Kiskessler?"

"Well, the knowing about, it's common for police and people with access to police, like Fischer himself, or the councilman, people in government, or someone with merely good social connections, like Wrangler—all those sorts of people could know. And possibly even have contacts within law enforcement willing to give them information about the whereabouts of such a person," said Ellard. Which would include getting him taken care of, once he was in jail.

"That would leave me out," said Li Ah.

"No, you were the wife of a person who might have that information."

"Me?" said Kakonis, looking for some way to be innocent of something.

"There's hardly any knowing what you might know or whom," said Bradley.

"I think Buzz Baxter deserves a mention," I said, which seemed to startle the man some.

"What, what?" he said.

"Just to get you off the hook, pal," I said.

"What hook?"

"Well, you provided Gabriella with an alibi when she was actually at Teri's, looking for the tapes she knew incriminated her. But your admission of that, plus our in-the-field research tend to exonerate you," said Bradley.

Meaning my take he wasn't together enough to put gas in the car, much less figure out a big conspiracy.

"I don't know what you're talking about," said Kakonis.

"It's all right, he does."

"I do?" said Buzz, proving we were right.

"I do," said Ellard. Adding points.

Harry Sanford wasn't saying anything. He hadn't been remotely accused of anything and was only here so far to protect his interest in the Sunset Center. Being a victim himself, Jeffrey Hong didn't have to defend himself, either.

Arthur Tsu kept quiet. He wasn't the sort to volunteer any information anyway. I decided to rattle his cage a little.

"Speaking of Gabriella's tapes, Mr. Tsu, it was you had the duplicate made, which we assumed was for her. But it's possible could of been for someone else."

"I not know what you talkin' about," said Tsu, suddenly Hollywood Asian. And went back to heavy inscrutness.

Charles Bolton, Taxi Man, also mum, deserved a mention.

"Just for our own information, Charlie," I said. "Why are you here?"

"Me? I'm a part-owner, too."

"Really? How so?"

"It's kind of complicated. Teri owed me some money for—whatever, purchases. It was understood I'd get a payback out of this."

I looked at Kakonis. He shrugged, but didn't deny it. Covering for actors and their dope was nothing new to him.

"So, in a way, you had a motive of sorts," said Bradley.

"Give me a break. Teri, long shot maybe. But Fischer? The other two guys, I don't even know their names? And Gabriella? Long way to go."

It was a long way to go.

"Why don't we quit the bullshitting," said Kakonis, a way I'd never heard him talk. "Let's deal with the principals. Who do you think and why?"

"Well, very little doubt you have the best motive of all," said Bradley. "The financial aspects, which I don't think we have to go into at this time. But as a given, the last thing you wanted was for this project to go forward." When the fact of the money he'd stolen would be discovered, before he had a fighting chance to replace it. And that Gabriella, for one, *had* found out. Or that's a good guess from her telling Baxter more or less that the shit had hit the fan.

"I really must protest . . ." he began.

"I wouldn't," said Ellard, which made him think a moment. His partners didn't know the details yet.

"Everybody else wanted the project to go forward," continued Bradley. "Teri, by way of her protector, the mysterious and elusive C.B., promised a share, certainly did. Gabriella, she'd invested the largest part of her estate. Even if it was a bad time and a likely money-loser, it was also a money launderer of all those U.S. Pictures residuals. Fabrisio, likewise, had a huge stake in it. Hong played a key part, with his influence at City Hall, to get the environmental-impact study overridden, and all kinds of variances. Given the large campaign contributions and the favors he could call in for his run at mayor, he certainly wanted it to go forward. Mei Ling, his associate— similar motives. Go forward."

"What's good for General Motors," I said, which made Bradley give me one of those generation-gap looks.

"Wrangler? Heavy investor, on the line—it's a go for him. Hildebrandt? What's good for Wrangler's good for him. And vice versa, a subject we'll come back to," I went on.

"So let me understand you," said Kakonis. "What you're carefully doing here is eliminating everyone in this room as a possible suspect but me?"

"That's the way it looks, isn't it?" I said.

"Well, that being the case, this meeting is over and I want you to get the hell out of my house."

"While you get yourself a good lawyer," said Ellard.

"Exactly. Now all of you, just get the fuck out."

Stress sure took language down a peg.

# 36

# Mark Bradley

But it wasn't all that electric. It wasn't as if everybody broke and ran for the phones. (Stop the presses!) It was more that a kind of stunned silence prevailed. And after what I deemed the proper dramatic pause, it was I who got the action back on track.

"Or," I said, "you could be patient for a few more minutes and we could clear this whole matter up to everyone's satisfaction—or nearly everyone's."

"Then you're retracting your accusation?" asked Kakonis.

"Sir, we never accused you," I reminded him. "We merely eliminated, or seemed to eliminate everyone else."

"I don't understand," he said. "Though on reflection I have to agree it was not a good place to end the discussion."

And he sat back down, as did the others.

"So," I continued, "if indeed we've found reasons to exclude everyone here as potentially guilty parties—including, belatedly, Mr. Kakonis—what does that mean?"

"Don't do that teacher shit," whispered Goodman.

"It means," I continued, not yielding to pique, "we gave somebody an alibi who doesn't really merit one. So maybe we should take another approach."

"And the way to do that," interjected Goodman, "is examine who might want what. Motive. Starting again first with Marvin Fischer. What motive besides jealousy—who else might want what?"

"Marvin Fischer was the mayor's right-hand man," I continued. "Uniquely situated to know what influence was being brought to bear and what backdoor deals were being made so that he could either block or demand a piece of the Sunset Center project. Which provides motive for all of you—ironically now with the *exception* of Li Ah—to want him dead."

"And also except me," said Jeffrey Hong. "While I may have had some peripheral interest ..."

"Peripheral?" I said. "With Lord knows how much in your campaign coffers—a hundred, hundred and fifty thousand, was it?—and continued backing from the most influential men in the city for your campaign for mayor—you'd *better* see that the project went through. You certainly had a more than *peripheral* interest in having Mr. Fischer eliminated."

"And getting myself shot in the bargain?" said Hong, making his point.

"There's that," I conceded. "So, let's then move on to the second victim, Teri. Teri knew where the bodies were buried, so to speak. She had contacts with and influence on various of you. *Mostly* she was the pawn of the mysterious 'C.B.'—whoever that is; substantiated by various documents and tapes and so forth. And, in fact, it seems to us that this C.B. would have the best motive, as far as she was concerned—since she also had very definite ambitions to become *Mrs.* C.B."

"Which I guess would eliminate us girls," said Mei Ling.

"That's right. It would certainly seem you and Li Ah are free and clear."

"She wanted this C.B., she planned to get him—it was a him," said Goodman. "It was almost like a Marilyn thing, she just would not face up to the fact the man was married and was going to stay that way."

"Leaves me out," said Fabrisio. "I'm available."

"Me, too," said Arthur Tsu.

"And me, too," said Buzz Baxter, trying to stay in the cast. "I'd've remarried her in a minute."

"Correct," I admitted.

"And I don't think we can make much of an argument she was all that crazy about me," said Harry Sanford. "A little, what, generous, time to time. But *want* me? An aging shnook going out of business? I don't think so."

"I don't think so, either," I agreed.

"I'm still in the game," admitted Charles Bolton, it seemed delighted by the potential to play a larger role.

"As are Wrangler Morangis, and Marshal Hildebrandt—you're married, aren't you, Hildebrandt?"

"Separated." (I can't imagine why.)

"And, of course, Harry Kakonis—who *is* a prize, indeed; who also has a wife, and who is, in some ways, as influential as a Kennedy, to complete the parallel."

"I thought we settled that."

"Going through the routine," I repeated, holding up a cautionary finger.

"All right," Goodman continued. "So then we come to Kiskessler. Who could know about and fix up taking care of Kiskessler? Have to say, probably Councilman Hong."

"Yes, but I'm eliminated since I was also a target."

"Unquestionably. Mr. Kakonis, though, would have that kind of connection." I held up another finger before he could protest. "Morangis definitely, a very good prospect as far as that's concerned; and if Morangis, then Hildebrandt as well."

More outbursts.

"Gentlemen, please—hold your horses!" (I was spending too much time with Goodman.) "Hear us out and we'll see where it leads."

"Singleton's next," said Goodman. "Our reading on that is whoever killed Teri killed Singleton. He was on the scene. A great candidate for patsy. Whoever came to kill Teri ran into Singleton. Unsuspecting, he gets beat to the punch and captured. And probably before his eyes, the killer cuts Teri to ribbons. Right-hand knifer, by the way, so that's not much help. Now he turns to Singleton, gets him to confess in a call to the police, hoping to save his life. Instead, he cuts him up, too. Takes him out to Benedict Canyon, does the fire thing with the car. And that's that one." Which seemed to send a chill through the group.

"And finally, Gabriella. Why kill Gabriella?" I asked. "It wasn't for jealousy, it wasn't for love. Gabriella was a smart, aware woman. She could only be fooled on a

limited basis for a limited time. She found out what Mr.
Kakonis had done with the syndicate's money . . ."

General hubbub over that—"Our money?" "What's
he mean?" "The money's gone?"

"*Which* we won't go into at this particular moment.
Suffice it to say, the bulk of the financing for the Sunset
Center was, let's say, in vague limbo—separate thing,
separate investigation, not our table," I said.

"Again, despite serious and unproven allegations,"
said Kakonis, "making it sound like I somehow had
something to do with killing her. Anybody who knows
me knows I'm not a killer. What would I gain by it?
Suppose she blew the whistle? If the deal were coming
apart, if I was exposed, it would come apart anyway,
sooner or later."

"Exactly," I said. "And that's the key part. While you
virtually all had an interest in the deal not falling apart,
there was only one person who had a specific interest in
its not falling apart *before a certain date.*"

"Gabriella had to be kept from blowing the whistle
and bringing the whole house of cards crashing down
and everybody finding out about influence peddling, and
high offices for sale," said Goodman.

"*Before* the election. It had to be held off before the
election," I clarified.

A moment to sink in.

There was only one person in the room running for
office.

"So let's get this straight, and I hope it *is* being recorded," said Jeffrey Hong. "You're saying *I* did all
this?"

I held up a finger, once again. "VCR?" I said to Kakonis, handing him a cassette.

He went to the machine, put it in, electronically lowered a large screen recessed in the ceiling, and projected
the tape. It was the Lambda Awards dinner.

"If you will just fast-forward a little to . . . there. OK,"
I went on. "You see Mei Ling get up from the table,
leaving an empty seat. Now, go forward a little. More.
There! You see Fischer come over to join Hong. Doesn't
seem happy to see him, does he? Go on."

The tape ran on.

"All right, here we go," I continued. "The shooting starts. Hong, who we thought was trying to push Fischer to safety, if you'll look closely, is actually trying to *separate* himself, get *himself* out of the way."

"That's some stretch," said Hong. "And even so, so what— self-preservation."

"Freeze it. Oh, we agree about that," I went on. "Evidently Kiskessler'd been hired through a third party and didn't know who you were, you just happened to be next to his target. Roll it. And you knew that, so look, you try to get away but can't. Stop. Go back. There. Roll. OK, OK—pow!—you take a bullet. In the *left* shoulder. Freeze that." Kakonis did. And after a moment I went over and turned off the tape.

"So, so?" said Hong.

"So, subsequently, every time we saw you, you were wearing a sling."

"If I can interrupt a minute," said Ellard. "A sling that was some kind of strange since at the time you didn't even go to a hospital. The paramedics said it was just a flesh wound."

"Right, it's against the law to wear a sling," said Hong.

"Not against the law," said Goodman. "But weird, especially considering you wore it on the *right* side. I noticed when we met at the Roxbury you shook lefty. Then later I touched you on the left shoulder and you winced. Because the wound was on the left."

"But it occurred to a smart fellow like you," I said, "that in the unlikely outside chance you happened to be connected to and suspected of stabbing Teri, you would seem to have an alibi. Since she was stabbed by a right-hander, you couldn't have done it because your right arm was apparently immobile. Not so, mister."

"Well, well," said Hong. "Now I've heard everything. What a crock. I'm sure I can find plenty of doctors who will swear wearing a sling on one shoulder can relieve pressure on another. To say nothing of the fact you haven't connected me to Teri."

"Well, it's true, your use of her, what, services to help

put the whole scheme together for weirdos like Wrangler, here, and Marshal ..."

"Hey, hey, podna," said Wrangler, managing small umbrage.

"... were all of the sort, 'here's a number of someone you might enjoy seeing.' "

"I had her number. Maybe. So maybe somebody gave me her number. That doesn't mean I even knew her, much less killed her."

"But the thing is," said Goodman, pulling the folded slip of paper he'd gotten from the now-beauteous Martina Gonsalves from his pocket, "she'd got *yours*. Your super private, in the drawer number. The one so private once you knew she had it, you changed it. Meaning it was private for someone else."

"Nothing, you have nothing," said Hong.

"Teri *was* a Marilyn, as my partner pointed out," I continued. "And she had similar expectations. She believed you'd divorce your wife. She believed you'd be elected mayor, and maybe governor, and who knows, president of these United States, God help us. And that you'd marry her and she'd share it all."

"Naturally, you had no idea of doing any of that," said Goodman. "Divorce your wife and marry *Teri*? A Hollywood joke? Fat chance. But you're no fool, you knew she could be trouble. So you were careful not to be seen, not to have a link. Only she surprised you, she stashed those videotapes you had her make with people you wanted to control. And you had a hell of a time getting out of her where she'd put them; didn't in fact, till you had her horse killed and your associates, whoever, found them up in Chatsworth. All but one, the one where you're almost showing. My guess is you hadn't seen it, and weren't positive. But weren't willing to take any chances."

"Not knowing, however," I went on, "that there was also a diary; a diary her dog buried and we found, that told all about 'C.B.' and what she had in mind for him."

"C.B. Who's C.B.? Does she say I'm C.B.? You've got nothing." He raised a deprecating hand as if to say "forget it."

"There's more," I said.

"No, no, no—I've heard enough. This is absolutely ridiculous. It's all wildly speculative, totally specious; there isn't one shred of evidence. I'm out of here." And he turned his back and started packing his attaché case.

"There is one thing more you really should hear," I said, in a moderate voice. "The other night my partner was lured to the site where you folks are building. And he was attacked; shot at and an attempt was made to bury him alive."

Hong ignored me. I raised my voice.

"That person was the guilty party, no doubt about it. Two things about that. Whoever did it had to know how to drive a bulldozer, a fact you made likely in a casual remark that you once worked in construction."

Hong continued packing papers. Everyone else was looking at him.

"And when I came on the scene, and fired back, that person escaped, and ran up the hill," I continued, raising my voice even more. "And as he got to the top, a huge siren went off, about the loudest sound you ever heard. Enough to pop an eardrum," I said and raised my voice still more. "At the very least loud enough to make someone temporarily very hard of hearing!"

Everyone was staring.

Hong closed his attaché case. Took a breath, and turned.

"What do you think of that?" I said.

"What do I think of what?" said Jeffrey Hong.

The timing was a little off. After all, it wasn't the movies. But Ellard, naturally, took custody of Hong, read him his rights, the whole shmear, *after* which one of the flunkies reported to Kakonis that several uninvited members of the police department were on hand and did he wish them admitted or turned away?

"Am I, uh, a part of this procedure here?" asked Kakonis of Ellard.

"You mean lock-up and that? No, not my department. I'm sure the matter will be investigated, is already being investigated, and I wouldn't count on charges not being lodged. But it'll be a while before you're in denims. You'll get to spend a lot of time and money on lawyers and appeals and stall and delay, still in your custom-made suits and two-hundred-dollar ties."

"Now, Lieutenant, I think that's sort of an impertinent remark."

"Well, I'll tell you, Mr. Kakonis, I tend to lose a little respect for guys with a hundred mil looking to steal another hundred mil. Forgive me if I was out of line."

"And what about the rest of us, can we go home?" said Buzz Baxter.

"Most of you. We'll want Mr. Morangis and Mr. Hildebrandt to stay."

"Anybody mind if I eat a little of that great spread out there?" asked Harry Sanford in a practical vein.

"I don't think they're going to be counting their pennies," said Ellard.

"So, we're all through?" said Li Ah Fischer.

"You can go," said Ellard.

"What do you mean, *we* got to stay?" said Hildebrandt.

"Oh, you don't actually stay. I'm taking you in. On a charge of conspiracy to commit murder by soliciting William Hobart Kiskessler to kill Marvin Fischer."

"Me? Me solicit Kiskessler?" shrieked Hildebrandt, his voice rising.

"Yeah, podna, I'm afraid they made me tell 'em," said Wrangler Morangis.

"Tell 'em what? *You* were the one did that for Hong; you told me yourself."

"Now, now, buckaroo, that old dog just ain't gonna hunt. Somebody gotta go down. You can't seriously think it's gonna be me?"

"Read him his rights," said Ellard to one of the gentlemen in blue. Who took out the little card and read the Miranda while his partner secured the prisoner's hands behind him.

And that part of the fix was in.

Then the procession moved slowly toward the door and out into the anteroom, and the bar.

"I do believe I will have that taste of spirits, now,"

said Goodman to the attendant on duty. "Vodka, tomato juice, no spices, no vegetables."

Ellard pushed the button for the elevator, his prisoner Jeffrey Hong, cuffed, at his side.

Mei Ling passed us and hesitated before joining them at the elevator.

"Mei Ling, listen—call Ron Silverman, see how he wants to handle this. Whether alone or with other legal talent. What the deal is, the bail, whatever," said Hong.

"Right. I still work for you," she said.

"Of course you still work for me. This whole thing is not going to hold water, I promise you."

"You made me some other promises, too," she said quietly. "I was patient about your wife. I understood the politics of that. At least till after the election. I even overlooked the little chippies at the discos; just some male preening. But I didn't know about Teri."

"There was nothing between Teri and me. She was a demented nutcase."

"A dead demented nutcase."

"Listen, now, I'm telling you, it's all circumstantial. This is not the time. Just do what I say. Get Silverman, find out when there'll be a hearing, arrange bail. I know it's Sunday, but I'm sure he can get a friendly judge . . ."

"Hold it, hold it, hold it," said Mei Ling. "You're talking to the wrong person. I just resigned."

"Oh, sure—the going gets tough."

"You know that's not it."

"The other stuff doesn't count."

"Hey! Murder was never part of the deal," she said. "China Boy."

And she turned away, electing to wait for the next elevator.

T.B., Toy Boy, D.B., Delivery Boy.

"C.B.," Goodman and I said, together.

China Boy.

"I believe I'll have a little libation myself," I added in my own imitation of W.C. Fields, joining the current incarnation at the bar.

# 37

# Rayford Goodman

There was a bit of milling around. And tagging evidence—the videotape of the awards dinner, for one; the audiotape of the meeting we'd just had, thanks to Kakonis, for another—admissible, since we'd been forewarned. And taking of statements. And general stalling till the arresting and investigating officers had managed a lot of walk-bys at the snack bar and finally finished off the brunch. To their credit (or fear) I didn't see any booze snatching.

Then I and a couple other principals (the arrestees) got to go to headquarters (in the case of Beverly Hills the *only* quarters). Where I regave my statement and signed stuff and all that

Then I was alone with Ellard in his spiffy new office in their quadrillion-dollar complex.

"You know," I said to him, "every time I see a movie, police headquarters always looks like a condemned slum. This looks like the Sultan of Brunei's summer palace."

"Well, we have a deal with the moviemakers, they never show it. We don't want to make law enforcement too attractive or the crooks'd want our jobs instead of being real estate or stockbrokers."

"I personally always felt anything with the word 'broke' in it couldn't be too good an investment."

And we smiled around like that for a while. Bradley'd gone home once he'd found out Christopher was available for afternoon tea and trumpets. Whatever had to be done here I could handle. And anyway, we had a date to meet later for dinner.

"I, uh," said Ellard, "suppose you expect me to make an apology and all that."

"You kidding? I'm thrilled you're not trying to make me a coconspirator."

"Well, I do appreciate the way you handled this. You could have hogged the glory."

"Hey, I figure next time your people start rioting and burning things I might need a friend. To help water the roof."

"Just paint a big sign 'Black Owned' on your house."

"My neighborhood, they'll think it means I have a slave."

Which was about when I started getting uncomfortable. I just wasn't that used to being friendly with a cop.

"It was a nice piece of work," he said.

"Got a little lucky, too."

"Hey, never hurts."

"Wasn't that the mutt decided to off me I don't know I could of proved it."

"I don't know, you pretty much had him nailed."

"Yes, but evidence. Would your D.A. have gone on what I had?"

"No, I guess not."

"Him calling me out to the site on the phony promise of naming the killer was a real break. Actually, of course, he did name the killer—himself."

"You mean by trying to murder you."

"Well, sure. But besides that, other than the cops and myself and Bradley, no outsider knew exactly where Gabriella's body'd been found. Whoever showed up right there had to be the guilty one."

He nodded. Agreed.

"So. There's nothing else, I guess I'll saddle up," I said.

"Nothing at the moment. You can go."

"Oh. I don't suppose you'd mind calling me a cab?"

"I could have a car drive you home."

"No, no—once we start that, no telling where it winds up. I'll be buying tickets to the Policemen's Prom."

"OK, maybe you're right." And he pushed a button on his intercom. "Sergeant, would you call a cab for Mr. Goodman?"

"Celebrity Cab?"

"Thanks for the compliment," I said.

"It's no compliment, that's the name of the cab company," he said to me. "That'll be fine," he said to the sergeant.

Forever Hollywood. As if celebrities took cabs. In fact, Los Angeles is probably the only place in America only poor people take cabs. Since there's no public transportation to speak of, if you can't afford a car, you take cabs.

The intercom buzzed. Ellard pushed down the button.

"Yeah?"

"They'll be here in five minutes."

"Thank you."

"I'll mosey on out," I said.

"Saddle up, mosey out—you been spending too much time with Wrangler Morangis."

"You may be right. Take care," I said, about to go.

"By the way," he said, stopping me. "Got something for you." And handed me an envelope. "The suspension's lifted on your P.I. license."

"Oh, thanks," I said, taking it.

"Don't thank me, I had nothing to do with it. They decided."

Yeah, right.

I gave him a little wave and split.

The cab cost eight-fifty. I could almost of walked it.

In addition to being terrific, and still feeling a lot like Old Hollywood, one of the nice things about Chasen's, it stayed open Sunday.

I never could understand so many restaurants closing on Sunday, I'd figure one of the better days. Why not Monday instead? With the exception of delicatessens sending out for Monday-night football, what kind of business could there be? A couple widows, maybe. Something like that. Just a thought.

It'd become kind of like a tradition for us to have dinner at Chasen's when we cracked a case.

Bradley was bringing Christopher and they were going direct.

I was bringing Francie, and since my car was still at the impound, she was picking me up.

I was waiting out front, where I'd been for a good fifteen minutes. But I know this generation. I'd already called and told Julius we'd be late. Who probably knew that anyway. I have a feeling another thing separated New York from Los Angeles was in New York everyone was on the pace and in L.A. twenty minutes behind.

Which is exactly how late Francie was when she showed up in her green Mustang convertible with the top up not to muss our hair.

"Thanks, Francie," I told her, climbing in. "I appreciate your picking me up. Sorry about my car."

"Hey, shmuts happens," she said, backing up about sixty miles an hour for ten feet, jamming on the brakes just before going over the cliff, and turning around. Giving me whiplash and palpitations.

I wasn't going to say anything I could risk my life other ways, why not driving with my good friend, there?

Here at the wheel, I could turn and stare without it seeming rude. She looked tired and pressed. Why not?

Still, the woman did ring my bell. With that great skin she had, like that Bernadette lady that sang? And her voluptuous figure. Which usually not my style, being propagandized by the Luanas of the world with their high-fashion bony huntress look. I guess I generally preferred that, especially now it came with boobs as standard equipment. But there was something to say for the lush, meet me in the jungle under the jacarandas look.

She was in a good mood, I could tell. She wasn't wisecracking. And didn't feel she had to talk to keep me from getting close. Then she did about the nicest thing she ever had. She slipped a cassette in the machine and turned it on. And it was Coleman Hawkins playing, "Body and Soul." Only the best tenor solo ever recorded.

I was beginning to feel like Sam Goldwyn must of when the President of the United States walked in his house—"Uh-oh, I guess I'm dying."

I didn't talk. Because you don't talk while that's going on. But when it was over, I said, "That was real sweet, Francie."

"Oh, shit, I must have picked up the wrong tape," she said back, lest life got in danger of turning out OK.

At Chasen's I was greeted by name, which always surprised me not being all that famous or that good a customer. Then we were led past the front room where whoever was richest or had the biggest grossing picture at the moment sat. I think they might of been one of the first restaurants to do that, seat all the best customers in front. Who, I guess, didn't mind the drafty doors and the traffic if they could be admired by everyone passing through. Me, if I was star, I think I'd like to be tucked in a quiet corner. But maybe not. Maybe not wanting that was one of the reasons I wasn't a star.

"Your table's ready, Mr. Goodman; and your guests are already seated," said Julius, leading us to my favorite booth back near the bar.

Bradley and Christopher were both leaning over something frothy with a straw. Since I knew Bradley really preferred gin and tonic, I think he just did that to amuse himself by trying to bait me. Which nothing was going to do tonight.

"Hi, guys," I said. "Come here often?"

We all went ha ha a little—very little. And the captain came over and asked whether we wanted something to drink.

I told him I'd have a Tanqueray Sterling vodka on the rocks with a small Perrier on the side.

And then it registered that Francie had said instead of diet Coke something on the order of Glenfish, or Gloccamora—one of those scotch numbers. I waited for the captain to leave.

"Excuse me, miss, I was under the impression you were a recovering addict of some sort."

"Right," she said.

"Are you supposed to be drinking?"

"Nope."

"Just so we understand each other."

"Look, you're not supposed to do anything. That's the problem with them, they get fanatic."

"I can't imagine why," said Bradley, joining in.

"You're not allowed any single thing that might possibly give you pleasure."

"I wouldn't go that far," said Bradley again.

"I know; and neither would I," said Francie. "Here's the Francine Rizetti formula. You don't give up everything. You just give up the thing you want most. Which, unfortunately, you have to do, because that's the thing you can't handle. But you take your abstaining in moderation, concentrating only on your really bad habits. That way you get partial clearing and a little sun peeking through the clouds now and then."

Made sense to me.

Enough that we all had a second drink, with both Bradley and Christopher switching from whatever to real drinks.

And got the menus.

And ordered.

Christopher checked out the room and found several celebrities I wouldn't know if they ran over me and just when I thought he wasn't really "one of us" surprised me with, "You'd be amazed how little these people spend on real estate."

I wouldn't be amazed. I would be amazed if one of them reached for a check.

"A fifty-million-dollar person only buys a three-million-dollar house," he complained.

"That's because it's their own money," I explained.

"Look who's at the bar," said Bradley. I figured some other celebrity. But I looked anyway.

It was Dick Penny, our erstwhile publisher.

He caught my look, mistook it for an invitation and came over. Or probably was just looking for an excuse.

"Gee, it's so good to see you folks eating so heartily when it's not on the expense account," he said.

"Am I to take it you're turning down the offer I faxed?" said Bradley.

"Well, I wouldn't say turning down," he answered. "How about I agree it's a good place to start?"

"Good night, Dick, nice to see you," said Bradley.

"Wait, wait, can't we talk?"

"About what?"

"All right. You've got me at gunpoint. It's a real holdup."

I wondered what he'd asked for. I didn't interfere in that sort of thing. Bradley knew much more than I did (since I didn't know anything) about publishing and what the traffic would bear.

"I don't see why; just that we've doubled our advance? Have you any idea what Jack Nicholson gets?"

"You notice that Jack Nicholson doesn't work for me," said Penny. "OK, you guys. I surrender. But you better give me a good book."

"Gonna give you more than that," I said. Bradley looked at me, surprised I might add any conditions.

"What's that?" said Penny warily.

"Gonna give you a dog," I said. "I call him Asta, but, you know—your dog, you can call him whatever you want."

"I don't want a dog," he said, a little whiney.

"Yeah, you do," I said. "Deal breaker."

He threw up his hands—not too hard—and made his way back to the bar.

The salads came.

And we filled Francie in. Which took to well into the main course. And would take as long to digest.

"So," she said, wiping her mouth daintily. "You guys really pulled it off."

"And we were lucky," I said. "Lucky, too, Ellard came through for us. It would of been a hard prove without him faking Kakonis out about the injunction."

"There's not going to be one?"

"Oh, there will be now," I said. "All that stuff'll come out."

"And C.B. was for China Boy—Teri's nickname for Hong."

"Right."

"Actually," said Bradley. "It's probably just as well we didn't know that in advance, we might have been misdirected to Arthur Tsu."

"How so? Or how tsu?"

"Once we found the tape Tsu had duped that was stashed at the stable in Chatsworth ..."

"Thanks to my valuable contribution," said Francie.

"Thanks to your valuable contribution," Bradley agreed. "We could have easily gone astray thinking Gabriella was guilty."

"Well, we did, really," I said.

"Yes. Well, true. But the fact is Tsu wasn't actually so much working for Gabriella as being Hong's spy at court."

"Sort of a chink in her armor," said Francie.

"I'll pretend you didn't say that," said Bradley, narrowing his eyes.

"You people are terrible," said Christopher, trying not to laugh.

"That's the trouble with ethnic humor—it's funny," said Bradley. But I knew better than to follow where *that* led. We all have lots of tolerance—till it's us. ("Today on *Geraldo*—transvestites who don't know how to masturbate!")

And we filled in most of the details over coffee.

"All right," said Francie finally. "What about my problem?"

"I think it's working out very nicely," said Bradley. "Wrangler was really guilty of setting up Kiskessler, but with his wealth and connections and the fact it was with the connivance of law-enforcement people there was no way he'd have gone to trial, much less be found guilty."

"So this way, we got him to give up Hildebrandt," I explained.

"Aren't you folks sort of playing God?" asked Christopher.

"Yeah," I said; Bradley nodding.

"It's no more than the D.A. does," he said. "Get one to squeal in order to nail the other."

"But Marshal didn't do it."

"This."

A moment's silence while that got absorbed. They didn't get Capone on murder, either.

"But it won't stand up," said Francie, after a bit.

"Neither will Hildebrandt, once Queen Kong gets through with him."

"Who or what is Queen Kong?" she asked.

"Queen Kong is a six-foot seven-inch weight-lifting

felon usually kept in solitary at County while he waits trial on four counts of raping male prostitutes."

"All the victims of which required hospitalization and extensive internal repairs," added Bradley.

We all sort of did a silent "ooh."

"Am I missing something here?" said Francie.

"Yeah. Ellard says a mistake's being made and Hildebrandt's being put in with Kong."

"Won't he cry rape?" said Christopher.

"That's the thing about rape," I said. "It's just one person's word against another."

And we all stared into our coffee for a while.

The waiter came with more coffee, which we didn't want. So we sent for ye olde l'addition.

When the captain came with the check, Bradley held me off (which some might say wasn't all that hard) and said to him, "Do you know Mr. Penny, at the bar?" With which he waved to Penny.

"Yes?" said the captain.

"He insists on paying."

The captain hesitated for the barest moment, but it was exactly when Penny waved back.

"Very good, sir," he said, taking the check back from Bradley.

And we made one of the quicker exits you're likely to see at Chasen's.

They brought both our cars about the same time.

"I got it," I said, and gave the head parker a tenspot.

I expected Bradley would do a fake faint or something. Instead, he gave me a big hug.

"Thank you," he said.

Hey, we just sold a book.

Then Francie drove me home to the house, and to my surprise said okay to a nightcap.

And another.

And between mumbling how men are all just rat-fuck bastards, and drinking one last nightcap, wound up on top of my bed, fast asleep, with her head on my shoulder.

I stayed awake and watched.

Sometimes you have to settle for the next-best thing.

# MYSTERY ANTHOLOGIES

☐ **MURDER ON TRIAL** *13 Courtroom Mysteries By the Masters of Detection.* Attorney and clients, judges and prosecutors, witnesses and victims all meet in this perfect locale for outstanding mystery fiction. Now, subpoenaed from the pages of *Alfred Hitchcock's Mystery Magazine* and *Ellery Queen Mystery Magazine*—with the sole motive of entertaining you—are tales brimming with courtroom drama.

(177215—$4.99)

☐ **ROYAL CRIMES, New Tales of Blue-Bloody Murder, by Robert Barnard, Sharyn McCrumb, H. R. F. Keating, Peter Lovesey, Edward Hoch and 10 others. Edited by Maxim Jakubowski and Martin H. Greenberg.** From necromancy in the reign of Richard II to amorous pussyfooting by recent prime ministers, heavy indeed is the head that wears the crown, especially when trying to figure out whodunit . . . in fifteen brand new stories of murder most royal. (181115—$4.99)

☐ **MURDER FOR MOTHER by Ruth Rendell, Barbara Collins, Billie Sue Mosiman, Bill Crider, J. Madison Davis, Wendy Hornsby, and twelve more.** These eighteen works of short fiction celebrate Mother's Day with a gift of great entertainment . . . a story collection that every mystery-loving mama won't want to miss.

(180364—$4.99)

☐ **MURDER FOR FATHER 20 Mystery Stories by Ruth Rendell, Ed Gorman, Barbara Collins, and 7 More Contemporary Writers of Detective Fiction.** Here are proud papas committing crimes, solving cases, or being role models for dark deeds of retribution, revenge, and of course, murder. (180682—$4.99)

*Prices slightly higher in Canada